"Kiss me, Alex."

Glynis remembered the taste of his mouth on hers. "Ye kissed me before. What's the harm in doing it again?"

His eyes went dark and he clenched his jaw for a long, long moment. When he finally gave in and leaned down, her stomach tightened in anticipation. The moment his lips touched hers, it was as if there was a fire beneath her skin. She pulled him down into a deep, open-mouthed kiss. Aye, this was what she wanted.

But Alex broke away. His gaze was smoldering and his breathing harsh.

"'Tis a dangerous game you're playing." His fingers shook as he brushed her hair back from her face. "One thing is bound to lead to another."

"I'm hoping it will." Glynis wasn't sure when she had decided that she wanted it all, but she had. She wanted to know what it was like to feel passion in the night, and she would never have another chance.

Or a better man to show her…

Praise for the novels of
Margaret Mallory

THE GUARDIAN

"4 ½ stars! Top Pick! Mallory imbues history with a life of its own, creating a deeply moving story. Her characters are vibrantly alive and full of emotional depth, each with their own realistic flaws. Her sensuous and highly passionate tale grabs the reader and doesn't let go."

—RT Book Reviews

"Masterfully written...Mallory has created a series that every romance reader must read. *The Guardian* is truly a sizzling romance with high-impact adventure that captures the Scotland readers long for. The characters created by Mallory have found places in my heart and I am impatiently awaiting the next of this spectacular series!"

—FreshFiction.com

"What is more tantalizing than a quartet of sexy men in plaids? *The Guardian* is very much a romance with plenty of adventure wrapped around it. Don't miss this terrific opening shot in a promising new series."

—RomRevToday.com

"A must-read for all historical and highlander fans...Ms. Mallory weaves a gripping story of heartbreak, intrigue, and trust...This one is a keeper."

—TheRomanceReadersConnection.com

"10 Stars! Top 20 Reviewed! Exquisite... An extraordinary medieval romance... Mallory has brilliantly set the stage for the next of three books... passionate characters and the women who love them [leap] off the pages... a true keeper to devour happily, knowing it remains on your shelf or in your e-reader to be re-read and savored over and over again!"

"A joyfully recommended read!... Vividly fierce, phenomenal... Breathtaking is not a good enough description... I've read a couple of Highlander books but none of them ever spoke to me the way *The Guardian* does!"

"I have always enjoyed [Mallory's] rich, lush historicals... The romance community now has a new star in Scottish tales... Characters that tug at the deepest corners of your heart, a love story that seeps into the very depth of your core, and a multiple sigh-worthy ending that sings to your spirit are all combined in the magic of this wonderful book. Bravo, Margaret Mallory!"

"An amazing introduction to what is fated to become a dangerously addictive series. With characters capable of breaching the most impenetrable of readers' defenses, riveting story lines (and even more intriguing subplots), quick, witty dialogue, as well as wild sexual tension—the only thing readers will crave, is more."

KNIGHT OF PASSION

"Top Pick! As in the previous book in her All the King's Men series, Mallory brings history to life, creating dramatic and gut-wrenching stories. Her characters are incredibly alive and readers will feel and believe their sensual and passionate adventures. Mallory raises the genre to new levels."

—RT Book Reviews

"An amazing story...a series that readers won't want to miss...Filled with hot romance as well as adventure with a fascinating historical background."

—RomRevToday.com

KNIGHT OF PLEASURE

"4 Stars! A riveting story...Such depth and sensuality are a rare treat."

—RT Book Reviews

"Fascinating...An excellent historical romance. Ms. Mallory gives us amazingly vivid details of the characters, romance, and intrigue of England. You're not just reading a novel, you are stepping into the story and feeling all the emotions of each character...*Knight of Pleasure* is amazing and I highly recommend it."

—TheRomanceReadersConnection.com

"An absolute delight...captivating."

—FreshFiction.com

KNIGHT OF DESIRE

"Spellbinding! Few writers share Margaret Mallory's talent for bringing history to vivid, pulsing life."
   —**Virginia Henley,** *New York Times* **bestselling author of** *The Decadent Duke*

"An impressive debut... Margaret Mallory is a star in the making."
   —**Mary Balogh,** *New York Times* **bestselling author of** *At Last Comes Love*

"5 Stars! Amazing... The fifteenth century came alive... *Knight of Desire* is the first in the All the King's Men series and what a way to start it off."
   —**CoffeeTimeRomance.com**

"A fast-paced tale of romance and intrigue that will sweep you along and have you rooting for William and his fair Catherine to fight their way to love at last."
   —**Candace Camp,** *New York Times* **bestselling author of** *The Courtship Dance*

"4 Stars! Mallory's debut is impressive. She breathes life into major historical characters... in a dramatic romance."
   —*RT Book Reviews*

ALSO BY MARGARET MALLORY

The Return of the Highlanders

The Guardian

All the King's Men

Knight of Desire
Knight of Pleasure
Knight of Passion

THE
SINNER

MARGARET MALLORY

FOREVER

NEW YORK   BOSTON

Forever
Hachette Book Group
237 Park Avenue
New York, NY 10017

www.HachetteBookGroup.com

Forever is an imprint of Grand Central Publishing.
The Forever name and logo are trademarks of Hachette Book Group, Inc.

The publisher is not responsible for websites (or their content) that are not owned by the publisher.

Printed in the United States of America

First Edition: November 2011

10 9 8 7 6 5 4 3 2 1

This book is dedicated to
the Wallace sisters, here and in Heaven:
My mother, Audrey, and my aunts, Priscilla and Dorothy

ACKNOWLEDGMENTS

I am grateful to my editor, Alex Logan, who reminded me to play to my strengths and helped make this a better book. Many thanks to her and the entire team at Grand Central Publishing for all they do for me. A warm thank-you to my agent, Kevan Lyon, for pretending I'm not troublesome and for giving me wise counsel and enthusiastic support.

I am indebted to Anthea Lawson, my critique partner, and to Ginny Heim, who reads all my manuscripts. Thank you with all my heart. When my confidence ran low, Erynn Carter, Theresa Scott, and Chris Trujillo kindly pitched in and read all or part of the draft manuscript for me. I am grateful to my RWA chapter-mates and fellow romance authors who continue to give me support and guidance.

A special thank-you to Josephine Piraneo at GlassSlipperWebDesign.com for making my website beautiful and doing endless updates for me. Thanks also to Sharron Gunn for her help with Gaelic, though any mistakes are mine, and to Mark Steven Long, who is an author's dream copy editor.

I apologize to my husband for all the evenings he is

left with the dog for company while I write. I am fortunate to have a family who supports me so completely in this writing adventure. Finally, I want to say a big thank-you to all the readers who have sent me messages telling me you enjoyed my books. You make it all worthwhile.

Chan ann leis a'chiad bhuille thuiteas a'chraobh.

It is not with the first stroke that the tree falls.

—Gaelic Proverb

PROLOGUE

Weeping will get you nothing," the woman said. "Be quiet if you want to go up."

Claire wiped her eyes on her sleeve and scrambled to her feet.

"You'd best learn to be tough, where you're going," the woman said, as she gathered her skirts to start up the rope ladder. "They say Scotland is full of wild warriors who would sooner cut your throat than bid you good day."

The rungs were too far apart for Claire's legs, and the woman's heavy skirts brushed her head as she climbed. When the ship swayed, she lost her footing. For a long, frightening moment, Claire swung by her arms, kicking in the air, until her foot found the rung again.

"I don't know how the Scots can call themselves Christian," the woman said in a muffled voice above her, "when they have wicked fairies hiding behind every rock."

Finally, a burst of cold night air hit Claire's face and blew her hair back.

"Don't speak to anyone," the woman said, grabbing Claire's wrist in a grip that pinched, "or the mistress will dismiss me, and then you'll have no one to take care of you."

Claire leaned her head back to look at the stars. Every night when the woman brought her food and allowed her to come up the ladder for a short while, she found the star and made her wish to go home to her grandmère and grandpère.

She did not understand why her grandparents had let this woman take her away, or why, despite making sure she made her wish on the very brightest star, she did not find herself in her own bed in the morning. But she knew Grandmère and Grandpère would not approve of how this woman was taking care of their special little girl. So tonight, she made a new wish.

Please, send someone better to take care of me.

CHAPTER 1

ON THE OPPOSITE COAST OF SCOTLAND
THE NEXT DAY

Y e are a devil, Alex Bàn MacDonald!"

Alex caught the boot the woman threw at his head. As he paused on the stairs to put it on, his other boot hit the stone wall behind him and bounced down the staircase.

"Janet, can I have my shirt and plaid as well, please?" he called up.

Her dark hair spilled over her shoulder as she leaned over the stairs to glare at him. "My name is not Janet!"

Damn, Janet was the last one.

"Sorry, Mary," he said. "I'm sure ye don't want anyone seeing me leave your house bare-arsed, so be a sweet lass and toss my clothes down."

"Ye don't even know why I'm angry, do ye?"

The woman's voice had a catch in it now that made him nervous. God, he hated it when they cried. Alex considered leaving without his clothes.

"I must go," he said. "My friend is here with the boat, waiting."

"Ye aren't coming back, are ye?" Mary said.

He shouldn't have come in the first place. He'd avoided Mary for weeks, but she'd found him at his father's house last night, drunk and desperate. After a week with his parents, he would have followed a demon to hell to escape.

"I was going to leave my husband for ye," Mary called down.

"For God's sake, lass, ye don't want to do that!" Alex bit his tongue to keep from reminding her that she was the one who had started the affair—and she'd made it very clear at the time that all she wanted from him was between his legs. "I'm sure your husband is a fine man."

"He's an idiot!"

"Idiot or no, he won't like finding another man's clothes in your bedchamber," Alex said, talking to her in the even tones he used to calm horses. "So please, Mary, let me have them so I can go."

"Ye will regret this, Alexander Bàn MacDonald!"

He already did.

His shirt and plaid floated down to him as the door slammed upstairs. As he dressed, Alex had a sour feeling in his belly. Most of the time, he managed to part on good terms with the women he bedded. He liked them, they liked him, and they understood it was only meant to be a bit of fun. But he had misjudged this one.

"Alex!" Through the open window, he heard Duncan calling from the shore. "There's a man walking up the path. Get your arse in the boat!"

Alex climbed out the window and ran for the boat. Not his finest moment. He took the rudder while Duncan raised the sail, and they headed for open water.

Duncan was in a foul mood—but then he often was. He stomped around the boat, making sure everything was tied down, which it already was.

"Are ye no tired of these antics with women?" Duncan finally said. "God knows I am."

Alex was weary to death of it, but he wasn't about to admit that. Instead, he said, "This was easier in France."

Alex and Duncan—along with Alex's cousins, Connor and Ian—had spent five years in France, fighting and swiving. It had been grand. Once a French noblewoman gave her husband an heir, no one got too excited if she discreetly took a lover. Ach, it was almost expected. In truth, Highlanders were no more likely to keep their vows, but bloodshed and clan wars were a too-frequent consequence.

"How did ye know where to find me?" Alex asked when his curiosity got the better of him.

"I saw Mary drag your drunken arse off last night just as I arrived," Duncan said. "Ye didn't look worth the trouble, but then, she doesn't strike me as particular."

Alex fixed his gaze on the horizon as they sailed past his parents' houses. When his mother left his father, she had only gone across the inlet, where she could watch him. His father was no better—both paid servants in each other's houses to spy for them.

"Why does my mother insist on returning to my father's house when I visit?" Alex asked, though he didn't expect an answer. "My ears are still ringing from the shouting."

When they reached open water, Alex stretched out to enjoy the sun and sea breeze. They had a long sail ahead of them, from their home island of Skye to the outer isles.

"Remind me how Connor convinced us to pay a visit on the MacNeils," Alex said.

"We volunteered," Duncan said.

"Ach, that was foolish," Alex said, "when we know the MacNeil chieftain is looking for husbands for his daughters."

"Aye."

Alex opened one eye to look at his big, red-haired friend. "Were we that drunk?"

"Aye," Duncan said with one of his rare smiles.

Duncan was a good man, if a wee bit dour these days—which just went to show that love could bring the strongest of men to their knees.

"And he didn't tell us that he wanted us to visit the MacNeils while we're in the outer isles," Duncan said, "until after he'd lured us in with the prospect of chasing pirates."

"Since Connor became chieftain," Alex said, "I swear he grows more devious by the day."

"Ye could make this easy by marrying one of the MacNeils' daughters," Duncan said, the corner of his mouth quirking up.

"I see ye do remember how to make a joke." Not many men teased Duncan, so Alex did his best to make up for it.

"Ye know that's what Connor wants," Duncan said. "He has no brothers to make marriage alliances with other clans—so a cousin will have to do. If ye don't like one of the MacNeil lasses, there are plenty of other chieftains' daughters."

"I'd take a blade for Connor," Alex said, losing his humor, "but I'll no take a wife for him."

"Connor has a way of getting what he wants," Duncan said. "I wager you'll be wed within half a year."

Alex sat up and grinned at his friend. "What shall we wager?"

"This boat," Duncan said.

"Perfect." Alex loved this sleek little galley that sliced through the water like a fish. They had been arguing over who had the better right to it ever since they had stolen it from Shaggy Maclean. "You're going to miss this sweet boat."

* * *

"Can ye hurry with your stitching?" Glynis asked, as she peered out her window. "Their boat is nearly at the sea gate."

"Your father is going to murder ye for this." Old Molly's face was grim, but her needle flew along the seam at Glynis's waist.

"Better dead than wed again," Glynis said under her breath.

"This trick will work but once, if it works at all." Old Molly paused to tie a knot and rethread the needle. "'Tis a losing game you're playing, lass."

Glynis crossed her arms. "I won't let him marry me off again."

"Your da is just as stubborn as you, and he's the chieftain." Old Molly looked up from her sewing to fix her filmy eyes on Glynis. "Not all men are as blackhearted as your first husband."

"Perhaps not," Glynis said, though she was far from convinced. "But the MacDonalds of Sleat are known philanderers. I swear on my grandmother's grave, I'll no take one of them."

"Beware of what ye swear, lass," Old Molly said. "I knew your grandmother well, and I'd hate for ye to cause that good woman to turn in her grave."

"Ouch!" Glynis yelped when a loud banging caused Old Molly to stick the needle into her side.

"Get yourself down to the hall, Glynis!" her father shouted from the other side of the door. "Our guests are arriving."

"I'm almost ready, da," Glynis called out, and sidled over to the door.

"Don't think ye can fool me with a sweet voice," he said. "What are ye doing in there?"

Glynis risked opening the door a crack and stuck her face in it. Her father, a big, barrel-chested man, was looking as foul-tempered as his reputation.

"Ye said I should dress so these damned MacDonalds won't soon forget me," she said. "That takes a woman time, da."

He narrowed his eyes at her, but he let it pass. After all these years of living with a wife and daughters, females were still largely a mystery to her father. In this war with him, Glynis was willing to use whatever small advantage she had.

"Their new chieftain didn't come himself," he said, in what for him was a low voice. "But it was too much to hope a chieftain would take ye, after the shame ye brought upon yourself. One of these others will have to do."

Glynis swallowed against the lump in her throat. Having her father blame her for her failed marriage—and believe that she had dishonored her family—hurt more than anything her husband had done to her.

"I did nothing shameful," she said through clenched teeth. "But I will, if ye force me to take another husband."

Glynis had a clear right to quit her marriage under the time-honored Highland tradition of trial marriage. Unfortunately, neither her father nor her former husband had taken her decision well.

"Ye were born obstinate as an ox," her father shouted through the six-inch crack in the door. "But I am your father and your chieftain, and ye will do as I tell ye."

"What man will want a woman who's shamed herself?" she hissed at him.

"Ach, men are fools for beauty," her father said. "Despite what happened, ye are still that."

Glynis slammed the door shut in his face and threw the bar across it.

"Ye will do as I say, or I'll throw ye out to starve!" That was all she could make out amidst his long string of curses before his footsteps echoed down the spiral stone staircase.

Glynis blinked hard to keep back the tears. She was done with weeping.

"I should have given ye poison as a wedding gift so ye could come home a widow," Old Molly said behind her. "I told the chieftain he was wedding ye to a bad man, but he's no better at listening than his daughter is."

"Quickly now." Glynis picked up the small bowl from the side table and held it out to Molly. "It will ruin everything if he loses patience and comes back to drag me downstairs."

Old Molly heaved a great sigh and dipped her fingers into the red clay paste.

CHAPTER 2

THE MACNEIL STRONGHOLD, BARRA ISLAND

Alex guided the boat to the sea gate of the MacNeil castle, which was built on a rock island a few yards offshore. A short time later, he and Duncan were surrounded by a large group of armed MacNeil warriors who escorted them into the castle's keep.

"I see we've got them scared," Alex said in a low voice to Duncan.

"We could take them," Duncan grunted.

"Did ye notice that there are twelve of them?" Alex asked.

"I'm no saying it would be easy."

Alex laughed, which had the MacNeils all reaching for their swords. He was enjoying himself. Still, he hoped that he and Duncan wouldn't have to fight their way out. These were Highland warriors, not Englishmen or Lowlanders, and everyone knew MacNeils were mean and devious fighters.

Almost as mean and devious as MacDonalds.

But the MacNeils had more dangerous weapons in their arsenal. Alex heard Duncan groan beside him as they entered the hall and saw what was waiting for them.

"God save us" escaped Alex's lips. There were three twittering lasses sitting at the head table. The girls were pretty, but young and innocent enough to give Alex hives.

One of them wiggled her fingers at him, then her sister elbowed her in the ribs, and all three went into a fit of giggles behind their hands.

It was going to be a long evening.

"Quiet!" the chieftain thundered, and the color drained from the girls' faces.

After exchanging greetings with Alex and Duncan, the MacNeil introduced his wife, an attractive, plump woman half his age, and his young son, who sat on her lap.

"These are my three youngest daughters," the chieftain said, waving his arm toward the girls. "My eldest will join us soon."

The missing daughter would be the one they'd heard about. She was rumored to be a rare beauty who had been turned out by her husband in disgrace.

She sounded like Alex's kind of woman.

Before the chieftain could direct them where to sit, Alex and Duncan took seats at the far end from the three lasses. After a cursory prayer, wine and ale was poured, and the first courses were brought out.

Alex wanted to get their business done and leave. "Our chieftain hopes to strengthen the friendship between our two clans and has sent us here on a mission of goodwill."

The MacNeil kept glancing at the doorway, his face

darker each time. Though their host didn't appear to be listening to a word, Alex forged ahead.

"Our chieftain pledges to join ye in fighting the pirates who are harassing your shores," Alex said.

That caught the MacNeil's attention. "The worst of them is his own uncle, Hugh Dubh," he said, using the nickname Black Hugh, given him for his black heart.

"Hugh is his half uncle," Duncan put in, as if that explained it all. "Two of his other half uncles have joined the pirates as well."

"How do I know these MacDonald pirates aren't raping and pillaging the outer isles on your chieftain's orders?" the MacNeil demanded.

This was precisely what Connor feared the other chieftains would believe.

"Because they've raided our own clansmen up on North Uist," Alex said. "Since we can't know when or where Hugh will attack, the best way to catch him is to find his camp. Have ye heard any rumors of where it might be?"

"They say Hugh Dubh has piles of gold hidden away in his camp," one of the MacNeil's look-alike daughters piped up, "and he has a sea monster that protects it."

"But no one can find Hugh," another girl added, fixing wide blue eyes on Alex, "because he can call up a sea mist by magic and disappear."

"Then I'll just look for a sea monster in the mist," Alex said to the girls, and Duncan glared at him for causing another round of giggles.

"Enough of these foolish tales," their father shouted at the girls, then turned back to Alex and Duncan. "'Tis true that Hugh's ship does have a way of disappearing into the mists, and no one knows where his camp is."

The MacNeil chief tilted his head back to take a long drink from his cup, then slammed it on the table, sputtering and choking.

Alex followed the direction of his gaze—and almost choked on his own ale when he saw the woman. Ach, the poor lass had suffered the worst case of pox Alex had ever seen. The afflicted woman crossed the room at a brisk pace, her gaze fixed on the floor. When she took the place at the end of the table next to Alex, he had to move over to make room for her. She was quite stout, though not in a pleasing sort of way.

Alex tried not to stare at the pockmarks when he turned to greet her. But he couldn't help it. God's bones, these weren't old scars—the pox were still oozing! Blood never troubled him at all, of course, but he was a wee bit squeamish about seeping sores.

"They call me Alexander Bàn." *Alexander the Fair-Haired.* He put on a bright smile and waited. When she kept her gaze on the table and didn't respond, he asked, "And you are?"

"Glynis."

Since she refused to look at him, Alex could stare freely. The longer he looked, the more certain he was that the pockmarks weren't oozing—they were melting. Amusement tugged at the corners of his mouth.

"I confess, ye have me curious," he said, leaning close to her ear. "What would cause a lass to give herself pockmarks?"

Glynis jerked her head up and stared at him. Despite the distracting red boils that were easing their way down her face, Alex couldn't help noticing that she had beautiful gray eyes.

"'Tis unkind to poke fun at a lady's unfortunate looks," she said.

It was disconcerting to hear such a lovely voice come out of that alarming face. Alex let his gaze drift over her, taking in the graceful swan neck and the long, slender fingers clenching her wine cup.

"Your secret is safe with me, lass," Alex said in a low voice. "But I suspect your family already knows it's a disguise."

He was hoping for a laugh, but he got none.

"Come," he said, waggling his eyebrows at her. "Tell me why ye did it."

She took a deep drink from her wine, then said, "So ye wouldn't want to marry me, of course."

Alex laughed. "I fear ye went to a good deal of trouble for no purpose, for I have no intention of leaving here with a wife. But does it happen to ye often that men see ye once and want to marry ye?"

"My father says men are fools for beauty, so I couldn't take the risk."

The woman said this with utter seriousness. Alex hadn't been this amused in some time—and he was a man easily amused.

"No matter how lovely ye are beneath the padding and paste," Alex said, "ye are quite safe from finding wedded bliss with me."

She searched his face, as if trying to decide if she could believe him. The combination of her sober expression and the globs sliding down her face made it hard not to laugh, but he managed.

"My father was certain your new chieftain would want a marriage between our clans," she said at last, "to show his goodwill after the trouble caused by the MacDonald pirates."

"Your father isn't far wrong," Alex said. "But my chieftain, who is also my cousin and good friend, knows my feelings about matrimony."

Alex realized he'd been so caught up in his conversation with this unusual lass that he'd been ignoring her father and the rest of the table. When he turned to join their conversation, however, he found that no one else was speaking. Every member of Glynis's family was staring at them.

Alex guessed this was the first time Glynis had tried this particular method of thwarting a potential suitor.

Glynis nudged him. When he turned back to her, she nodded toward Duncan, who, as usual, was putting away astonishing quantities of food.

"What about your friend?" she asked in a low voice. "Is he in want of a wife?"

Duncan only wanted one woman. Unfortunately, that particular woman was living in Ireland with her husband.

"No, you're safe from Duncan as well."

Glynis dropped her shoulders and closed her eyes, as if he'd just told her that a loved one she'd feared dead had been found alive.

"'Tis a pleasure to talk with a woman who is almost as set against marriage as I am." Alex lifted his cup to her. "To our escape from that blessèd union."

Apparently Glynis couldn't spare him a smile, but she did raise her cup to his.

"How could ye tell my gown was padded?" she asked.

"I pinched your behind."

Her jaw dropped. "Ye wouldn't dare."

"Ach, of course I would," he said, though he hadn't. "And ye didn't feel a thing."

"How did ye know I didn't feel it?" she asked.

"Well, it's like this," he said, leaning forward on his elbows. "A pinch earns a man either a slap or a wink, and ye gave me neither."

Her laugh was all the more lovely for being unexpected.

"Ye are a devil," she said and poked his arm with her finger.

That long, slender finger made him wonder what the rest of her looked like without the padding. He was a man of considerable imagination.

"Which do ye get more often, a wink or a slap?" she asked.

"'Tis always a wink, lass."

Glynis laughed again and missed the startled looks her father and sisters gave her.

"Ye are a vain man, to be sure." She took a drumstick from the platter as she spoke, and Alex realized he hadn't taken a bite since she sat down.

"It's just that I know women," Alex explained, as he took a slab of roasted mutton with his knife. "So I can tell the ones who would welcome a pinch."

Glynis pointed her drumstick at him. "Ye pinched me, and I didn't want ye to."

"Pinching your padding doesn't count," Alex said. "You'd wink if I pinched ye, Mistress Glynis. Ye may not know it yet, but I can tell."

Instead of laughing and calling him vain again, as he'd hoped, her expression turned tense. "I don't like the way my father looks."

"How does he look to ye?" Alex asked.

"Hopeful."

* * *

Alex and Duncan slept on the floor of the hall with a score of snoring MacNeils. At dawn, Alex awoke to the sound of soft footfalls crossing the floor. He rolled to the side and leaped to his feet, leaving his host kicking the empty space where Alex had been lying.

"You're quick," the MacNeil said, with an approving nod. "I only meant to wake ye."

"That could have gotten ye killed," Alex said, as he slipped his dirk back into his belt. "And then I'd have no end of trouble leaving your fine home."

Duncan was feigning sleep, but his hand was on the hilt of his dagger. If Alex gave the signal, Duncan would slit their host's throat, and the two of them would be halfway to their boat before anyone else in the hall knew what had happened.

"Come for a stroll with me," the MacNeil said. "I've something to show ye."

"I could use some fresh air after all the whiskey ye gave me last night."

Because it was difficult to discover a man's true intentions when he was sober, Alex had matched the MacNeil drink for drink far into the night. No doubt his host had the same goal in mind.

"No one forced it down your throat," the MacNeil said, as they left the hall.

"Ah, but ye knew I am a MacDonald," Alex said. "We don't like to lose, whether it be drinking games or battles."

The MacNeil cocked an eyebrow. "Or women?"

Alex didn't take the bait. His problem had never been losing women, but finding a graceful way to end it when the time came—which it always did.

Alex followed the MacNeil out the gate and onto the narrow causeway that connected the castle to the main island.

The MacNeil halted and pointed down the beach. "My daughter Glynis is there."

Alex's gaze was riveted to the slender figure walking barefoot along the shore with her back to them. Her long hair was blowing in the wind, and every few feet she stopped and leaned over to pick up something from the beach. Ach, she made a lovely sight. Alex had a weakness for a woman who liked to get her feet wet.

"Ye strike me as a curious man," the MacNeil said. "Don't ye want to know what she truly looks like?"

Alex did want to know. He narrowed his eyes at the MacNeil. He was more accustomed to having fathers hide their daughters from him. "Are ye not fond of your daughter?"

"Glynis is my only child by my first wife. She's verra much like her mother, who was as difficult a woman as was ever born." The MacNeil sighed. "God, how I loved her."

More proof if Alex needed it—which he didn't—that love led to misery.

"The other girls are sweet, biddable lasses who will tell their husbands they are wise and clever and always in the right, whether they are or no," the chieftain continued. "But not Glynis."

The younger sisters sounded too dull by half.

"I didn't raise Glynis any different, she just is," the MacNeil said. "If we were attacked and I was killed, the other girls would weep and wail, helpless creatures that they are. But Glynis would pick up a sword and fight like a she-wolf to protect the others."

"So why are ye so anxious to see Glynis wed?" Alex asked. She seemed the only one worth keeping to him.

"She and her stepmother are like dry kindling and a lit torch. Glynis needs her own home. She doesn't like being under the thumb of another woman."

"Or a man's," Alex said. "Judging from what I heard she did to her former husband."

"Ach, he was a fool to tell the tale," the MacNeil said with a wave of his hand. "What man with any pride would admit his wife got her blade into his hip? Ye know what she was aiming for, of course."

Alex winced. He'd had women weep and occasionally toss things at him, but none had ever tried to cut off his manly parts.

But then, Alex had never married.

CHAPTER 3

The pungent smell of low tide filled Alex's nose as he followed Glynis MacNeil over the barnacled rocks and seaweed along the shore. Each time the wind blew against her skirts and revealed her slender frame, he smiled to himself. She was absorbed in collecting shells and did not appear to hear his approach over the cries of the gulls and the rhythmic crash of the surf.

When she hiked her skirts to create a makeshift basket for her collection, a sigh of appreciation escaped Alex's throat. He could see no more than slender ankles and a precious few inches of calf, but his gaze slid upward, imagining long, shapely legs.

Glynis paused over a tide pool. Something caught her eye, and she dropped down for a closer look, wrapping her arms around her knees. Her rich brown hair formed a curtain, hiding her face from his view. Would the lass's face be as alluring as her long, slender body?

It was time to satisfy his curiosity. In a few long strides, he stood over her.

"I see ye found a purple starfish," Alex said. "That means good luck is coming your way." He made that up, of course.

When Glynis tipped her head back to look at him, Alex's heart missed several beats—and then made up for it by hammering in his chest. He'd noticed the beauty of her wide, gray eyes the night before. But in that face, they were arresting.

Her features were a tantalizing mixture of wholesomeness and sensuality, from the sprinkling of delicate freckles across her nose to her full, rosy lips. The unusual combination set off warring urges within him. He had a wild desire to lay her back on the sand and watch those gray eyes glaze with pleasure as he had his wicked way with her. At the same time, he felt an odd urge to protect her.

Alex knew he should reassure her, for he had clearly startled her, but words failed him. This was so unlike him that he wondered for a moment if a fairy had cast a spell upon him.

But then the lass fell backward onto her arse, and he knew she was human.

* * *

The man's voice startled Glynis, and she looked up with her heart pounding.

She recognized the golden warrior looming above her to be Alex MacDonald, the man she'd spoken to last night. At least, part of her knew that was who he was. But with the glow of sunrise shining all about him, he looked like a Viking marauder come to blazing life out of the old stories her father's *seannachie* told.

She could imagine him standing in the prow of his ship with his white-blond hair blowing behind him and carved gold bands encircling his bare, muscled arms. When he fixed green eyes the color of the sea on her, she felt as if something slammed into her chest, and she fell backward.

The shock of cold water jarred her from her trance. Heat flooded her cheeks as she realized she was sitting in a pool of seawater, soaking the back of her skirts to her skin.

"Sorry, lass. I shouldn't have startled ye like that." The glint of humor that touched his eyes as he held out his hand should have made him less threatening—but it did not.

Glynis swallowed and gave him her hand, which was gritty with sand. He hoisted her up effortlessly, as if she were as petite as her sisters. Tall as she was, Glynis had to tilt back her head to look into his face. She was vaguely aware that she was staring, but she couldn't seem to help herself.

What was God thinking, allowing a man to be this handsome?

He stood so close that the heat radiating from his body drove the chill right out of her. The humor that had touched his eyes was gone, replaced by something darker that pulled her toward this MacDonald warrior as if an undertow were dragging her out to sea.

"Ye should be more aware of your surroundings, lass," Alex said, still standing far too close. "I could have been a dangerous man."

"And ye aren't one?" she asked.

"Me?" His teeth were white, and his smile had the force of the summer sun on a clear day. "I'm dangerous as sin."

"My father's guards can see us from the castle."

Alex glanced over his shoulder. "I could have ye behind the trees or in my boat before they were out the castle gate." He paused, eyes glinting. "Especially if ye were willing."

She rolled her eyes. "No fear of that."

"Are ye certain?" he asked in a husky voice that resonated somewhere deep in her belly.

Glynis held her breath, unable to move, as Alex lifted his hand to her face. Even though she anticipated his touch, her stomach fluttered when he brushed the back of his fingers against her cheek. Her gaze dropped to his wide, sensuous mouth, and her throat went dry. This man would know how to give a lass a proper kiss—not like that wretched Magnus Clanranald she'd wed.

She felt herself leaning forward and snapped her head back. "I warn ye, I've got a dirk, and I'm no afraid to use it."

"So I've heard, but ye won't need your dirk," Alex said. "I like my women willing."

And she'd wager there were plenty of those.

"You've nothing to fear," he said. "I never harm women."

"If ye don't count breaking their hearts."

Glynis didn't know what made her blurt out the words. But he stiffened, and she saw the truth reflected in his eyes. Alex MacDonald had broken hearts, but he didn't glory in it. Nay, it pained him.

Of course, that only added to his appeal. A heartless man would be easier to resist.

"You're safe from me." Alex gave her a wink, and she could almost see him pull on his charming mask. "I don't dally with women who are looking for husbands."

"I'm no looking for a husband." Her cheeks grew warm as soon as the words were out of her mouth. "I didn't mean I wish to d…d…" Try as she might, she could not get the word *dally* to cross her lips.

"I can't say the same." He gave her a devilish grin that sent hot darts of awareness across her skin. "But even if ye aren't looking for a husband, your father is, and that amounts to the same thing. Besides, ye deserve better than me."

"I do," she snapped. "God save me from another handsome philanderer."

Something flickered in his eyes before the smiling mask dropped into place again. It was a blindingly handsome mask, but Glynis found herself wondering about the part of Alexander MacDonald that he hid from the world.

She felt guilty for being sharp with him, when the man had done nothing more than tease her, so she asked, "Do ye want to see my favorite spot?"

"It might be more fun to let me find it myself," he said.

Her breath caught as his eyes traveled over her slowly from head to toe.

"I meant on the beach!" She punched his arm, and it was like hitting iron. "Ach, ye are the worst rogue I've ever met."

He laughed and took her hand. "Lead me where ye will, fair lady."

Alex's hand was big and warm around hers. She'd

never walked hand in hand with a man before, and she felt a wee bit wicked for it—in a good sort of way.

She took him to the far end of the bay.

"The seals like to gather here." She pointed to a huge, flat rock that jutted out of the water a few yards offshore.

They found a dry, sandy area high on the beach and sat down. As she removed her hand from his, her gaze slid over his arm, taking in the golden hairs against his tanned skin. Alex stretched out his long, muscular legs, which were covered with the same golden hair.

"Ye should lie on your stomach," he said, "so the sun can dry the back of your gown."

Glynis was tempted. Her stepmother was bound to make unpleasant remarks about Glynis's slovenly ways if she returned to the castle with her gown soaked. But she couldn't very well lie down when she was alone with a man.

"I wouldn't want your father to think I had ye on your back in the sand," Alex said. "We'd be wed before noon."

Glynis flopped down on her stomach and leaned on her elbows. They watched in companionable silence as several seals hauled themselves out of the sea to nap on the flat rock.

Alex nudged her with his knee. "What other tricks have ye used to drive away potential husbands?"

"I tell them I'm barren." She kept her voice flat to cover how much this hurt. "That's sufficient to discourage most of them."

"Ye can't know that for certain, can ye?" Alex asked. "You're young yet."

Glynis shrugged. Since she was never going to marry again, it was of no consequence.

"What about the men who already have heirs?" he asked. "How do ye discourage them?"

"I've rubbed onions on my clothes and chewed garlic."
She sighed. "If that isn't enough, I say I dreamed I was
wearing widow's clothes on my next birthday."

Alex's laugh rumbled deep in his throat. It was a surprisingly pleasant sound.

"Are ye the one who started the story about stabbing
your husband?" he asked.

"I fear that one is true," she said. "I do find it useful."

This time, his laughter roused two or three seals, who
lifted their heads to look at them before resuming their
slumber.

"I doubt your father is trying to marry ye off to make
ye suffer," Alex said. "He needs alliances, just as my
chieftain does."

"And the wrong alliances will bring disaster," Glynis
said. "I told my father not to join this rebellion, but, of
course, he wouldn't listen to me."

Half the clans in the Western Isles had risen against the
Scottish Crown in yet another doomed rebellion.

"The rebellion will fail eventually," Alex said. "But
until it does, any clan that takes the side of the Crown
risks being attacked by its neighbors."

"'Tis clever of your chieftain to let each side court
him," she said.

"Court him?" Alex said. "Connor feels like he's strad-
dling two sea monsters, while each tries to snap his head
off and dump him into the sea."

She couldn't help but smile at his colorful description,
but she was worried about her clan. "You're lucky to be
a man. Ye can serve your clan without being bought and
sold like a cow."

"I've never met a woman with such a low opinion

of marriage," Alex said, then he added something under his breath that sounded very much like "except for my mother."

"I'd do anything for my clan but wed," Glynis said.

"Since we are of one mind on that," Alex said, "we can be friends, aye?"

She looked over her shoulder at him. "Do ye mean it?"

"Usually I become friends with women *after* I bed them," he said. "But I'll make an exception for ye."

"Ye are teasing me again," she said.

"Ye are so serious, I can't help myself," Alex said in a soft voice. "But if we should meet again, ye can trust me to be a friend."

Glynis met his sea-green eyes. "Then I'll be your friend as well, Alex MacDonald."

When she shifted her gaze back to the seals, several of them lifted their heads. Then, one by one, they began slipping into the water.

"Get up," Alex said with steel in his voice.

Before she could move, his hands encircled her waist, and he lifted her to her feet.

"Damn," Alex said between his teeth, as a war galley glided around the point of the bay.

"They could be friendly," Glynis said, but her heart was pounding hard in her chest.

"That's Hugh MacDonald's ship," Alex said, his gaze fixed on it. "We'll try to outrun them and get back to the castle."

Alex grabbed her hand, and they flew over the sand and rocks. The pirate galley must have been spotted in the castle as well. Across the small bay, two dozen men poured over the causeway from the castle. The pirates were sailing for the beach midway between them and the castle in an attempt to cut them off before her father's men could reach them.

It looked as if the pirates would succeed. Though her bare feet were cut and bleeding from the barnacles, Glynis ran faster and faster. But the castle guards were too far away—and the pirates too close.

The guards were still a hundred yards away when the pirate's boat grounded. Glynis jerked to a halt and watched in horror as men dropped over the side of the ship and started splashing toward shore.

Alex lifted her onto a high rock.

"Stay here so I know where ye are," he ordered. "I won't let them get to ye."

As Alex turned from her, he reached behind him for his claymore, and the steel of his blade whistled through the air. His battle cry "*Fraoch!*" thundered in her ears as he ran straight at the pirates coming toward them through the surf.

Without breaking his stride, Alex cut down the first two men. As he leaped over the blade of a third, he swung his claymore into the man's side.

Glynis screamed as another pirate charged Alex before he could recover from his last swing with the big, two-handed sword. With flowing movements, Alex released one hand from his claymore, pulled his dirk from his belt, and plunged it into the man's chest. His attacker sank to his knees with a cry, and his blood colored the water around him in rusty clouds.

Alex glanced over his shoulder at her as if to be sure none of the pirates had gotten past him. His eyes were murderous, and his every muscle taut and ready.

This was not the laughing man who sat beside Glynis watching seals a short time ago. Nay, this Alexander Bàn MacDonald was every inch a fearsome Highland warrior—and he was magnificent to behold.

Her father's men were running the last few yards to join the fight, with Duncan MacDonald in the lead. The two groups crashed together with shouts and grunts and swords clanging.

Glynis could not take her eyes off the two MacDonald men. Despite the pirates' greater number, the pair were lethal. They forced the pirates back, and back again, under a unified and ferocious assault. Although her father's men fought well, they fought individually. The MacDonald warriors fought as a merciless unit.

Their violence had a grace and control that bespoke years of practice. After a time, she could catch some of the silent signals between them. *You take this one, I'll take that one.* The pirates fell before them, one after another.

Something drew her attention from the fierce battle raging on the beach to the pirate ship. A man stood alone in the prow with his arms folded across his broad chest. He was staring at her. As their eyes locked across the distance, a cold shiver went up her spine.

She sensed this man meant her harm—and not just the harm he meant to anyone who crossed his path. She didn't know why, but she felt as if he was fixing her in his mind, as if he had a particular, evil plan for her.

With his eyes still on her, the man put his fingers to his mouth and made a piercing whistle. The pirates on the beach ran to the boat and scrambled up the sides like rats.

Alex ran after them into the surf until he stood in water to his waist.

"Hugh Dubh MacDonald," he shouted, waving his claymore in the air. "Come back and fight, ye miserable coward!"

"Tell my nephew I'll see him dead," the man in the prow shouted back. He ducked just as Alex's dirk sailed through the air where his head had been.

While her father's men congratulated themselves on their success in driving the pirates off and Duncan cleaned his sword, Alex stood in the water raining curses on the departing ship. Finally, Alex turned and strode through the surf toward the beach with the sun glinting on his hair and fire burning in his eyes.

"'Tis safe to go to the castle now, Mistress Glynis," one of her father's men said. "Let me help ye down."

As the man reached up to grasp her about the waist, Alex's shout stopped him.

"Take your hands off her!"

The guard jumped back and stared at Alex. Glynis's heart was in her throat as Alex stormed up the beach dripping water and blood, looking like his Viking ancestors who once terrorized these coasts. His eyes bored into her as if no one else existed.

When Alex reached her, he clamped his hands around her waist and lifted her off the rock. His eyes never left her face as he slid her down his body, every inch of her rubbing against the scorching heat of his muscular frame. Glynis's knees were weak before her feet touched the ground.

Alex's eyes had a wild fierceness and a hunger that sent her pulse racing.

"Aye," she whispered and held on as he leaned her backward.

* * *

Battle lust throbbed in Alex's veins and left him hard. When he turned and saw Glynis on the rock, he would have killed to have her. He had never wanted a woman as much as he wanted Glynis MacNeil right now.

From the moment their bodies touched, he felt as if it had been ordained that they should join. Her body melded to his as if she had been made for him alone. Alex kissed her with all the lust pounding through him, his tongue thrusting, possessing. He had to have her.

He heard Duncan call his name through the haze of lust, but he didn't give a damn. Nothing mattered but this woman's sweet mouth on his. She was a wonder under his hands, responding with an awakening passion that had him yearning to lie her down and take her on the sand.

The sharp prick of a steel point in the middle of his back was a bit harder to ignore than Duncan.

"I appreciate ye saving my daughter from your miserable pirate relations," the MacNeil said close to Alex's ear. "But unless ye want to leave here with a wife, you'd best release her now."

Alex wanted her so much that he could almost have agreed to a life in chains just to have her this once. But when Glynis's eyes went wide with panic, he came to his senses. Slowly, he straightened and forced himself to release her.

Glynis swayed on her feet, as if her legs might not hold her. When Alex started to reach for her, her father gave him a quelling look and put a firm arm around her shoulders.

Alex glanced left and right, taking in the circle of men around them. What madness had taken hold of him to kiss the chieftain's daughter—*and to kiss her like that*—in front of all of her father's warriors? Alex hadn't given a thought to the other men on the beach. Nay, he hadn't even seen them.

Stealing a kiss from a willing lass was no grave offense, so the MacNeil probably wouldn't kill him. On the other hand, his timing was verra poor, and any fool could see that he hadn't meant to stop with the kiss.

"What do ye have to say for yourself, Alex Bàn MacDonald?" the MacNeil chieftain demanded.

"If I said I was sorry for kissing your daughter, we'd both know I was lying," Alex said. Then he turned to Glynis, who looked as dazed as he felt. "I am sorry, lass, if I embarrassed ye."

Alex wished he could speak with her without all the others watching, so he could ask her if she was all right. But if he did have Glynis MacNeil alone now, he knew damned well they wouldn't waste the opportunity talking.

CHAPTER 4

Alex waved to his cousin, the chieftain of the MacDonalds of Sleat, who was making his way down to the shore from Dunscaith Castle to meet him. Connor's shoulder-length black hair blew behind him as he jumped from rock to rock.

"Have ye started to regret taking the chieftainship yet?" Alex asked, as Connor helped haul the boat up onto the beach.

"Every day," Connor said with a dry laugh. "How do our clansmen on North Uist fare?"

"They've lost a good deal to the raiders, but they won't starve," Alex said. "The fishing is good, and the other supplies I delivered should see them through until the next harvest."

After climbing up the hill, he and Connor crossed the narrow bridge to the castle, which was built on a rock off the headland.

"Ian and Duncan are here as well," Connor said. "We have clan business to discuss."

Inside, the hall had clean rushes, and the servants were sober. This was a far cry from the condition the castle had been in when they took it from Connor's uncle Hugh. The cleanliness and order were the work of Duncan's sister, Ilysa. Though they weren't actually related, Ilysa was the closest thing Connor had to a female relative to perform the castle duties in place of a wife.

Their cousin Ian, who looked so much like Connor they could pass as brothers, was sitting at the chieftain's high table with Duncan.

"Ian, ye look like shite," Alex greeted him.

Ian grinned. "The twins are keeping Sìleas and me up most nights. They're getting more new teeth."

Ach, no. The last time Alex had seen Ian's bairns, one of them crawled up his leg, sank her teeth into his knee, and held on like a limpet.

"'Tis only the start of the trouble those pretty babes are going to cause ye," Alex said. "Ye know that, don't ye?"

"I do," Ian said with a weary smile. "They are beauties, aren't they?"

The thought of raising daughters gave Alex the shudders, but Ian's eyes shone when he spoke of his wee, red-haired devils.

At Connor's signal, the other men in the hall moved away to allow the four of them to speak in private. Connor had a formal council of senior clansmen, as was expected, but everyone knew that Ian, Alex, and Duncan were his closest advisers.

"We need to forge strong alliances to survive these troubled times," Connor said, taking the seat across the table from Alex. "Our clan is still weak after losing my father and so many other men at the Battle of Flodden."

The four of them had been in France when they received the news of the Scots' disastrous loss to Henry VIII's forces at Flodden. They had returned home to find their king and their chieftain among the dead and their clan in a dire state.

"We succeeded in throwing Hugh out of the chieftain's castle," Alex said.

He did not mention that Connor's uncle was still a source of dissention within the clan. Some of their clansmen mistook Hugh's brutality for strength and, if given the chance, would support him as chieftain.

"We have much to do yet," Connor said, his voice hard. "We cannot rest until we have control over all of the lands that rightfully belong to our clan."

"Aye!" Duncan said, and they all raised their cups.

They had secured their base here on the Isle of Skye, with Connor holding Dunscaith Castle on one side of the Sleat Peninsula and Ian holding Knock Castle on the other. It pained them all, however, that the MacLeods had stolen the Trotternish Peninsula while the four of them were still in France. And now, Hugh and his pirates were ravaging their lands on the island of North Uist.

"We don't yet have the strength to fight the MacLeods for the rest of our lands here on Skye," Ian said. "That will be a bloody battle when it comes."

"Our first task should be to protect our kin on North Uist," Alex said. "Our clansmen there live at the mercy of these pirates." Seeing how his kinsmen were preyed upon had eaten a hole in his stomach.

"I agree," Connor said. "Before the fall harvest, I want

one of ye to rebuild our castle on North Uist and remain there to protect our clansmen."

"It's high time we took on your marauding uncles." Alex had a burning desire to strangle Hugh with his bare hands for taking food out of the mouths of his own kinsmen. "Give me a few warriors, and I'll set sail in the morning."

"If it weren't for this damned rebellion, I'd send ye now," Connor said, shaking his head. "Unfortunately, we have other business that can't wait."

"What's happened?" Duncan asked.

"The new regent has summoned me to court in Edinburgh," Connor said.

When the Scottish king was killed at Flodden, he left a babe as his heir, and the court factions had been fighting for control ever since. The king's widow, who was also the sister of the hated Henry VIII, was regent for a time. But when the queen remarried, the Council had called John Stewart, the Duke of Albany, from France to take her place.

"Albany wants to see the new chieftain of the MacDonalds of Sleat bend his knee and swear allegiance to the Crown," Ian said.

"Ach, no, ye can't go," Duncan said. "Ye know how many times a Highland chieftain has obeyed a summons to court and ended up dead or imprisoned."

"We can't risk losing ye," Ian said.

They were not just speaking out of affection for Connor. By tradition, their chieftain must be a man who had the chieftain's family blood in his veins. Ian and Alex were related to Connor through their mothers so they couldn't replace him—praise God. The only men still

alive who could be chieftain besides Connor were his half
uncles, and their clan would not survive under the leadership of one of them.

"Aye, but if I don't go, Albany will believe I've joined
the rebellion." Connor heaved a deep sigh. "'Tis getting
harder and harder to stay out of this fight between the
rebel clans and the Crown, though I see no gain for our
clan either way."

"Send one of us in your place," Ian said. "Whoever
goes can concoct an excuse why ye can't make the long
journey to Edinburgh at this time and appease the regent
with vague assurances of your goodwill."

Ian was almost as conniving as Connor.

"The man who goes will risk being held hostage by the
Crown," Alex said, "but it's a good plan."

"The rebels are also pressing me to choose sides,"
Connor said. "There is a gathering of the rebel clans at the
Maclean stronghold. If I'm not there, we could face at-
tack by the neighboring clans who support the rebellion.
The MacLeods, for one, would be happy for an excuse to
try to take more of our lands."

"Again, send one of us," Ian said. "We must straddle
the two sides for as long as we can."

"Which brings me back to our need for alliances," Connor said, looking directly at Alex. "Marriage alliances."

"No," Alex said, meeting his cousin's gaze. "Ye will
not ask that of me."

Connor rubbed his hand over his face. He looked even
more tired than Ian, and considerably less happy.

"What I propose is that Alex wed a lass whose clan is
on one side of the rebellion," Connor said, "and Duncan
wed a lass whose clan is on the other side."

Duncan gave Connor a sideways glance that could freeze a loch.

"Thought ye were safe from his schemes, did ye, Duncan?" Alex said.

"No chieftain will want me for his daughter," Duncan said to Connor. "I'm just your former nursemaid's son."

"You're the captain of my guard and as close as a brother to me," Connor said. "You'll make a good catch for a chieftain with daughters to marry off."

Duncan looked into his cup and didn't argue, but he would be as obstinate as Alex in this.

"Ye will marry sooner or later, as all men do," Connor said, as he refilled Alex's and Duncan's cups with more whiskey. "I'm merely suggesting ye do it sooner."

"I won't do it," Alex said in a hard voice. "Not now. Not ever."

"We need allies," Connor repeated.

"Then I'll look for a wife for you," Alex said.

If anyone needed a woman to stir his blood, it was Connor. He hadn't touched one since he'd become chieftain.

"I'm even willing to take the chieftains' daughters to bed," Alex said, "just so I can tell ye which one is dull enough for ye."

"If I take a wife, it would be interpreted as choosing sides in the rebellion," Connor said, "and I'm no ready to do that."

Damn, but Connor was hard to ruffle these days.

"I see," Alex said. "Ye are the prize to be dangled before them all until the last possible moment."

Connor sighed. "All I'm asking is that ye meet the daughters of these chieftains and see if there is one to your liking."

"We've made up a list of women for ye to consider," Ian said, pulling out a sheet of parchment and spreading it on the table.

"What?" Alex said.

"As ye can see, we've given ye plenty to choose from," Ian said. "I've divided them into those for and against the rebellion."

"We left out the Campbells because an earl's daughter seemed beyond our reach," Connor said, his eyes twinkling. "But if ye can enchant one, I'll no complain."

Alex refilled his cup, wondering when this would be over.

"I want both of ye to go to the rebel gathering at Duart Castle on Mull," Connor said. "From there, one of ye can go on to Edinburgh to see the regent."

"Should be a pleasant time at Duart Castle, consorting with rebels and a host who tried to murder us," Alex said, and they all laughed.

Connor tapped his finger on the parchment. "While ye are at the rebel gathering, ye can meet some of the prospective brides on my list."

Connor shoved the list across the table toward Duncan and Alex. Neither of them would take it, but the names were plain enough to see.

"Ahh, McNeil's eldest daughter is at the top of the list," Duncan said.

"Alex, I understand ye showed considerable interest in the lass," Connor said. "Kissing her in front of her father and clansmen."

Alex glared at Duncan. "Traitor."

"Shall I send a message to her father?" Connor asked with a wicked glint in his eye.

"The kiss meant nothing," Alex protested. "Ye know I have a weakness for pretty lasses. I forgot myself for a moment, that's all it was."

Duncan took a slow drink and set down his cup "'Twas a rather *long* moment, Alex."

Alex couldn't help joining in the laughter. But he was thinking that the kiss had not been nearly long enough.

"I almost forgot, Alex," Connor said, reaching inside his shirt. "Father Brian was here, and he brought a letter for ye."

CHAPTER 5

W ho would write me a letter?" Alex asked. Anyone who wished to speak to him could just get in his boat and come find him.

"Looks like it's been through many hands to get here," Connor said, holding out the battered parchment. "Do ye recognize the seal?"

As he studied the rose seal, vague recollections of France, perfumed messages, and assignations flitted through Alex's head. He sniffed the letter. The faintest hint of lavender remained.

Alex broke the seal and unfolded the parchment. The loopy French script tugged at his memory. This time, the image of perfect, full breasts came into his mind.

"How long are ye going to keep us waiting?" Connor asked.

"Just savoring the moment," Alex said. "Do ye remember Sabine de Savoisy, that countess who took me to her bed soon after we arrived in France?"

"Ye cannot expect me to remember all your women," Connor said. "I can't count that high, let alone recall their names."

"There was only one countess. Ye must remember Sabine—she had the enormous house outside Paris."

Connor nodded. "And lovely breasts."

It was unlike Connor to speak crudely in front of a woman, but he didn't appear to notice that Ilysa was standing nearby.

"So ye do remember Sabine." Alex looked at the date at the top of the letter. *The 10th of May in the year of our Lord 1515.* "It took a long time to get here."

The four of them had almost no secrets, so Alex began reading aloud.

I am in Edinburgh visiting the French Ambassador's wife. Such miserable, damp weather you have here and so little entertainment. I am bored beyond reason and would welcome a visit from you.

"The woman must have a vivid memory," Ian said, "to ask ye to make such a long journey for a tumble."

"Good as I am," Alex said, tapping the edge of the letter against the table, "I suspect Sabine could find a man in Edinburgh if that were her only purpose. No, she has some other reason for wanting me there."

I shall languish in this dreadful city through the month of July. Have mercy on me and come quickly. Your friend D'Arcy is here, adding to the tedium.

They had fought with D'Arcy in France.

"D'Arcy has close ties to Albany," Connor said.

So did Sabine, but Alex kept that to himself. He took a sip of his whiskey and then read the rest of the missive.

I have a special gift for you. I know how you like surprises so do come. I promise you will regret it if you do not.

                                                    S

Alex set his cup down and read the letter through twice more to himself. The message was veiled, the signature indeterminate, and the seal not her official one. But then, the countess was always careful.

"Do ye have any notion what this 'special gift' might be?" Connor asked, reading over his shoulder. "Other than the obvious."

Alex shook his head. "No, but I'll go to Edinburgh for ye and find out."

"Ye should take the letter to Teàrlag," Ilysa said.

Connor started at the sound of her voice. "Forgive me, Ilysa, I didn't see ye there," he said. "What do ye say, Alex? It can't hurt to show the letter to the old seer."

* * *

The wind whipped Connor's hair as he adjusted the sail. "It feels good to be out on the water."

"Ye should get out sailing more often." Alex was concerned about his cousin. The weight of his responsibilities showed in the lines of weariness on his face.

It was a short sail to the seer's cottage, which sat on

a ledge between the mountains and the sea. The four of them had done it countless times as lads, but today, it was just Alex, Connor, and Ilysa in the boat. Duncan had gone with Ian to visit Sìleas and the babes—despite Alex's warning that the twins were biters. Brave man.

"How is it that you have Shaggy's boat and not me?" Connor asked.

"Because I love her best," Alex said, patting the rail.

Connor laughed, a welcome sound. Ilysa, who fretted about Connor more than anyone, gave Alex a grateful look.

A short time later, they pulled the boat into the cove below Teàrlag's house and climbed the slippery steps cut into the stone cliff. Teàrlag was waiting for them outside her cottage. Despite the mildness of the early summer day, she was hunched over with two shawls wrapped around her, as if facing a bracing wind.

"I saw ye coming," she said, by way of greeting.

With her one good eye, Teàrlag couldn't see much in the usual sense, but she was a seer of great repute. Most folk avoided her, for she had an unnerving proclivity for predicting death.

They went inside, and Ilysa unloaded the basket of food she'd brought while Alex and Connor sat down with Teàrlag at her tiny table.

"Hush, they'll be gone soon," Teàrlag said to her cow, who was mooing in complaint on the other side of the half wall that divided the cottage. "Ilysa, get my whiskey. 'Tis no every day I have a visit from our chieftain."

"We need your help with a letter," Connor said after they'd downed their drinks.

Alex unfolded the parchment and held it flat on the table. Of course, the seer couldn't read, but that wasn't the point of bringing it.

"It's from a woman who says she has a special gift for me," Alex said. "Can ye tell me what it might be?"

Teàrlag cackled. "A special gift? Is that what they call it now?"

Ach, even the old seer had to joke.

Ilysa helped Teàrlag to the hearth, took a small bowl of herbs from the shelf, and tossed a pinch onto the fire. After breathing deeply from the burst of pungent smoke, the old seer shuffled back to her stool and placed her hands on the letter.

"I see three women, Alex Bàn MacDonald," she said in a far-off voice.

Only three? Alex hardly needed a seer to tell him there were women in his future. In fact, Teàrlag had been seeing women in his future since he was twelve.

"On your journey, three women will call on ye for help, and ye must give it," she said. "But beware! One brings danger and another deceit."

Alex rarely refused a woman anything, so this did not concern him. And a little danger and deceit just made things interesting.

"What about the third lass?" he asked.

"Ach." Tearlag gave him a sour look. "One has the power to fulfill your deepest desires."

Alex grinned. "Danger, deceit, and deep desires—I'm looking forward to this journey."

Teàrlag closed her eyes and rocked side to side, making a strange humming sound. Alex often wondered how much of Teàrlag's performance was for show.

"Ye are a sinner, Alexander Bàn," she called out.

"And the time will come soon when ye will pay for your sins."

Teàrlag was not the first to make this particular prediction. Alex was almost certain she was merely lecturing him now, as she had since he was a lad.

"What about the gift?" Connor asked.

Teàrlag was silent for so long that Alex thought she might have gone to sleep.

"I see brightness, like a moonbeam," Teàrlag said, waving her hand in front of her face.

Alex snorted. A moonbeam. Ach, that would be a useful gift. Now, if it was a sword, well, a man could always use another good sword.

"'Tis no a sword," Teàrlag said, snapping her eyes open. "This is an important gift, and ye must fetch it. Now go!"

They left Ilysa with Teàrlag, who was teaching her the old remedies. Duncan had forbidden his sister from training with the old seer, but Ilysa was one of the few creatures on God's earth who was not intimidated by him.

"That was even stranger than usual," Alex said, as soon as they were outside the cottage. "But I hope ye noticed that Teàrlag did not foresee a marriage for me."

"I want Duncan looking for a wife as well while ye are at the rebel gathering," Connor said, undeterred.

"He won't," Alex said. "Duncan still loves your sister."

"Moira's married," Connor said. "'Tis time Duncan forgot her and found a wife."

"He won't."

"We shall all do what we must to protect the clan," Connor said.

Connor was sounding more like a chieftain all the time.

"And Alex, ye have a bad habit of attracting women ye shouldn't," Connor said. "Try not to make us any new enemies while you're gone—we have enough to spare already."

CHAPTER 6

Glynis pulled the hood of her cloak low over her face as she and her father entered the castle's courtyard, which was already crowded with guests. The MacNeils of Barra and the Macleans of Duart had a long friendship, and she had been to Duart Castle many times. But this was her first large clan gathering since the end of her marriage.

When the Maclean chieftain saw her father, he broke away from his other guests to greet them. "Chieftain MacNeil, I welcome ye once again to my home."

Not many people made Glynis uneasy, but Lachlan Cattanach Maclean, otherwise known as Shaggy, was one. She was accustomed to fierce warriors, but Shaggy was unpredictable. In truth, she thought him a little mad.

"I had to leave my wife at home, as she is with child," Glynis's father said.

"A wife who does her duty by providing her husband with children," Shaggy said, "is the only kind of wife worth keeping."

Glynis wasn't sure if Shaggy meant to insult her or his current wife, Catherine Campbell.

"As ye can see, I brought Glynis instead," her father said. "I'm hoping to find her a new husband."

Glynis ducked her head still lower, though what she wanted to do was kick her father.

"Your daughter has grown shy," Shaggy said.

Her father coughed.

"Not beating up the lads like ye used to?" Shaggy said to her. "Just stabbing them, aye?"

"Only when provoked," she murmured while Shaggy laughed, and her father rammed his elbow into her side.

"If my wife, *the earl's daughter*," Shaggy said with sarcasm so heavy it scraped the floor, "would lower herself to greet my guests, I'm sure she would show ye the chamber set aside for the visiting lasses."

"Glynis can find it," her father said. "We'll visit with the other guests in the hall first."

Glynis had barely set foot in Duart Castle, and already she was counting the hours until they left. Once inside the keep, they stood at the entrance to the hall surveying the noisy room. Many clans were represented, judging by the number of men dressed in the saffron shirts and fine wool plaids of highborn clansmen.

"The young chieftain of the MacDonalds of Sleat is an elusive man," her father said, his voice rasping with displeasure. "It doesn't appear he has come."

"You shouldn't have either, da," Glynis said. "Joining this rebellion was a mistake, and ye should quit it now."

"Did I ask your advice, daughter? These are no matters for women to decide."

"Please, da," Glynis said, and pulled at his arm. "Don't agree to do anything more."

Preventing her father from becoming more deeply involved in this rebellion was the sole reason she'd agreed to come to the gathering without being bound and gagged.

"Your chances of catching a chieftain are poor now," her father said, his eyes traveling the room. "If ye had proven yourself a good breeder, it might be different."

Glynis told herself that her father didn't realize how his harping on her failure to conceive was like a blade in her heart. It was the only way she could forgive him for it.

"Remember," he said, " 'Honey may be sweet, but no one licks it off a briar.' "

Glynis sucked in her breath.

"What is it?" her father asked.

Her hands shook as she smoothed her skirts and tried to gather herself. Her former husband, Magnus Clanranald, the man who had humiliated and shamed her, was in the hall. She hadn't laid eyes on him since the night she left him. As usual, Magnus was giving his full attention to the breasts of a buxom lass who was on his lap.

"I didn't know Magnus would be here," her father said, following her gaze.

Her face burned, and her eyes stung. She should have stuck her blade into Magnus's black heart when she had the chance.

"I don't believe ye," she said. "Ye knew damned well Magnus would be here."

Glynis turned and bolted out of the keep.

* * *

"How did Connor convince us to visit Shaggy Maclean?" Alex eyed Duart Castle looming ahead of them on a rock cliff.

Duncan was playing his whistle and didn't trouble himself to respond. It was a sad tune, of course.

"I hope the accommodations are better than on our previous visit," Alex said. The last time they were at Shaggy Maclean's castle, they were prisoners in his dungeon.

Duncan tucked his whistle inside his shirt. "Then keep your distance from Shaggy's wife this time."

"Ye can't blame that on me," Alex said. "She took advantage of me when I was weak from the beating they gave me. I hadn't the strength to resist her."

"Ye never have the strength to resist a willing lass."

"Willing? I thought the woman would eat the meat off my bones," Alex said. "And ye owe me thanks, for she did help us escape Shaggy's dungeon."

"We would have found another way out," Duncan said. "We always do."

"Shaggy's wife is a Campbell," Alex said to annoy Duncan. "I should do my part to bring us closer to such a powerful clan."

Shaggy had wed the Campbell chieftain's sister in a bid to bring peace between their clans. The two hated each other, however, which just went to show that marriage was a poor basis for forming an alliance.

That made Alex think of Glynis MacNeil's disastrous marriage. In truth, he thought of Glynis surprisingly often. She was a damned intriguing woman, though not his sort at all. He liked women with easy natures—and easier virtue.

"Why don't ye just get a mistress like a normal man?" Duncan asked.

Alex made a face. "Ach, no. A mistress can become too much like a wife."

He had seen that happen too many times. As a lad, it was always his shoulder they wept on when his father sent them away. Alex used to warn the women, but it was no use. After a few months, they always expected a permanent arrangement of one kind or another.

"At least I like the women I bed. I even talk to them— something ye might try," Alex said. "Do ye ever speak to your mistress, other than to say 'pass the fish' and 'take your clothes off'?"

"Time to lower the sails, lads," Duncan called out to the other men. "Take an oar."

Unfortunately, they couldn't arrive at Shaggy's in the boat they stole from him, so they were sailing one of the war galleys. Though it was large enough to carry fifty warriors, Connor had been able to spare only the eighteen needed to man the oars.

"I expect Rhona believes that behind all that silence you're thinking deep thoughts about her," Alex said, as he leaned on the rudder. "You've had her in your bed for months, and yet ye wouldn't care if she left tomorrow, would ye?"

"I don't mind her." Duncan shrugged. "We meet each other's needs, and she doesn't cause a fuss like your women do."

"*Meet each other's needs.*" Alex snorted. "That sounds like a fine time."

"Rest your oars," Duncan called out, and they glided into shore below the castle.

* * *

Alex was already bored listening to the men who were gathered in the castle courtyard. As always, there was a lot of pointless talk about returning to the glory days when half the Highlands answered to the Lord of the Isles, rather than to the King of Scotland.

For a hundred and fifty years, the Lord of the Isles had been the leader of all the branches of the Clan MacDonald and their vassals, which had included the Macleans, the MacLeods, the MacNeils, and the rest. Under the Lordship, the clans had followed old Celtic law and customs. That part had not changed much—they still ignored Scottish law and directives from the church in Rome, except when convenient.

But it had been more than twenty years since the Lord of the Isles had been forced to submit to the crown. Without a single leader, the clans fought among themselves all the time. That did not, however, keep them from rising against the Crown again and again.

"We'll burn Inverness!" one young man shouted, clenching his fist in the air.

"Not again." Alex sighed and turned to Duncan. "How many times has Inverness been burned?"

"Some men are practicing in the field behind the castle," Duncan said. "Since we may fight these rebels one day, let's see how good they are."

As Alex and Duncan entered the field, the men halted their practice. Twenty pairs of hostile eyes fixed upon them.

"What are the MacDonalds of Sleat doing here?" one man said loud enough for all to hear. He was a MacLeod warrior with a long scar down the side of his face.

"We're not your enemies," Alex said.

"Then why has your clan not joined the rebellion?" another man asked.

"Because we're just brimming with goodwill to all," Alex said, spreading his arms out.

Most of the men laughed and that might have been an end to it, if not for a young man with a weedy beard and weasel eyes.

"I say the MacDonalds of Sleat refuse to join us because they are poor fighters." The man paused, then added, "Or else they are just cowards."

"That's it," Duncan said, as he unsheathed his claymore. "Who's first?"

"I'll fight ye," the same fool said, and stepped forward to meet Duncan.

"Who's next?" Alex whipped out his sword—he couldn't let Duncan defend the honor of the clan alone. "How about you with the ugly face?"

As Alex fought the MacLeod warrior, he watched the other fight out of the corner of his eye. Duncan fought with his usual cool control. His opponent was red-faced and cursing as he fell back, again and again, under the pounding assault of Duncan's claymore. In no time, the man was flat on his back with Duncan's foot on his chest and the point of Duncan's sword just beneath his weedy beard.

After Alex and Duncan defeated three or four opponents each, tempers cooled, and the other men resumed their practice as if nothing had occurred.

"That felt good," Alex said, as he and Duncan rested against the castle wall. They watched the others, commenting in low voices on their skill or lack of it.

But then Alex's attention was caught by a woman who came out of the castle gate. She made an abrupt turn and walked toward them at a furious pace with her head down.

"Is that Glynis MacNeil?" Duncan asked.

"Aye. What in the hell is she doing out here alone?" There were other women at the gathering, but they had the sense to stay inside the keep or stick close to their men.

Alex caught her arm as she charged past him.

"Ye can't go—" The words dried in his mouth. He'd forgotten what an impact her face had on him. He tried telling himself that she wasn't any more beautiful than a hundred women he knew—but there was something about her that stole his thoughts away.

Glynis was staring right back at him with her luminous gray eyes. Though he knew it was a mistake, he let his gaze drop to her mouth. Her lips were parted. The memory of that kiss on the beach sang through his body, bringing everything to full attention.

Alex gave himself a mental shake. He couldn't let that happen again.

"You look upset," Alex said. "What's wrong?"

"Nothing." But then she glanced back toward the gate, and the color drained from her face.

A heavily muscled warrior with a full black beard and black eyes to match had just come into the field. He had his claymore strapped to his back and looked as if he meant to join the practice. But when his gaze fell on Glynis, he stopped in place. The tension running between the two of them was as palpable as a taut rope holding a sail in a storm.

"Who is he?" Alex asked.

"The chieftain of Clanranald," she said so low he could barely hear her. "Magnus, my former husband."

"He looks as if he harbors a grudge against ye," Alex said.

"He would have preferred I left our marriage for the grave."

"You!" Magnus roared, as he pulled his claymore from his back.

"Take her." Alex shoved Glynis toward Duncan and positioned himself a few paces in front of them, his stance wide and his sword ready.

"Watch yourself," Duncan said in a low voice behind him. "This one knows how to fight."

The Clanranald chieftain raised his claymore over his head and roared again as he ran headlong toward them. The blow was so strong that Alex felt the vibration to his feet.

"Ye forget you're a guest here," Alex grunted between their next exchange of blows.

The man's eyes were wild with rage, and he swung his sword with the force of a boulder crashing down a cliff. For a man so heavy with muscle, he was quick, too. It took all of Alex's skill and strength to force him toward the middle of the field. When Alex had him well away from the wall, he risked a glance to be sure Duncan had gotten Glynis inside the castle gate.

Diverting his attention for even a moment was a mistake. Alex had to drop to the ground to avoid the Clanranald chieftain's next swing. He felt the wind of the blade in his hair. Before he could get to his feet, his opponent brought his sword straight down with a loud grunt.

Alex rolled out of the way just before the blade thudded to the ground.

This was no practice fight—the Clanranald chieftain was trying to kill him.

The two of them crossed swords up and down the yard. Alex spun around and hit Magnus's back so hard with the flat of his sword that he nearly knocked the chieftain off his feet. When a cheer went up, Alex became aware that a crowd had gathered to watch them.

But Alex wasn't putting on a show this time. He was fighting for his life.

Sweat poured down his back as he alternately blocked Magnus's sword and swung his own. At last, he sensed his opponent tiring. They leaned into each other, swords crossed, and faces inches apart.

"Only a weak man would let a lass upset him so much," Alex taunted him.

"She doesn't upset me," Magnus hissed, his black eyes bulging with fury.

When they broke apart, Magnus came at him hard, but his swings were less controlled. Alex spun and danced around him, swinging again and again, wearing him down.

"I hear she cut your ballocks off," Alex said just loud enough for Magnus to hear him, "and left ye less than a man."

This time when Magnus charged him, Alex stepped aside—and stuck his foot out. The Clanranald chieftain crashed to the ground. In an instant, Alex sat astride his opponent's back and held his head up by his hair. Duncan appeared with a bucket of water and drenched the Clanranald chieftain, who sputtered and coughed.

"Ye can thank me for saving ye from murdering a lass who doesn't upset ye," Alex said, still breathing hard. "And by the way, I believe we are cousins of some sort— my mother is a Clanranald."

"Get off me!"

Alex leaned down to speak in the man's ear. "Stay away from Glynis MacNeil if ye know what's good for ye. Next time, I'll kill ye—and now ye know I can do it."

Magnus Clanranald was a chieftain and a man of pride. Threatening him was not wise, but it was necessary. Alex left the man with his face in the dirt.

"Let's go for a swim," Alex said, as he and Duncan started off the field. "I'd say we're doing a fine job of following Connor's orders to make friends among the rebel clans."

"'Tis good to remind them that we MacDonalds know how to fight," Duncan said. "Better that they respect us than like us."

"I did refrain from killing the Clanranald chieftain," Alex pointed out.

"That was probably a mistake," Duncan said. "I was watching his clansmen while ye were fighting, and at least half of them were ready to thank ye for doing away with him."

* * *

Glynis ignored Duncan's order to go inside the keep and stood transfixed watching the fight through the open gate. Apparently, the MacDonald captain of the guard was used to being obeyed, for he left her without a backward glance.

"Ye don't want to miss this fight!" someone shouted.

People jostled her as they pushed past to go out into the yard. Fortunately, no one seemed to realize the fight had anything to do with her. A large crowd encircled the two men who were clanking swords ferociously up and down the field.

"I don't blame ye for watching. Alex MacDonald is sinfully handsome."

Glynis started at the sound of a woman's deep, rich voice beside her. She turned to find it belonged to the mysterious beauty, Lady Catherine Campbell, who was Shaggy Maclean's wife. With her wavy dark hair and voluptuous curves, the woman exuded a sensuality that left men gasping. Catherine was every man's dream—and she knew it.

Next to her, Glynis felt like a doll her father once made for her from sticks and frayed rope.

"Praise God," Glynis said when Alex and Duncan left Magnus sprawled on the ground.

"I knew Alex would win," Catherine said. "He has the twin gifts of skill and the devil's own luck."

When Magnus started to get up, Glynis picked up her skirts to go inside before he saw her again. But as she turned, the glint of sun hitting metal caught her eye. Magnus was pulling a short blade from his sleeve.

"Alex!" Glynis shouted.

The warning was unnecessary. Alex had read his man well and was already spinning around in a crouch. He moved so fast that it was difficult to tell exactly how he did it, but his boot met Magnus's hand with such force that the dirk flew into the air.

A moment later, Magnus's own men caught him under

the arms and dragged him away. Attempting to stab another guest in the back was a serious breach of the rules of Highland hospitality.

Alex wiped his brow on his sleeve and headed down toward the water with Duncan. Glynis watched as the two men waded into the sea and dove under. When Alex emerged after his swim with his shirt clinging to his broad chest, and his hair slicked back and hanging to his shoulders, a small moan escaped her.

She had forgotten Catherine was still standing next to her until she spoke again.

"Save yourself some heartache—don't set your sights on Alex MacDonald," Catherine said. "You're not his sort at all."

"I've set my sights on no man," Glynis said, feeling unreasonably annoyed by the remark. "And what do ye mean, I'm not his sort?"

"Ye may be twenty, but you're still a girl," Catherine said with a laugh in her voice. "A man like Alex needs a woman."

CHAPTER 7

Alex looked for Glynis when he and Duncan entered the castle, thinking he deserved to collect a kiss from her after that fight. He was ready to risk it—though not in front of her father. But Glynis was not among the crowd congratulating him.

"That was some fine bladework," Shaggy Maclean said, slapping Alex on his back.

Alex refrained from telling Shaggy to keep his goddamned hands off of him. He hadn't forgotten Shaggy's attempt to help Hugh take the chieftainship from Connor.

"I hear the men tested your mettle as well," Shaggy said, and took his life in his hands by squeezing Duncan's shoulder. "We need warriors like the two of ye fighting for the rebellion."

"We'll discuss it with our chieftain," Duncan said.

He and Duncan excused themselves to rinse off the salt water from their swim at the well in the castle courtyard. Afterward, Alex climbed the stairs of the keep, looking for an empty chamber where he could stretch out away from the noise in the hall. He should ask his hostess, but he intended to avoid Catherine Campbell for as long as he could.

Alex stripped off his wet clothes and put on the dry shirt he had retrieved from their boat. His muscles ached pleasantly from being worked hard. With a sigh, he lay down on top of the bedclothes.

He had no idea how long he'd been sleeping when he awoke to the delicious sensation of a woman's fingertips caressing his stomach. He smiled to himself and indulged in the completely inappropriate fantasy that it was Glynis MacNeil running her fingers over his skin.

Ah, that feels good, Glynis.

Long hair tickled his chest, and he imagined her thick chestnut-brown hair sliding over him. *Aye.*

It was bound to be a disappointment, but he supposed it was time to find out who this really was. When he slit open his eyes, Catherine Campbell was leaning over him with her hair spilling over his chest.

"I'd been watching for ye," she said in her husky voice. "And now I've found ye."

She had found him, indeed. Her hand was wrapped around his cock.

Catherine was a gorgeous woman, and he was tempted. God knew, his body was ready. But contrary to what many thought of him, Alex did abide by certain rules.

"I can't do this, Catherine," he said. "Not when I'm a guest in your husband's home."

"That didn't trouble ye last time," she said.

When she started moving her hand up his shaft, he held her wrist—no small act of will.

"I was a prisoner in Shaggy's dungeon, not his guest," he said. "The customary rules of courtesy did not apply."

Catherine gave a throaty laugh. Alex tried hard not to notice that her skirts were hiked up to reveal lovely thighs—or that every time she leaned over him, her even lovelier breasts pressed against the low-cut bodice, as if begging to be released.

"Ye needn't be concerned about Shaggy because I'm going to leave him," Catherine said, and Alex's throat went dry as she ran her hands from the sides of her breasts down to her hips and then the tops of her bare thighs. "Ye see, I need a man who can please me."

There was nothing Connor would like better than a close connection to the Campbells. And Catherine was clearly suggesting a close connection of some sort.

"But ye haven't left Shaggy yet," he said. "So let me get up."

When she didn't budge, Alex decided he would have to move her off him, but there seemed no safe place to put his hands.

"Let's get naked, Alexander." She leaned against him, pressing her full breasts against his chest, and wound her arms around his neck.

It was not like him to say nay to a beautiful woman who wanted him naked. He made a practice of following the old saying *The oar that is close at hand, row with it.*

With her rubbing against him, his body was in favor of giving in. And yet, he didn't truly want Catherine. It wasn't just that bedding the wife of his host was against one of his few principles, or that he felt used—though he did. Catherine wanted to punish her husband. And worse, he suspected she wanted to get caught.

She was a beautiful, willing woman. And yet, Alex couldn't get rid of her fast enough to suit him. As he sat up he took hold of her waist and lifted her to the floor. *There.*

When he stood, Catherine came behind him and put her arms around his waist. Her hands roamed over his chest and hips, and it took him a moment too long to remember why this was a bad idea. By the time he did, she had tugged his shirt over his head.

"Catherine. I told ye I can't do this."

When he turned around and took his shirt from her, she pressed herself against him. Ach, Catherine would try a saint. As soon as he peeled her fingers from around his neck, they ended up on his arse.

She felt very, *very* good. As she kissed his chest, he closed his eyes and checked his resolve.

"Ye know ye want me," she said against his skin.

"Not now, Catherine." Gently, he pushed her away.

Before she could grab him again, Alex gathered the rest of his clothes from the bench. When he turned and started toward the door, it was already open. *Oh, God, no.*

CHAPTER 8

The clatter and voices from below grew muffled as Glynis climbed the circular stone stairs. She should find Alex in the hall and thank him for what he did, but she didn't want to risk seeing Magnus again so soon. When she reached the third floor, she paused, trying to remember which bedchamber the Macleans usually set aside for the visiting women of high rank.

Since everyone else was in the hall for the midday meal, she didn't have to worry about disturbing anyone, so she opened the door to her right. Glynis took one step inside and froze. Somewhere deep in the back of her mind, a voice was telling her to *get out*. But her feet would not obey.

Alexander Bàn MacDonald stood with his back to the door—and not a stitch on him. How she knew it was him from the back was a question she'd ask herself later. But one look at the blond hair, the broad shoulders, the long, muscular legs, and that perfect, manly arse, and Glynis knew for certain that this naked man was Alex.

A woman's fingers were laced at the back of his neck. Glynis still could not move—her hand held the door latch as if melded to it. She forced her gaze to the floor, but there was nothing she could do to slow her heartbeat. When the woman gave a throaty laugh, Glynis could not help looking up again.

She could not breathe. The woman had her hands on Alex's bare backside. Glynis imagined how his muscles would feel beneath her fingers.

"Not now, Catherine." Alex's voice penetrated her daze.

Glynis had to leave before Alex saw her. And still, she felt as if her feet were nailed to the floor.

Alex turned.

Ach, it was a sin for a man to be so tall and handsome. It wasn't fair at all. Her eyes skimmed over him, slowly moving from his damp blond hair and striking face to his broad chest. She longed to feel the rough hair and hard muscles beneath her palms. And then her gaze fell lower still.

Her mouth fell open, and she felt an odd squeeze inside her as she stared at his fully erect shaft. Suddenly, she realized what she was doing, and she jerked her gaze back up to his face.

Alex had halted where he was. A dark smile played over his lips.

"Glynis." He spoke her name slowly, as if tasting each letter. His voice was thick honey, golden like the rest of him.

Glynis was so bewitched that she had forgotten there was someone else in the room. When the woman came out from behind Alex and slipped her arm around his waist, Alex looked as startled as Glynis was.

The woman was Catherine Campbell, the Maclean chieftain's wife. With her shining black hair tousled, her gown loosened to reveal the tops of her generous breasts, and her eyes dark with desire, she was breathtaking.

Alex called Glynis's name as she ran down the stairs. His voice echoed off the stone walls and inside her head, but she did not stop. She ran out of the keep, across the yard, and out the gate. Only after she scrambled down to the shore did she finally stop. She sat on a rock and pressed her palm to her chest, trying to get her breath back. Her hands shook, and her heart pounded as if it would burst.

Why was she so upset? She hardly knew Alex MacDonald. And from what she did know about him, she shouldn't have been surprised to find him in bed with a woman. Still, it had been a shock to see the pair of them like that. She covered her face, remembering how she had stared at him naked. Ach, she had stared at his manly parts! How could she?

Of course, it would be the most beautiful woman in all the Highlands who was in bed with Alex. But his host's wife? Foolish, but Glynis had thought better of him than that.

*   *   *

Alex tried to find Glynis as soon as he had untangled himself from Catherine. Why he felt the need to explain himself to Glynis, he did not know. But for some reason, it was important to him that she not think he was even worse than he actually was.

He still hadn't seen Glynis when he and Duncan entered the hall for supper. He scanned the room for her. He didn't have much time left—he was leaving for Edinburgh in the morning.

"Who are ye looking for?" Duncan asked.

"No one," Alex said.

"Hmmph," Duncan grunted, but he let it pass. "These rebels are up to something. Donald Gallda and the other chieftains met this afternoon without any of their men present."

Donald Gallda MacDonald of Lachalsh was the latest MacDonald to take up the leadership of the rebellion. The king had taken him to be raised in the Lowlands after his father's rebellion, which was the reason Highlanders called him Donald *Gallda*, the Stranger.

"Let's split up and see what we can find out," Alex said.

"I'll see if that drunken lot knows anything," Duncan said with a nod toward a table of Maclean warriors. "I assume you'll talk with the MacNeils."

Before Alex could ask Duncan what he meant by that remark, Duncan was gone.

Alex found the MacNeil chieftain near the hearth. Judging from his hearty greeting, the man had forgiven Alex for that kiss on the beach.

"I have a warning for ye," the MacNeil said below the noise of the hall. "No one but the chieftains is to know ahead of time, but we're attacking Mingary Castle tomorrow."

"That's poking a stick in the hornet's nest." Mingary was held by the MacIains, who were close allies of the Crown. The Crown would be up in arms over this, which

made it all the more important for Alex to get to Edinburgh to reassure the regent.

"If ye don't want to be part of it, be gone by morning."
The MacNeil glanced about to be sure no one was listening. "They intend to give you and Duncan the choice to
fight with us or be the first to die in the battle."

If Connor's close cousin and the captain of his guard
participated in the attack, the Crown's allies would hear
of it, and their clan would be committed to the rebellion.

"The sly dogs." Alex should have expected it.

"I don't agree with forcing a chieftain's hand like that,"
the MacNeil said. "But after the others saw ye fight, they
were determined to see ye on the right side or dead."

"I appreciate the warning." They would all have to
leave tonight, he to Edinburgh, and Duncan and the rest
of their men to Skye.

"Being Highlanders, these other chieftains will be all the
more impressed if ye succeed in sneaking out of here under
their noses," the MacNeil said, and they both laughed.

"They'll never hear us leave," Alex said with a wink.
He was anxious to talk with Duncan, but that would have
to wait until after the meal. "Shall we find your daughter
and sit down?"

"She's sitting at the high table tonight."

Alex turned and saw Glynis was indeed at the high
table, sitting next to the weasel with the weedy beard.
"Who is that?"

"Shaggy's second son, Alain." The MacNeil elbowed
him. "He would be a good match for my Glynis."

"*Him?*" Alex stared at the pair at the head table for a
long moment, trying to decide if the MacNeil chieftain
was having a joke on him.

"Aye," the MacNeil said, nodding. "Alain is a chieftain's son from a strong clan that supports the rebellion, and she's known him all her life."

"He's not a man I would trust," Alex said.

For a brief moment, Glynis met his eyes. But when Alex smiled and nodded, she turned her head.

"And you are?" MacNeil asked him.

"Are what?" Alex asked, with his gaze still on Glynis.

"A man to be trusted."

That got his attention. Alex knew exactly what the MacNeil chieftain was asking him. He heard his mother's voice in his head, as if she were standing right next to him. *Ye will be just like your father!*

And Alex had turned out to be like his father. He enjoyed women, though never the same one for long. But in one regard, Alex was determined to be different from his father. He would not make the mistake of marrying a good woman and causing her to hate him.

"Your daughter would have her dirk in me in no time," Alex said. "And I'd deserve it."

"Alain will do," the MacNeil chieftain said. "Of course, I'd prefer that she and Magnus Clanranald patched up their differences."

Alex spun around to stare at him. "Ye can't mean it," he said, struggling to keep his voice low. "Magnus is a vile man—and he's a danger to her."

"Ach," MacNeil said, dismissing this with a wave of his hand. "They got off to a bad start. A little time is all they need—and a babe, of course. A babe would solve the problem. Ye can't blame Magnus for wanting an heir. Every man does."

He'd send her back to Magnus? Alex wanted to pound

the MacNeil's thick head on the table, but knocking sense into the man was clearly a hopeless task.

Alex drank down his ale, wishing to God that Shaggy served whiskey instead.

*   *   *

The bar across the door creaked as Glynis slid it back. Over the pounding in her ears, she heard one of the women on the bed behind her sigh. Her hands shook as she waited for the woman to call out to her.

There was a rustle of bedclothes, and she held her breath, waiting. Silence settled over the room again. Moving as quickly as she dared in the blackness, Glynis picked up the cloth bag she had left beside the door, lifted her cloak from the peg, and slipped out.

Panic surged through her limbs as a large hand covered her mouth.

CHAPTER 9

Don't scream. It's me." Alex didn't release his hand from Glynis's mouth until she nodded.

"I asked ye to meet me outside the kitchens," she whispered.

"Quiet. We can't talk here." He put his arm around her and swept her down the stairs before someone in one of the bedchambers heard them and came out to investigate.

When they reached the main floor, he continued down into the undercroft. With so many guests in the castle, they could find servants sleeping or still working in the kitchens, so he grabbed a lit torch off the wall and shoved her into a storeroom.

"What were ye thinking asking me to meet ye at this hour?" he said, as he rammed the torch into the sconce on the wall.

Alex had been on the galley sorting out the supplies he needed to take with him to Edinburgh when a young boy appeared and told him that a lady wanted him to meet her at midnight outside the kitchens. This was not the first time he'd had that sort of request. He was about to send the lad away, but something made him ask the lad to describe the lady first.

"I'm glad ye came," Glynis said.

"Ye gave me no choice," he said. "I couldn't have ye wandering around a castle full of warriors—half of them drunk— looking for me in the dark."

He took a deep breath. He had wanted to say goodbye to her—and to explain about what she'd seen when she walked in on him and Catherine—but he didn't have a lot of time. He was meeting Duncan soon, and then they were all leaving.

"Why did ye want to see me?" he asked.

"When I talked with your friend Duncan this afternoon, he told me you're going to Edinburgh."

How had she gotten closemouthed Duncan to share their business with her?

"I want ye to take me with ye," she said.

Alex could not have been more stunned if she'd sprouted fairy wings and flown over the pots and bags of grain in the storeroom. Just what was Glynis suggesting? His heart gave a big lurch as he considered the possibility that she might actually want to run off with him. Apparently, she liked what she saw of him earlier today.

But it seemed so unlikely that he had to ask. "Why?"

"I've decided to live with my mother's family," she said. "They are Lowlanders and live in Edinburgh."

Alex waited for the relief he should feel upon learning that her request had nothing to do with him, but it didn't come. A bad sign.

"Ye know verra well that I can't just run off with ye across Scotland," Alex said.

"Ye must," she said, clenching her fists. "My da wants to marry me to *Alain*."

Alex wanted to hit something. He didn't have time for this, and her father hadn't listened to him before, but he wanted to help her if he could. "Do ye know where your father is? I'll speak with him."

"Does my father strike ye as the sort of man who takes advice well?"

She had a point, but he said, "I can be verra persuasive."

"So I've heard," Glynis said with more than a touch of sarcasm. "But it will do no good. My father is too stubborn by half."

As was his daughter. "Have ye considered a compromise? Is there no man ye are willing to wed?"

Glynis gave her head a firm shake and folded her arms. "Ye said ye would be my friend."

"Stealing a lass away from her father is no being a friend," he said, though his words felt hollow. Her mother's family could hardly do worse by her.

"Take me, Alexander Bàn MacDonald," she said, her gray eyes turning to hard flint. "Or I'll go tell the Maclean chieftain right now that I saw ye swiving his wife."

"That wasn't what it looked like!" Alex was so used to having committed whatever offense he was accused of that he hardly knew how to defend himself. "My clan needs ties to the Campbells, so I couldn't offend her."

"Ye sacrificed yourself for the sake of your clan, did ye?"

"I didn't do what ye think," Alex protested. "Though it wasn't easy, mind ye."

Judging from the grim line of her mouth, Glynis was not impressed with his forbearance.

"Catherine is close to her brothers," he explained. "If you've forgotten, they are the Earl of Argyll and the Thane of Cawdor, so I had to be verra careful about how I told her nay."

"It looked like 'aye' to me—your being naked and all."

Ach, she was full of sarcasm tonight. Glynis took a step closer and tapped her finger against his chest. Despite the anger in her eyes, the point of her finger sent heat radiating through his body.

"How about I tell Shaggy Maclean what I saw and let him sort it out?" she asked.

God preserve him, she was a determined woman. If she went running to Shaggy with this tale now, none of the MacDonalds would escape tonight. Alex ran his hand through his hair. He could tie her up and leave her in the storeroom. But he didn't like the idea of leaving her helpless, not knowing how long she might lie here—or who might find her.

"If ye tell Shaggy, he'll kill me," Alex said, attempting to reason with her.

"It wouldn't be my fault," she said. "A man should pay for his sins."

Hadn't Teàrlag said something like that to him?

"Ye wouldn't be that heartless," he said, though Glynis was looking as if she damned well would. "And I'm telling ye, I didn't sin with Catherine."

Not this time, anyway.

"I'll do what I must," Glynis said with that stubborn look in her eyes. "There are hundreds of men here. My father won't know it was you I left with, if that's your concern."

With her father attacking Mingary, he wouldn't even know she was missing for days. Still, it was too foolish.

"The truth has a way of coming out." Alex folded his arms across his chest. "Have ye thought of what your father will do if he finds out I'm the one who stole ye away? Angry as he would be, he'd demand a wedding."

For the first time, Glynis looked uncertain. It grated on him that the possibility of being forced to wed him was the only part of her ridiculous plan that gave her pause.

"I'll have to take the risk," she said in a hard voice. "Now, do I go bang on Shaggy's bedchamber door, or will ye take me?"

CHAPTER 10

"Let's go," Alex said.

Glynis sucked in her breath as he pulled her tight against his side. Her feet barely touched the ground as they passed the kitchens and started up the stairs.

What was she doing, putting herself into the hands of a man she barely knew? What made her trust this too-handsome warrior from a different clan? He owed her no allegiance. And he was angry that she'd coerced him into taking her. He could abandon her in the wilderness.

This was the most outrageous thing she had ever done, except perhaps stabbing her husband. But sticking Magnus was something that just happened—she hadn't planned it.

The cool night air hit her face as they left the keep, but Alex's heat radiated through her. He had a warrior's body, powerful and graceful, and he held her with a sureness that sent her heart hammering.

Would Alex expect to be more than her escort?

That might be a reasonable assumption for a man to make—especially if he was the sort of man who was accustomed to having women offer themselves to him. If half of what she'd heard about Alex Bàn MacDonald was true, he was that sort of man.

"If anyone sees us," Alex said in a low voice, "we want them to believe we're a pair of lovers sneaking off for a tryst."

Alex only meant to pretend they would. Glynis was, of course, relieved that Alex had not mistaken her intentions.

"'Tis fortunate I have a companion with so much useful experience," she whispered.

"Keep your head down," Alex said. "We don't want anyone to recognize ye."

"I suppose it won't matter if they recognize you," she said. "In fact, it might seem suspicious if a night went by without someone seeing ye sneak off with a lass."

"Shhh."

They were walking along the castle wall, in sight of the gate now. Glynis's heart raced. Would the guards stop them? Would they demand to know who she was and call her father? Alex slowed his steps. When he leaned down, the warmth of his breath in her ear sent a tingle all the way to her toes.

"Play along with me," he whispered.

She nearly yelped when he slid his hand under her cloak and along her ribcage. It was far too close to her breast.

She grabbed his wrist and hissed, "I cannot breathe with your hand there."

He chuckled deep in his throat, but he didn't remove

his hand. Instead, he nuzzled her neck. "Have ye changed your mind?" he said against her skin. "Because if ye want to go to Edinburgh, we must first get out of the castle."

She heard the sound of boots coming around the corner of the keep. The next thing she knew, Alex had her flattened against the stone wall. His mouth was on hers before she could think, *Oh, God, he's going to kiss me!*

And it didn't seem like a pretend kiss at all. His body was hard against hers, but his mouth was soft and warm. As Alex kissed her again and again, her knees grew so weak she had to put her arms around his neck to keep from falling. He held her tighter as he deepened their kisses, his tongue in her mouth, probing, seeking.

Her insides turned to liquid, and her head spun. The things other women said about kissing were true after all. That was her last clear thought.

His hands were moving under her cloak, gripping her hip, sliding up the sides of her breasts. When she felt his hard shaft against her belly, a groan escaped her throat. She tangled her fingers in his hair, urging him closer still.

Suddenly, Alex broke the kiss. He was breathing hard, and he still had her pressed against the wall so that she felt every inch of his heat through her clothes.

He framed her face with his hands and looked into her eyes. She blinked, trying to take in what had just happened to her and what it meant.

"Do ye think we convinced the guards," he asked, running his thumb across her cheek, "or should I kiss ye again to be sure?"

She was mortified. It was all a joke to him.

* * *

How had he lost control like that? God help him, he'd wanted to lift Glynis's skirts and take her right there against the castle wall with the guards walking by.

Alex thought he could rely upon Glynis's good sense. Ha! She melted in his arms from the first touch of their lips—and he'd lost his mind.

How would he ever manage to make it all the way to Edinburgh?

This was Teàrlag's fault. He should have tied Glynis up instead of following the seer's admonition to help the women who called on him. And if he fulfilled his deep desires with this one, she was sure to bring him danger. Bedding an unmarried chieftain's daughter was a grave offense that justified the harshest possible punishment—death or *marriage*.

Alex ignored the guards' jibes about getting sand in their hair—and various private places—as the men let them out the gate. Glynis tried to tug her hand away, but he ignored that, too. Holding her tightly, he led her down to the shore.

"Over here," Duncan called.

Alex followed Duncan's voice until his friend's outline emerged from the darkness.

"I 'borrowed' this skiff from the Macleans for ye," Duncan said. "It's old, but it should get ye across to the mainland."

"You're a good man," Alex said. "You'd best be off as well."

Their men and galley were ready and waiting for Duncan in the next cove. Despite Glynis, all had gone well so far. But at any moment, someone in the hall could wake and notice that all the MacDonalds of Sleat were missing.

Duncan's gaze shifted from him to Glynis and back again, asking for an explanation.

"Ye never saw her," Alex said. "This was her plan, not mine. She wants me to take her to her relatives in Edinburgh."

"Mistress Glynis," Duncan said, "are ye certain ye want to do this?"

"I can take ye back to the keep, and no one would be the wiser." Alex held his breath, waiting for her answer.

"I'm going," Glynis said, and climbed into the boat.

It appeared Alex was in for an adventure. Teàrlag said three women would require his help, and he hoped to hell the old seer had miscounted.

"We aren't the only ones leaving in the dark tonight," Duncan said to Alex, after they had stepped away to speak in private. "I saw another boat go out a couple of hours ago."

Alex waited, sensing Duncan had something more to say to him.

"Glynis is a good woman," Duncan said at last.

"I know she is," Alex said. "I don't intend to take advantage of the situation."

"Good luck," Duncan said, squeezing Alex's shoulder. "I suspect ye will need it."

*　*　*

The moon shone between the fast-moving night clouds, revealing the occasional rock poking above the sea. Alex maneuvered the boat around them easily. He did not know the waters around the Mull as well as he did those around the islands to the north and the west. But the Viking blood was strong in him, and gave him a sixth sense on the water.

The only sound was the soft splash of his oars. The water was flat and silent, and neither he nor Glynis had spoken a word in the hour since they left the shore.

"Ye didn't have to kiss me," Glynis said.

He smiled to himself. Obviously, Glynis had been dwelling on those kisses, too.

"Ye could have pretended," she said. "It was too dark for the guards to tell the difference."

"And why would I want to do that?" he asked.

Glynis cleared her throat. "I fear I didn't make myself clear. When I asked ye to take me with ye—"

"Forced me, ye mean," Alex said.

"I didn't mean it as an invitation to...to..."

Alex couldn't help himself. "To make love to ye morning, noon, and night, all the way to Edinburgh?"

"Alex!"

Glynis sounded so scandalized that he laughed.

"Don't jump overboard—I know ye were only looking for an escort, not a bedmate." Under his breath, he added, "A shame, that."

A damn shame. This was going to be one hell of a long trip.

"What do ye know of your mother's family?" he asked to divert himself.

"I've never met them, but I understand they are a wealthy and respected merchant family," she said. "One of my uncles is a priest."

Alex would make sure that her mother's family were good people before he left her with them. If they weren't, heaven help him, for he didn't know what he'd do with her then.

"Why do ye travel to Edinburgh?" Glynis asked.

"I have business for my chieftain," Alex said. "And some of my own as well."

He should have kept his mouth shut about his own business. Before she could ask about that, he said, "'Tis a dangerous world, Glynis. Like it or no, ye need a husband to protect ye."

His own words caused an annoying sensation in his gut.

"Like my last husband protected me? No thank ye," Glynis said. "My mother's family will look after me. Besides, Edinburgh sounds like a tame place."

Alex didn't like the idea of her alone with only a family of Lowlanders and priests to protect her. "Ye should find yourself a strong Highland man."

"Hmmph. I've had one of those," she said

A heavy fog had rolled in. Alex heard a faint mewling sound in the distance and lifted his oars to listen.

"What is that?" Glynis asked in a hushed voice. "It sounds like a cat caught in a tree."

That was no cat. Alex rowed the boat toward the sound through the billowing fog.

CHAPTER 11

Help! Someone help me!" The cry came through the dense fog.

"It's a woman," Glynis said, leaning forward and grabbing Alex's knee.

"Aye." He had known it was a female from the start. The question was, what kind?

Alex wasn't a superstitious man—for a Highlander—but every story he'd ever heard about selkies came back to him as he rowed closer. A selkie was a sea creature who was known to take the form of a beautiful woman and lure sailors to their deaths. In nearly all the stories, selkies appeared to men when a dense fog lay over the water.

"Help me!"

In front of him, the black shape of a rock emerged out of the mist.

"I can see her!" Glynis stood in the boat, pointing. "She's clinging to that rock."

Alex saw the outline of the upper half of a figure

with long flowing hair above the water line. Her legs—or tail—were beneath the water.

"Hold on," he called out. "We're coming for ye."

"She's just there!" Glynis said.

"Get in the back of the boat." Knowing Glynis was not the sort to follow orders without an explanation, he added, "I need ye to keep the boat steady while I pull her in."

But if Alex saw a tail, he was dropping this creature back into the sea.

He brought the boat up next to the rock. When he leaned out to lift her, she kept her arms wrapped around the rock. Ach, this was no selkie. The poor thing was shaking like a newborn lamb.

"Ye can let go now," he said, using the same soft tone he would use with a riled horse. "I've got ye."

Only two feet of the rock remained above water, and the tide was still coming in. Another hour or two, and she'd have nothing left to hold on to. How long had she been here, clinging to it as the water rose around her? No wonder she was afraid to let go.

"Don't worry, lass," he said. "You're safe now."

"Alex?" the woman asked in a hoarse voice. "Is that you?"

God in Heaven, the woman clinging to the rock was Catherine Campbell.

"Aye, it's me," he said. "Put your arms around my neck. I promise I won't drop ye."

Catherine's skirts were heavy with water as he lifted her into the boat. Moving quickly, he loosened his plaid and wrapped it around them both, then he set to rubbing her back and limbs to get her blood moving. She was so cold her teeth were chattering.

Glynis found a blanket and draped it around Catherine's shoulders.

"What happened, Catherine?" Alex asked. "How did ye get out here?"

"Sh-sh-aggy did it." Her teeth chattered as she spoke. "He-he brought me out here and left me."

"Are ye saying Shaggy meant for ye to drown?"

She nodded against his chest.

The saints have mercy! Alex had seen a good deal of violence in his life, and he knew of instances when men murdered wives or lovers in a rage. But the cold ruthlessness of this shocked him. Shaggy had wanted his wife to watch the water rise for hours, knowing all the while that she would drown in the end.

"We've got to go to shore and get a fire going for her," he said to Glynis. "Then we'll need to get her to her family."

"What do ye want me to do?" Glynis asked. "I can row."

Thank God Glynis wasn't the sort of woman to lose her head in a crisis.

"I'll row," he said. "Just keep her as warm as ye can."

A second woman had asked for his help.

*   *   *

Glynis tried to lift Catherine Campbell to the back of the boat as Alex took up the oars, but the woman slid from her arms like an eel. When Glynis tried again, Catherine wrapped her arms around Alex's waist from behind and clung to him, just as she had to the rock.

"It's all right. Just tuck my plaid around her," Alex

said. "My body will give off plenty of heat while I row."

As he rowed, Alex calmed Lady Catherine with a steady, low murmur, as if he were soothing a babe in his arms. Glynis felt useless.

She bit her lip against her own disappointment. After what Lady Catherine had suffered, it was small of her to think about how her own plans were ruined. Alex would insist upon seeing Catherine safely to her brother's castle, as well he should, and Glynis would never make it to Edinburgh.

The Campbell chieftain would send word to Glynis's father. And she would go home in worse shame than before.

"The fog is lifting, and the wind is picking up," Alex said to Glynis after a while. "We can put the sail up now, and we'll be on the Campbell side of the loch in no time."

After Glynis helped him raise the boat's small sail, Alex gathered Lady Catherine in his lap and sat with one arm around her and one guiding the boat.

"Catherine, if ye feel well enough to talk," Alex said, "can ye tell us why Shaggy left ye on that rock?"

"He wanted to be rid of me without earning the wrath of my brothers," she said. "He wanted me dead, without blood on his hands."

"Who else was involved?" Alex asked.

"Shaggy rowed me out to the rock himself—he didn't want to risk any loose tongues," Catherine said, anger strengthening her voice. "While he had me trussed like a pig for roasting, he took considerable pleasure in telling me how the water would creep up until I'd have no rock to hold on to."

Glynis thought Lady Catherine sounded sufficiently

recovered to sit on her own. Catherine did not, however, remove herself from Alex's lap.

"Shame I didn't succeed in poisoning him," Catherine said. "I tried twice, but Shaggy is a tough old bird."

Glynis exchanged glances with Alex, but he showed no surprise at this remarkable confession.

"The poison did no more than make him ill for a day or two," Catherine said. "I tell ye, it was verra disappointing."

Alex cleared his throat. "I take it he planned to inform your brothers that ye met with an accident."

"Aye, and he'd have a few hundred men to say he was fighting the MacIains at Mingary Castle the day I disappeared," Catherine said, her voice hard with bitterness. "Shaggy will pay for this. My brothers will see to it."

They were finally drawing near the far shore, where several fishermen were at the water's edge readying their boats for the morning's fishing.

"They should be Campbells," Alex said. "You two stay in the boat while I talk with them."

Glynis took one of the oars and held it against the bottom of the loch to steady the boat while Alex climbed out. As he and the fisherman spoke in murmured voices, Glynis felt the eyes of the men on her and Lady Catherine.

"Catherine, these fishermen are your clansmen," Alex said when he returned to them. "We can rest here at their camp before starting the journey to Inveraray Castle."

Glynis wondered how many days and miles they would have to walk to reach the Campbell fortress, and her spirits sank lower.

The fishermen seemed in awe of their chieftain's sister and took pains to make them comfortable. After providing them with food and blankets and stoking the fire, they left the three of them to rest and took their boats out to fish.

Glynis was so tired after being awake all night on the water that she fell asleep almost before her head touched the ground. When she woke, it was near dusk, and the fishermen were back. Alex was sitting next to her, whittling a stick with his dirk. She sat up and looked around her. Lady Catherine stood several yards away surrounded by several men who had just arrived.

"Who are they?" she asked Alex.

"The fishermen felt their chieftain's sister needed Campbell warriors to escort her home," Alex said, with his eyes on the men. "They fetched these."

The Campbell warriors scowled at Alex when Catherine left them to sit next to him.

"These men will see ye safely to Inveraray Castle," Alex said. "But save your story about what Shaggy did for your brothers' ears alone."

Catherine slid her hand through Alex's arm. "I want you to take me there."

"Glynis and I must be on our way to Edinburgh in the morning," Alex said.

Relief flooded through Glynis. He would take her to her mother's family after all.

"Why are ye traveling with her?" Catherine glanced sideways at Glynis as if she were mud stuck on her shoes.

"I'm taking Glynis to her mother's relations, nothing more," he said. "We don't want her father to hear of it, so don't tell the men who we are."

"Surely your trip can wait," Catherine said, sounding her usual haughty self.

"I must meet someone in Edinburgh before the end of the month." Alex gave Catherine a smile that would melt a witch's heart. "Come, Catherine, ye know damned well no one on Campbell lands would dare harm a hair on your pretty head."

Ach, the man could charm the wings off a fairy. Glynis was disgusted with them both.

"I'll forgive ye if ye promise to visit on your return," Catherine said, taking his arm again.

"I'll do that," Alex said.

"My brothers will want to reward ye for saving me." Catherine tilted her head and looked at Alex from under her dark lashes. "And I'll want to reward ye as well."

*   *   *

"We'll leave as soon as the camp is quiet," Alex said close to Glynis's ear.

"I thought we were leaving in the morning."

"I'd rather not be dragged off in the night to have my throat cut," Alex said. "These men don't follow Catherine's orders, and they are mistrustful of strangers passing through their lands."

Well, that was true of all Highlanders.

"In the meantime, I'll encourage them to be cautious."

Alex stood and, taking his time, met the eyes of every man around the fire. Then he whipped his claymore out so fast it was a blur. Glynis felt the tension of the men as they exchanged glances and silently debated which of them would take on this bold stranger. She prayed Alex knew what he was doing.

Alex swung his claymore through the fire several times, back and forth. At first he did it with both hands, and then he shifted the heavy blade from hand to hand as he sliced it through the fire in smooth, deadly arcs.

After this display, he stood in front of Glynis and said, "No one touches her."

Glynis swallowed. She suddenly felt very warm. When Alex sat down next to her again, she could feel the power rolling off him.

He turned and spoke to her in a low, commanding voice. "You'll sleep with me."

CHAPTER 12

That was not how Glynis had imagined Alex would ask her to lie with him—not that she had imagined it, of course. But if she had, it would most definitely have involved kissing her as he had against the castle wall. His mouth hungry, his hands urgent. His voice rough with desire.

I must have ye, Glynis. I don't want anyone but you.

Glynis shook her head to clear it. By all the saints, what was she thinking? Alex was not the sort of man who wanted only one woman. All the same, when Alex lay down behind her and pulled her against him, she let herself pretend, just for a moment, that he was whispering in her ear, *I want ye badly. Only you.*

The arm around her held a dirk.

"I'll wake ye when it's time," he said.

He thought she could sleep? Between waiting for the Campbells to slice her throat and having Alex's body wrapped around hers, that seemed an unlikely prospect. She lay wide awake listening to Alex's breathing as the others settled down around the campfire. Despite Catherine's complaints, the Campbell warriors had insisted that she make her bed far from the "strangers."

"They have two men keeping watch by the horses," Alex whispered in her ear. "I'll take them first and then come back for ye."

Before Glynis could say no, he was gone without a sound. How would he subdue both guards? And even if he managed that, surely he would startle the horses and wake the other men.

What was she doing, waiting here to be murdered or worse?

She nearly shrieked when she felt a tap on her shoulder. She turned to find Alex squatting beside her. How had he returned so quickly? He put his finger to his lips and motioned for her to come with him.

The snores and snorts of the sleeping men seemed unnaturally loud, as did every twig under her feet. With each step, she expected to hear a shout behind her. But the angels must have been watching over them, for none of the Campbell men awoke. When she and Alex were thirty yards from the camp, Glynis heard a horse's neigh. In the darkness, she made out the outline of two horses. One of them nickered and trotted toward them.

"Ah, Buttercup, there's a good horse," Alex said in a low voice, as he rubbed the horse's forelock. The other horse followed and nudged Alex with its nose. "Now, don't be jealous, Rosebud."

"Ye know these horses?" Glynis asked.

"We just met," Alex said. "'Tis a long journey overland from here to Edinburgh so we're borrowing them from the Campbells."

"But if we steal their horses, they'll be after us for sure."

"We should hurry," Alex said in a calm voice, as he rubbed the second horse. "Do ye know how to ride?"

The saints preserve her. "Aye, but—"

Without waiting for her to finish, he lifted her up onto the horse, which was already saddled, and handed her the reins. "We can talk on the way."

"Which horse am I on?"

"I named that one Rosebud," he said, as he swung up on the other one. "Be good to her."

"I've never ridden in the dark before."

"We'll ride slowly," Alex said as he moved his horse into the lead. "Just give Rosebud her head, and you'll be fine."

"What if the Campbells chase us?" she asked.

"Their first duty is to get their chieftain's sister safely to Inveraray, so they probably won't," Alex said over his shoulder. "And I scattered the other horses."

After what seemed like a couple of hours, Alex dismounted and led their horses across a creek. Then he lifted her down from her mount.

"We'll sleep here, where we'll be hidden by these bushes," he said.

"Shouldn't we get farther away?"

"We have a good lead on the Campbells, and they won't be able to look for their horses until daylight," Alex said. "Besides, it's dangerous to ride in the dark."

Dangerous to ride in the dark? Glynis stood with her arms crossed while Alex rolled out two blankets.

"We must rest while we can," he said, as he lay down on one of them. "We'll need to be moving again at first light."

Glynis lay down on the other blanket, facing him.

"Did ye sleep when the fishermen left us at their camp today?" she asked.

"Of course not."

"How did ye do that with the horses?" she asked.

"I just have a way with horses," he said in a fading voice. "I always have."

Just like he had a way with women.

*   *   *

"Time to be on our way," Alex said after they ate their cold breakfast in the predawn light.

He couldn't understand why Glynis seemed surprised that he had collected the dried beef, cheese, and oatcakes from their boat before he got the horses last night. Did she want to go hungry?

He was anxious to put more distance between them and the Campbells. There had been no point in worrying her last night, but he was not as certain as he pretended that none of the Campbells would follow them.

Glynis rolled up the blankets and packed away the food while he saddled the horses.

"Traveling across other clans' lands is dangerous with just two of us," Alex said, as he lifted her onto Rosebud's back. "I don't want ye out of my sight, understand?"

Glynis fixed him with her serious gaze and nodded.

They rode steadily for hours. Though Alex saw no one behind them, twice he had to quickly pull their horses off the path to avoid meeting other travelers. Because of Glynis, he couldn't take any risks.

To pass the time, he told her stories. Glynis liked the

one about how Ian fell in love with his wife Sìleas best, judging by all the questions she asked.

"Ian left her for five years after they wed?" she asked.

"Ach, he didn't take it well, being forced to say vows with a dirk at his back," Alex said. "And he blamed Sìleas for it."

"I'm glad their story ended happily," Glynis said with a soft smile.

"Do ye need to stop and stretch your legs?" he asked, but she shook her head. "For a lass with a sour disposition, ye don't complain much."

"It's my stepmother who says I'm sour." Glynis heaved a sigh. "And it's true I do complain when she expects me to sit indoors doing needlework for hours."

"Well, ye are a fine traveling companion," he told her. "Ye have several advantages over the ones I usually travel with."

"I do?"

"For one thing, ye are prettier to look at than my cousins and Duncan," he said. "And for another, ye haven't heard all of my stories before."

On the other hand, if he were traveling with one of them, he wouldn't have to dive off the path like a frightened Lowlander every time a group of warriors was headed their way.

"Ye have a gift for storytelling," Glynis said with a faint blush. "I wouldn't mind if ye told them to me more than once."

"You'll regret those words," he said, and laughed. "We have a long journey ahead of us, and I've only got three days of stories." Of course, Alex had a good many more that he couldn't tell her.

"Ye told me about Ian," she said. "Will ye tell me about your friend Duncan next?"

Why did she want to know about Duncan?

"Duncan is a fierce warrior," he said, after a moment. "I've never seen him beaten. Not once."

"I liked him," she said. "He seems...dependable."

Alex stifled a groan. "Aye, Duncan is exceedingly dependable. He's steady, never wavers. Decides what he wants and that's that."

All the things that Alex was not.

"There is a good deal of mystery about Duncan's birth," Alex said. "And some say a bit of magic."

"Ye must tell me," Glynis said, turning wide eyes on him.

"When Duncan's mother was a lass of sixteen, she was stolen from the beach one day," Alex said, settling into his story. "A year later, she was returned to the same beach with a babe in her arms. That babe was Duncan."

"Who took her?"

"His mother never breathed a word—not about what happened, or where she'd been, or who the father of her child was." Alex paused. "Eight years later, it all happened again."

"And she still hasn't told?" Glynis was leaning so far out of her saddle that he feared she might fall off her horse.

"She took her secret to the grave."

As they rode and he told his stories, Alex scanned the green hills sprinkled with summer flowers. The Campbell men should have turned back by now, but there were plenty of other dangerous men who traveled this trail through the mountains.

"Who is it ye must meet in Edinburgh before the end of the month?"

Alex winced. He had hoped she wasn't listening when he mentioned that to Catherine.

"Ah, I see this is a story ye don't wish to tell me," Glynis said, raising her eyebrows. "Of course, now it is the only one I wish to hear."

Alex rubbed his neck. He did not want to discuss the Countess or her letter with Glynis MacNeil.

"So who would be waiting for Alex Bàn MacDonald in Edinburgh?" She tapped her finger on her chin—it was a very pretty chin. "Definitely a woman."

This lass, who was usually so serious, was teasing him. Alex might have enjoyed it for the sparkle in her eyes, if she had chosen a different subject.

"This particular woman must have something special ye want," Glynis said, narrowing her eyes. "Not the same 'reward' Lady Catherine was offering, since ye clearly don't need to travel all the way to Edinburgh for that."

"All right, I'll tell ye." The tale he told about Sabine was short since he left out the bedding parts.

"A countess," Glynis said, and there was a harder edge to her wit now. "I suppose that is even more impressive than an earl's daughter."

Alex never pretended to be other than what he was. Most women liked him, and he never cared much one way or the other whether they approved of him. And yet, it rankled like hell to have Glynis MacNeil think ill of him.

* * *

Glynis's legs were so stiff when they finally stopped for the night that she could hardly walk. And yet, the hours had flown by. Alex Bàn MacDonald had a magical quality about him that she suspected drew females from age three to threescore. It wasn't just his looks—though they were very fine indeed. When he was talking with you, he had a way of making you feel as if there was no one else in the world he'd rather be with.

Glynis realized that she was following Alex around the camp like a puppy and stopped herself. While he took care of the horses, she gathered dry moss and twigs for a fire.

"You're a helpful lass." Alex handed her the rolled blankets and squatted down to start the fire.

Glynis looked down at the blankets in her arms. Last night, Alex had been exhausted after rowing most of the night before. But now, with Alex wide awake and charm flowing from him like honey, the placement of the blankets seemed to take on more importance. How far apart should she spread them? On opposite sides of the fire, or side by side?

"Ye must be tired." The glow of the sunset touched Alex's hair as he smiled up at her. "Sit down, lass."

She dropped down on a rock. Holding the blankets to her chest, she looked about her to avoid looking at him. Alex had chosen a lovely spot next to a loch surrounded by hills.

"In the morning, I'll catch us fish for breakfast," he said as he handed her dried meat and another oatcake. "We'll make a quick meal of it tonight and get to bed."

The oatcake caught in her throat. He'd spoken as if both the meal and bed were activities they would share. Glynis took a big gulp from the flask of ale and told herself this was not a good time to remember how he'd kissed her against the castle wall.

And yet, now that the memory had come into her head, there was no removing it.

Alex tugged at the blankets in her lap, reminding her that she still had them. When he laid them out side by side, she took another swallow of the ale. Would she have the strength to resist him?

A new question fluttered across her mind. *Did she want to resist him?*

* * *

Alex lay awake staring at the dark clouds moving against the darker sky and forced himself to think of his parents. Reliving their screaming battles in his head was his only hope for keeping his hands off the woman beside him.

His cock, however, didn't want to listen to reason.

He knew damned well that Glynis did not want marriage any more than he did. And yet, she tried his will. Though she didn't touch him, he could feel her leaning toward him in the darkness. Her desire vibrated through him. That made it damned difficult to keep his parents in his head.

Ye cannot have this woman. Ye cannot have this woman. He chanted the words over and over to himself. He gave up on his parents and imagined swimming through icy cold water.

Then he and Glynis were naked in a warm loch, with her hair streaming around them in the water …

Alex shook his head. There were no warm lochs in Scotland. Ach, this journey to Edinburgh was going to kill him for certain.

CHAPTER 13

Alex called on every saint he could think of to give him strength. Three days and nights alone with Glynis—*especially the nights*—and he was losing his mind.

He felt a prickle at the back of his neck again. He was so twitchy from unrelenting lust that he didn't know if someone was on the trail behind them or if a flea was scratching itself a hundred miles away.

"We'll go off the trail here to make our camp," he said, in case there truly was someone coming up behind them. He was glad it had begun to rain, for that would wash out their tracks.

A short time later, he was cursing the weather. Only in the Highlands would it hail in mid-July. Now he'd have to make a lean-to for them to sleep under with one of their blankets—leaving them one blanket to share. The fairies were making mischief and laughing at him in their fairy hills.

"I'll look for dry moss to start a fire," Glynis said.

"No fire."

"But I'm freezing," she said, clutching her cloak close about her.

Alex refrained from suggesting the obvious method for two people to keep warm on a cold night.

"There might be someone behind us on the trail," he said. "'Tis nothing to worry about, but we'll wait until morning to build a fire."

The icy pellets caught in her hair as Glynis helped him tie two corners of the blanket to a tree and stake the other corners to the ground with sticks.

"Duck inside while I take care of the horses," he said. "I'll be back shortly."

The wind was picking up as he led Rosebud and Buttercup into the brush by the creek that ran along the base of the valley.

A mix of hail and icy rain pelted his face as he hurried back to check on Glynis. When he crawled inside their makeshift lean-to, he found her shivering so hard that her teeth were chattering. Alex swore he could hear the fairies laughing as he put his arms around her and rubbed her back. The scent of her hair filled his nose. How could a woman smell so good after a long day of riding? He forced himself to release her as soon as she stopped shivering.

He opened the bag with their dwindling supply of food. "I'm afraid it's dried beef and oatcakes again."

"It tastes wonderful," Glynis said, ripping a hunk of the meat off with her teeth.

She ate with an enthusiasm that had him imagining her other appetites. Lord above, sleeping in such close quarters with her was going to make this an even longer night than the others.

"Have some ale," he said, handing her the flask. Ach, he needed whiskey.

"This is bound to put me right to sleep," she said with a smile, as she handed it back.

There was only one thing that would put him to sleep. Laying her back on the blanket and making love to her two or three times.

"We had a long day of riding," she said.

He took a long pull from the flask, his mind on another kind of riding.

"I haven't thanked ye properly for all you've done for me." When she lowered her eyes, her eyelashes fanned against her cheekbones. It was a reflection of the state he was in that he found this unbearably arousing.

"Thank ye for bringing me with ye even though ye didn't want to, and for helping me escape Duart Castle without being caught. And for remembering the food and blankets, and stealing the horses, and telling me stories, and keeping me safe...and...for everything."

Alex heard the hesitation in her voice but didn't know what it meant. He cursed himself for hoping she was getting up her courage to suggest they make love until neither of them could walk.

"Well, good night then." She lay down abruptly and curled herself into a ball.

The storm made it seem later than it was, and Alex wasn't tired. In the dimming light, he watched the rise and fall of her chest. He took another long drink of the ale, wishing again he had something stronger.

A sigh escaped him as he unfolded himself and felt the heat of her body along his side. He stared at the blanket strung above them, bouncing in the wind. Until the last few nights, had he ever slept beside a woman without making love to her first? Nay, he was quite certain he had never suffered this particular form of torture before.

He was so hard that if Glynis breathed on him he might explode.

"I'm freezing," she said, and huddled closer to his side.

Alex gritted his teeth and pulled her into his arms. When she rested her head on his chest, he lay still and tense, trying to control his breathing. For the hundredth time, he reminded himself that he never bedded virtuous women—especially unmarried ones—and it would be wrong to take advantage of the situation.

And yet, desire, dark and twisted, tested his will like the storm pounding against their fragile shelter. He wanted her deeply, and he wanted her *now*.

He wanted to bury his face in her hair and taste the salt of her skin on his tongue. To roll her on her back and feel her long legs wrapped around him as he buried himself inside her. Now. Now. Now.

Though Alex wished he could pretend otherwise, this throbbing lust was for Glynis alone, and only she could slake it. Her intensity drew him; her seriousness challenged him. He wanted to shatter her self-control, to set a torch to her steady calm, and to hear her cry his name as she turned into liquid fire beneath him.

When she rolled to her side, he rolled with her, desire pulling him as if she were a lodestone. Tension curled in his gut as he breathed in the fragrance of heather and pine in her hair. Squeezing his eyes shut, he rested his hand lightly on her hip.

The storm outside was nothing compared to the tempest raging inside him. After all the women who had come so easy, it was as if a special hell had been devised just for him, trapping him under this small lean-to with a woman he could not have.

Perhaps God was a female after all.

*   *   *

The howling wind woke Glynis, and she huddled against Alex, cocooned in the heat of his body folded around hers. She'd never slept with a man's arms around her before—if she didn't count her husband falling into a drunken stupor on top of her after he was done poking her.

The dim gray light of dusk still filled their shelter so she had not dozed long. With Alex lying behind her, touching her, she would not get back to sleep soon.

Alex was in a deep slumber, judging by how still he was. She felt edgy and restless. When she scooted closer against him, she felt his shaft, hard and urgent against her bottom. If he were awake, she'd have to move away. His hand moved to cup her breast. Each time she moved it away, it returned as if it belonged there—when, of course, it had no business being there at all. She felt guilty, but so long as he wasn't awake to know she liked the feel of his big hand covering her breast, was it truly a sin?

Did she care if it was a sin?

"Glynis."

She sucked in her breath at the sound of Alex's voice in her ear.

"I can't be responsible if ye keep moving against me like that," he said. "I'm begging ye to stop."

The devil made her press against him.

"Ahh, ye feel so good," he said, and she sighed with him as he ran his hand all the way down her side to her thigh and back up again.

She willed him to do it again. When he did not, she rolled onto her back to look at him. He propped himself up on his elbow and leaned over her with his face so close that she could feel his breath. Unable to resist, she cupped his cheek with her hand. The scratch of his rough beard felt good against her palm.

"We can't do this, Glynis."

"Why not?"

Alex gave her that smile that always made her stomach leap. "Ye know the reasons."

Glynis had been responsible all her life—putting her clan first, taking care of her sisters and brother, offering guidance to her father, whether he took it or not—and what had it got her? Magnus Clanranald was what. Doing as she ought had bought her a foul husband who shamed her—and who would murder her now if he could.

"Ye kissed me before. What's the harm in doing it again?" She ran her tongue over her top lip, remembering the taste of his mouth on hers. "Kiss me, Alex."

His eyes went dark, and he clenched his jaw for a long, long moment. When he finally gave in and leaned down, her stomach tightened in anticipation. The moment his lips touched hers, fire spread beneath her skin. She pulled him down into a deep, openmouthed kiss. Aye, this was what she wanted.

The heat from his body sizzled through hers. Her breasts ached, her head spun, and she felt as if she were falling backward, though she was flat on the ground. When he cupped her breast, she moaned into his mouth.

Their legs became entangled as their kisses grew deeper, more frantic. She wanted to feel his weight on her, to feel his bare skin beneath her fingers.

But Alex broke away. His gaze was smoldering and his breathing harsh.

"'Tis is a dangerous game you're playing." His fingers shook as he brushed her hair back from her face. "One thing is bound to lead to another."

"I'm hoping it will." Glynis wasn't sure when she had decided that she wanted it all, but she had.

Magnus had been such an oaf. He had claimed it was her fault that she didn't warm to his touch, but she understood now that Magnus hadn't the slightest notion how to touch her. She wanted to know what it was like to feel passion in the night, and she would never have another chance.

Or a better man to show her.

"Ye may think this is what ye want," Alex said, "but ye don't really."

"I do." Her fingers still gripped the front of his shirt, and she wasn't letting go.

"Perhaps ye do right at this moment, but ye would regret it later." He sighed as he traced the side of her face with his finger. "I don't want to be a regret."

She shook her head vehemently from side to side. "I won't regret it. I promise."

Alex gave her a faint smile. "Then I will. Ye are precisely the sort of woman I avoid bedding."

Her stomach clutched, and she turned her face to the side.

"What's wrong with me?" she asked, her voice coming out high and thin.

"Ach, 'tis not that I don't want to," Alex said, grazing his knuckles against her cheek. "I've never wanted a woman this much."

No doubt he was stretching the truth, but there was such longing in his voice that she did believe he wanted her.

"Then why not?" she asked.

"Ye would expect more of me than I am able to give," he said in a soft voice. "Ye would want me to be there tomorrow and the next day—and a year from now. I can't make a woman happy for that long."

"You're wrong about what I want," she said. "I don't want a husband—but I do want this."

He made a low sound in the back of his throat that sent a thrill vibrating through her.

"I'm careful," he said, "but there's always a chance I could get ye with child."

She had no idea what he meant by being "careful," but she shook her head again. "I told ye that I'm barren."

From the time Glynis started her fluxes, her stepmother had lectured her that it only took once for a lass to get pregnant. But even fertility charms had not worked for her. Glynis had lived with Magnus for three interminable months before she stabbed him and fled, and she had not conceived.

"You're not the sort to have affairs," Alex said.

"How can ye say I'm not the sort when I'm the one asking?"

"Because ye couldn't take it as just a bit of fun," he said, twisting a strand of her hair around his finger. "Ye don't have a frivolous bone in your body, Glynis MacNeil."

"I won't have this chance again," she said. "I'm always watched over—I'm never free."

Her family criticized her for being too serious-minded. Now that she'd decided to do something wholly irresponsible and wicked, she was determined to succeed. She was never one to do things by halves.

"I won't wed again. Before I spend my life alone, I want to be with a man." She sensed Alex was weakening and ran her hands up his chest. "I want to be with you."

Lightning cracked and flashed through the gap in the hanging blanket. For an instant, its white light shone on Alex, making him look like the fairy king himself come to work his magic on her. Every young lass in the Western Isles was warned that the fairy king could not be resisted without a special protective charm.

If Glynis had such a charm, she would toss it away.

She let her gaze drop to Alex's mouth and whispered, "Show me your magic."

CHAPTER 14

Alex knew it was wrong, but it would take a saint to resist her.

And God knew, he was no saint.

Though he rarely paid for his sins, they would both pay a penance for this. No matter what Glynis said now, she would regret it. And even though he knew that, Alex was helpless against the pull of desire, both hers and his. He had wanted her from the moment he'd seen her collecting shells on the beach at Barra. All he could do was make sure he gave her enough pleasure that the sin might seem worth the cost to her.

But every plan, every thought, every bit of reason left him when his lips met hers. He sank into her, their tongues moving in a slow, passionate dance that left him wanting more. He kissed her eyebrows, her cheeks, beneath her delicate ears. Then he buried his face in her neck and breathed in the smell of her skin.

When she wrapped her arms around his neck, he

moved his hands over her, following the sleek lines of her body. She was like the sea, both mysterious and familiar at once. He wanted to discover every mystery, to know every secret place.

Lust surged through him as Glynis melted in his arms like soft wax. Alex thought he knew women, but he felt as if he was sailing in uncharted waters. And if he fell off the edge of the world, he would not care because no woman had ever felt this good.

He needed to feel her against his skin. He got up on his knees and jerked his shirt over his head. When he tossed it aside, he felt as much as saw her gaze move over his chest in the near darkness. Her gaze dropped further to his staff, which was standing up begging to be noticed. Her lips parted as she stared at him, sending another bolt of lust shooting through him.

"Are ye warm enough to take off your gown?" he asked, trying and failing to keep the note of desperation from his voice.

She gave him a solemn nod. His serious lass.

As he leaned over her and eased her gown up over her long, slender legs, he wondered if he was too young to have his heart give out. She was like a doe, graceful and made for running. He wanted to run with her, to go wherever she would let him.

He lifted her knee and kissed it. It was perfect, like the rest of her. She drew in a sharp breath as he slid his hand up the silky skin of her inner thigh. His mouth followed his hand as he worked his way up, inch by inch, torturing them both. When his fingers brushed the curls between her legs, she jolted.

"Shh," he soothed her. "I'll make ye feel good, I will."

God in Heaven, she was already wet for him. He wanted to bury his face between her legs and taste her, but she had tensed, and he sensed that would be a new experience for her best saved for a wee bit later. For having been married a year, she seemed innocent. But then, some fools never took the time to savor a woman.

Alex intended to savor every inch of Glynis MacNeil until she was weak and sated from their lovemaking. And then he would do it all again.

"Can ye sit up so we can get your gown off the rest of the way?" he said, as he pulled her up.

When she wrapped her arms around him, they fell into deep kisses again, and he found it hard to concentrate on unfastening the hooks at the back of her gown. Finally, he eased the gown up over her head. He pulled her against him again and closed his eyes against the sensation of her soft skin beneath his hands and her breasts pressed against his chest.

They fell back onto the blankets. It was too dark to see her now, but his hands and mouth explored her body. He kissed her breasts, teasing the nipples with his teeth and tongue, then sucking until she whimpered and arched against him.

He moved to lie beside her and kissed her as if he would die if he could not—because he believed he would. She was slick and hot beneath his hand. The little sounds she was making as he touched her were driving him mad with desire. He ached to enter her, to feel her tight around his shaft.

He rolled with her until she lay on top of him. It was too soon, too soon. He tried to catch his breath, to slow himself down. Her heartbeat matched his as he held her tightly against him.

"I want ye inside me," she said.

Heat surged through him—and he was certain he'd never heard sweeter words in his life. He took hold of her hips to ease her down. Sweat broke out on his forehead as the top of his shaft pressed against her center.

"God in Heaven, ye feel good, Glynis," he said, closing his eyes.

"We can do it like this?" she asked.

"Have ye never been on top?" What in God's name had been wrong with her husband?

"What do I do?" she asked.

"Sit up. Aye, like that." He groaned, and Glynis gasped as she slowly sank down on him. As he held her hips to guide her, he said in a tight voice, "It's like rocking to the motion of the sea."

Her ancestors must have been sea nymphs. In no time, she was making him blind with desire. He was mindless of anything except the rhythm of her hips and the feel of her tight around his shaft. Her breathing was already ragged when he ran his hand up her thigh and found her sensitive nub with his thumb. It was too dark to see more than her outline. But over the howling wind, he heard her gasps and whimpers.

Then she fell forward and gripped his shoulders as if she were drowning and he was the only one who could save her. Each sweep of her hair across his chest sent tendrils of sensation to his core.

Lightning struck again, and he felt as if it ran through his body. His every nerve and muscle strained and jangled with mounting tension. When her body clenched around him and she cried out, he was lost in the tempest with her. His heart thundered in his ears as he pulled her hips against him again and again. As if in the distance, he heard his voice calling her name as he exploded inside her.

He wrapped his arms around her and held her so tightly that he knew he was crushing her, but he could not make himself let go. He wanted to stay inside her forever.

How foolish he had been to think that they would not end up like this. From the start, it was inevitable. From that first mindless kiss he gave her on the beach in front of her father and all her clansman. From the night he had her against the wall at Duart Castle, and they couldn't keep their hands off each other. Once they met, they were bound to end up lying in each other's arms like this.

"I didn't know," she said against his chest, and he felt the wetness of her tears on his skin. "I didn't know. I didn't know."

Alex hadn't known, either. In all his experience, he had never felt a need that strong. Never been so completely lost to passion. Glynis MacNeil had caught him completely by surprise.

CHAPTER 15

Whe Glynis awoke, the sun was shining in a hazy glow through the weave of the blanket that somehow still hung over them. Had last night truly happened? It must have, for Glynis's imagination was not as good as that. She understood now why women were willing to take Alex Bàn MacDonald into their beds for as long as he was willing to stay.

She risked turning to look at him. Ach, Alex was handsome enough to make the fairies jealous. She let her gaze travel over every perfect, manly feature—the straight nose, high cheekbones, and strong jaw stubbled with golden whiskers. Even in his sleep, his mouth was curved up at the corners, as if he had a wicked secret to tell ye that would make ye laugh.

Her cheeks grew hot as she recalled all the places his mouth had touched her. Three times he had reached for her in the night and made her feel things she'd never felt before.

She had wanted to know passion with a man. Too late, she realized that she might be better off not knowing the pleasures that were possible between a man and a woman. It would certainly be easier to live without them if she were still ignorant. She recalled the bliss she had felt in his arms and sighed.

Nay, she could not regret the night.

* * *

"Tell me about your marriage," Alex asked.

Glynis turned in his arms, all warm and sleepy-eyed. "Why do ye want to know?"

He shrugged. "I'm curious, that's all."

Her eyes, as always, seemed to see right into his lying heart. In truth, he had wanted to ask her about her marriage to Magnus all along. He felt the unfamiliar tug of jealousy over this man who had touched her in all the places he had.

"The two of ye have such animosity toward each other that I figure ye must have cared deeply once." Alex had learned from his parents how love could turn to hate.

"Hmmph." She crossed her arms and stared up at the blanket strung above them. "Magnus Clanranald doesn't care about anyone but himself."

She hadn't said that she had not cared for Clanranald.

"Magnus doesn't like to lose his possessions," she said. "He thought I was one of them."

"Why did ye leave him?" Alex asked.

"The marriage took place at my family's castle on Barra, so I didn't know what was waiting for me at his home." Glynis was quiet for a long moment before she spoke again. "His mistress was there to greet him, along with a couple of other verra friendly lasses. Magnus made no effort to hide them—and saw no reason he should. He even let his mistress take my place at the table."

Ach, it sounded too much like his father. But Alex's mother fought back just as hard in the bitter war between them.

"Magnus is the worst of chieftains," she said, her voice hard now. "While my father sometimes makes errors in judgment, he always *tries* to do what is best for our clan. Magnus puts his own interests before his clan's, always."

Alex suspected that the true reason she left Magnus was that she didn't respect him.

"I tried to protect his own clansmen from him, but I couldn't." Glynis brushed a tear away with an impatient hand. "I saw him murder one in a fit of temper and another because the man objected to Magnus's interest in his daughter."

Alex cupped her cheek with his hand. "Magnus's temper seemed fixed on you when we saw him at Duart Castle. Did he ever harm ye?"

"No. He knew that if he did, my father would come with his war galleys full of men," she said. "Magnus didn't want the trouble—but that was before I stabbed him and left."

For all Alex's sins, at least he'd brought Glynis far enough away to be safe from her former husband.

* * *

"Enough of this serious talk." A slow smile spread over Alex's face as he leaned over her, and his green eyes danced. "If ye have the strength to make love again before breakfast, I do."

Letting Alex touch her all over in the dark of night was one thing, but it was broad daylight now.

"Ach, I'm sorry, lass," he said, frowning. "Did I make ye too sore?"

She was sore, but not *that* sore.

"We could try other things," he said, giving her a look so full of sin that it made her pulse flutter.

"I'm all right," she said, her voice coming out high.

"Then what do ye say, Glynis? In for a penny, in for a pound?" Her breath hitched as he stroked the inside of her thigh. "When ye confess to the priest, the penance is likely to be the same, whether we do it two times or twenty."

"Twenty times?" Her voice went higher still.

"Have ye changed your mind about this?" Alex asked, his expression suddenly serious. "Just tell me if ye have, and I'll let ye be."

"No," she said. "I just didn't expect ye to want to do it again."

"Me not want to?" he said and laughed. Then he got on his knees and started unfastening the blanket from the tree. "It's stuffy in here."

Glynis watched the muscles of his back as he stretched to unhook the corners. Besides being able to ask her the most private questions as if he were discussing the weather, the man was completely unselfconscious about his nakedness. But then, he was beautiful.

The blanket fell to the ground, and sunlight washed over him. When he turned, the warm light kissed the skin over his sculpted muscles and glinted off the golden hair on his broad chest. Her gaze drifted downward, and she swallowed when she saw how ready he was to make love again.

"Come, let me see ye," he said, tugging at the blanket she held to her chest.

She remembered how Magnus ridiculed her, saying her breasts were too small. It was the least of the sins for which he would burn in hell, but the memory stung all the same.

"Can't we do this without ye looking at me?" she asked.

"Ye aren't going to be shy now, are ye?" Alex folded his own arms across his chest. "We'll stop right now if I can't see. I've been looking forward to this for too long."

"You were expecting me to go to bed with ye all along?" She was horrified.

"Nay, I wasn't expecting it." His grin grew wider. "That doesn't mean I wasn't imagining ye naked."

"That's no the same thing," she said.

"Of course, I did see ye last night, but the light was verra poor," he said, making a face.

"My breasts are too small," she blurted out. Her face was scalding.

"What fool told ye that?" He tugged at the blanket again. "Please, Glynis. I had my hands on ye enough last night to have a fair idea of what your breasts look like. *Please.*"

It was clear that the man was going to beg until she relented. When he tugged at the blanket again, she let go.

"Ah, lass, my imagination was sorely lacking," he said. "Ye are as beautiful as the selkies that lure men to their death at sea."

His words both pleased her and embarrassed her further. "Alex, will ye lie down now?"

Instead, he knelt by her feet and kissed her from her toes upward until his warm lips tickled her knee. Heat pooled in her belly as he moved up her thigh to her hip. By the time he reached her breasts, she was breathless.

He cupped her breasts in his hands. "They are perfect," he said, his eyes intense on hers. "You're perfect."

In the sunlight streaming over them, she watched as he flicked his tongue over her erect nipple. When he took it into his mouth and groaned, she closed her eyes and gave herself over to the sensations spiraling through her.

Just when Glynis thought she could not bear it anymore, he moved up to kiss her shoulder and run his tongue into the hollow above her collarbone. He worked his way along the side of her throat to beneath her ear with his warm lips and tongue. She felt as if she were melting into the ground by the time he claimed her mouth again.

With every stroke of his strong hands, he wiped away another bad memory of Magnus touching her. She wanted him to replace every ounce of unpleasantness and humiliation with pleasure and joy. Oh, God, how she wanted him. She wrapped her legs around Alex's hips, urging him forward.

"I don't want to rush this time," he said against her ear. "I'm going to make certain ye don't forget me too soon, Glynis MacNeil."

Not likely. She almost laughed, but then her breath caught as his hand moved between her legs. At first, her muscles went all weak as he worked his magic on her. Then the pleasure became a tension building inside her until she thought that she would burst into pieces.

"Please, Alex, please," she said, pulling at his shoulders.

He hovered over her, teasing her and kissing her senseless until at last he gave in. A high-pitched moan came out of her throat as he finally slid inside her. *At last.*

Alex seemed to know how to keep her on the edge, moving just so, slow and deep, until she wanted to pound her fists against his chest.

"Harder," she said, trying not to shout. "Harder."

"Tell me ye won't forget me," he said, as he thrust deep inside her. "Tell me."

"I won't forget," she said between gasps. "I won't."

Not for as long as she lived.

Glynis could tell the moment that he lost control because a wildness replaced his skilled movements. He was pure want and need and full of the same joy that she felt. They came together in an explosion of white heat and stars.

But afterward, as she lay beside him staring up at the blue sky above her, the joy seeped from her bit by bit. She realized that Alex MacDonald could hurt in a way that Magnus never could. She'd cared nothing for Magnus. Nay, she despised him. Before their wedding night was over, she had closed her heart to him.

But this was different. She would have to guard her heart closely to keep Alex from walking away with it. He would not intend to take it—he did not want it any more than she wanted to give it to him. But with every wink and smile, he stole a piece of it. And when he made love to her, he held it in his hands.

CHAPTER 16

Alex could not trust himself with this woman. He felt too much. He wanted too much. This was not like him at all.

After several days of making love to her morning, noon, and night, his desire for her had not slacked one whit. In his pride, Alex had thought he would light up the nights for Glynis and give her plenty of pleasure to remember him by. But each time he made love to her, he was as amazed as the first.

As he watched the light of dawn break over the hills and cast a golden glow on her sleeping face, his father's voice pounded in his head.

Beware of a woman who can grab your soul, for she'll make your life a misery.

Ge milis am fìon, tha e searbh ri dhìol. The wine is sweet, the paying bitter.

And why was he so determined that she not forget him? He'd never cared before. Nay, he hoped that the women he bedded would forget him and leave him alone when it was over. But Glynis had nothing in common with the easy, laughing, overtly sensuous women he usually bedded. Nay, she was not his usual sort at all.

She was the sort his father had warned him about.

It was lucky for them both that Glynis was barren, for he was a lunatic when he was with her. After telling her he was always careful, he kept forgetting to pull out as he should. Hell, he never even thought of it. He had to get control of himself.

When Glynis opened her eyes and smiled at him, he felt so closed in he couldn't breathe.

"We'll have to make better time, or I'll be late getting to Edinburgh," Alex said, not that he gave a damn anymore about arriving in time to see Sabine.

He got up from their warm blankets and threw on his clothes. It wasn't like him to panic and run, but he was desperate to get moving.

"I need to check the snares I set last night before we go," he said as he strapped on his claymore. They were camped in a wood well below the trail, so she should be safe, and he needed to get away from her to clear his head.

"I'll pack up," Glynis said, and Alex heard the hurt in her voice.

"Be careful and stay close to camp." He crouched beside her and touched her cheek. "Don't go where ye can be seen from the path."

Looking into her face, with those big, solemn eyes and that sweet sprinkling of freckles across her nose, Alex could not escape the knowledge that he had corrupted a wholesome lass. The fact that she'd wanted corrupting did not excuse him.

This had been a big mistake.

*   *   *

Glynis gulped in deep breaths as she rolled up the blankets. She should have expected that Alex would tire of her this quickly. In the midst of saddling Rosebud, she paused to rest her head against the horse's shoulder. She wanted to blame Alex for the hurt welling up in her chest, but he had tried to warn her that she could not do this lightly. She clenched her fists and told herself that once she was in Edinburgh, she would make herself forget Alex MacDonald.

Since Alex was in such a damned hurry to get there, she wasn't waiting for him to return to water the horses. The walk down to the small loch where they had taken them last night was a bit longer than she remembered, but it was well hidden by the trees.

After letting the horses drink, she tied them at the edge of the nearby clearing where they could munch on the grass, then she took off her shoes and waded into the water. Closing her eyes, she leaned her head back and let the sunshine wash over her. She took deep breaths until she felt calmer.

Her eyes flew open as a sudden unease swept over her.

She turned, and her heart dropped to her stomach. Over the tops of the trees, she saw a man up on the path. He was too far away for her to tell if he saw her, too.

Glynis held her breath and forced herself to move slowly out of the water so as not to draw his attention.

When she reached the cover of the trees, she paused, listening hard. But she heard nothing except the birds and the breeze in the branches overhead.

She hid behind a thick bush and curled herself into a ball. Would the man look for her? Her heart thudded in her ears as she waited. *Please, God, let Alex return soon.*

Glynis forgot about the horses until she heard a loud whinny. She scrambled low over the ground until she could see into the clearing where she'd left them.

"Goddamned beast!" A tall warrior with a claymore strapped to his back was trying to grab Rosebud's rope, but she was snorting and pawing at the air. "I'll show ye who's master!"

Glynis watched in horror as the man brought a switch down on Rosebud's neck again and again. Now both horses were rearing up and straining against their ropes.

She had to do something. There was only one man, and she had surprise on her side. She picked up a hefty stick from the ground. While his back was to her, she should do it. Still, she hesitated, hoping Alex would burst through the trees.

But the horses were frantic, their whinnies like screams in her ears. She couldn't bear it. Raising the stick over her head with both hands, she ran toward the man.

Argh! With all her might, she whacked him on the back of the head. It made a sickening thud, and he crumpled to the ground. Oh, God, had she killed him?

"Hush, hush." She tried to soothe the horses. But their eyes rolled back, and they grew wilder still. Glynis felt a prickle at the back of her neck—and suddenly she knew why the horses were still upset.

She screamed and pulled her dirk as she turned. A

half dozen warriors had entered the small clearing.

"Stay back!" She stood in front of the horses, holding the bloodied stick in one hand and her dirk in the other.

Her gaze flew from one to another. God, no. She recognized these men. They were members of Magnus's personal guard.

"We've been looking for ye for days." The one who spoke was Fingall, a huge man with broken teeth who was known for terrorizing the weak among his clansmen. "Magnus sent men in every direction looking for ye, but we got lucky when we came upon some Campbell fishermen who saw ye."

"We were beginning to wonder if they lied to us about which way ye went," another of the men said. "But we couldn't go back and ask them again because we left them all dead."

This brought a round of laughter from the others.

"Ye murder defenseless fishermen, and ye call yourselves warriors?" Glynis said. "Ye disgust me!"

"Ye always did have a sharp tongue." Fingall said. "But we'll soon wear the fight out of ye."

He signaled to the others, and they all started moving toward her. Behind her, the horses were rearing and whinnying again.

"Magnus wants ye back alive, that's all," Fingall said. "We'll have some fun with ye on the way back."

* * *

Alex whistled to himself as he walked down the side of the hill through the tall, wet grass. Glynis wasn't just another woman, but this was just another affair for him. All he'd needed was some time to roam on his own to realize he'd exaggerated it all in his mind. When it came to women, it didn't pay to think too much.

A scream echoed off the hills and reverberated through his bones.

Glynis.

Alex ran hard for the camp, icy fear coursing through his veins. The camp was empty. Without pausing, he continued running in the direction from which her scream had come.

"Alex!" Glynis screamed his name this time.

His feet pounded down the path toward the lake. He drew his claymore as he burst through the low-hanging trees into the clearing.

The details of the scene before him ticked in his mind in an instant. Glynis, her dirk in one hand, a stick in the other. A body at her feet. Six warriors, their weapons out, in a half circle in front of her. They had Glynis backed up against the horses, who were rearing dangerously close to her.

Alex shouted to draw the men's attention as he ran straight at them. As he jumped over a log, he threw his first dirk. It caught the man closest to Glynis in the chest and dropped him. Another of the attackers reached for her, and Alex threw his second dirk into the man's throat.

Four men left. Alex swung his claymore into the one brandishing an axe. When Rosebud reared, he shoved another under her hooves. Red fury pounded through him as he swung his claymore into yet another.

"Move away from the horses before they trample ye!" he shouted at Glynis, as the last man came at him.

Alex pulled another dirk from his boot as he ducked

below the swing of the man's sword. As he came up, he buried the dirk under the man's rib cage.

The last attacker was down. Alex blew out his breath.

Then Glynis screamed again. When he turned, Alex saw that the man he'd thought was dead when he first came into the clearing had gotten to his feet. Blood poured from a wound on his head as he stumbled toward her. She swung too soon with her dirk.

Alex was running hard toward them as the wounded man caught Glynis's arm that held her knife. Before the man could pull Glynis in front of him to use her as a shield, Alex skewered the wretch. He pried the dying man's fingers from Glynis's wrist and pulled her into his arms.

"Are ye all right, lass?" he asked when he could get the words out.

"Aye," Glynis said into his shoulder. "They were Magnus's men."

Christ have mercy. He never should have left her for a moment.

"I'm sorry," she said in a shaky voice. "I didn't realize I could be seen from the loch."

"It's my fault. I never should have brought ye." Alex was so accustomed to these sorts of dangers that he hadn't recognized how foolish it was to take a woman by himself on this journey.

"I did hide," she said, "but then I saw one of them hurting the horses."

"*O shluagh!*" Alex called on the fairies for help. "Ye risked your life for the horses?"

"He was whipping Rosebud." Glynis leaned back and looked at him with wide eyes. "I only saw the one man at first, and I knew ye hadn't gone far. As soon as I saw the others, I screamed for ye."

"What if I hadn't gotten here in time?" In the blink of an eye, one of those men could have slit her throat or had her on the ground with her gown up to her waist. "Ye are a danger to yourself, woman."

He was furious with her. And at the same time, he wanted her so badly his teeth ached.

* * *

The hillside was covered with wildflowers, with a few sheep grazing here and there.

"I thought you had tired of me," Glynis said, in her usual direct way, as she lay in his arms.

After the attack, Alex had brought Glynis straight up to the top of the highest hill where he could see for miles and miles. Once he was certain no one else would surprise them, he'd made love to her first frantically and then quite thoroughly.

"The truth is, I can't get enough of ye," Alex said, brushing his thumb across her bottom lip.

There was no point in pretending he could resist her. They would be in Edinburgh in a few days, and it would end. Why deny themselves the pleasure in the meantime?

Alex noted how high the sun was and knew they should be on their way. But the smell of her hair was in his nose and the silk of her skin under his fingertips. So, instead, he watched two hawks soar back and forth against the blue summer sky as he and Glynis talked about the rebellion, the new regent, and whatever else came into their heads.

When Glynis snuggled closer, Alex exhaled a breath and closed his eyes. God help him, he wanted her again. Surely, this could not go on. His desire for her would eventually fade, as it did with every single woman he had ever been with.

In the meantime, he would enjoy the present, as he always did. When he tilted her head up with his finger to kiss her, Glynis's gray eyes searched his, as if she were trying to see into the heart of a sinner.

But this sinner's heart was buried far too deep for her to find it.

CHAPTER 17

Glynis held Alex's arm tightly as they climbed the cobblestoned High Street through the heart of the city. Bells clanked, and carts rattled by her. Edinburgh was a buzzing hive of activity with people hauling goods up and down the crowded streets.

Unlike the Lowlanders scurrying around her like rabbits, Glynis felt as if she had weights on her feet. As soon as they found her relatives' house, she and Alex would part. She tried telling herself that she dreaded having him leave her because of the uncertainties ahead—but she was never good at lying.

The High Street followed a ridge through the city like the spine of a sitting dog. Between the buildings, Glynis caught glimpses of an enormous fortress rising from black rock above the city.

"That's Edinburgh Castle," Alex said, following her gaze.

"Is that where ye are going to meet the regent and your countess?" she asked.

"She's no my countess," Alex said in a clipped tone.

Still, Glynis wondered what it was about the Frenchwoman that could draw Alex all the way to Edinburgh to see her.

"The royals find it is too windy and cold up on the rock," Alex said, nodding toward the castle. "They prefer the comforts of Holyrood Palace, which is behind us at the other end of the city. That's where I expect to find the regent—and the countess."

"Ach, it seems wasteful to have two castles in one city," she said.

"I fear being sensible is no requirement for being royal," Alex said, and gave her arm a squeeze. "But if the English attack, the royals will run up the hill to Edinburgh Castle, for it is an impregnable fortress. Ye don't want to be held prisoner there."

"Is that where they have Donald Dubh MacDonald?" she asked.

Donald Dubh was the true heir to the Lordship of the Isles. As a child, he was held captive by the Campbells, who were his mother's family. After he escaped from them, the clans united behind him, and he led a great rebellion.

"Aye, they've kept Donald Dubh imprisoned in Edinburgh Castle since they caught him ten years ago," Alex said. "If it was possible to get him out, whether by force or trickery, the rebels would have done it long ago."

How she would miss talking with Alex and hearing his stories. At night, after they made love, he would tell her tales as enchanting as any bard's for as long as she wanted. She would fall asleep to the sound of his voice and wake up in his arms. The memory made her eyes sting.

"What is that horrid smell?" Glynis asked, as she wiped her eye with her sleeve. "It's so foul it makes my eyes water."

"Too many people living close together." Alex pointed to one of the many narrow passages off the High Street. "The buildings are ten and twelve stories high on these passageways that they call closes. Everyone living on the close empties their waste out their doors or windows, and it all flows downhill to the loch below. The loch has no outlet, so the filth of the city stagnates there."

"That's disgusting," she said, wrinkling her nose.

"Not so disgusting for the wealthy who live near the High Street, farthest from the loch." Alex paused in his explanation as he guided her around a man carrying loaves of steaming bread on his head. "As ye go down the closes, those who are better off live on the upper floors, while the poorer souls live on the lower ones. The poorest of the poor live on the ground floor at the base of the hill next to the loch."

"How do they survive it?" she asked.

"If they are born here, I suppose they are accustomed to it," he said, "just as we islanders are accustomed to the sound of the sea and the feel of the wind in our faces."

"Will ye be in the city long?" she couldn't help asking.

"A couple of days. Only as long as it takes to get an audience with the regent."

It was fortunate Alex would not be staying. Otherwise, she feared she would behave like all the other women he left wanting more. She'd be weak enough to keep watch for him, hoping to meet him in the most unlikely places. And worse, she'd pray he would miss her and seek her out.

Foolish thoughts! Even if Alex remained in the city, she could never risk continuing the affair. She had allowed herself this one wild folly before settling into her life as a spinster.

"Here is St. Giles," Alex said, as they came to an enormous church on a square.

Alex had asked after her relatives when he boarded the horses at a tavern near the edge of the city. The tavern keeper told them that her uncle, the priest, was attached to St. Giles and lived close by with his sister.

Alex flipped a coin to a dirty boy begging across the street from the church. "Where can I find the Hume family?"

Alex spoke to the lad in Lowland Scots, which Glynis could understand if it was not spoken too quickly. She did not catch half of the lad's reply, but he pointed down the close behind him.

"He says it's the one with the red door, just here," Alex said.

Glynis tightened her grip on Alex's arm as they turned into the narrow close. The buildings rose so high on either side that only a sliver of the sky showed between them.

"They can't see the weather coming," she said, startled by the notion.

"I suppose they don't need to know, since they neither farm nor sail," Alex said.

They stood in front of the impressive red door. Instead of knocking, Alex turned and took both her hands.

"Are ye sure ye want to go in?" he asked.

In truth, she was frightened to death to go inside. But what else could she do after traveling all across Scotland to get here? Crawl home in greater shame than the last time?

When she managed a stiff nod, something flashed in Alex's eyes that she couldn't read. Concern? Regret? Before she could be sure, he dropped her hands and banged on the door.

*   *   *

There was nothing about the house that should make Alex uneasy, and yet he was.

Clearly, it belonged to a prosperous family, and the serving woman who answered the door was clean and respectful. After Alex stated their business, she led them upstairs to a parlor with costly furniture and tapestries.

While they waited for the serving woman to announce their presence, Alex watched Glynis. She was pale as death.

He turned as a plump, middle-aged woman with a pleasant face entered the parlor. Ach, she looked like everyone's favorite aunt—the sort who always had a smile and a treat in her pocket for a bairn. She halted just inside the doorway, her eyes fixed on Glynis.

"I did not believe it when Bessie told me," she said, holding her plump hand against her bosom. "But ye look so much like my baby sister that it's like seeing her ghost."

When the woman crossed the room and embraced Glynis, Alex noted the contrast between the aunt's short, rounded figure and Glynis's slender, graceful body. He stifled a sigh as he recalled running his hands over Glynis's long, naked limbs.

"I'm your aunt Peg," the older woman said, as she dabbed at her eyes. "My husband Henry will be overjoyed to meet ye. And I'll send a lad over to tell your uncle at St. Giles. After all these years, to finally lay eyes on my sister's child..."

The woman chatted incessantly, but Alex could see no harm in her.

"Is this handsome man your husband?" Peg asked, turning to him with a twinkle in her eyes.

"Nay," Glynis said with unnecessary force. "This is Alexander MacDonald. He...and his large party, which included several women, escorted me here."

"So where is your husband then?" Peg asked. "Surely ye are of an age to have one?"

"I was married," Glynis said, "but..."

"Oh, my dear, ye have been widowed," Peg said, her face all pinched with concern.

Glynis threw Alex a desperate glance, and he gave her a slight nod to let her know her secret was safe.

"It seems ye will be well cared for here," Alex said, and the aunt beamed at him. "With your permission, I'll leave ye now."

He went to stand in front of Glynis and took her hands. Though there was nothing more he could do for her, he felt unsettled leaving her.

Despite the panic in Glynis's eyes, she would be fine. She was the most capable and determined woman he'd ever met. This sweet auntie would prove no challenge for a lass who put a blade into one Highland warrior and convinced another to take her across the breadth of Scotland. In a week's time, Glynis would have this household running like she thought it ought—and the Humes would be the better for it.

No matter what Glynis believed now, Alex was certain

she would end up married again. Any man who wanted a wife would be a fool to pass her by. The next time Alex saw her—if he ever saw her again—she would belong to another man.

"I wish ye happy, Glynis," he said, squeezing her hands. "Ye deserve it."

"You as well," she said, her voice a bare whisper.

Since they were not related, it was not proper for him to kiss her cheek. But when had he cared about propriety? He cupped her face and pressed his lips against the soft skin of her cheek for the last time. Despite the foul city air, her hair still smelled of the pine needles they had slept on the night before.

"I'll miss sleeping with ye," he whispered in her ear to make her blush.

But that was not all he would miss. For the first time in his life, Alex was close to making a fool of himself over a woman.

He was escaping just in time.

CHAPTER 18

After checking on Rosebud and Buttercup, Alex paid for a bed and a bath at the tavern. An hour later, he was on his way to Holyrood Palace. He tried to pry his mind away from Glynis and focus his thoughts on his meeting with the regent. But he felt on edge, as if he had left Glynis in the hands of pirates instead of her sweet aunt.

Fortunately, Alex was at his best when acting on his instincts. If Connor wanted someone who would plan it all out ahead of time like a chess game, he should have sent Ian or come himself. Alex's goal was clear: reassure the Crown that his clan did not support the rebellion, while avoiding any specific commitment to fight the rebels.

As for his personal business, he'd lost interest in Sabine's gift, whatever it was. Still, it had been foolish to arrive on the very last day of July and risk missing her. He had slowed his pace to spend a couple more nights with Glynis.

Ach, he hardly knew himself. And now, he felt irritable

that Glynis had made no fuss when he left her. What had he expected? That Glynis would weep and beg for him to stay? There was no point in that.

The guards at the palace gate were MacKenzies, with whom his clan had no current feud, so they let him pass with no difficulty. At the entrance to the palace building, Alex found the Scottish court guarded by Frenchmen. This annoyed him, though he should have expected it. The new regent had spent little time in Scotland and spoke neither Scots nor Gaelic. According to the tavern keeper, the regent had brought a huge entourage with him from France, including jugglers, for God's sake.

"Your weapons," one of the guards said to him in French.

As Alex unstrapped his claymore, he scanned the crowded hall. Sabine had mentioned in her letter that D'Arcy, a French nobleman Alex had fought with in France, was here with the French contingent. Since both D'Arcy and Sabine knew the regent well, he hoped to get advice from one of them before his audience.

"Those as well," the guard said, pointing at the dirks that hung from Alex's belt.

Alex removed them, since he had no choice if he wanted to go inside.

"Your name and your business?" one of the other guards demanded.

"I am Alexander MacDonald of Sleat."

Before he could state his business, the guards began shouting. "*Il est un MacDonald!*" He is a MacDonald! "*Un rebelle!*" A rebel!

In an instant, two dozen guards surrounded him with their swords drawn.

O shluagh. Alex briefly considered fighting his way out, but killing a few of the regent's guards inside the royal palace probably would not serve his clan well. Still, a man couldn't be faulted for throwing a few punches.

From the guards' excited shouts as they dragged him up the stairs, Alex gathered that they thought he was Alexander MacDonald of Dunivaig and the Glens, who was one of the rebel chieftains. Apparently they didn't know that half the warriors in the Western Isles were named Alexander or Donald after former Lords of the Isles.

Alex suspected he would have his audience with the regent sooner than expected.

The guards led him through double doors into an elaborately decorated parlor—painted pink, no less. Inside, courtiers and ladies dressed in silks hovered around a man in an ornate chair who had the beard and shrewd blue eyes of a Stewart. So this must be John Stewart, who was the Duke of Albany, the current regent, and third in line to the throne after the two royal babes.

When the two guards holding Alex's arms attempted to toss him onto the floor at the regent's feet, Alex knocked their heads together and let them fall. He glared over his shoulder at the other guards before dropping to his knee.

"Your Grace," Alex said in French. "Your men have mistaken me for a rebel leader because the fools don't know one damned MacDonald clan from another."

Albany raised his eyebrows. Whether it was in admiration for his perfect French or because he had called Albany's guards fools, Alex didn't much care.

"And which MacDonald are you?"

"I am Alexander MacDonald of Sleat," Alex said.

"And if ye don't mind a bit of advice, I suggest ye replace your French guards with men who know who is your enemy and who is not."

"That is no easy task," Albany said, touching the fingertips of his hands together as he glared at Alex, "even for someone who can distinguish one MacDonald from another."

Touché.

"You will forgive us our vigilance against traitors," Albany bit out. "A group of MacIains just arrived to report that the rebels have laid siege to Mingary Castle and lain waste to all the surrounding lands."

"My clan had no part in this attack," Alex said.

"I would prefer to hear that from your chieftain." Albany stood and began pacing in front of Alex. "I assume he is here with you in Edinburgh, as ordered?"

"I am our chieftain's cousin," Alex said. "I've come in his stead to assure you—"

"I am not assured." The regent stopped pacing and fixed his piercing blue eyes on Alex. "I summoned your chieftain, not his cousin."

"He would have come himself, but he was badly injured at the time he became chieftain and has not yet fully recovered," Alex said, knowing that a partial truth was always more credible than a complete lie.

"Or he is laying siege to Mingary Castle with the other rebels." Albany's face was growing red. "I will not tolerate it! Make no mistake, the clans in the Western Isles will be brought to heel."

"My clan has no dispute with either the Crown or the MacIains," Alex said, wishing he had arrived before the news of this latest rebel attack.

"I need proof," the regent said, his eyes narrow angry slits.

"If my clan were fighting, I would be with them." Alex spread his arms out. "As ye can see, I'm here."

"While your chieftain is at Mingary with three hundred warriors, raping and pillaging with the rest of these traitorous heathens," Albany shouted.

"We don't hold with rape," Alex said, offended.

Being called traitorous heathens, however, didn't bother him overmuch. A Highlander's only true allegiance was to his clan, and though Highlanders were as good of Christians as anyone, they didn't let that interfere with the old customs more than they had to.

"If your clan is not in league with the rebels, then I expect your chieftain to send warriors promptly to fight them."

"He will as soon as he can spare the men," Alex said. "For now, my chieftain must keep his warriors at home to protect our clan from the MacLeods, who have already stolen some of our lands, and from the pirates, who are raiding all up and down the Western Isles. In fact, Your Grace, we could use some assistance ourselves."

Judging from the regent's thunderous expression, he didn't like Alex's suggestion.

"Perhaps the MacDonalds of Sleat need a chieftain who is willing to fight for the Crown," Albany snapped. "I've been told that Hugh MacDonald would do so if he were chieftain."

Alex usually held his temper, but the regent's veiled threat to support Hugh in a bid to take the chieftainship from Connor had it rising fast.

"We call him Hugh Dubh, *Black Hugh*, because of his

black heart," Alex said. "He is one of the pirates terrorizing innocent folk, and you'd be a fool to trust him."

The courtiers observing their exchange gasped as one.

"I will use whoever and whatever I must to put down this rebellion." Albany's voice was soft now, but his fists were clenched so tight that his knuckles were white. "Tell me, does your chieftain have a son or a brother?"

"His brother is dead, and he has no son yet." A prickle of unease began working it's way up Alex's spine.

"You are his closest kin?"

"I'm as close as any, after his sister in Ireland," Alex said.

"Then we'll have to make do with you for a hostage," the regent said. "You shall be our guest at Edinburgh Castle until your chieftain commits his warriors to fighting the rebels."

The urge to escape pulsed through Alex. In a flash, he knew how he would do it. He saw himself pulling his hidden blade and springing on the regent. With his dirk at Albany's throat, he could use him to get out of the palace. From there, it would be easy to escape the city.

Alex was quick, and he was bold. He knew he could do it.

There was nothing he would hate more than to be locked in a confined space for months or years. He would rather fight a hundred battles, die a dozen ugly deaths.

And yet, a man must make the sacrifice that is needed, not the one he would choose for himself. If serving as the Crown's hostage would buy Connor time for the clan, Alex must let them take him.

Albany waved his hand at the guards and shouted, "Seize him!"

CHAPTER 19

"My, don't ye look lovely," Glynis's aunt Peg said, clasping her hands together in front of her. "The gown fits ye like a glove."

Glynis ran her hands over the soft wool. It felt strange to be wearing her mother's clothes. Bessie, the slight, middle-aged maid, had found the trunk with her mother's things in the attic.

"Ye are just her size," Bessie said, as she fastened the last button at the back of Glynis's neck. "And just as pretty."

"My father always said how much I was like her." And he never seemed to notice the look of irritation on her stepmother's face when he said it.

For the first time, Glynis felt guilty, knowing how worried her father must be about her. They had always had a close bond, though their fights since she left Magnus had strained it badly.

"I'll never understand what possessed my sister to run

off and wed that wild Highlander," Aunt Peg said, touching the back of her pudgy hand to her forehead.

"He was devilishly handsome," the maid said in a voice too low for her aunt to hear.

Glynis did not believe that was the reason her mother had followed him across Scotland, though her father must have been handsome as a young chieftain.

"It was because he loved her so much," Glynis said.

She felt a sting in her eye, thinking of her father's daily visits to her mother's grave. How many times had she spied on him there as a child and heard him having a discussion with his long-dead wife? If Glynis had grown up expecting to have love in her marriage, it was her father's doing, however inadvert.

"Love doesn't put food on the table," her aunt said. "Henry's left his shop to take us on our errand, so we must not keep him waiting."

Glynis had a hundred questions she wanted to ask about her mother, but her aunt had had little to say on the subject when she inquired earlier.

In far too short a time, Glynis found herself on the High Street again. The city was nothing like the soft, dreamy images she had of it. Her nursemaid, Old Molly, had told her stories about her parents falling in love here when her father was called to court. According to Old Molly, her father had been a lost man from the moment he first saw her mother on this very street. How had he noticed her in the midst of this chaos?

"Is it always like this?" Glynis asked. The constant noise of voices, carts, and clanking bells made her head throb.

"Aye," her aunt said. "Exciting, isn't it?"

"There's no place like it, except for London," her aunt's husband said. Henry was a squat, bald-headed man who seemed as mild and pleasant as her aunt.

As Glynis followed them through the doorway of yet another shop, she had to turn sideways to avoid a woman carrying a large basket. They had visited half a dozen shops, and her aunt and uncle had not purchased anything.

"What is it you're looking for?" Whatever it was, Glynis hoped they found it soon.

Glynis felt an elbow in her side and looked down to find her aunt beaming up at her with a smile so big that her eyes nearly closed above her plump cheeks.

"A husband," her aunt whispered in a giddy voice. "Henry says two of the unmarried merchants are interested in ye already—and we've only been out an hour!"

* * *

Blackness settled over Alex's soul as the door clanked shut behind him. In the dim torchlight coming through the door's iron grate, he took in his cell. He was in the undercroft that carried the weight of the castle and rested on the black rock on which it was built.

The curved ceiling was too low for him to stand, so he sat on the uneven rock floor and held his head in his hands. His freedom was everything to him. Sailing, fighting, swiving. That was his life. His cell didn't even have a window.

He had known it might come to this when he agreed to come to court for Connor, but he hadn't let himself think about it. Most hostages were kept in better quarters—apparently he'd made a poor impression on the regent.

As the hours ticked by, Alex wondered how he would keep his sanity in the months to come. He felt the weight of the tons of stone above him.

He heard muffled footsteps and assumed they were bringing him his first meal. But when a guard with missing teeth unlocked the iron grate to his cell, he was empty-handed.

"Ye have friends in high places," the guard said. "Follow me."

Alex leaped to his feet and nearly banged his head in his hurry to get out. Feeling like a rat, he followed the guard through the tunnel-like corridor between the cells. Impatience thrummed through his muscles as the guard fumbled with the keys at the last door. Finally, it opened, and Alex stepped out into a burst of sunshine that was like entering Heaven.

A tall, dark-haired Frenchman with a white scarf around his neck was waiting there. By the saints, it was the White Knight, Antoine D'Arcy, Sieur de la Bastie.

"You are free, Alexander," D'Arcy said.

Alex didn't quite believe it until D'Arcy signaled to a man standing behind him, who came forward to hand Alex his claymore and his dirks.

"God bless ye, D'Arcy," Alex said, as he strapped on his claymore. "Ye can consider the debt ye owe me repaid."

"Saving a man from prison is not equal to saving a man's life," D'Arcy said.

"It is to me," Alex said and squeezed D'Arcy's shoulder. "How did ye do it?"

"It was fortunate I was in the hall and saw the guards take you," D'Arcy said, as they started walking in the direction of the castle gate. "I told the regent that you and your chieftain had fought the English with us in France, and so you could not be traitors."

Why fighting the English should ensure their loyalty to the Scottish Crown was something of a mystery to Alex, but he didn't say so. "The regent accepted that?"

"I told him I would defend your honor to the death."

Despite all he'd been through, Alex had to fight a smile. D'Arcy lived for the old knightly virtues that seemed naïve to a Highlander.

"I suspect that your being rich, titled, and famous throughout France for your fighting skills may have been persuasive as well," Alex said.

"Of course," D'Arcy said without the slightest bit of humor.

D'Arcy had horses waiting for them in the castle's lower courtyard next to the massive stone gatehouse. As Alex rode through the gate, he eyed the iron spikes of the raised portcullis above his head. He blew out his breath when he reached the other side.

"Albany asked ye to come to Scotland?" Alex asked.

"He needed help persuading the queen and her English faction to give up the regency," D'Arcy said. "We had to lay siege to Stirling Castle before she would hand over the royal children."

They continued talking royal politics as they rode down the hill. Even the city air smelled good to Alex.

"What will the queen and her new husband do now?" Alex asked.

The handsome Douglas chieftain had wormed his way into the queen's bed in a bid for power almost before the king's body was cold.

"The queen fled to England to her brother, King Henry VIII, but her husband...," D'Arcy paused, lifting an eyebrow, "...accompanied her as far as the border and turned around."

Alex laughed. "There's true love for ye. I suppose the Douglas was afraid of being labeled a traitor and losing his lands."

"I'm glad your clan is not part of this rebellion," D'Arcy said. "I'd rather not face you and your cousins and that big fellow Duncan in battle."

Alex grinned, recalling the last time they had practiced together. It had been a hard fight, but it had ended with D'Arcy on his back and the point of Alex's blade at his throat. To his credit, D'Arcy had conceded with his usual grace.

"You'll find that rebellions are like mud in the Highlands," Alex said. "Everywhere ye step, more squishes through your toes."

"Albany is intent on putting an end to them," D'Arcy said. "He and the Council have appointed Colin Campbell, the Earl of Argyll, as Protector of the Western Isles, and they've given him authority to put down the rebellion 'by sword and by fire.'"

"Ach, 'tis dangerous to give that much power to the Campbells," Alex said.

"Albany is aware of the risk," D'Arcy said. "But as the Scottish Crown has no army of its own, he must rely on chieftains who can command large numbers of men to enforce the Crown's authority. In this case, that is Colin Campbell."

Alex had come to Edinburgh to appease the Crown, but it was the Campbell chieftain who now wielded immediate power over the clans in the Western Isles. Fortunately, the Campbell chieftain owed Alex a favor for rescuing his sister. He hoped he could use it to benefit his clan.

"Albany has charged me with delivering the decree to the Campbell chieftain," D'Arcy said. "If you are leaving for your home, you must travel with me as far as Inveraray Castle. It would be like old times."

"I'm leaving as soon as I collect my horses," Alex said. "But I'll wait for ye outside the city."

"I can't let you go yet," D'Arcy said. "Sabine de Savoisy insisted I bring you back to the palace to see her."

Alex groaned. He had forgotten all about Sabine.

CHAPTER 20

The guards at the door to the palace looked as if they would like to gut Alex, but they let him through with D'Arcy. Once they were inside, D'Arcy sent a message for Sabine with one of the servants.

"Ah, the exquisite Sabine de Savoisy has arrived," D'Arcy said a short time later.

Alex turned in time to see her descending the wide staircase. All the men in the hall seemed to be watching her as she paused on the stairs to survey the room. When her eyes met Alex's, she gave him a slight nod.

"Weren't you and she once...," D'Arcy said.

"A very long time ago," Alex said.

"If you wish to ride to Inveraray with me and my men, meet us at noon tomorrow outside the palace gates," D'Arcy said. "Of course, I won't blame you if you decide to stay longer to visit with Sabine."

Alex bid D'Arcy farewell and crossed the hall to greet Sabine.

"You're as lovely as ever," he said, as he brought her hand to his lips.

Sabine was a few years older than Alex, so she must be about thirty now. The planes of her face were sharper, giving her a starker, more austere beauty. Her hair was drawn up into a high, elaborate headdress that drew the eye to the graceful line of her neck.

"I am delighted you could visit me at last." As she took his arm, she added in a low voice, "I'll take you to a room where we can be alone."

Her skirts rustled and shimmered as they crossed the crowded room. When she led him through a low doorway, up a back stairway, and into a chamber with a large canopied bed in the center, Alex wondered what kind of fool's errand he was on. Surely Sabine could not have asked him to travel all this way to roll around on a bed for an hour or two.

When she settled on the settee by the windows, Alex sighed with relief and took the chair opposite her.

"You look well, Alexander," she said with a bright smile.

He held her gaze and let the silence grow between them while he waited for her to state her purpose.

"Does your clan support the faction that favors France, or do you favor ties with those dreadful Englishmen?"

"I fear we Highlanders have been too occupied cutting each other's throats to give the question our full consideration," Alex said.

Sabine leaned her head back, revealing her ivory throat, and gave a light, musical laugh. There were those who would be surprised to know it was Sabine's laugh, and not her lush body, that had first drawn him to her.

"Did ye ask me to travel across the breadth of Scotland—and into Lowlander territory, no less—to discuss politics with ye?"

"You used to be better at taking your time with ... the preliminaries," she said, her lips curved in amusement.

"Sorry, but your friend Albany had me tossed into a prison cell today."

"I heard you made a memorable entrance." She laughed again, but this time it was a nervous laugh. "You're the talk of the palace."

"What is this gift ye have for me?" he asked.

She dropped her gaze and ran her fingers along the edge of the settee. This hesitancy was unlike the Sabine who had taken hold of a young Highlander and let him know in no uncertain terms what she wanted of him. Alex leaned back and waited her out.

"I had a child," she said.

"Congratulations." Alex shrugged. "That must have pleased your husband at his advanced age." Her husband was eighty if he was a day.

"Hardly, since the child could not possibly have been his," she said, giving Alex a piercing look. "It was fortunate for me that my husband died before my pregnancy showed."

A swell of unease settled in Alex's gut. "When did ye have this child?"

She lifted her gaze to the ceiling and touched a finger to her powdered cheek. "Let me try to remember," she said with a sharp edge to her voice. "Oh yes, the child was born precisely eight and a half months after we ended our affair."

Surely she was not suggesting that the child was his?

What puzzled him was why she would tell him this lie.

"Our affair began and ended shortly after I arrived in France," he said, cocking his eyebrow at her. "But I was in France for five more years. If the child was mine, a woman as resourceful as you could have gotten word to me."

"I had no reason to tell you," she said. "I didn't want anyone to know, and mourning the death of my husband gave me the excuse to retire from society for a few months."

That would explain why he had never heard of Sabine having a child. It did not mean, however, that the child was his.

"Why not tell me, if ye believed the child could be mine?" he asked.

"I feared you would make a fuss," she said, turning her head to gaze out the window.

Alex sat up straight. "A fuss? A man doesn't make a fuss."

"No matter how devil-may-care you are about women," she said in a thin voice, "I understand that you Highlanders have…unusually strong feelings about blood relationships."

"No more games, Sabine." Alex leaned forward and took hold of her arms. "If there truly is a child, what makes ye think it's mine? And I won't believe I was your only lover."

"You were my only lover at the time I conceived," she said, glaring at him.

"Or the only one ye think is gullible enough to believe the child is his."

"If you recall," she said, her voice as sharp as a razor,

"we did not leave my house for a fortnight. *Resourceful* as I am, it would not have been possible for me to carry on another affair at the same time."

Never left her house? Ach, they rarely left her bed— except to make love on the floor or against the wall. He recalled how her well-trained servants left trays of food and drink outside the bedchamber door. Still, Sabine could easily lie about when the child was conceived.

"You will know the child is yours when you see it," she said, and folded her hands in her lap.

She must think he would accept any fair-haired child as his own. And yet, if the child was his, he had cause to be furious with her.

"Ye believed the child was mine all along," he said, raising his voice, "and ye didn't tell me?"

"I wanted to keep the child's existence a secret."

And Alex wanted to shake Sabine until her teeth rattled. He made himself take a deep breath before he spoke again. "So why tell me now?"

"I've run out of money." She looked up at him from under her lashes. "So I must marry again."

Alex's heart sank to his feet with a thud. Did she want him to claim her child and marry her? He could not imagine a worse wife. Why, Sabine was exactly like him.

"I'm not a poor man," he said, "but I'm no a rich one, either."

Sabine's expression clouded for a moment, and then she tilted her head back in a genuine laugh. "Alex, I'm not suggesting we marry!" She lifted her hand toward the window and said, "Can you see me living in this wilderness?"

If she considered Edinburgh a wilderness, then going

to Skye would seem to her like crossing the River Styx to Hades.

"*Mon dieu!*" She wiped the corners of her eyes with a lace handkerchief, still shaking with laughter. "Finding a wealthy man was not difficult. In fact, I'm already betrothed."

Another man would raise his child? Alex got up and started pacing the room.

"The problem is that I cannot take the chance that my betrothed will discover I had a child outside of my marriage." She cleared her throat. "He is generous to a fault, but his steward takes his duties far too seriously. Why, the wretch tracks every penny!"

"What has this to do with me?" Alex asked.

"I fear that if I continue to support the child, my secret will be discovered." She paused and licked her lips. "So I brought the child here."

"The child is here?" Alex thought he must have heard wrong.

"Not here at the palace, of course." Sabine fanned herself with her hand. "But, yes, she is here in Edinburgh. I thought it wise to speak alone with you first, before you see her."

"*She?*" Good God, was Sabine telling him this child was a girl?

"I'm told she is an…*unusual*…child," Sabine said.

"You're *told*?"

"You can't believe that the child has been living with me?" Sabine rolled her eyes as if she found him desperately slow-witted.

"Of course not," he said. "Having a child about would be too inconvenient."

"Don't be foolish," she snapped, her expression suddenly angry. "Men can raise their bastard children if they wish, but for a woman it would be a catastrophe."

Alex had to acknowledge that there was some truth to that, at least in France.

"So where has your daughter been living?" he asked.

Sabine shrugged one elegant shoulder. "With an elderly couple in the country."

What did Sabine want? Was it money? Did she think a wee visit with the child was necessary to convince him to pay?

"Tell me why ye went to the trouble of bringing the child here," he said.

"Why indeed!" Her hand fluttered to her chest. "It was a risk, but it would have been a greater risk to keep her in France."

It finally dawned on him that Sabine wanted him to take the child. He began pacing the small parlor again, feeling like a trapped animal.

"Ye say this child is a girl?" He could hear the desperation in his voice.

"Why yes, she is," Sabine said, cool as could be.

"And now, after all this time," he said, flinging his arms out wide, "ye want to give her away, like some garment you've grown tired of?"

"Hardly that."

Alex felt as if he'd been tossed overboard in a rough sea, and the waves were too high for him to see which way was the shore.

"You must take her, Alexander."

He ran his hands through his hair as he walked back and forth. "What is the child's name?"

"I believe," she said, shifting her gaze to the side, "that the couple she lived with called her Claire."

"Christ above, Sabine, ye didn't even give the child a name?" He was incensed, but he may as well be angry with a cuckoo bird for being a bad mother. Sabine was who she was.

Alex felt sorry for the child, having a mother with so little regard for her. While his own parents fought like hungry dogs, he never doubted that they cared for him. They simply cared more about making each other miserable.

"I have provided for her from birth," Sabine said. "Now you must take her."

He heard Teàrlag's voice in his head: *Three women will ask for your help, and ye must give it.* No, not this.

"What would I do with a wee girl?" he demanded, raising his hands in the air. The notion was ridiculous.

"You must know someone who could care for her," Sabine said, as if she were talking about a pet dog. "I heard your cousin Ian has wed. Perhaps he could take her? If you've no one else, you can always put her in a convent."

"A convent?" he said, raising his voice. "The child is what—five, six years old?"

Sabine got to her feet and smoothed her gown. "Before you decide to abandon her—"

"*Me* abandon her?"

"I suggest you meet your daughter," Sabine finished, ignoring his interruption.

His daughter. Could it be true that he had a daughter?

"My ship leaves in two days." Sabine pulled a slip of paper out of her sleeve and handed it to him. "Meet me at this address at dawn, and I'll take you to her."

Alex heard the rustle of Sabine's silk skirts as she walked to the door, but he did not look up from the folded paper clenched in his hand.

"One last thing, Alexander," she said. "Albany intends to have you arrested as soon as D'Arcy leaves the city."

CHAPTER 21

Skrit scrit, scrit. Claire drew her feet in as the mouse crossed the floor. It was bigger and bolder than the mice in the fields at home.

The old woman had not brought food yet today, so she and her doll were hungry. Poor Marie was dirty as well. If Grandmère was here, she would scold Claire for not taking better care of her doll. Grandpère had made Marie specially for his little girl from straw and rope, and then Grandmère had sewn her pretty gown from scraps.

The girl pressed her nose against Marie's soft belly and sniffed, but the smell of Grandmère and Grandpère had been gone for a long, long time.

CHAPTER 22

When Glynis came down for supper, a man dressed in a priest's robes was already sitting at the head of the table. He looked at her with gray eyes that were the same color and shape as her own, but they were as cold as a frozen pond.

"She does look like our former sister," the priest said in a flat tone.

"Ye are my uncle?" Glynis asked.

After growing up in a family in which she looked like no one else, Glynis had been disappointed to see no resemblance between herself and her aunt. She could see herself in this tall, gaunt priest—but she did not like what she saw.

"Yes, I am Father Thomas," he said, as if being himself was a great responsibility. "You may sit."

Glynis's backside was barely on the bench before her uncle started the prayer. He recited it rapidly with no inflection, giving Glynis the impression that his mind was elsewhere. When he finished the prayer, he helped himself to the choicest piece of meat on the tray and began eating before the rest of them had any.

"I hope you have a more obedient nature than your mother did," he said, looking at her with a grim expression. "I pray you will not bring more shame upon our family."

He did not expect an answer, and Glynis had to bite her tongue to prevent herself from giving him one he was sure not to like.

Glynis's lively aunt Peg and Henry seemed to wilt in the priest's presence, and the supper conversation was stilted. Midway through the meal, the priest put away his eating knife.

"Gavin Douglas has been imprisoned," he announced.

Aunt Peg gasped, and Henry went pale.

"How can that be?" Henry asked. "He was supposed to become the Archbishop of St. Andrews."

"The queen nominated him, and she is no longer regent," Father Thomas hissed. "Now the Douglases are out of favor."

"What does this mean?" Peg asked in a hesitant voice.

"It means, dear sister," Father Thomas said, turning his venomous eyes on her, "that I will not be going to St. Andrews with Gavin Douglas."

Glynis was tempted to suggest that Father Thomas should be grateful he was not following this Gavin Douglas to prison.

"What in the name of God possessed Gavin to advise his nephew to marry the queen?" Father Thomas raised his hands as he spoke, as if beseeching Heaven. "As her lover, Archibald Douglas had the queen in his pocket. And the council could do nothing because the king's will provided that the queen should be regent *so long as she did not remarry.*"

Glynis dropped her gaze to the food growing cold in front of her.

"Damn him to hell," Father Thomas said. "Gavin should have stuck to his poetry."

"He is a poet?" Glynis asked, hoping to divert Father Thomas to a topic less upsetting to him.

"Gavin Douglas is famous for his own poetry as well as for his translations of ancient poems," Father Thomas said. "A useless activity, of course, but one that would not have cost him a bishopric."

"Useless?" Glynis said. "We Highlanders hold our poets in high esteem."

From the way Father Thomas's eyebrows shot up, he was not accustomed to disagreement.

"Why has the poor man been imprisoned?" Glynis asked, her curiosity overtaking her caution, as it often did.

"He is accused of attempting to buy the bishopric from the Pope." Father Thomas shrugged one bony shoulder. "If Albany's faction did not suspect Gavin had also advised the queen to flee to England with the Scottish heir, no one would care if he bought it."

Glynis cleared her throat. "Are ye aware, Uncle, of what this new regent's attitude is toward the Highland clans?"

"Of course I am," he snapped. "'Tis fortunate that you escaped that God-forsaken place, for Albany has given the Campbells the crown's blessing to destroy this Highland rebellion 'by sword and by fire.'"

Glynis put her hand to her throat, fearing for her family back home. "What does that mean?"

"It means they have a free hand to lay waste to the rebels' lands and murder anyone who stands in their way, including women and children," Father Thomas said, "When the rebels submit, as they will, the Campbells are to collect the rebel chieftains' eldest sons as hostages to assure their father's good behavior."

"My brother is only four years old." Glynis felt sick to her stomach.

"Then it may just be possible to teach him civilized ways."

If her father knew of this plan, surely he would see sense and leave the rebellion. Before Glynis could question Father Thomas further, he got to his feet.

"I must pursue my advancement independent of Gavin Douglas now," he said, fixing his hard gaze on Henry. "It will be costly."

Father Thomas did not wait for a response. Without so much as a fare-thee-well, he left the room with long-legged strides.

"Thomas is an important man in the church," Peg said when he had gone, as if that should excuse his rudeness.

"Eat up," Henry said to Glynis, as he stuffed an apple tart in his mouth. "A man likes a woman with some flesh on her bones."

Glynis could not recover her good humor as quickly as her Aunt Peg and Henry, but she managed a weak smile and took a bite. The apples were not as tart as at home. Nothing tasted good here.

"What do ye think about James the Baker?" Henry said, looking at her aunt. "He's a fine man. Wouldn't he make our bonny niece a good husband?"

Glynis choked on the bite of dry tart caught in her

throat. "Thank ye for your concern," she said when she could speak, "but I don't wish to marry again."

"Don't wish to marry?" Henry said, then repeated it more loudly: "Don't wish to marry?"

When Glynis shook her head, Henry and her aunt exchanged startled glances.

"James is a steady man with a good future before him." Her aunt reached across the narrow table and patted her hand. "It can't hurt to meet him."

"Thank ye kindly," Glynis said. "But meeting the man will no change my mind."

Bessie came in then and stooped to speak to Henry in a low voice.

"James is here," Henry said, and gave Glynis a wide smile. "Make yourself pretty while I fetch him."

Two hours later, Glynis was so bored she wanted to stab herself in the eye. James was easily the most tedious man she had met in her life. Alas, he was unattractive as well.

"Do ye never leave the city?" she asked after listening to him drone on about meetings of his guild. "Surely ye must long to take a sail or a walk in the meadows now and again?"

"There are pirates roaming the seas!" Poor James looked genuinely alarmed. "Besides, the sea makes me sick as a dog."

The sea made him ill?

A wave of homesickness swept over Glynis, leaving a sense of hopelessness in its wake. She had always lived on the sea and had no notion how much she would miss it. Even when she was married to that despicable Magnus, she could hear the sea from her window and walk on the shore every day.

Glynis's attention was brought back to the present by the sudden damp heat of a heavy hand on her thigh.

"Ye are a pretty thing," James said, leaning close enough for her to see the spittle on his chin. "And I believe I'm just the man to tame a wild Highland lass."

CHAPTER 23

Alex walked the city streets in the bleak hours before dawn. Occasionally, women of the night called out to him from doorways. No one else was out at this hour save for thieves and groups of drunken young men looking for a fight. But with his claymore strapped to his back and dirks hanging from his belt in plain sight, no one gave Alex trouble.

After tossing and turning on the too-small bed at the tavern, Alex had given up on sleep. He wished he could talk with Glynis about the problem of this wee girl Sabine claimed was his daughter. Glynis would give him honest advice. But he could not very well wake up her relatives' household by pounding on their door in the middle of the night.

When the first streaks of dawn speared through the sky, he unfolded the paper that Sabine had given him and read the directions written there. What in the hell was wrong with Sabine keeping the child in the most wretched part of the city?

Alex turned down a close and held his plaid over his mouth and nose as he walked farther and farther down the hill. He was nearly to the sewage-filled loch before he finally reached the place. He pounded on the door with murder running through his veins.

A woman opened the door just wide enough for him to see her greasy hair and careworn face. Her eyes grew wide as she took him in.

"Alexander MacDonald?" she asked in a hoarse voice.

"Aye."

When the woman opened the door wider, Alex ducked his head and stepped inside. He found himself in a low-ceilinged room lit by a single, smoky lamp. There was no one in it but the two of them.

"Where is the Countess?" he asked, though he had realized as he walked down the close that Sabine would never ruin her delicate slippers coming to this desperate place.

"I never saw the lady," the woman said. "Her maid said ye would be the one to pay me."

One brings deceit.

"Their ship has sailed?" Alex asked, though he already knew it had.

The woman nodded. "Aye, at dawn."

"And the child?"

"I have her, but ye must pay me first."

Sabine had known that, regardless of whether the girl was his or not, Alex would not be able to leave a child in this squalid place with no one to care for her. At least, he hoped Sabine had known that when she abandoned her daughter.

A ragged strip of cloth hung over the doorway to a connecting room, and he suspected the child was there. Though Alex could have fetched her himself, the woman deserved her pay. He dropped the coins into her waiting palm.

His heart raced as the woman disappeared into the blackness behind the curtain. What in God's name was wrong with him? He was fearless sailing into a squall or charging into battle, and yet an unfamiliar frisson of terror traveled up his knees over meeting a wee bairn.

Before he had time to prepare himself, the woman flipped back the cloth and reentered the room leading a child by the hand. Sabine's gift to him.

Alex had never lacked for words in his life, but he was too stunned to speak. Looking at the child, he had the oddest sensation that he was seeing a feminine version of himself as a wee lad. Her hair was the same white-blond his had been as a bairn, and she was long-legged as a newborn colt.

"She's a strange child," the woman said. "Can't speak a word."

"Maybe she has nothing to say to ye." Alex noticed how dirty the child was, and a horrible thought occurred to him. "How long have ye kept her here?"

"Since she was brought to me a couple of months ago," the woman said. "As ye can see, I've taken good care of her."

God have mercy. The child must have been here since Sabine arrived in Edinburgh. That had probably sucked the words right out of the poor wee thing. Alex remembered how desperate he had felt in that cell after just a couple of hours, and he could have wept for the child.

Alex dropped to his knee to have a closer look at her. Eyes the same shade of green met his. Though her face was heart-shaped, rather than square-jawed like his, she had a delicate version of his straight nose and his generous mouth with its full bottom lip.

Alex heard the woman leave, but he did not take his eyes off the child. He had a strange compulsion to touch her. He smiled at her as he cupped the wee lass's cheek—and felt a surge of relief when she did not flinch. She had the soft skin of a baby. His heart hurt as he thought of her closed up in this dark, wretched place for so long.

"I'm told your name is Claire," he said, speaking to her in French.

She nodded. While the child might be mute, she was not deaf.

"Do ye know what your name means?" he asked.

She shook her head a fraction.

"Bright and shining. Radiant," he said, fanning his fingers out. For once he was grateful for the Latin that had been forced upon him in university. "In Gaelic, the language where I come from, we say *Sorcha*."

Claire was a lovely name, but it sounded fragile to his ear.

"Sorcha is a powerful name," he said. "Would it be all right if that is what I call ye?"

Her gaze never faltered as she paused to consider this and then gave him a slow nod.

"Sorcha, are ye ready to leave this foul-smelling place and come on an adventure with me?"

The girl nodded again. She was a brave lass, of course.

"We have a long journey ahead of us," he said. "I'm taking ye home to Skye."

That was as far as his plans went. He had no notion what he would do with her once he got her there.

"Skye is an island surrounded by sea," he said, stretching his arms out. "And it's as beautiful as Heaven."

She put her thumb in her mouth, but he could tell she was listening hard.

When he picked her up, he was unprepared for the swell of emotion that filled his chest at holding his wee daughter for the first time. Her long hair fell in tangles over his arm as she tilted her head back to examine him.

"If ye are wondering who I am," he said, touching his finger to her wee nose. "I'm your father, lass."

CHAPTER 24

A woman could do worse than James," Glynis's aunt said over breakfast. "He is a steady man, and you'd never need to fret about other women with him."

That was for certain. "I couldn't marry a man who hates the sea," Glynis said, since they would not hear that she did not wish to marry at all. "We would never get along."

Henry looked at her as if she were mad. "What has one got to do with the other?"

A vision of Alex jumping over a log brandishing his claymore in one hand and throwing his dirk with the other came to her. Even if she had wanted a husband, how could she let one of these pitiful men touch her after Alex?

"If ye don't like James, what about Tim the Silversmith?" her aunt asked. "Ye must remember him—his was the third shop we visited yesterday."

Unfortunately, she remembered the silversmith all too clearly.

"He's shorter than I am." It was the least of Glynis's objections, but the first that burst out of her mouth.

"'Tis a shame ye are so tall," Henry said, shaking his head as if it were a great misfortune. "But I don't believe Tim minded."

"He's pale as a fish's belly," Glynis said. "And he has bad breath."

"What is important is that he could support ye very well," her aunt said.

Glynis was a chieftain's daughter, and her father would provide a significant *tochar*, or dowry, if she should marry again. But she was becoming suspicious about the state of her Edinburgh relatives' finances and decided not to enlighten them.

"There are hundreds of merchants in our grand city." Henry got to his feet and stretched his stubby arms. "We're bound to find one to your liking."

"We are delighted to have ye visit us," her aunt said after Henry left. "But what is your plan, child, if ye don't intend to marry?"

Glynis had intended to be the spinster relative who grew old in the attic.

"Surely ye didn't come here expecting to live with us forever?" her aunt asked, pinching her brows together.

Glynis sat up straight. In the Highlands, hospitality was a sacred duty. It was unthinkable to toss out any guest, let alone one who was also a close relation. One suffered with them as long as one had to.

"I apologize," Glynis said, feeling her face go hot. "I did not realize I would be imposing."

"All we want is for ye to be happy, but for that, a woman needs a husband," her aunt said, giving her a sweet smile.

"And the wealthier he is, the happier you'll be."

"Are ye expecting this wealthy husband to help support Father Thomas's ambitions?" Glynis asked.

"That would be an added blessing, of course." Her aunt patted her hand. "We don't want to go to the moneylenders again."

* * *

The bright sun hurt Claire's eyes, but it felt good on her face. She could not remember the last time she had been outside. She was high above the people on the street, sitting on the shoulders of the man with the laughing eyes.

S-o-r-ch-a. She practiced the name the man had given her in her head. Grandmère had only called her Claire when she was angry—her real name was ma chère. But perhaps she was wrong. When Grandmère first gave her the doll, she had called Marie by different names until she had found the right one.

The man spoke to her in words that were familiar, and sometimes she tried to understand what he was saying. But she had grown accustomed to listening for other things in voices. She knew from the rise in the old woman's voice when she was going to slap her.

But the man's big, deep voice made her happy.

* * *

Alex carried the child on his shoulders to keep people from stepping on the wee thing.

"Ye see that water in the distance?" he asked, turning around and pointing. "That's the Firth, where the boat ye came on sailed into Edinburgh. Did ye like sailing?"

When he looked up her, she nodded. Since the child needed to learn Gaelic, he said everything to her first in French and then in Gaelic.

"We are going to say good-bye to a friend of mine before we leave," he said, starting up the hill again. "It won't take long."

As anxious as he was to leave the city, he needed to see that Glynis was happily settled with her aunt. At least that was what he was telling himself.

When they reached the house, he set Sorcha on her feet. It seemed much longer than a day since he had stood before this red door with Glynis. At his knock, the same maid as yesterday answered it.

"I've come to speak to Mistress Glyn—"

He stopped when he saw Glynis descending the stair, looking as fresh as a spring breeze in a pale green gown. The only sign of surprise she showed at seeing him with a wee girl holding his hand was a slight widening of her eyes.

"Glynis, this is my daughter."

Alex waited for her to call him a philanderer, a sinner, or worse.

"I can see that she is," Glynis said with a light in her eyes. She leaned down with a warm smile and touched Sorcha's shoulder. "What's your name, child?"

"She doesn't speak," he said.

"She has no Gaelic?" Glynis asked, looking up at him.

"Her mother was French, so she has no Gaelic," he said. "But what I meant is that she has not yet said a word of any kind."

"Where is her mother?" Glynis asked in a soft voice.

"On her way back to France."

Glynis met his gaze, and he was grateful she asked for no further explanation.

"I thought perhaps your family here might know of a good woman I could hire to look after my daughter on the journey home," he said. "I haven't the slightest notion how to take care of a bairn—especially a lass."

"I could do it," Glynis said in a rush.

Alex stared at her, wondering if he had heard her correctly.

"I have three younger sisters, so I know how," she said, her voice unnaturally high. "And ye wouldn't have to pay me."

It was one shock too many before breakfast. "What are ye saying? Have pity on a hungry man and speak plainly."

"I feel foolish after all the trouble I put ye to bringing me all the way here to Edinburgh," she said.

"I enjoyed it quite thoroughly," he said, causing her to blush. "But ye just arrived. Why would ye be wanting to go back so soon?"

"I didn't know what it would be like here, with all the people and the noise and so far from the sea," she said, worrying the skirt of her gown in her hands. "And my mother's family is dead set on wedding me to a merchant."

"To a merchant? Are they mad?"

"Nay, but they are short of money." Glynis gripped his arm and looked up at him in a most appealing way. "I'd rather be unhappy at home than unhappy here. Please, Alex, don't leave me in this city."

"Get your things," he said.

"Thank ye." Glynis threw her arms around his neck. Too soon, she released him.

"Best not tell your relatives," he said, catching her arm

before she could fly up the stairs. "We don't want an argument."

He and Glynis both turned to look at the maid, who was still standing behind Glynis.

"I'll tell ye the same as I told your mother," the woman said. "You'll find no happiness in this house, so go with your handsome Highlander as quick as ye can."

"Bless ye, Bessie," Glynis said, picking up her skirts and heading toward the stairs.

"But take me with ye, mistress," the maid said.

The two women turned pleading eyes on Alex.

"Can Bessie come? Please?" Glynis asked. "It won't be proper if I don't have a maid with me when I arrive home. We can tell my father that she traveled with us both going and coming."

"Aye." God help him, he'd be traveling with three females now. He did not point out that a serving woman was what he'd asked for in the first place.

As Alex watched the two women disappear up the stairs, he felt an unfamiliar tug on his hand and looked down. By the saints, he had forgotten his wee daughter already. What kind of a father was he going to make?

Sorcha gave his hand another tug and pointed at the stairs, as if asking for an explanation.

"Mistress Glynis is coming with us," he said. "She'll take care of ye."

His daughter gave him the faintest of smiles—her first—and it made his heart go all soft like butter on a hot day.

"So ye like Mistress Glynis?" he asked her.

Sorcha put her thumb in her mouth and gave him a solemn nod.

Alex sighed. "I do as well."

CHAPTER 25

Alex was in the stable behind the tavern getting the horses when he heard running footsteps behind him. But it was only the tavern keeper's daughter, so he put away his dirk. She was a stout lass of seventeen or so, and it took her a moment to get her breath.

"Were ye able to find a clean gown for the wee lass with that coin I gave ye?" he asked.

Alex was relieved that Glynis had insisted on giving the child a bath at the tavern because he never would have attempted it himself. Sorcha was so filthy, however, that he had planned to dunk her in the first loch they came to.

"I found a gown, but that's not what I've come to tell ye," the young woman said between gasps. "There are royal guards inside asking for ye. I told them we hadn't seen ye since yesterday, but they won't leave, and they're watching the door."

Damn, they'd come early. The regent was anxious to lock him away again.

"Can ye bring my friends out the back without the guards seeing ye?" he asked. When the young woman gave him an earnest nod, he took her by the shoulders and kissed her cheek. "Thank ye. This is kind of ye."

The lass blushed almost purple and hurried back inside.

A short time later, Alex and his three female charges rode out the back with the guards none the wiser.

"See how well Sorcha sits on a horse," Alex said, as he held his daughter in front of him on Rosebud. "She must get that from me—'tis in the blood, ye know."

Glynis gave him an indulgent smile. She was looking as pretty as could be on Buttercup.

"Relax, Bessie," Alex told the maid because she was sitting as stiff as poker behind Glynis and holding her in a death grip.

"Ye call this enormous beast with the devil eyes Buttercup?" Bessie asked. "It tried to bite me!"

"Ach, ye are upsetting her." He reached over and patted Buttercup.

Glynis covered her mouth to stifle a laugh.

"Those are D'Arcy's men," Alex said, pointing at the group gathered in front of the palace gate. He wished they were meeting anywhere but here, but he didn't think the regent's men would try to take him in front of D'Arcy.

D'Arcy spotted him and rode toward them, his white scarf blowing in the breeze.

"I feared you would not be joining us." D'Arcy flashed a white-toothed smile at Glynis and Sorcha. "Are these lovely ladies here to see us off?"

"They are traveling with me," Alex said.

"What a delightful surprise," D'Arcy said, his gaze lingering on Glynis.

Alex turned to Glynis. "I apologize for speaking in French, but I don't know if my friend here speaks anything else."

"Is that Gaelic you are speaking to this lovely lady?" D'Arcy said. "I can't speak Gaelic, but I know a bit of Scots."

"She doesn't," Alex lied. "Shame, but I fear ye won't be able to speak to her at all."

"With women, it is possible to speak with only the eyes," D'Arcy said, his gaze never leaving her face.

Ach, Frenchmen.

"What did he say?" Glynis asked.

"He wants to know where the privy is," Alex said. "He needs to take a piss before we leave."

Glynis's eyebrows shot up, and she flushed a becoming shade of pink.

"What is the lady's name?" D'Arcy asked.

"Glynis MacNeil." Alex begrudged him the information. But since they would be traveling together all the way to the Campbell stronghold of Inveraray, he could not very well keep her name a secret.

"Is she yours?" D'arcy asked.

"Nay, she's no mine." Then, for no good reason, he added, "Not precisely."

Why was he doing this? There could be no better man for Glynis. Lord Antoine d'Arcy was a champion knight who held important titles and lands in France and was closely connected to Scotland's new regent. In addition, he had the personal virtues of being brave, honest, and conscientious. It was those qualities—rather than that ridiculous white scarf—that had earned D'Arcy the nickname the White Knight.

In fact, D'Arcy was so virtuous as to be a trifle dull. And he was not a Highlander, but the man could not help his birth.

"What has he been doing in Scotland?" Glynis asked.

Alex translated her question and groaned under his breath when he heard D'Arcy's response.

"D'Arcy designed the new artillery and blockhouse at Dunbar Castle, to secure it in preparation for Albany's return." Alex cleared his throat. "And he designed the new artillery works here at Edinburgh Castle as well."

Ach, being rich and titled was not enough? Must the man be brilliant as well?

"My, that is impressive," Glynis said, nodding at D'Arcy.

"I suspect he also walks on water." Alex found his friend's list of accomplishments rather tedious.

"Your current lady is quite unlike the ones you had in France," D'Arcy said, drawing Alex's attention again. "She has a subtle beauty that is far more intriguing."

"She is not my 'current lady,'" Alex said between his teeth. He did not want D'Arcy thinking Glynis was that sort.

D'Arcy took his eyes off Glynis long enough to raise his eyebrows at Alex. "Then she is available, no?"

"Not in the way that ye are suggesting," Alex said. "Shouldn't ye be gathering your men? 'Tis no getting any earlier."

"I have an extra mule the maid can ride," D'Arcy said. "The lady will be more comfortable riding alone."

When D'Arcy turned his horse to rejoin his men, Alex looked down to find that Sorcha had her face pressed against him. He could have kicked himself for letting his irritation with D'Arcy show. The child was so sensitive to his moods that he would have to be more careful.

"Nothing to worry about, little one," he said, patting her soft hair. "No one here will harm ye."

"'Tis fortunate we could join Lord d'Arcy's group," Glynis said, as they started off.

"Hmmph." Alex would have preferred to travel separately, but traveling with D'Arcy's men would be safer. With three females in his care, Alex had no choice.

As they rode out of the city, Alex tried desperately to think of what he would do with his daughter once they reached Skye. He could give her to his mother to raise—but he feared his parents would fight as much over a grandchild as they had over a son.

For a mile or two, he considered leaving Sorcha with his cousin Ian and his wife, as Sabine had suggested. But those twins were going to be terrors. Having been one himself, Alex could recognize the trait. Nay, that would not do at all.

He looked down at Sorcha, who had fallen asleep against him, and sighed. The deeper truth was that he did not want to give up his daughter. He never would have predicted that he would feel this way, but he did not question it, either. The problem was that he could not raise her alone—a girl needed a mother.

Alex tried mightily, but there was no avoiding the obvious conclusion. To keep his daughter close, he would have to shackle himself to a wife. He had been fooling himself, in any case, to believe he could escape matrimony forever. Neither his parents nor Connor would give him any peace until he stepped off that cliff.

He did not want a wife. But, like it or not, he had a sudden need for one.

The image of Glynis standing in front of rearing horses with a dirk in one hand and a bloody stick in the other came into his mind. She would make a fiercely protective mother. After Sabine's indifference, that was precisely the kind of mother his daughter needed and deserved.

Múineann gá seift. Need teaches a plan. He could solve all his problems with one stroke—and the answer was riding right beside him.

Glynis was at the top of Connor's list of marriage prospects, so Alex could do his duty by his clan and provide a good mother for Sorcha at the same time. And it didn't hurt that he had this abiding itch to bed the very woman who would suit both purposes so well.

Glynis needed a husband, and he needed a wife. Alex was sure he could work out a sensible arrangement with her.

He turned and gave Glynis a wide smile.

As the saying went, get bait while the tide is out.

* * *

What was Alex doing, smiling and winking at her like that, for anyone to see?

"I'd like to sneak off with ye and share a blanket under the stars tonight," Alex said.

Glynis glanced about her, blushing to her roots. Fortunately, the riders had strung out along the trail so that no one else was within earshot. Bessie appeared to be enjoying herself overmuch, chatting with D'Arcy's manservant at the back of the group.

"Ye have your daughter with ye," she hissed.

"I missed ye in my bed last night," Alex said. "I couldn't sleep at all."

"Alex, hush!" she said. "I'm sure ye say that to all your women."

"Nay, I never tell women I miss them."

Glynis did not know what to make of that. Despite herself, she was flattered that Alex still wanted her. But then, they had a long journey ahead, and there were no other women, save for Bessie, who had a good twenty years on him.

"What happened between us should not have," she said, turning to speak to him in a low voice. "And ye know verra well it cannot happen again."

"Why not?"

What a maddening man. "I only did it because no one would ever find out," she hissed. "And because I never expected to see ye again."

"Ye do want to," Alex said, giving her that smoldering look that made her chest so tight she could hardly draw breath.

His hair brushed his shoulders, and she remembered gripping it in her fingers. And how it felt to have him deep inside her, saying her name over and over.

Aye, she wanted to.

"It doesn't matter whether I want to or no," she said. "I cannot, and I will not."

CHAPTER 26

Glynis sat with Sorcha on her lap while Alex fed sticks into the fire. After four nights, they had their routine. They ate supper with D'Arcy and his men around the main campfire, and then Alex built them a separate fire several yards away from the others. He had also fashioned a tent from extra blankets for Glynis, Bessie, and Sorcha, to give them privacy from the men. Bessie, who was not accustomed to long days of riding, was already asleep inside it.

The firelight glinted off Alex's fair hair and the strong lines of his perfect face. Though it was growing chilly, he pushed his sleeves up, revealing his tautly muscled forearms. When he caught her staring at him, he pinned her with a sizzling look. Then he slid his gaze over her from head to toe, with pauses in between, making her feel as if he was running his fingers over her naked skin.

Glynis knew what he wanted because she wanted it, too. Her resistance had worn thin, riding next to him all day and then sleeping a few feet away from him each night. Traveling the same trail made her recall all too clearly how they had spent their nights on their way to Edinburgh.

She would not bring shame upon herself and her family by having an open affair with Alex. But she had come to the conclusion that if there was any way she could have a secret one again, she would. Since that appeared utterly impossible with the child and the maid and twenty men a stone's throw away, Glynis resolutely focused her attention on Sorcha.

"One, two, three...four," she repeated in Gaelic, as she held up the child's fingers. "Five...six...seven..." Glynis felt Alex's eyes on her and turned to him. "Stop looking at me like that."

A slow smile spread over his face. "Like I want ye? I can't help it, Glynis. I do."

"Watch what ye say," she whispered. "Ye don't know how much Gaelic the child understands already." Despite the fact that Sorcha's head lay heavy against Glynis's chest and her eyelids were drifting shut, Glynis continued. "Eight, nine—"

"For God's sake, Glynis, let the poor child sleep." Alex scooped Sorcha up in his arms, then he paused and looked down at his daughter with a soft smile. "I'm looking forward to taking her sailing. Ye can see that the Viking blood is strong in her, just as it is in me."

"Aye," Glynis said, thinking they made an extraordinary pair with their fair hair shining in the firelight. "And when ye took her in the loch today, she swam like a wee fish."

Alex laid Sorcha inside the tent next to Bessie. When

he returned, he sat close enough to Glynis that his sleeve brushed hers. She stared into the fire and tried to make herself breathe normally.

"I have a proposition for ye," Alex said.

Glynis's stomach did a little flip. "A proposition?"

She hoped her voice didn't sound as stiff and prim to him as it did to her. Did he have to put it to her formally? This would be easier if he sneaked off with her into the darkness, swept her into his arms, and covered her with kisses. But it was like Alex not to let her pretend he had seduced her. Nay, he would make her acknowledge that she chose to sin with him.

"I want to." She was gripping the skirt of her gown so tightly that her knuckles were white. Could he not just get on with it?

"I haven't told ye the proposition yet."

"Must ye always tease me?" Glynis was so embarrassed she could not look at him. "I told ye the answer is aye. But not now—we must wait until we are certain all the men are asleep so no one sees us."

Alex touched her elbow, sending sparks of heat up her arm.

"I don't mean to tease ye," he said in a low voice that reverberated through her. "And I'm not propositioning ye, if that's what ye think."

Heat drenched through her. It was ten times—nay, a hundred times—more embarrassing to say aye to a proposition that was not given, than to one that was.

"Wait," Alex said, holding her arm as she tried to pull away.

She felt hurt, as well as humiliated, and she wanted to be away from him.

"Glynis, listen to me." She struggled against him, but he held her in a firm grip. "I do want to bed ye."

This was too mortifying. "Let me go, Alex."

He turned her face toward him. "Believe me, I do want ye."

The roughness in his voice and the heat in his eyes made her feel confused and flustered. Did he want her or no?

"Bedding ye is part of what I'm asking ye," he said, his green eyes intent on hers. "But it's no the most important part."

There was something more important to Alex MacDonald than swiving? Now there was a surprise.

"What else do ye want of me?" She could not think with him so close.

Alex released her and cleared his throat. For a man who was usually so at ease, he suddenly seemed uncomfortable in his own skin. All her instincts were on alert, telling her to be wary. Whatever Alex was about to ask her, he surely did not want to.

"Marriage." Alex said it on an exhale, as if forcing the word out. "That's what I'm asking."

"Marriage?" Glynis could not have been more astonished if a dozen fairies had joined them at their campfire.

"Ye will have to take another husband," Alex said. "Surely ye can see that now?"

She had been trying to reconcile herself to the notion since discovering that her mother's family was just as adamant as her father was about seeing her remarried. But it was a bitter medicine to swallow.

"As distasteful as it is to me to wed again, I admit that I may have no choice in the end," she said. "But you, Alex, ye cannot seriously want a wife."

"My daughter needs a mother," he said.

Of course, that was what prompted this. Why had she not thought of it at once?

"Why me?" she asked. "There are plenty of women—including chieftains' daughters—who want a husband."

"Sorcha warmed to ye from the start," Alex said. "She's become attached to ye, and I believe ye have to her as well."

An unexpected swell of disappointment filled Glynis's chest.

"You'd be a good mother to her," he said.

"And that is the reason ye ask me to be your wife?" Her voice was sharper than she intended.

"We get along well enough." Alex shrugged and gave her his devilish smile. "Especially in bed."

"So going to bed with ye would be part of my duties, in addition to playing nursemaid?" she snapped. "For how long, Alex?"

When his eyes darted like a trapped animal, Glynis felt as if her heart were being squeezed by a fist.

"Ye heard what I did to my first husband." She deliberately looked at his crotch. "Are ye no afraid I'll cut it off?"

* * *

Alex threw his head back and laughed. "I do like your spark, Glynis."

If he could keep things light and easy between them, all would be well—or, at least, well enough. He was determined to raise his daughter in a home without the fights and screaming that he grew up with. From his par-

ents, he'd learned that one strong emotion led too easily
to another, that love could turn to hate. And hate lasted
far longer.

Magnus Clanranald had made the same mistake that
Alex's father had, embarrassing his wife by being brazen
about his other women. There was no need for that. A
good husband was sensitive to his wife's feelings. If Alex
could not control his urges, then he'd keep his affairs brief
and out of Glynis's sight.

"I'd always respect ye." Alex looked into the fire and
spoke to her from his heart. "I promise I would never embarrass ye. I would always be discreet."

Both his parents had told him countless times that it
was not in his blood to be content with one woman. But
at the moment, at least, all his urges involved Glynis. He
would not be satisfied until he had her a hundred different
ways. By the saints, he wanted this woman as he'd never
wanted another. The last four days and nights had nearly
killed him.

He turned, intent on dragging her off into the bushes at
last. But he stopped short when he saw that the fire burning in her eyes was not the sort he had been hoping for.

"Oouu!" The sound she emitted as she sprang to her
feet made him glad there was no crockery about for her
to throw at him. Apparently, promising to be discreet had
been the wrong thing to say. He stood up and considered
how best to soothe her.

"What woman," she said, planting her fists on her hips,
"could say nay to having such a considerate husband?"

"I don't want to lie to ye," he said. "I've never tried to
be faithful, so I don't know if I can."

"Ye are a born romantic, Alexander Bàn MacDonald."

Good lord, did hardheaded Glynis MacNeil expect love? He'd had no notion she harbored such hopes.

"I thought your first marriage would have cured ye of unreasonable expectations," he said—and knew at once he had made another a mistake.

"So, I am the unreasonable one?" Her eyes were narrow slits like a wildcat's ready to strike. "And yet, ye would expect me to mother your daughter, manage your household, and be your bedmate for as long as ye like. And then, when ye tire of having me in your bed, I'm to stand aside while ye have one 'discreet' affair after another with every willing woman in the Western Isles?"

Alex shifted from foot to foot. He did not sleep with *every* willing woman, but it seemed best not to mention that just now.

"And because ye are such a handsome, charming man," she said, spreading her hands out, "I would, of course, agree to this arrangement."

"Ye are a sensible woman," he said, though he was having serious doubts about this. "Ye have to marry someone, and I'm no worse than most."

Not much worse, anyway.

"Besides," he added, "ye already went to bed with me, so we ought to marry."

"I presume," she continued, as though he had not spoken, "that I could have affairs as well, so long as I was *discreet*."

"Nay." The word was out of his mouth before he thought it. He would have to kill any man who touched his wife, but he thought better of telling her this. "Suppose ye became pregnant? I'd need to know that the child was mine."

"Setting aside the fact that I'm verra likely barren," she said. "You're saying it would be well and good for me to raise your children by other women, but no the other way around."

"Aye." That was the way of the world. Why did she make it sound as if he had invented it? "But I only have the one child."

"So far." She folded her arms. "I appreciate that ye blessed me with your kind offer, but I will not marry another philanderer. If I am forced to take another husband, I'll wed a steady, serious man I can rely on."

He reached for her hand, but she snatched it away.

"You, Alexander Bàn MacDonald," she said, poking her finger into his chest, "are the verra last man in all of the Highlands I would want for a husband."

* * *

Sorcha opened her eyes to blackness, and fear rushed through her. When she heard the soft breathing of the women on either side of her, she knew she was not back in the room with the big mice. Still, she wanted to see the stars to be sure.

Taking care not to wake Glynis and Bessie, she crawled out of the tent on her hands and knees. Across the cold campfire, her father sat alone in the dark. He was no more than a black shape, but she knew it was him. And he was sad.

The grass made her feet wet as she walked around the campfire to him.

"Ye couldn't sleep either?" he asked in a soft voice when she crawled into his lap.

She nodded against his chest and pointed up at the stars.

"A wish?" He always seemed to understand her. She felt him chuckle, and he said, "I suppose it can't hurt."

Together they found the brightest star so he could make his wish.

Sorcha didn't need to make one. Hers had been granted when her father found her.

CHAPTER 27

By the saints, Glynis MacNeil was a stubborn woman. In the week since Alex suggested they marry, she had not spoken to him except when absolutely necessary.

Worse, she spent far too much time riding beside D'Arcy. They were in front of him and Sorcha now, engaged in a lively conversation that involved hand motions as much as words. It appeared that she was teaching D'Arcy Gaelic. Still, Glynis had kept her promise to care for Sorcha on the trip. Every night, she sat by the fire with his daughter in her lap and then slept with her—instead of him.

Alex usually let women come to him, but he was not above seducing Glynis to persuade her to wed him. It should not be difficult—he could tell she wanted him. He was always catching her eyes on him, because he was always looking at her as well. Unfortunately, the opportunities to seduce her while riding out in the open with twenty men and his daughter were few, so Alex was biding his time until they reached the Campbell stronghold.

In the meantime, he was wooing her with his stories around the campfire. Glynis was a constant surprise, for beneath that sober, sensible demeanor was a lass with a weakness for a good tale. Alex hoped her weakness would extend to the storyteller.

"That castle ye see across this loch is Inveraray Castle, the seat of the Campbell clan," Alex said, pointing it out for Sorcha. Sometimes now he spoke to her only in Gaelic, and she would tap on his arm to let him know when she did not understand. "We'll reach it tomorrow."

Glynis slowed her horse to ride beside them.

"The Campbells are a powerful clan, and this is just one of their castles," Alex continued. "The Campbell chieftain can raise hundreds of warriors."

He glanced at Glynis's stiff form and decided that a wee bit of jealousy might help his cause. "Glynis, do ye think I should look for a wife among the Campbells? Nothing would please my chieftain more."

"Nor mine." She gave him a look that would slice through granite. "I suspect a chieftain's daughter would appeal to those land-grabbing Campbells."

"If ye wish to catch a man, I suggest ye work on your charm," Alex said. "Men like sweet, *agreeable* women."

Sorcha tapped on his arm, but he shook his head. This was not a conversation for a child.

"Is that what ye will tell your daughter?" Glynis asked. "That she must be sweet and agreeable?"

"If I wanted her to wed, I would," he lied.

"Hmmph."

Sorcha was tapping furiously on his arm. Finally, he

tore his gaze away from the infuriating woman riding beside him to look at his daughter.

"Why are we arguing, is that what ye want to know?" he asked Sorcha. When she nodded, he said, "Because Mistress Glynis is stubborn as a mule and can't see what is good for her."

He repeated it in three languages to be sure Glynis did not miss his meaning.

* * *

Sorcha had fallen asleep with her head in Glynis's lap long ago, and Bessie was yawning beside her, while the men took turns telling stories. Glynis had steeled herself against Alex attempting to get her alone on this, their last night before reaching Inveraray Castle, but he appeared in no hurry to leave the main campfire.

She should rouse Sorcha and Bessie and go off to bed, but she was enjoying the tales. If she were truthful, she was only waiting to hear Alex. No one could tell a story like he did—and it gave her an excuse to watch him.

When at last it was Alex's turn, Glynis smiled in anticipation.

"Since we are about to visit the Campbells, I'll tell ye the true story about how the Campbell chieftain's brother became the Thane of Cawdor."

Alex stretched out his legs, settling himself for a long tale. As he told it, his voice carried around the circle, drawing them in and warming Glynis as much as the fire.

"Seventeen years ago, the last Thane of Cawdor died, leaving no heir but a wee red-haired babe. Her name was

Muriel, and she was the last of her line, the sole heiress to the ancient seat of Cawdor.

"Chieftains from all over the Highlands started scheming, each set on making a match between young Muriel and his son—for whatever man the wee lass wed would become the next Thane of Cawdor. The lass was but a babe, so they had plenty of time to work their plans, or so they thought.

"But all that land and wealth in the hands of one wee lass proved too great a temptation to the Campbells. One day, when wee Muriel was four years old, her nursemaid took her outside Cawdor Castle to enjoy the fine weather. And that's when a party of Campbells, who had been waiting for just such an opportunity, burst out of the woods and stole her away."

Glynis gasped, and Alex's eyes twinkled at her as he met her gaze across the fire.

"Muriel's uncles gave chase, of course. The Campbells were far from home, and it looked as though Muriel's clansmen would catch them. But the Campbells saw them coming and inverted a large iron kettle on the ground. Then one of the Campbell men ordered all seven of his sons to defend the kettle to the death, pretending wee Muriel was inside it.

"The seven sons fought hard, and every one of them died. When Muriel's clansmen lifted the kettle to rescue her, they found nothing but the green grass on the ground. While they had been fighting the seven brothers, the rest of the Campbell party had escaped with the lass."

"'Tis a long journey from Cawdor Castle to the Campbell lands," one of the men around the campfire said. "Did wee Muriel survive?"

"Ye will have to decide that for yourselves," Alex said. "When one of the Campbell warriors asked what would happen if the child died before she reached marriageable age, the chieftain said..."

Alex paused until someone called out, "Come, Alex, tell us what he said."

"The chieftain said that the wee heiress would never die so long as a red-haired lass could be found on either side of Loch Awe—which, as ye know, is in the heart of Campbell territory."

"Conniving bastard," one man said amidst the laughter around the campfire.

"It was to prevent just such a scheme," Alex said, lifting his finger, "that Muriel's nursemaid had the foresight to bite off the end of the wee lass's finger when she saw the Campbells burst out of the wood."

"Ach, the poor child!" Bessie murmured beside Glynis.

"Now do ye suppose, that after the trouble the Campbells went through to get their hands on Muriel, they would let a missing joint on one wee finger come between them and all that land and wealth?" Alex let his gaze move slowly around the circle. "Who's to say that they didn't find another red-haired lass and bite off the end of her finger?"

There was a long silence around the campfire.

"But Muriel did live?" Glynis could not help asking.

"Most believe she did," Alex said. "The red-haired lass was raised in the Campbell chieftain's household, and on her twelfth birthday she was wed to the chieftain's son John."

That was young to wed, though it was legal age of consent.

"Ach, the poor thing must be miserable," Glynis said.

"'Tis true that the pair was wed for the most practical of reasons," Alex said, giving her a pointed look across the campfire. "That was five years ago, and by all accounts, they are a remarkably happy couple."

Glynis did not mistake Alex's meaning. Holding his gaze, she said, "*Devoted* to each other, no doubt."

"Aye, despite the fact that the Campbells killed all of Muriel's uncles after the marriage," Alex said, then he shifted his gaze to the men around the fire. "The lesson, lads, is to avoid getting yourself between the Campbells and what they want."

"I could listen to that man's stories every night and never tire of them," Bessie said with a long sigh.

Glynis could, as well—if she did not have to wonder who the storyteller was taking to bed afterward.

CHAPTER 28

Glynis forced herself to drag her gaze from the young red-haired woman's little finger—which was missing the last joint—to her face. From the way Lady Muriel gazed up at her husband, it was obvious that she adored the man. What was a pleasant surprise was the way John Campbell's hard expression softened when he looked at Muriel. Happiness radiated from them.

Glynis swallowed back the well of emotion choking her at the sight. Long ago, she had believed that she would find love like that when she wed. She had decided never to marry again, rather than accept something less a second time.

Against her will, her gaze traveled down the head table past Muriel and John to Archibald Campbell, who had become earl and chieftain when his father was killed at the Battle of Flodden. The Campbell chieftain was black-haired and broad-chested, and he had the piercing eyes of a hawk. It was not the chieftain, however, who drew her attention, but his sister.

Catherine Campbell sat on the other side of the chieftain sharing a plate of food with Alex. With her lush curves, creamy skin, and dark, luminous eyes, Catherine was the sort of woman every man lusted after. And anyone could see that she wanted Alex. Catherine was not a subtle woman.

Catherine's deep, sensuous laugh seemed to flow below the noise in the hall straight into Glynis's ears. Glynis stabbed her knife into a slab of pork and cut it into tiny bites for Sorcha, who sat beside her. She chewed her own food with such resolve that her jaw ached.

Glynis was so intent on keeping her gaze on the food before her that she was unaware of the hush in the hall until Sorcha poked her in the side. When she looked up, the only sound in the room was a furious whispering between the Campbell chieftain and his brother and sister, who sat on either side of him. The seat next to Catherine was empty.

"Glynis."

Glynis jumped at the sound of Alex's voice behind her.

He rested his hand on her shoulder and said close to her ear, "We are leaving the hall."

"Why?" she asked.

"Shaggy MacLean has just come through the gate," he said. "'Tis best we not get caught in the middle of this play."

Alex did not wait for her to agree. He picked up Sorcha, pulled Glynis to her feet, and whisked them through a side door near the end of the head table. The door led into a narrow passageway between the castle's stone wall and the decorative wood paneling of the interior wall of the hall.

"What is Shaggy doing here?" Glynis whispered.

"I believe he's come to share the infinitely sad news of the *accidental* death of his beloved wife, Catherine, with her brothers."

"Nay, he would not!" Glynis said.

"Come," Alex said with a broad smile. "There's a peephole behind the head table through which we can watch the fun."

Peepholes in a castle were family secrets. Either Catherine Campbell had an appalling lack of discretion— or she was anticipating bringing Alex into the family.

"Who was that sitting next to ye?" Alex asked. "Ye seemed friendly."

Glynis forgot she had even spoken to the man, and it took her a moment to recall his name. "Malcolm Campbell. He seemed a quiet, steady man."

"Ye mean dull and tedious," Alex said.

"I'm sure he's a good man," she said. "Still waters run deep."

"Stagnant, more likely." Alex turned to Sorcha and held his finger to his lips. "I'll explain to ye later, sweet one."

Alex came to a halt and pointed out two peepholes, close together. He put his arm around Glynys's shoulders as they leaned down to look. She closed her eyes for a moment, enjoying his touch, before she remembered what she was supposed to be doing.

"I see him," she whispered.

Shaggy was walking down the length of the great hall with head down, as if he could hardly bear the weight of his grief. Midway down the room, he staggered. And then he commenced to weeping and wailing, making the most wretched sound Glynis had ever heard.

"Ach, the man is playing the part for all he's worth," Alex said beside her.

Lady Catherine had left the table. Glynis remembered how much it had shaken her to see her former husband and couldn't blame Catherine for wanting to avoid seeing Shaggy after what he'd done to her.

Shaggy's shoulders shook as he paused to mop his face with a big handkerchief. He continued in this fashion, weeping and wailing, until he was a few feet in front of the chieftain's high table.

Then, suddenly, he halted midstride. His mouth fell open, and his hand went to his heart. Glynis followed his wide-eyed stare and saw Catherine taking her place next to the Campbell chieftain.

Glynis heard Alex's deep chuckle as Shaggy looked over his shoulder, evidently expecting the Campbell guards to converge on him.

"Will they kill him?" Glynis asked.

"The Campbells will observe the time-honored tradition of Highland hospitality," Alex said, "and refrain from murdering Shaggy while he is a guest in their home."

The Campbell chieftain gave one of the servants a slight nod, and the man guided Shaggy to a seat. While Shaggy looked ill, the Campbell siblings sat at the head table eating and drinking as if nothing was amiss. They were a cold-blooded lot.

"Sorcha is getting restless," Alex said. "There will be nothing more to see tonight except for watching Shaggy sweat."

Alex led Glynys out of the narrow corridor and up a back stairway.

"What will the Campbells do about Shaggy?" she asked.

"They'll bide their time and toy with him," Alex said. "Shaggy will never know what day they will strike. But one day he'll be found dead with a dirk in his belly, and everyone will know it was a Campbell who put it there."

Alex opened a door at the top of the stairs, and Glynis found herself outside the bedchamber she shared with Sorcha and Bessie.

"How is it that ye know about the peepholes and secret passageways in the Campbell stronghold?" she asked.

"People like to tell me secrets," Alex said.

By people, he meant women. And in this particular instance, Lady Catherine Campbell.

Glynis helped Sorcha get ready for bed, and then Alex sat on the floor beside his daughter's pallet and told her a long story, easily going back and forth from French to Gaelic. Though Glynis was familiar with the tale, Alex made it more exciting than her father's *seannachie* ever had.

"She looks like a wee angel," Glynis said when Sorcha had fallen asleep.

"'Tis early yet," Alex said with a glint in his eyes that made her nervous.

"Bessie will be up soon," she said.

Alex shook his head. "I believe your maid has found herself a man."

"Bessie?" Glynis was shocked. "Ye must be joking."

"Ye can trust me on that," Alex said, as he stepped toward her. "We won't be seeing her for at least a couple of hours."

Glynis backed up until her heel clunked against the wooden door.

"All the same," Alex said, as he reached behind her and slid the bar across, "we should make certain we won't be interrupted."

"Your daughter is asleep on the floor!"

"That's what bed curtains are for," he said. "Come, Glynis, let me take ye behind them and show ye how much I missed ye."

"Isn't Catherine waiting for ye?" she asked.

"So ye *are* jealous." He chuckled deep in his chest. "I suspect Catherine and her brothers will be watching Shaggy for half the night."

"I see. Ye have some time on your hands, is that it?"

"You're the only one I've asked to be my wife," he said.

She closed her eyes when he lowered his head and pressed his warm lips to the side of her throat.

"It is you I want, Glynis MacNeil," he said against her skin. "Don't send me looking for another wife."

"I can't do this," she said, pushing him away. "We aren't even wed yet, and ye have another woman expecting ye later."

"But I don't want her," he said. "I want you."

He looked so sincere that it would be easy to believe him. Still, he had not denied that Catherine was expecting him.

"For how long would ye want me?" she asked. "A week? A month? That won't do for me."

"What if I were to give ye my promise that I wouldn't stray?" he said, sounding pained. "Will ye take me then? Sorcha and I need ye."

"How could I trust ye?" she asked, though with Alex's hands running over her, she was sorely tempted to. "Ye told me before that ye didn't know yourself if ye could be faithful."

"If I give my word," he said with steel in his voice, "I'll keep it."

She wanted him to be faithful because he wanted no one but her. Ach, she was foolish to want the impossible from Alexander Bàn MacDonald. If he loved her, she might throw her fate to the four winds and hope for the best. But Alex only wished to wed her for the sake of his daughter.

"Please, Glynis," he said, his voice like a caress across her skin. "Say ye will marry me and come to bed."

CHAPTER 29

Alex was flirting shamelessly with Catherine, though his heart was not in it. He'd spent half his life trying to avoid jealous women, and here he was doing his best to make one jealous. And it wasn't working, damn her.

Last night, he was certain Glynis was going to give in—but she had not. If she continued to refuse him, he would have to choose another. His daughter needed a mother.

Alex caught sight of his daughter and Bessie going through the doorway that led to the upper floors. Glynis was not with them. When he glanced about the hall, he did not see her.

D'Arcy was missing as well.

Under the table, Catherine's hand was moving up his leg—and heaven knew his cock was suffering from lack of attention. But he did not have time for this now.

"Come to my chamber tonight," she said close to his ear.

Alex was used to avoiding promises, and he did not make one now.

"I am meeting with your brothers soon, and I must look in on my daughter first," he said, as he eased Catherine's hand off his leg. He did intend to see Sorcha—as soon as he found out where Glynis was.

"Your daughter?" Catherine leaned toward him until her breast pressed against his arm. "Surely her nursemaid can look after her?"

"Sorcha is not accustomed to having so many strangers about," Alex said. "She's had a difficult time, and she becomes anxious if she does not see me for long."

"Poor child," Catherine said, pursing her full, red lips. "She's lucky to have such an attentive father."

Alex smiled, pleased by the compliment and by Catherine's concern for his daughter. "I'm glad ye understand."

If he could not persuade Glynis to see sense, perhaps he should consider wedding Catherine.

* * *

Glynis felt so unsettled that she had asked Bessie to take Sorcha up for a nap while she went for a walk along the shore of the loch. She was staring off at the mountains, wishing she was home, when she felt someone beside her and turned.

"Ye startled me, Lord d'Arcy," she said, putting her hand to her chest.

"Please call me Antoine," he said in his lovely accent. "May I walk with you?"

"Of course," she said. "Ye have a remarkable gift for

languages, Lord—Antoine. Your Gaelic improves by the day."

"I have a good teacher," he said, taking her arm. "I hope you will continue to practice with me."

"I will be here at Inveraray only a short while longer." She hoped. "But I am happy to help ye until I leave."

After they walked for a time, D'Arcy came to a halt and turned to face her.

"I have an important question to ask you." He took her hand and kissed it, as if she were a princess. "Albany has appointed me castellan of Dunbar Castle, a great fortress on the sea to the east. Would you consider joining me there and being the queen of my castle?"

A marriage proposal was the last thing she had expected.

Glynis knew she should shout *aye* and throw her arms around his neck. D'Arcy was perfect in every possible way: handsome, serious, principled, and a renowned warrior. Most important, he was closely connected to the regent and therefore in a position to protect her clan.

D'Arcy was so far above her father's expectations for her that she was tempted to agree to be his wife just for spite. And he would be a most considerate husband.

So why did she stand here saying nothing?

Because Alex MacDonald's face, full of laughter, flooded her vision. Alex was wrong for her in so many ways, and yet the devil tempted her to choose the sinfully charming man.

"Thank ye for your kind offer," she said. "Please give me a day to consider."

"Of course."

D'Arcy kissed her hand again. It was a romantic gesture that should have made her sigh. But, as handsome and gallant as D'Arcy was, she felt no spark.

It was a grave disappointment. She did not, however, need to ask him if he would honor his vows—a man like D'Arcy would always be honorable.

* * *

Alex winked at Catherine and left her to find Glynis. On the steps of the keep, he met D'Arcy.

"I've just been speaking with your lovely friend Glynis." D'Arcy gave Alex a smile like a cat that has gotten its paw into the cream. "I fear you must make the rest of the journey without her. She is going to leave with me."

"*What?*"

"She asked for a day to consider my proposal," D'Arcy said, "but I believe she will say yes."

"Ye asked Glynis to be your wife?" Alex felt as if he were falling down a deep well with no rope to hold on to.

"Of course not," D'Arcy said. "I already have a wife."

"Ye have a wife?"

"As you should, my friend," D'Arcy said, putting his hand on Alex's shoulder. "My dear Isabelle was with child when I left, and so we agreed that she must remain in France for the time being. Frankly, I am not at all certain your wild country would suit her."

"If ye have a wife already," Alex said, "then just what did ye plan to do with Glynis?"

"Make her my mistress, of course," he said. "If Isabelle is able to join me in Scotland later, then I will make other arrangements for Glynis. I would not embarrass my wife by keeping another woman in our home while she was there."

"Ye don't seriously believe Glynis would agree to be your mistress, do ye?" Alex asked.

"I know you are concerned for Glynis's welfare," D'Arcy said. "So I want to assure you that if there are children from our liaison, I will provide for them."

"Ye misunderstand," Alex said, wanting to shake him for his stupidity. "I am certain Glynis believes ye are offering her marriage."

"Marriage?" D'Arcy's eyebrows shot halfway up his forehead. "Why, even if I were not already married, that would be absurd."

Alex's head felt in danger of exploding. "And why would it be absurd?"

"I could never marry that sort of woman."

Alex grabbed D'Arcy by the front of his tunic. "Just what do ye mean by 'that sort of woman'?"

"The sort who has affairs with you, Alexander."

"Glynis is no that sort." Alex drove his fist into D'Arcy's jaw, which hurt his hand like the devil, but was very satisfying nonetheless.

"It was an honest mistake," D'Arcy said, rubbing his jaw. "I can tell you've had her from the way the two of you look at each other. So no matter what you say, Glynis is no innocent."

"We have a saying here: *Many a time a man's mouth broke his nose*," Alex said. "If ye don't want your nose broken, I suggest ye remember that Glynis is a chieftain's daughter and a woman deserving of your respect."

"I was not disrespectful," D'Arcy said, looking offended. "I simply made her an offer."

"I would have thought the White Knight was too pure to look at another woman once ye had a wife."

"No man is *that* pure." D'Arcy paused to wipe the blood from the corner of his mouth with a white handkerchief. "I fail to understand why you are upset. There's no harm in my keeping a mistress, especially when my wife is not here."

"Ye will tell Glynis your true intentions," Alex said, leaning forward until they were nose to nose.

"I did not mean to deceive her," D'Arcy said, and took a step back.

"Ye will tell her today."

"I will be honest with Glynis, of course." D'Arcy raised an eyebrow. "Will you do the same, my friend?"

"I haven't misled her." In fact, he had made her an honorable proposal.

"Yet, I do not believe you have told the lady your true feelings," D'Arcy said, studying him with narrowed eyes. "If I'd known them myself, I would never have approached her."

* * *

Sorcha hid behind Bessie's skirts when she saw the black-eyed woman coming toward them. Sometimes the woman looked at Sorcha like a mean dog that bites.

"You can go," the woman said to Bessie. "I'll take her to her father."

"The mistress told me…," Bessie started to say, but her voice faded.

Sorcha understood how words could get stuck inside you.

Bessie left them with a long look over her shoulder. When the woman took Sorcha's wrist, Sorcha tried to pull away, but the woman gave her that mean-dog look.

"Don't fuss," the woman snapped, and started dragging her down the path.

Sorcha wanted to call out for her father or Glynis, but her throat was closed tight.

"Do ye understand a word I say? Ach, how did a clever man like Alex sire an idiot?"

The woman's voice was like her eyes, full of jagged teeth.

"The man dotes on ye like a pet," she said. "I can't have my husband putting his idiot child before me and the children of Campbell blood that I intend to give him."

CHAPTER 30

Glynis stared out the bedchamber window at the distant hills as she brushed her hair. Like a child, she had spent the entire afternoon in here to avoid seeing either Alex or D'Arcy before she made up her mind. Although she knew it would be the sensible thing to do, she could not quite convince herself to give D'Arcy permission to approach her father to negotiate a marriage contract.

From the corner of her eye, Glynis caught a flash of hair the color of moonbeams. She stepped closer to the narrow window for a better look.

What was Catherine Campbell doing leading Sorcha down the path that ran along the loch? The child missed Rosebud and Buttercup, as they all did, so Glynis had sent her with Bessie to see if Alex could take her for one last ride before the horses' owners came to claim them. Alex must have let Catherine take Sorcha for a walk instead.

This was a ploy of Catherine's to win Alex, for the woman did not like the child. Glynis had seen how

Catherine looked at Sorcha when Alex was not watching. To be charitable, perhaps Catherine was attempting to forge a bond with the child.

But there was something about the determined way Catherine was walking that made the hairs on the back of Glynis's neck stand up. And the child was dragging her feet. When Glynis saw how Sorcha kept glancing over her shoulder, she dropped her brush and flew out the door.

She was probably being foolish, but fear pulsed through her veins, urging her feet faster. When she reached the hall, she forced herself to slow to a fast walk and took care not to meet anyone's eyes, lest they try to speak with her. She could not see Sorcha and Catherine when she stepped out of the doors of the keep. Sweat broke out on her palms.

As soon as she reached the bottom of the keep steps, Glynis picked up her skirts and ran across the castle yard, through the gate, and down to the loch. She continued running along the path that disappeared into the tall brush by the loch. Though she had no reason to suspect Catherine would harm the child, Glynis could not talk herself out of her fear. She ran faster, heedless of the briars that tugged at her gown. Branches slashed at her arms and face.

When she reached a split in the path, she paused, heart racing. One fork went up the hill, while the other continued through the thicker vegetation along the shoreline. She took the shoreline path, instinct telling her the greater danger lay in that direction.

When she still did not see them, panic pounded through her veins. Had she taken the wrong fork? She started to turn around when she thought she heard something.

Glynis paused to listen. At first she could hear nothing over the thundering of her heart. But then, she heard it again. A child's whimper.

"Your father will be disappointed," she heard a woman's voice, cajoling, "when I tell him ye are afraid of the water."

Sorcha did not fear the water—Glynis had never seen a child less afraid of it.

Glynis left the path and pushed her way through the brush to the edge of the loch. The sight that met her should have been a peaceful image: a beautiful dark-haired woman leading a fair-haired child out for a swim in a quiet loch on a golden afternoon.

The water was up to Sorcha's chest. Instead of splashing and playing in the water as she did when Alex took her swimming, her slight body was stiff. Catherine was pulling on her arm.

"Can I join ye?" Glynis called out, as she pushed her way through the last of the bushes. "There's nothing I like better than a swim in the late afternoon."

When Catherine looked up, Glynis pretended not to notice her furious expression and gave her a bright smile. But her heart turned in her chest when she saw that Sorcha's eyes were brimming with unshed tears.

"Oh dear," Glynis said, looking about her as if she were dimwitted, "it looks as if ye forgot to bring dry clothes."

"A maid is following with them," Catherine said. "I don't know what's keeping her."

"Ach, maids," Glynis said, shaking her head. "It appears she has forgotten, so you'd best come in. Alex MacDonald is verra protective of his wee daughter, and he won't be pleased if she catches cold."

Catherine looked down at Sorcha. "I'll bring ye back another day, I promise."

As soon as Catherine released Sorcha's wrist, the child ran out of the water and straight into Glynis's arms.

"Such a fearful child," Catherine said. "Ye can tell she was not born a Highlander."

A murderous rage pounded through Glynis. But while in the heart of the Campbell stronghold, it would not pay to call the chieftain's sister the liar that she was.

Pretending nothing had happened while she walked beside Catherine and held the shaking child in her arms was one of the hardest things Glynis had ever done. If she had not left her dirk in the bedchamber, Catherine's dead body might well have been found on the path later that day.

Clearly, Catherine had decided she wanted Alex—and not his child.

"As ye say, Sorcha was not born a Highlander," Glynis said. "I fear she will have a difficult time adjusting to Alexander MacDonald's home. 'Tis a lonely, desolate place."

Of course, Glynis had never been there. If she could dissuade Catherine from pursuing Alex, however, Sorcha would be safe from her.

"What is Alex's home like?" Catherine asked.

"It sits on a high cliff facing north over the sea, where the wind is always blowing." Glynis shuddered. "They don't get many visitors there. Ye could go weeks without seeing a soul outside the household."

Catherine frowned. "How many are in the household?"

"I fear the family has hit on hard times," Glynis said, and shook her head.

"But Alexander's cousin is chieftain, and he holds Alex in high esteem."

"That is true enough, but the chieftain must keep all his warriors at his own castle, Dunscaith," Glynis said. "Unfortunately, he can offer little help when pirates attack, as they frequently do. And then, of course, there are the MacLeods."

"Ach, you're just jealous," Catherine said, a smile curving her lips. "I've seen how ye look at Alexander."

Damn, Glynis was never good at lying. What else could she do to protect the child? If she told Alex what she'd seen, he would not believe Catherine intended to murder the child. And she could not blame him, for no one would. And yet, Glynis had never been more certain of anything in her life.

Glynis kept her gaze fixed ahead as she marched along the path. Her skin itched from the child's damp heat soaking through the front of her gown. Though her arms grew weary, she held Sorcha tight against her. When they reached the fork in the path, Catherine stopped her with a hand on her shoulder.

"Let go of me," Glynis said, her façade breaking.

"I'm doing ye a favor, Glynis, for we both know ye couldn't keep a man like Alex satisfied," Catherine said with her cat's smile. "He'll be in my bed tonight—and he won't want to leave it."

With that, Catherine turned and started up the fork that climbed the hill, her wet gown clinging to every curve.

Glynis understood why Shaggy had left the woman on a tidal rock.

* * *

Alex was in a foul mood as he waited for the guards to admit him into the Campbell chieftain's private chamber. By now, D'Arcy would have told Glynis of his true intentions. Alex had put off visiting his daughter because he didn't want to find Glynis weeping her eyes out over the Frenchman.

"The chieftain is ready for ye," one of the guards said. "I'll take your weapons."

The Campbell chieftain had hundreds of warriors at his command and far more guards protecting his person than the regent had. Parting with his claymore and dirks worsened Alex's mood. He never felt right without his weapons close to hand.

Inside the chamber, the Campbell chieftain and his brother John, the Thane of Cawdor, sat on ornately carved chairs with rich tapestries hanging on the wall behind them. Alex needed to keep his wits about him. This pair had proven they were crafty enough to hold on to power in the ever-changing currents of royal and clan politics.

The Campbell chieftain waved for his guards to leave the room, a symbolic gesture of trust. Unlike Alex, the two Campbells wore their weapons.

"My sister Catherine tells me you are the one who saved her from drowning," the chieftain said when Alex had sat down in the single chair opposite them.

"'Twas fortunate I was there to offer assistance," Alex said.

"We're no pleased that ye stole horses from our men," John, the Thane of Cawdor, said. "But we are impressed."

"I only borrowed them," Alex said.

"Someone murdered the Campbell fishermen ye met." The chieftain's black eyes burned bright with anger. "One of them lived long enough to tell us it wasn't you."

That was lucky.

"D'Arcy tells me ye had some difficulty with our new regent," the chieftain said.

"Difficulty? Ach, the regent liked me so well he wanted to keep me as a permanent guest," Alex said, and the two Campbells laughed.

"I like to discharge my debts," the chieftain said. "I'll make certain the MacDonalds of Sleat are not *falsely* accused of being traitorous rebels."

"I appreciate that," Alex said, and the chieftain nodded, accepting his due. Now for the difficult part. "As ye know, the Western Isles are swarming with rebels. By not joining them, my clan risks being attacked. For us to take the Crown's side in this fight, we need a strong ally."

The Campbell chieftain nodded and folded his hands. "That would be wise."

"A marriage alliance is one means of binding our clans in friendship," John said. "Once this matter with Shaggy Maclean is settled, our sister will be free to remarry."

Sweat rolled down Alex's back. He hoped they were not suggesting what he thought they were.

"I don't have the authority to agree to a marriage on my chieftain's behalf," Alex said and hardly felt guilty for throwing Connor to the wolves.

"Catherine seems to favor you," John said.

"Ach, I'm no more than a chieftain's cousin." Alex's head was pounding. Now that the offer was being made, he was suddenly very certain he did not want to marry Catherine. "I'm sure ye will want someone more important."

"After the marriage I arranged for her nearly ended in

her death," the chieftain said, "I'm inclined to let Catherine have her way this time."

O shluagh! Alex silently pleaded for help from the fairies.

"Your sister is as fair a lass as ever graced the Highlands," Alex said, "but I've already asked another to be my wife." Though Glynis had refused him, he did ask.

"That pretty MacNeil lass?" John asked.

"Aye, and I've already bedded her," Alex said. Under Highland custom, a promise to marry followed by a bedding made you as good as wed. Alex wasn't telling them that the bedding had come before, and not after the promise. "I intend to negotiate the marriage contract with her father when we return."

"I wish ye well," John said, "but I suggest ye hide your wife's dirk."

Alex forced a laugh, though he did not find the remark amusing.

"I believe my chieftain would be honored to enter into an agreement of manrent, instead." Alex was suggesting an agreement under which his clan would have the protection of the powerful Campbells in exchange for sending warriors when the Campbells called on them.

"Tell your chieftain I'm agreeable to it," the Campbell said. "I understand he has his own troubles to deal with now, but I'll expect him to come with his warriors when I need them."

Alex could go home now, knowing he had accomplished the best he could for his clan. Of course, they could count on the Campbells only so long as their interests coincided. The Campbells looked out for the Campbells, first, last, and always. But for the time being, the

Campbells would mind their backs vis-à-vis both the Crown and the other clans. That would free them to turn their attention to subduing the pirates on North Uist.

Glynis could ruin it all. If she did not become Alex's wife in the very near future, the Campbell chieftain would take offense over Alex's refusal of his sister. And the only way to fix that would be to marry Catherine.

Alex was in a grim mood when he knocked on Glynis's bedchamber door.

"Where are they?" he demanded when he found only Bessie there.

"I don't know where Mistress Glynis is, but I thought Sorcha was with you."

"With me?"

"Aye, Lady Catherine said she would take Sorcha to ye," Bessie said. "As the two of ye seemed uncommonly friendly, I didn't think ye would want me to tell her nay…"

"If your mistress had agreed to marry me, then I wouldn't need to be uncommonly friendly in pursuit of another wife!"

Alex turned on his heel and stormed off, though it was not like him to be so irritable. After searching all the common areas of the castle without finding Glynis, Sorcha, or Catherine, he went up to the walkway that ran along the top of on the castle's wall to see if he could spot them from there.

He was pacing back and forth, annoying the guards, when he saw Glynis emerge from the path that skirted the loch. He saw at once that something was amiss. Her hair was loose, and she was swaying with the weight of something she was clutching against her chest. An instant later, he realized that the burden she carried was Sorcha.

Alex ran down the wall steps two at a time. He was across the yard and through the gate before Glynis reached the castle. When he saw that his daughter's clothes were wet and her hair hung in wet clumps down her back, his stomach dropped to his feet.

"What happened?" He tried to lift her from Glynis's arms, but Sorcha clung to her like a monkey.

"Sorcha had a bad fright in the water," Glynis said, "but she is unharmed."

He took a deep breath, trying to calm himself. How did Ian survive with two daughters? Alex supposed that with practice not every spill his daughter took would take a year off his life.

"I've changed my mind," Glynis said, and she had the fiercest look in her eyes.

"Changed your mind about what?" he asked.

"If ye still want me, I'm ready to wed ye."

CHAPTER 31

Truly, Glynis was the most surprising woman. Just when Alex thought she would never agree to wed him, she decided she would, with no persuasion. This was what he wanted. And yet, he did not feel much relieved.

Why would she change her mind so suddenly? Alex considered the question as he waited outside the bed-chamber while Sorcha and Glynis changed out of their wet clothes. Perhaps Sorcha's little mishap, whatever it was, made Glynis realize how attached she was to the child.

More likely, it was because D'Arcy had told her that his offer was to be his mistress. It grated on Alex to know that Glynis had finally agreed to wed him in the wake of her disappointment over D'Arcy.

Glynis came out of the bedchamber and closed the door softly behind her. "Sorcha needs a rest. Bessie will stay with her."

"Good," he said, grabbing her wrist. "We need to talk."

He pulled her up the stairs to the chamber above, which was unoccupied. After sliding the bar across the door, he turned to face her.

"What do ye want, Glynis?"

"I want to marry ye," Glynis said. "Do ye still want me?"

"I do," Alex said, though he would be considerably happier about it if he thought her reasons for changing her mind had anything to do with him.

"I do have conditions," Glynis said.

"Why does this no surprise me?" He folded his arms and narrowed his eyes at her. "And what might these conditions be?"

"The first is that we leave Inveraray Castle at once."

"I must bid farewell to the chieftain and his family," Alex said. "But we can be gone in an hour's time."

Her shoulders relaxed a bit. Evidently, she was desperate to get away from D'Arcy and put that disappointment behind her.

"What else?" he asked, keeping his voice even.

Her face was strained, and she could not look him in the eye. Whatever this second condition was, it was difficult for her to say it.

And he was certain he would not like it.

"I will no share your bed."

What? If there was one thing he had been confident of, it was that he pleased her under the blankets. Did she dislike him so much that she would give up the pleasure they shared in bed?

"If all I wanted was a nursemaid, I would hire one. And I believe the chances are good that I could find a pretty one and bed her as well." He added the last part because he was angry. "I want a wife. In every sense."

Glynis flushed and bit her lip. She could not truly have expected him to agree to this. He waited to hear what she really wanted.

"I'll share your bed—but only so long as ye are faithful." She lifted her serious gray eyes to meet his. "If ye take another woman, I shall never willingly share your bed again."

"Never *willingly*?" he said, white-hot anger sending sparks across his vision. What did she think of him? "I'm no the sort of man who forces women."

"If ye take another woman, then ye must agree to give me a separate house to live in," she said. "A small cottage would do."

The anger welled in his chest, threatening to explode. Nay, he would not live as his parents did.

"Do ye agree?" She held his gaze as if she were trying to see into his soul for the truth.

He pulled her against him and covered her mouth with his. He kissed her with all the fury and passion pent up inside of him, until she was like liquid fire in his arms. When he pulled away, her eyes were dazed—just as he wanted.

"Ye want me to make love to ye," he said, "until ye hear the blood thundering in your ears and see the flashes of light as I make ye come again and again."

Her breath was ragged, and her lips parted and soft from his kisses.

"Say it," he demanded.

"I do," she said, her voice barely above a whisper.

"Ye want me to be your husband and to share my bed every night. Say it!"

"I do."

He kissed her again until she moaned in his mouth and swayed against him. By God, she would want him and only him. His anger still was not spent when he released her a second time.

"I'll agree to a full marriage, then," she said, primly running her hands over her gown to smooth it. "If we decide after a year that we do not suit, we'll part with no hard feelings. Unless, of course, ye take another woman before then, in which case, it will be as I said before."

It was time to settle this between them.

Alex pulled his dirk from his belt and heard her suck in her breath as he used it to cut a strip of cloth from the bottom of his shirt. He grasped her hand and interlocked his fingers with hers. Holding their hands up between them, he locked eyes with her as he wound the strip of cloth around their wrists three times.

"I take ye as my wife, Glynis MacNeil, daughter of Gilleonan MacNeil of Barra, and I will be your husband." Alex paused, and then he said in a deliberate voice, "'Til death, Glynis. Did ye hear that? 'Til *death*."

Under Highland tradition, a man who was unhappy with a marriage could return the woman to her father, along with her dowry, or *tochar*, at the end of a year. This was most commonly done when the woman failed to conceive, but if there was a child, the child was considered legitimate. Unfortunately, the woman could quit the marriage as well.

Alex could not hold Glynis to more than a year without a priest—and priests were few and far between in the Highlands—but he was demanding it anyway.

She pressed her lips into a tight line and glared at him.

"You've done this before," he said. "Ye know what to say."

When he saw the flash of hurt in her eyes, he regretted bringing up her prior marriage. But for reasons he did not understand himself, he was far too angry to apologize.

"All right," she said between clenched teeth. "I take ye as my husband, Alexander MacDonald, and I promise to be your wife."

"Until death," he finished for her.

"Until death," she said, her eyes shooting daggers at him. "Or until ye stray, as we both know ye will."

"Don't mistake me for Clanranald, for I will hold ye to your promise," Alex said.

"I was no the first to break my promise with him, and I won't be with you either," she said. "But if ye take another woman, I'll never share your bed again."

"I'll do my damnedest to make sure ye can never bring yourself to tell me nay," he said.

She gasped when he pulled her hard against him again. As he leaned down, she made a high-pitched sound at the back of her throat, then her eyes fluttered closed, and she tilted her head back. He stopped just short of her parted lips.

"Pack up your things," he said. "I promised ye that we would leave at once, and I am a man of my word."

CHAPTER 32

Why was Alex so furious with her? She had agreed to the full marriage. And right now, she wanted the marriage rights quite badly.

"We could stay the night," Alex said, his breath tickling her lips. "But only if ye are willing to release me from my promise to leave at once."

He was supporting her back with one strong arm while he ran his other hand up her side. When he brushed the side of her breast, she bit her lip to keep from sighing aloud. How she'd missed his touch.

"If this is what ye want, ye must tell me," he said.

Why did he insist that she say it? Because she had pricked his pride, suggesting he might force her one day if she refused. She should not have said it, for she knew he was not like that. She remembered how her first husband had pushed her back on the bed and taken her virginity with little preamble—and certainly without waiting for her permission.

But Alex demanded that she give her consent explicitly. It was hard to confess that she wanted him, for it forced her to admit that this was not purely a selfless act to protect a child. Nor was it merely a practical decision to choose a husband before her father did it for her.

"Aye, this is what I want," she whispered. "I want you, Alex MacDonald."

He walked her backward until the bed was against her back. She was grateful for the support because her knees grew weak as he ran kisses down her throat. When he pressed his warm lips to the hollow above her collarbone, a sigh escaped her. His breath on her skin made her breasts ache. When his hands finally covered them, she closed her eyes.

When Alex kissed her mouth again, their tongues moved in a primal rhythm that filled her with longing. She twined her arms around his neck and slid her fingers through his hair. When he pulled away, her body followed, pressing against him.

"Do we delay our departure and stay the night?" he asked in a voice rough with desire.

"Aye," she said again. "Take me to bed."

"The right answer, wife."

Alex swept aside the bed curtains, sat her on the high bed, and lit the candle on the table beside it. He was often playful in bed, but there was nothing lighthearted about the way he was looking at her now.

"Your gown," he said in a strained voice. "Take it off."

Glynis swallowed and decided to start with her shoes. She slipped one off and then the other, letting them drop with soft thuds in the silent room. As she eased her stocking down her calf, she looked up and saw Alex's chest rise and fall in slow, deep breaths.

He was staring at her so fiercely that her fingers shook a little as she removed her head covering and unwound her hair from the coil Bessie had pinned up only a short time ago. After unfastening the first two hooks at the back of her gown, she dropped her arms.

"I can't do the rest myself."

Alex's jaw was clenched tight, but he gave her a curt nod, so she slid down from the bed. She was so tense that she felt light-headed as she took the three steps to reach him and turned around. When his fingers grazed the back of her neck, she drew in a sharp breath at the shock of his touch.

A little of her confidence returned when she realized that Alex, who was usually disconcertingly adept at removing women's clothing, was fumbling with the hooks. Once he had them undone, he dragged the gown off her shoulders and let it fall in a pool around her feet.

His lips were gentle as he brushed soft kisses against her neck, but his hands gripped her upper arms so tightly it almost hurt. When she leaned back against him, she felt his solid heat through her thin shift. He kissed her hair and the side of her face as he eased her shift off her shoulders. She felt the cool air on her breasts for an instant before he held them in his hands.

"Ah, Glynis." His breath was hot in her ear. "I was going to die if ye held me to my promise and made me wait."

He scraped his teeth along her shoulder as he slid one hand beneath the shift that still clung to her hips. He groaned when his hand cupped her between her legs.

Then pleasure shot through her as his fingers dipped and explored.

Her legs grew weak, and she sagged against him as heat pooled low and heavy in her belly. But then he began to move against her, pressing his hard shaft into her, and she strained against him.

She turned in his arms, wanting his kiss. His clothes were rough against her sensitive nipples. Gripping her hips, he held her tight against him as he gave her long, deep kisses.

She tore her mouth away. "Alex, I must lie down."

He threw the bedclothes back with one hand, and then swept her off her feet and laid her on the bed in one easy motion. Before she could blink, Alex had unfastened his plaid and pulled his shirt over his head.

Glynis watched the muscles of his back and thighs as he stretched and leaned over to remove his boots. Then he stood upright facing her in all his glory. Ach, he was magnificent. The candlelight played across every contour of his muscular arms and torso. Glynis swallowed as her gaze moved down from his chest to his flat belly and full staff.

When she lifted her gaze back to his face, Alex's eyes scorched her skin.

Her heart pounded against her chest and her breath came fast as he climbed onto the bed. Anticipation sparked through her as he reached for her. At once, she was enfolded in his heat, under his weight, and drowning in reckless passion. His hands were everywhere—and every part of her ached for his touch. She tried to catch her breath as he kissed her eyebrows, her cheeks, her jaw, her ear. As he worked his way down her throat with his lips and tongue, she tilted her chest upward.

"Aye," she breathed when his hands covered her breasts and found her nipples. She heard herself making incoherent sounds as he pressed openmouthed kisses down her breastbone while teasing her nipples with his thumbs. She thought she might die from the pleasure—and that was before he dragged his tongue across her breast to her nipple.

She clenched her fingers in Alex's hair as he first circled her nipple with his tongue and then drew it into his mouth. He suckled her breast as if his whole being was focused on drawing sensations from the depth of her soul. It was too much. She clawed at his shoulders, not certain herself if she was begging him to stop or begging him not to.

Then he ran his tongue along the underside of her breast and pressed kisses over her ribs. His hair left a trail of sparks as it brushed across her skin. Anticipation grew by leaps and bounds when his kisses moved lower, down her belly and over her hip, and he wrapped his arm around her thigh.

At last, he rested his hand on her mound and found the sensitive spot between her legs with his thumb. She sank into the whirl of sensations. What this man did to her!

She tensed when she felt the heat of his breath and his tongue move close to where his hand was. He'd done this before, but she still couldn't quite believe it. She dragged her head up from the bed. Her breath went shallow as he moved his hand away to kiss her between her legs. Then he shot her a sizzling look that made her insides squeeze.

"Ye know ye like this," he said in a low voice that vibrated through her.

Like it? She loved it. She dropped her head back down on the bed. If she had to spend some time in purgatory for this, she was willing.

She sucked in her breath as he ran his tongue over that same sensitive spot. *Oh, my.* She clenched the bedclothes in her hands and gave herself over to the storm of sensations as Alex licked and sucked and ran his tongue over and into her. She tried to be quiet, but sighs and moans and a kind of pleading sound came from her throat.

She tossed her head from side to side, but Alex was relentless. When she felt herself rising to a peak, he clutched her body tighter. He would not let her move away from him until her body spasmed into an explosion of pleasure.

She shuddered when he ran his tongue lightly up her stomach. When he stretched out beside her, she turned into him, still shaken from the intensity of her release, and wrapped her arms around him. She buried her face in his neck.

"I've been wanting to do that for days," he said, as he ran his fingers up and down her side and her back.

"That felt so good that I'm certain it must be verra sinful," she said against his skin.

She felt the low rumble of his chuckle. "Nothing is sinful between a man and wife, but if it pleases ye to think it is, then I won't argue with ye."

When she scooted closer, his shaft pressed against her belly, reminding her of his need. And just like that, she wanted him all over again. She pulled him into a deep kiss. Alex groaned in her mouth as she rubbed her palm up his shaft.

He needed no more encouragement. When he rolled

her on her back, she wrapped her legs around him. She closed her eyes against the rush of pleasure as he slid inside her. When she opened her eyes again, he held her head between his hands and stared down at her.

"I missed being with ye like this," Alex said, as if the confession was torn from him against his will.

"I missed ye too."

With their eyes locked on each other, he started moving in and out. His breathing was ragged, and his face strained. She knew Alex prided himself on his control, but she sensed that he was barely hanging on to it—and she wanted it to snap. She wanted to feel his raw need, to know that he was as affected as she was.

As he moved faster and deeper, she gripped his shoulders and wrapped her legs more tightly around him. She had so many emotions swirling inside her—desire, affection, hope, longing—that she felt as if her chest might burst.

I love you. The words were in her mind and almost on her lips.

Waves of blinding pleasure coursed through her as he thrust inside her again and again. He cried her name as he drove deep inside her one last time.

Then he collapsed on top of her, his weight heavy but reassuring. He was hers. At least for now, he was hers.

After a short while, he rolled to his side, bringing her with him. Her limbs felt limp, as if they would bend in the waves like seaweed. She lay with her head on his chest and his heart thundering in her ear.

Something profound had happened, and it had altered her forever. It wasn't that she had agreed to wed him, though that would certainly change her life. God help her, but there was no avoiding it—she had fallen in love with him. Was she alone in this, or had Alex felt as much as she did when he was inside her?

Alex lay on his back with one arm about her and his other hand holding hers on his chest. Glynis watched his profile while he stared at the ceiling.

"What are ye thinking?" she finally asked.

"That it's strange to be married without Connor, Ian, and Duncan knowing it," Alex said.

She swallowed back her disappointment. "Ye are close to them, aren't ye?"

"Aye. The four of us have been through everything together," he said with a smile in his voice. "They are the first ones I will tell."

"What about your parents?"

He blew his breath out. "I'll tell them when I see them."

Would his parents not be pleased with the marriage? Did they have someone else in mind for him?

Alex turned toward her and cradled the side of her face with his hand. "We shall wed properly when we return to Skye," he said, with his eyes intent on hers. "I'll send word to your father. As soon as he arrives, we'll say our pledges again before witnesses and have a great wedding feast at Dunscaith Castle."

"I'll meet your parents at this wedding feast?" she asked. "What are they like?"

"We can talk about my parents later," he said, as he brought his lips to hers.

* * *

It was not like Glynis to go back on her word. All the same, Alex would not be content until he had a formal marriage contract with her father, and they had said their pledges before a dozen of their clansmen. If Alex could find a priest, all the better.

While they made love, his anger and resentment had burned away in the hot flame of desire. He was so lost in his passion for Glynis that nothing else mattered. And then after, as she lay in his arms, happiness took told of him for long moments, blinding him to truths he should not let himself forget.

But with the dawn, his caution returned with his resentment.

Alex knew he had no right to resent that Glynis only agreed to wed him after she learned D'Arcy was not offering her marriage. Nor should it have angered him that Glynis saw him as the least offensive of undesirable choices, for Alex had made that very argument himself. And if she also did it because she wanted to be a mother to his daughter, he should be glad of that.

And yet, all these things ate at him.

Alex had not wanted to marry any more than she did. But when he decided to, Glynis MacNeil was his first and his only choice. No one else would do.

And that troubled him most of all.

CHAPTER 33

Poor Bessie had shown herself to be a Lowlander by spending much of the long sail with her head over the side. While Glynis tucked a blanket around the sleeping maid, she heard Alex laughing and talking with the Campbell men who were sailing them to Skye.

The Campbell chieftain had provided a boat to take them home, and Alex had persuaded the Campbell men sailing it to let him take the rudder. Under his sure hand, the boat glided over the water and around the rocks as smoothly as a fairy flying through trees in a forest.

Glynis bit her lip and fixed her gaze on the Isle of Skye ahead on the horizon. Alex had not laughed with her once since they left Inveraray Castle days before. From the moment she had told him she would be his wife, he had lost his easy cheerfulness.

Clearly, Alex did not want this marriage. He *needed* a wife—or rather, a mother for his daughter—but he was not happy about it. She should have taken heed from her first conversation with him back on Barra. *Ye are quite safe from finding wedded bliss with me.*

Wedded bliss, indeed. Misery seemed more the way of it. What had she got herself into?

Glynis sat back down next to Sorcha and combed the child's windblown hair with her fingers. When Sorcha smiled at her, she was reminded that the marriage did have its good side. It brought her motherhood, a precious gift she had thought she would be denied. And Alex did not constantly criticize her and expect her to be other than what she was, as both Magnus and her stepmother had. He would protect her with his life, no doubt of that.

But Alex was bound to break her heart. When Magnus took other women, it had hurt her pride, but that was all. It would be different with Alex. When they lay together, he not only gave her pleasure—though there was plenty of that, to be sure—he showed her parts of herself she had not known before. After what they had shared, she could not bear to know he was going to another woman's bed.

Because she loved him. God help her.

When Alex turned his sea-green eyes on her, the laughter left his face, and her heart sank. He gave the rudder to one of the other men, crossed the boat to sit beside her, and took Sorcha into his lap.

"The land to our right is the Sleat Peninsula of Skye." Alex rested his hand on Glynis's shoulder and tilted his head down to hers as he pointed. "And the castle ye see there is Dunscaith, my chieftain's castle."

Glynis's body felt pulled to his. She longed to lean into him—but she did not.

"Dunscaith got its name from Scáthach, the warrior queen who had her legendary school of heroes on the verra spot where our chieftain's castle now stands," Alex said, speaking first in French for Sorcha and then in Gaelic. "Those mountains ye see beyond the castle are the Cuillins, which are named for Cúchulainn, the most famous of the heroes Scáthach trained."

Glynis could not help smiling, for she recognized the start of one of his stories. She added Alex's storytelling to her list of good things that the marriage brought her.

"Now, Scáthach would only train the bravest and most skilled young warriors. To prove himself worthy, a man first had to penetrate her fortress, which had many defenses, including magical ones. Cúchulainn traveled here from Ireland as a young man, after the father of the lass he loved said he would only agree to their marriage if Cúchulainn was trained as a warrior by Scáthach.

"Young Cúchulainn succeeded in getting inside the castle and was accepted by the warrior queen. Later, as part of his training, he helped Scáthach subdue a neighboring female chieftain who was causing Scáthach trouble. In the process of fulfilling this task, Cúchulainn had a child with the woman. And though his heart was always with the young lass he loved back in Ireland, he also became friendly with Scáthach's daughter. Unfortunately, he had to kill the daughter's husband in a duel, which I'm sure he regretted. I believe it was after the daughter that Cúchulainn became friendly with Scáthach herself."

"What kind of story is this to tell to a wee girl?" Glynis interrupted.

"I can't change the story," Alex said, lifting his shoulders. "'Tis the legend of our castle."

"The MacDonalds would have legends of philanderers and call them heroes," Glynis said, folding her arms.

"Cúchulainn was no a married man at the time." Alex cleared his throat and began again. "When Cúchulainn returned to Ireland, the lass's father refused to let them marry, although Cúchulainn had fulfilled the condition. Ye see, the father never intended to allow the marriage and believed he had set an impossible condition. Well, that was a mistake for certain. Cúchulainn captured the father's fortress, took the man's treasure—and his life—and then he married his love."

Glynis had been lost in the story and was startled when Alex stopped speaking. They were close enough to Dunscaith now that she could see the guards on the walls.

"I'll tell ye more stories about Scáthach and Cúchulainn later," Alex said to Sorcha. "But now, it's time for ye to meet the Clan MacDonald."

As the boat pulled beside the sea gate, Glynis stood to thank the Campbell men. They were anxious to return to their homes and had refused Alex's offer of hospitality. One of them, however, insisted on carrying Bessie into the castle, as she was still quite ill from the journey.

Alex picked Sorcha up in one arm and held his other hand out to Glynis. When she looked into his grim face, her heart sank lower still.

"Don't fret. They never thought I'd find a woman willing to put up with me," Alex said, but his humor seemed forced. "They will all be verra pleased to see ye."

If only Alex were pleased himself, she wouldn't care about the rest of the MacDonalds. She felt as if she were a weight tied around his neck.

No sooner had they climbed up the steep stairs into the castle courtyard than Glynis was surrounded by MacDonalds. It seemed to her that all the MacDonald men were extraordinarily tall. She had to tilt her head back to breathe.

In the midst of this sea of strangers, she saw Duncan walking toward them. He nodded at her, and the corners of his mouth went up a fraction in what she took for a smile. On either side of Duncan were two dark-haired, handsome warriors who looked to be brothers.

"Come meet my cousins," Alex said, pushing her forward with his hand at her back.

Before Alex could introduce her and Sorcha, Glynis heard a familiar bellow come from behind the gathered men. "Alexander Bàn MacDonald!"

Glynis put her hand to her forehead. Nay. That could not be her father.

"Alexander Bàn MacDonald!" This time, the roar cleared a path through the MacDonald warriors like Moses parting the Red Sea—and at the other end of it stood her father. As he strode toward them, Alex set Sorcha down behind him and took Glynis's hand.

"After stealing my daughter from under my nose and dragging her to God knows where for weeks," her father shouted, all red in the face, "ye will either be my son-in-law before the day is out, or you'll be a dead man!"

Glynis flushed to her roots. Why was her father doing this?

"Da, Alex did no—," she started to explain, but Alex cut her off.

"I beg your forgiveness for stealing your daughter from ye," Alex said, putting his hand over his heart. "But sometimes a man must act boldly to get the woman he wants."

Alex was taking the blame for all of this. She might

have appreciated the gesture if he'd done it out of affection for her, rather than manly pride.

"I believe ye are aware that your daughter was...disinclined toward marriage," Alex continued. "So I had no choice but to force her hand by kidnapping her."

Ach, her father could not have looked more pleased. She felt like a hog caught between two cooks.

"I succeeded in persuading her to take me as her husband," Alex said, "and we have made a marriage pledge to each other."

"An alleged hand-fasting with just the two of ye under the stars will not do," her father said, planting his hands on his hips. "Glynis is a chieftain's daughter, no a penniless lass. Ye will do this proper, Alexander MacDonald, with a contract, a *tochar*, and pledges made before both clan chieftains."

"That is precisely my desire as well, sir," Alex said.

The two of them were having a fine time trying to outdo the other in their resolve to have her good and properly bound in marriage. Each had his reasons, which had nothing to do with her feelings on the matter.

"The MacDonald chieftain and I have already worked out the agreement," her father said.

How did her father know she would be returning with Alex, when she herself had no idea? And, by the saints, how long had her father been waiting here? He should have gone home and pretended nothing was amiss. Ach, it was humiliating.

"I've been waiting here for weeks," her father said, confirming her worst fear. "Let's get this wedding under way!"

One of the two handsome, dark-haired warriors with

Duncan stepped forward. "A thousand welcomes to you, Glynis, daughter of Gilleonan MacNeil of Barra," he said. "I am Connor, chieftain of the MacDonalds of Sleat, and I am most happy to have ye here at Dunscaith Castle."

After her father's shouting, she appreciated the chieftain's formal greeting and replied in kind. "A blessing on the house of the grandson of Hugh MacDonald and great-grandson of the Lord of the Isles."

The chieftain gestured toward the other dark-haired warrior, who had the bluest eyes Glynis had ever seen. "This is Ian, who is my cousin as well as Alex's."

She was introduced in quick succession to a few dozen MacDonalds and then greeted by the few MacNeil men who were here with her father. Her head was spinning when two women had mercy on her and interrupted the greetings. One was small and brisk and dressed in a gown too large for her slender figure, and the other was a lovely redhead who carried two look-alike babes in her arms.

"Come with us." The small woman smiled as she put her hand at Glynis's back and took Sorcha's hand. "I have a chamber ready for ye upstairs. I've already seen to your maid, the poor dear."

Glynis let the two women lead her and Sorcha inside the keep and up the stairs to a tidy bedchamber that smelled of heather.

"We thought ye needed rescuing," the redhead said, giving Glynis a wide smile. "I'm Sìleas, Ian's wife."

"And I'm Ilysa, Duncan's sister," the other woman said. "I've sent someone to bring up a bit of food and drink. If ye need anything at all, you've only to ask."

Glynis was puzzled as to why Duncan's sister appeared to be managing the chieftain's household, but perhaps the chieftain had no close female relative to fill the role in lieu of a wife. It was odd that he didn't have a wife, though, for a chieftain had an even greater duty than other men to produce heirs.

"Ye know from my father that I'm Glynis," she said. "And this is Sorcha, Alex's daughter."

"I knew ye were Alex's child the moment I saw ye, Sorcha," Sìleas said with a soft smile.

Sorcha could not take her eyes off the twins and took a couple of cautious steps toward them.

"This one is Beitris," Sìleas said, tilting her head toward one of the look-alike babes. "And this one is Alexandra, named for your father."

When Alexandra grabbed hold of Sorcha's nose, both babes squealed in delight at her mischief—and Sorcha laughed. Glynis put her hand to her chest. Hearing Sorcha laugh for the first time felt like a small miracle.

"I'm glad Alex found ye," Ilysa said, after they had talked about the babes for a time. "Frankly, none of us was certain he would show such good judgment."

"I happened to be the closest woman at hand when he needed a wife," Glynis said. Realizing she had said too much, she tried to make light of it. "*An ràmh is fhaisg air làimh, iomair leis.*" The oar that is close at hand, row with it.

"Alex has never had trouble finding women, so I'm sure that wasn't the reason," Sìleas said. "Now we'd best get ye ready, for I believe they intend to have this wedding tonight."

Tonight?

CHAPTER 34

Glynis felt ill. Her stomach hurt, her head throbbed, and dread weighed down on her chest, making it hard to breathe. Although Sìleas and Ilysa were kindness itself, their glowing faces only made Glynis feel worse.

Every time one of them mentioned how delighted they were that Alex had chosen a bride who was so different from "his usual sort," she wondered how long it would be before he went back to his usual ways and his usual sort.

Bang, bang, bang. Ach, Glynis knew that knock.

"It's my father." She jumped to her feet to get to the door first and then slipped outside so that they could speak in private.

"Ye had me worried, lass." Her father lifted her off her feet in a crushing embrace. That raised her spirits—until he set her back down and said, "Praise God he's marrying ye. I feared I'd have to kill him."

"It didn't happen like ye think, da," she said. "Alex doesn't really want me."

"Ach, that man wants ye," her father said. "He has since he first saw ye on the beach at Barra."

She sighed. "What I mean, da, is that he doesn't want me for *a wife*. Not truly."

Her father lifted her chin. "I know I made a mistake with Magnus Clanranald."

This was the first he had admitted that.

"But Alex sees ye for what ye are, and he likes what he sees," her father said. "This man is going to love ye, whether he wants to or no."

Glynis swallowed against the lump in her throat. Even if her father could not be more wrong, it warmed her heart to know that he wanted this for her.

"How did ye know it was Alex I left with?" she asked.

"I watched the two of ye, and I figured ye just needed some time together for this to happen," he said. "So I let ye both believe I was going to make ye wed that Alain Maclean, though he is even madder than his father Shaggy."

"Ye did that on purpose?"

"Aye," her father said, grinning from ear to ear.

She couldn't believe it! Despite all her efforts to thwart her father's plans for her—from putting her fate in the hands of a stranger to traveling all the way to Edinburgh—she had ended up doing exactly what he wanted.

"I went home to Barra before coming here to wait for ye," he said before she could gather herself to shout at him. He stooped to reach into a cloth bag at his feet and pulled a soft blue gown from it. "Your stepmother made ye a new gown to be wed in."

"It's lovely!" Glynis said, holding it up. "That was kind of her, truly. Oh, da, I wish I could see the rest of the family."

"They all miss ye," her father said. "Tell that new husband of yours to bring ye for a long visit soon."

Glynis prayed she would not be coming home alone and in shame again.

* * *

Alex stood at the front of the hall, flanked by Connor and Duncan on one side and by the MacNeil chieftain and Ian on the other, waiting for his bride to make her appearance. And waiting. When Glynis's father took a step, looking as if he meant to fetch her and drag her down the stairs by her hair, Alex grabbed his arm in an iron grip.

"Give her time." Alex locked eyes with her father and did not let go of him until the chieftain nodded and stepped back.

When the voices in the hall hushed, Alex turned and sucked in his breath at the sight of Glynis at the far end of the hall. She wore a soft blue gown that drew attention to her slender, elegant figure and flowed about her as she walked. With her rich brown hair pulled up in a crown of flowers and ribbons, and then cascading down her back, she looked like a wood nymph come from the forest to enchant him.

But beneath her crown of flowers, Glynis's face was strained. Her wide gray eyes had the same look of panic Alex had seen in a wounded doe's as it lay on the ground with an arrow in its side. Glynis hesitated at every step, looking as if she might bolt if someone made a loud noise. It seemed to take her forever to cross the length of the hall. Finally, she stood before him.

Glynis had not changed her mind. But it had been close.

* * *

Alex was breathtakingly handsome, tall and striking in his saffron shirt and plaid with greens that matched his eyes. Most of the people gathered in the hall—particularly her own clansmen—must be wondering how such a skinny, difficult lass had come to be the one that Alex chose to wed.

Glynis darted glances left and right as she traversed the endless hall, a different question dragging her steps. How many women in the room had Alex slept with? Two? Three? A dozen?

"Ye look beautiful," Alex said, playing the part of bridegroom, when she finally reached the end of the gauntlet. "I believe we sign the contract first."

By *we*, he meant her father, of course. All the same, Alex took her with him to the small table where the contract had been laid out. She had learned to read, but she was too overwrought to make sense of any of the words.

"Is it acceptable to ye?" Alex asked, which was kind, but pointless, since her father had already signed it.

She could not get a word through her throat, so she nodded. When Alex signed, his signature was big and bold with a flare, just like he was. She felt like a skinny, brown mouse next to him.

After she and Alex returned to their places, the two chieftains made speeches about a glorious union, fertility, and such. She saw no priest, so it appeared Alex had not succeeded in finding one on short notice. Glynis ignored the speeches and closed her eyes to say her own prayer.

Please, God, give me a few months with him before he breaks my heart.

"Glynis!" When she heard her father say her name, she opened her eyes to find both chieftains staring at her. "Say your pledge," her father hissed.

Her heart hammered so loudly she thought they must hear it.

"I…" Her throat was too dry, and she had to stop to swallow. It took her three tries, but she got the words out. She fixed her gaze on the floor as she waited for Alex to say his vows.

He was silent. The longer Alex did not speak, the more his silence seemed to expand and fill the hall. When Glynis risked a sideways glance at him, he was staring at her with a fiercely grim expression on his face.

Alex grabbed her by the wrist. She had to struggle to keep her feet under her as he proceeded to haul her out of the hall with his long-legged strides.

"*O shluagh!*" she whispered. What had she done to deserve this?

CHAPTER 35

Alex dragged Glynis into a large bedchamber that she assumed must be the chieftain's because it adjoined the hall, though it was plainly furnished and the walls had no decoration at all. After sitting her down in a chair, Alex pulled another up opposite so that they sat face-to-face with no more than a foot between them.

"Glynis, I cannot go ahead with this marriage when ye look as if you're going to your own hanging," Alex said. "We'll end this right now if it makes ye this unhappy to be my wife."

She was too shocked to speak. After doing everything he could to persuade her to wed him, now he wanted to release her from her pledge?

"I hoped ye would come to see me as a man ye could be content with and reconcile yourself to the marriage," he said. "But it appears ye cannot, and I will no raise my daughter in a house filled with anger and unhappiness."

Glynis's heart was pounding so hard that her chest hurt.

"It won't be easy convincing your father that I haven't taken ye to bed and given him cause to force the marriage," he said with a resigned sigh, "but I will."

She did not want to return to her father's house to be put on display for an endless stream of unsavory suitors again. "What about all those people waiting out there for us?"

Alex dismissed them all with a wave of his hand. "I know I pressed ye hard to do this, but you're a stubborn lass who knows her own mind. So tell me, why did ye agree to wed me?"

Glynis paused to lick her lips. She was unsure whether to tell him the truth, but she had nothing else to say. "Because I feared ye would wed Catherine, and I believed she would harm Sorcha."

Instead of dismissing her accusation as foolishness or demanding proof, Alex simply looked at her steadily and waited for her to explain herself.

"Because Sorcha is silent, she senses things that others miss."

"Aye, I've noticed that," Alex said.

"I found Catherine taking Sorcha out in the loch where no one could see," Glynis said. "I could tell that Sorcha was frightened to death of her." She told him the rest of what happened, though there was not much more to tell.

"*One brings danger*," he muttered as he ran his hands through his hair. "I had no notion Catherine would want to harm Sorcha."

Glynis was used to her father—and everyone else— dismissing her judgment. It touched her that Alex did not question her perception of what had happened at the loch that day.

"Well, I was right about one thing," Alex said with a sad smile. "Ye would be a good mother to Sorcha."

"A child alone cannot bind us," Glynis said, blinking hard to keep back tears. "As ye said, being a wife is more than being a nursemaid."

"I wanted ye for myself as well," he said, and touched the back of his fingers to her cheek. "I know it is important to ye that your husband is faithful. Is that part of what is making ye so miserable about the prospect of being married to me?"

Glynis dropped her gaze to her hands folded in her lap and nodded.

"Then I would give ye my promise that so long as we share a bed as man and wife, I'll take no other."

When he first spoke of marriage, he had only promised to be discreet in his affairs. He was willing to give her the promise she wanted now, but could she trust him? Even if Alex meant it now, would he still mean it in a month?

"I can't do more than give ye my word on it." He got to his feet and looked down at her. "I wish that were enough."

If Alex had shouted at her and stormed off, Glynis might not have stopped him. But instead, he leaned down and kissed her cheek, a tender gesture that left her blinking back tears again. Then he turned and walked quietly toward the door.

As Alex said, he was the best of her choices, by far. But more than that, he was the only man she wanted. Was she brave enough to take the risk that he would hurt her? Was she strong enough to survive if he disappointed her? All Glynis knew for certain was that she could not bear the thought of him wedding another.

"Alex!"

When he turned around, his face, which was normally so full of humor, looked ragged.

"Ye were right. I did not fulfill my side of the bargain," she said. "Since I said I would wed ye, I should not have done it begrudgingly. That was wrong of me, and I'm sorry."

"Ye needn't apologize," Alex said, sounding tired. "I'll go tell the others now, and I'll have someone bring ye supper so ye don't have to face them."

When he started to leave again, she sprang to her feet. "Wait. Ye don't understand me."

"That's true enough," he said, giving her a bittersweet smile.

"What I mean is, I think we should marry," she said in a rush. "I'll make the best of it."

He gave a dry laugh. "Make the best of something ye hate? Nay, that's no good enough."

"I want to marry ye, Alex," she said, and it was the truth. With all her heart, she wanted him. "And I will try to trust ye."

"Are ye certain ye want to go ahead with this?" His expression was solemn. "I told ye, I don't want a trial marriage. My daughter already lost whoever raised her until now."

Alex had told her that he wanted her for himself as well, and she would hang on to that. Though he would not be marrying at all if not for Sorcha, he must care for her a little.

Glynis quelled her doubts and nodded.

"All I ask is that ye make a peaceful home for me and my daughter." Alex held out his hand, and when she took it he gave her a genuine smile. "Duncan has been entertaining everyone with his pipes, but let's no keep them waiting any longer."

*   *   *

"Ready?" Alex asked, as they stood together just outside the hall. He gave her hand a reassuring squeeze, then flung the door open.

The buzz of voices died, and every head turned toward them. In another moment, Duncan abandoned the mournful strain he had been playing and began a lively tune that sounded like pure happiness. When the MacDonalds broke into wild cheers, signaling their approval of the marriage, Glynis felt herself blush with pleasure.

Hope flooded her heart.

She smiled up at Alex as they walked hand in hand to the front of the hall. This time, they said their vows in strong voices and without hesitation. Then Alex gave her a kiss that caused the crowd to hoot and shout again. As soon as he released her, Sorcha, who had been standing with Sìleas and Ilysa, threw her arms around Glynis's waist.

And suddenly, Glynis had both a husband and a daughter. With Alex's arm about her shoulders, her new daughter at her side, and all the MacDonalds giving her such a warm welcome, Glynis set her doubts aside and decided to enjoy her day of happiness.

Alex's clansmen came up one after another to wish them well, giving them the traditional greetings. *Saoghal fada dhuibh.* Long life to you. *A h-uile là sona dhuibh gun là idir dona dhuibh.* May every day be happy for you without a single bad day.

Alex was laughing at something his cousin Ian had said when Glynis felt him go rigid beside her.

"So, 'tis true that ye let a lass catch ye," a deep voice called out.

When Glynis turned to see who had spoken, she felt as if she were looking into the future and seeing Alex thirty years hence. The tall, fair-haired warrior could be none other than Alex's father. Ach, it was a sin for a man to still be so handsome at his age.

"I caught her, Father," Alex said, his voice as stiff as his back. "I am a lucky man."

Alex said it with a fierceness that made it sound more like a challenge than an expression of good fortune.

"Ah, ye are a pretty lass," his father said, giving Glynis a wink and taking her hands.

It was easy to see where Alex got his charm, but the older man had a hardness in his eyes that Glynis had only seen in Alex when he fought—and right now.

When his father leaned down to kiss her, Alex put his arm out to stop him.

"'Tis past time ye did your duty and wed," his father said, meeting Alex's glare. "A man needs an heir."

A dark-haired woman broke through the group surrounding them and threw her arms around Alex. "Is it true? Ye are taking a wife at long last?"

"Aye, Mother," Alex said in a strained voice, as he gently pushed her away. "What are the two of ye doing here?"

"We heard that the MacNeil claimed ye had run off with his daughter and was waiting for ye here," his father said. "And then our chieftain sent word today that ye were here with the lass."

Alex shot a glare at Connor.

"We couldn't miss our only son's wedding," his mother said, "so we came at once."

"Ye came together?" Alex asked. "On the same ship?"

"There wasn't much time," his mother said.

"I'm pleased ye can join us for the wedding feast," Alex said, though he did not sound pleased at all. "Mother, Father, this is my bride, Glynis, daughter of Gilleonan of Barra, chieftain of the MacNeils."

"I didn't think there was a lass in all the Highlands who could capture my son," his father said with another broad wink. "But ye proved me wrong."

"What a horrid thing to say to a new bride," his mother snapped. "I can only hope our son is a better husband than ye were."

Glynis was beginning to understand where Alex's aversion to marriage came from—and why he was so set on having a peaceful home.

"However ye did it, dear," his mother said, patting Glynis's arm, "I praise God, for I feared I would never see a grandchild of mine."

"Then ye will be glad to hear my other news." Alex drew Sorcha out from where she had been hiding behind him and rested his hands on her shoulders. "This is my daughter, Sorcha."

His mother shrieked and threw her hands up in the air. Before his father and mother could close in on the poor child, Alex lifted Sorcha in his arms. He spoke in French to her—without translating into Gaelic for once—then turned his attention back to his parents.

"Sorcha hasn't chosen to speak yet," he said in a firm tone. "She will in her own good time, so don't press her."

What a family. Glynis suddenly realized that she had never asked Alex where they would be living. By the saints, she hoped it was not with his parents.

*   *   *

Alex felt as if he were suffocating. His mother and father were in the same room, his bride was looking as if she'd rather be at the bottom of the sea, and his daughter was cowering against his chest with her hands covering her face.

His parents' arrival made him remember every reason he had never wanted to marry.

CHAPTER 36

After the food had been taken away and the old and young began leaving for their beds, Alex's friends gathered around to tell Glynis tales and jokes about the groom. They were all drinking and enjoying themselves considerably, as men did on such occasions. Her new husband, however, appeared to be enjoying his drink a good deal more than the jokes.

"'Tis a special day for me as well," Duncan said. "'Tis not often a man gets a present on his friend's wedding day."

"What present is that?" Alex asked.

"Why, that sweet galley we stole from Shaggy belongs to me now," Duncan said. "Don't ye recall our wager?"

"What wager?" Alex asked.

"I bet ye would have a wife within half a year," Duncan said. "And here ye are wed, when it's only been three months."

"Ach, no!" Alex said. "Ye wouldn't take her from me."

"I would," Duncan said with a slow smile.

"By the saints, I hate to lose that boat," Alex said. "Ye know how much I love her."

Glynis pressed her lips together. Must Alex announce to his entire clan that he favored a stolen boat over his new wife?

"I'd say ye got the better end of the wager," Duncan said, and turned to her. "Alex is a lucky man. I wish ye every happiness with the damned scoundrel."

Glynis pasted a smile on her face as the men laughed.

Then Duncan turned and collected coins from all the other men. It appeared that every one of them had wagered against Alex marrying.

"Ye look good for a dead man," a small, wiry man said, as he slapped Alex on the back.

"What are ye saying, Tait?" Alex asked.

"Didn't Alex tell us all he'd be dead before he'd be wed?" Tait shouted to the others.

Connor grabbed Tait by the back of his shirt as if he were a cat. "Ye know what a joker Alex is."

But Tait was undaunted. "If Alex said it once, he said it a hundred times: 'Better to tie an anchor to my leg and toss me into the sea than to tie me to a wife. Better to beat me with a...'"

The sound of Tait's voice faded as Connor marched him off.

Ian gave Glynis a smile that she was certain had stopped a few lasses' hearts. "We didn't have an opportunity to go off with the groom the night before the wedding, as is customary. Do ye mind if we take your husband for a wee bit before we give him to ye for good?"

"Or for bad!" one of the other men called out to another round of laughter.

* * *

Married. How had it happened?

Alex took another long pull from the jug of whiskey. From the time he was a wee lad, he'd vowed he'd never do it.

He had a *wife*. Despite the fact that he'd spent the last fortnight cajoling, charming, seducing, and almost begging Glynis to agree to marry him, it was hard to fathom.

"Be brave," Ian said, squeezing his shoulder.

"What if I can't do this?" Alex said, desperation rising in his throat.

"Is it the basic instruction ye need?" Duncan asked with a straight face. "What goes where and such?"

"I don't mean in bed—I *know* how to please a woman." Alex punched Duncan's arm, then turned to Ian. "It's all the rest of the time. What do I do with her?"

"Ye do the same as ye always do—the difference is that ye have someone to talk to about it." Ian grinned. "Whether ye want to talk about it or no."

Alex took another long drink while the others laughed.

"Glynis seems a good sort," Connor said. "I'm sure ye have nothing to worry about."

Worried? He glanced over at Glynis, with Sorcha asleep against her shoulder. He was petrified that he would fail them.

Oh, God, no. Alex closed his eyes as his father pushed Ian aside to sit next to him and put his arm around him. *Ge b'e thig gun chuireadh, suidhidh e gun iarraidh.* Who comes uninvited will sit down unbidden.

Ian, Connor, and Duncan had sensed he was sinking below the waves and had dragged him to a corner of the hall for a private talk. Alex did not want to speak with anyone else—particularly his father.

"Don't ever love a woman," his father said, staring at Alex's mother across the hall, "or she'll tear your heart out and feed it to the fish."

*   *   *

Sorcha yawned and leaned against Glynis's shoulder. Glynis kissed the top of her head, pleased to have the comfort of the child's presence. Across the hall, she saw Sìleas enter on light feet and come straight toward them.

"Sorcha can sleep with us and our two babes," Sìleas said, holding her hand out to Sorcha. "The twins are already upstairs with their nursemaid."

"Sorcha isn't used to strangers—," Glynis started to say before Sorcha bounded to her feet and took Sìleas's hand.

"It's your wedding night," Sileas said with a soft smile. "Sorcha will enjoy being with the twins."

Glynis felt bereft without her. Alex's mother came to sit beside her, which was unlikely to cheer her up. His mother must have been beautiful before lines of disappointment etched the skin around her eyes and mouth.

"Alex has a good heart," his mother said, patting Glynis's hand. "Unfortunately, he has bad blood from his father."

His mother was slurring her words. Were all the MacDonalds drunkards?

"To the one man who could tame my wild daughter!"

her father shouted across the room, as he lifted his cup high—proving that the MacDonalds had nothing on the MacNeils when it came to drink.

Glynis closed her eyes and wished she were anywhere but at her wedding.

Glynis could tell that the drunker the men became, the more colorful were their stories. Memories of her first wedding swirled through her head and weighed down on her chest. Magnus was not the sort of man to be sensitive about a lass's first time, and drunk he was worse.

Glynis stood, intent on slipping out of the hall and up the stairs to the bedchamber Ilysa had prepared for them—and barring the door when she got there.

But before she took two steps, one of the men shouted, "Alex, your bride is tired of waiting for ye. Time for the bedding!"

CHAPTER 37

Alex did not remember his wedding night.

God help him, he was a bastard. A useless man. A poor excuse for a husband. And his head hurt like the devil. *Oh, Jesus, take me now.* What had he been thinking?

His mouth was dry, he had sand in his eyes, and he was still drunk, but he had this blinding headache. And worst of all was the sinking feeling in his stomach that came from knowing he had fooked up badly. As awful as he felt, he rolled over toward his bride, intending to make up for his lack of attention with a bout of morning lovemaking.

He stretched his arm out and felt around. But his bride was not in the bed.

Alex crawled out of bed and poured the pitcher of water into the basin. He splashed water on his face, and when that did not do the job, he stuck his head in the basin and closed his eyes. God's bones, he felt ill. And it was going to get worse.

Alex spent the next hour searching the castle high and low for Glynis—while trying to avoid telling anyone that he had already lost his wife. He finally found her in one of the boats pulled up on the shore. She was sitting as straight as an arrow with her arms crossed over her chest, a grim look on her face, and her eyes fixed on the sea.

Glynis did not turn to look at him as he climbed into the boat.

"What are ye doing here?" he asked after a while.

"I'm waiting to leave," she said. "I want to put our wedding night behind me as soon as possible."

He had slept through his wedding night. God help him, because the bedding was the only part about being a husband that Alex had been certain he could do well.

Glynis just sat there with her arms folded and her mouth clamped shut again. At least she didn't shout and throw things like his mother. He considered pointing out to her that their *true* wedding night had been after they had made their vows alone to each other—and he'd acquitted himself quite well. But he thought better of it.

Just when he thought she might never speak again, Glynis said, "Ye never told me where we will live."

"Well, that is something I wanted to discuss with ye."

"Don't pretend I have a choice, and ye haven't already decided," she said with her gaze still fixed on the horizon.

He drew in a deep breath and reminded himself that she was used to having her opinions ignored. Perhaps this gave him an opportunity to make up lost ground.

"My father's lands will be mine one day, so there is good reason for us to live there." Alex thought her back went stiffer, though he didn't see how that was possible. "But Connor needs a man to go to North Uist, where our clansmen have been living at the mercy of his pirating uncles."

Alex wanted to go there. Fighting the pirates appealed to him, of course, and living with either of his parents was his own vision of hell. But even more than that, he wanted to take on the responsibility of securing North Uist for his clan.

"Before I left, I told Connor that when I returned I would go live on North Uist and bring order to the island," he said. "But that was before I had a wife and daughter to consider. 'Tis far more dangerous there than on my father's lands, so I'm inclined to ask Connor to send Duncan instead."

Glynis slanted her eyes at him. "I'm no frail lass, like the sort ye knew at court or in France."

"I didn't say ye were, but ye are my responsibility now."

"North Uist is a short sail from Barra, so I doubt it's any more dangerous," she said. "And if ye needed help fighting, my father would send men."

If he had to have a wife, praise God she was a fearless lass. Still, he wanted to be honest with her about what awaited them there.

"Our clan has an old castle there, Dunfaileag, that should provide sufficient protection once it is repaired," he said. "But it will take a good deal of work before it is either comfortable or secure."

"I like to be busy," she said. "And have ye forgotten I traveled to Edinburgh and back sleeping outdoors on the hard ground?"

"Nay, I haven't forgotten a single night." He met her eyes and gave her a smile that made her blush. He was glad for the opportunity to remind her that he knew how to please her under the blankets when he wasn't dead drunk.

"I could see my family more often," she said. "Please, Alex, I want to go."

Praise God.

"My parents are expecting us, so we'll have to pay them a visit on the way," he said. "But then we'll sail for North Uist."

Glynis finally gave him a smile. They'd had a civil conversation and come to an agreement on an important matter without a fuss or fight. It bode well for the future.

Alex didn't want to mention her former husband, but North Uist had one other advantage over Skye—it was further away from the Clanranald chieftain's base at Castle Tioram.

"We took this boat from Hugh Dubh when we removed him from Dunscaith Castle," Alex said, patting the rail. "How did ye know this was the one Connor wanted me to take?"

"Ilysa told me."

Of course. Alex looked down the length of the boat. It was a full-size war galley, so Connor also had to give up the eighteen men it took to row it.

"I'll need a war galley on North Uist," Alex said, reconciling himself to it. He leaned his elbows on the rail to admire Shaggy's boat, which was looking so pretty sitting out on the water. "Shame about losing that sweet little galley."

"If I hear another word about that galley, which didn't belong to ye in the first place," Glynis said, "I swear I'll set fire to it."

And Alex had prided himself that he understood women. He had no idea why mention of Shaggy's boat should upset her. Fortunately, he saw Ilysa making her way down to the shore with Sorcha and Bessie. Deciding it was best to let Glynis calm down, Alex went to meet them.

"I didn't have a chance to tell ye before," Ilysa said, when he reached them. "Teàrlag gave me a message for ye."

"Wait in the boat for me, Sorcha." Judging from past experience, Teàrlag's message would not be something he wanted his daughter to hear. After Sorcha skipped off with Bessie, he said, "Teàrlag couldn't wait to admonish me in person?"

"No admonishments this time," Ilysa said, smiling. "She sends blessings on your marriage."

"So that's how ye knew to have enough food and drink on hand for a feast," Alex said. "Thank ye for that."

Connor had no notion of all that Ilysa did. Though she was young, Connor would never find a wife who could keep the castle half so well. *Cha bhi fios aire math an to-bair gus an tràigh e.* The value of the well is not known until it goes dry.

"Teàrlag did say to remind ye that she was correct about the three women," Ilysa said, "and about the gift being special and bright as a moonbeam."

Alex glanced over his shoulder at his wee daughter, whose hair was the color of moonbeams and whose name meant "radiant." "Aye, she is a special gift."

"And the three women?" Ilysa asked.

"Three did require my help, though I can't say any of them gave me a choice about giving it," he said. "Glynis threatened me, Sorcha's mother sailed off without her, and I couldn't very well let the other one drown."

Ilysa laughed. "I suppose not."

"As Teàrlag predicted, one brought deceit and another danger," he said, and his heart missed a beat as he thought of how he could have lost Sorcha. Attempting to regain his light tone, he said, "And I'm hoping my new bride will fulfill a few of my deepest desires tonight."

Ilysa gave him a soft smile and touched his arm. "Open your heart to Glynis."

"And why should I take advice from Duncan's baby sister?" Alex asked.

"Because, while some say ye got a better woman than ye deserve," Ilysa said, "I believe ye can be as good a man as ye want to be, Alexander Bàn MacDonald."

* * *

Sorcha leaned against her father and waved good-bye to Dunscaith Castle as they sailed away. She missed the little red-haired girls already. Though they made lots of funny sounds, they had only one word between them. Sorcha didn't mind that they screamed it over and over— *Da! Da!*—because it made them so happy.

But she was disappointed she did not get to see the warrior queen her father told her about.

Unless her new mother was the warrior queen. Glynis dressed like the other women, but Sorcha could imagine her fighting with a great sword.

She felt safe with Glynis.

CHAPTER 38

Glynis intended to stay angry with Alex for a very long time.

Of course, having her husband sleep through their wedding night was a vast improvement over her first wedding night. Ach, Magnus was a disgusting, selfish pig both in and out of bed.

Glynis felt herself softening toward Alex as she watched him at the rudder, with Sorcha on his lap, pointing out landmarks on the shore and the small islands they passed. Alex had such an easy, generous nature. As her curiosity overcame her stubbornness, she inched her way along the rail until she was close enough to hear what Alex was saying.

"That is where your grandmother lives," Alex said, pointing to a two-story house on an offshore island to their right. Then he pointed to an older, larger fortified house a short distance up the coast on their left. "And that is your grandfather's, which is where we'll be staying."

Sorcha tugged at his arm and held up two fingers.

"Why do they have two houses?" Alex paused for a long moment before he answered. "They needed room for all their friends."

Glynis should have taken that as a warning.

Alex's mother and father had an earlier start from Dunscaith and were both waiting in the hall for them. As the serving women came in and out with drinks and platters of food, they gave Alex overly friendly greetings. Not one of them was old or unattractive.

This household was altogether too much like Clanranald's. It made Glynis physically ill to be here. Although Alex's jokes and laughing remarks were not as blatant as Magnus's pinches and squeezes, his relationship with several of the women was clear, nonetheless.

Glynis was rapidly losing her appreciation for her new husband's generous nature.

"Hello, Anna," Alex called out to a buxom redhead, who winked at him. "You're looking well, Brigid," he said to the dark-haired beauty who made a point of brushing up against his shoulder when she brought him a cup of ale.

Sweat broke out on Glynis's palms as she fought another wave of nausea. She fixed her gaze on the far wall and held on to the table as she got to her feet.

"I'd like to get settled in my chamber, if someone will show me where it is."

* * *

"Here we are," Alex said, as he opened the door for Glynis and Sorcha.

It felt strange to be in his old bedchamber, and stranger still to be settling his new family in it. From the time he was old enough to sail on his own, he had spent as little time here as possible. He was always off having adventures—or getting into trouble, depending on your point of view—with Connor, Ian, and Duncan. He'd made himself a regular guest at both Dunscaith and Ian's house.

Sorcha went to the window to look out, and Glynis looked everywhere but at him. Alex glanced at the small bed. His feet would hang off the end, but Glynis could not avoid him in a bed that size. He was desperate to have some time alone with her—both in and out of bed. He would ask his mother to take Sorcha to sleep with her.

He was pleased then when his mother appeared in the doorway.

"Do ye have what ye need?" she asked.

Though his mother had moved out years ago, she always assumed the role of hostess the moment she stepped foot into his father's house. Before Alex could ask her about changing the sleeping arrangements, his mother forged ahead with what she had come to tell them.

"Our clansmen on this side of Skye didn't get word in time to come to the wedding feast at Dunscaith." She clasped her hands together and beamed at them. "So I've invited them all here tonight for another wedding feast!"

Alex was furious with his mother. The last thing he needed tonight was a second wedding feast.

"That was kind of ye," Glynis said, but she had gone pale as death. "I'm a wee bit tired from all the...excitement...of last night. So if ye don't mind taking Sorcha, I'd like to take a rest."

"I could use a lie down myself," Alex said, feeling hopeful.

"I'm sure ye can find a bed somewhere," Glynis said, giving him a look that would sour milk.

"What in the hell have ye done, Mother?" Alex demanded, as they went down the stairs. "Ye should have asked me before inviting everyone."

"I wanted to make your wife and daughter feel welcome," his mother said, smiling down at Sorcha.

Alex was not appeased by his mother's professed good intensions. Both his parents always did precisely as they wanted with no thought to anyone else. The deed was done, however, so tonight would be spent entertaining every man, woman, and child within a half day's journey of his father's house.

A short while later, he was sitting in the hall contemplating his grim future with a cup of ale when his parents' voices pierced his thoughts. When he turned, he saw his daughter squeezing the life out of her old doll as she looked back and forth between his parents.

"I don't care what ye say," his mother said, leaning forward with her hands on her hips. "I'm taking Sorcha home with me tonight."

"Ye will no take my granddaughter out of this house," his father shouted.

His parents were far too engrossed in their argument to notice Sorcha was watching them with eyes as big as platters. Alex stormed over and picked up his daughter. When she leaned against him with her thumb in her mouth, he brushed her hair back and kissed her forehead.

"I won't have this," he said to his parents, who had paused long enough to look at him. "The two of ye will get along in my daughter's presence, or ye will not see her."

His parents spoke over each other. "But she is my only grandchild!" "You've no right!"

"I do have the right," Alex said, fixing his gaze on each of his parents in turn. "And I will no allow ye to fight over her the way ye did with me."

Alex had never voiced his feelings about their fighting before, and they were both—for once—too shocked to speak. He supposed that was often the way of it with families. The obvious truths were never spoken aloud, as if that somehow made them less true.

"I won't tell ye again," he said. "If ye can't be civil to each other in front of my daughter, we'll leave and we won't come back."

*   *   *

Things were going from bad to worse. Ach, why did Mary have to come to the feast?

Alex felt lower than dirt as he greeted her husband. Now that he was a husband himself, he saw the whole situation quite differently. Mary's husband was a sniveling ass, but that did not excuse Alex taking his wife to bed. Alex would kill any man who did the same to him. The mere thought of another man's hands on Glynis sent murder roiling through his veins.

Through seven courses, Mary tried to catch Alex's eye. Alex steadfastly ignored her and tried his best to converse with Glynis.

"I'm sorry for all the guests tonight," he said, leaning close to Glynis's ear.

"Why would ye be sorry?" she said, her back as stiff as a board. "Is it me or your daughter that ye are ashamed to have them meet?"

Alex clenched his jaw to keep from shouting at her.

"Ye know damned well I'm no ashamed of either of ye," he said, when he could manage to speak in a low voice. "Can ye no meet me halfway and attempt to be pleasant?"

"If ye wanted a pleasant wife, ye should have picked someone else," she said in a fierce whisper. "I warned ye from the start about my sour disposition."

With that, Glynis turned her back on him to talk to his mother, who sat on her other side. Ach! His head was already pounding when Mary got up and gave him a broad wink over her shoulder as she left the hall. Damn it, at least he could put a stop to that.

He waited in the vestibule for Mary to come back from the privy. When she came in and saw him, she broke into a wide smile.

"Alex—"

"Quiet!" He grabbed Mary by the wrist and hauled her outside into the dark courtyard. As soon as he had her around the corner of the house where they couldn't be seen from the door, he jerked her around to face him.

"So ye did miss me," she said and started to run her palm up his chest.

"What in the hell are ye doing, Mary?" he said, pushing her hand away. "I brought ye out here to tell ye to stop this foolishness before my wife notices."

"Frankly, your bride doesn't look as if she'd care one way or the other."

"She would," Alex said, though he was beginning to

doubt it himself. "She just isn't as obvious in her attentions as some."

Mary gave a light laugh. "Indeed."

"I want ye to go home now and don't come back," he said, keeping his voice low.

"Where do ye want to meet, then?" she asked.

"Keep your voice down," he hissed. "Ye are no understanding me. I'm a married man now, and I've no intention of starting another affair with ye—or anyone else."

"Ye know what they say about good intentions," Mary said with a smile in her voice.

"I mean it, Mary," Alex said. "I don't want to make trouble for ye, but I will if I have to."

"I was made for trouble." She laughed and leaned against him.

"I'm warning ye," he said, pushing her away from him by her shoulders. "Take your husband and go home."

Alex left her standing alone in the dark and stomped up the steps of the house. God in Heaven, what had he seen in such a woman?

* * *

Glynis was certain everyone in the hall was laughing at her behind their hands. All evening, that woman named Mary had been glancing and winking at Alex. Mary's husband must be half blind, but there was nothing wrong with Glynis's eyesight. When Alex and Mary both disappeared, Glynis should have had too much pride to follow them—but she simply could not stay in her seat. She had to know for certain that Alex had truly gone to meet a lover on the second night of their marriage.

When she stepped out into the vestibule and saw neither of them, her chest felt too tight. Though Glynis had feared Alex had left with the woman, she had wanted to be proven wrong. Still, she told herself she must not judge him without actually seeing him with the wretched woman. There were only two places one could go from the vestibule—outside or up the stairs to the bedchambers.

Glynis could not face finding them in a bedchamber, so she slipped out the front door, taking care to not make a sound. As she eased the door closed behind her, she heard a murmur of voices. She followed the sound down the steps to the corner of the house.

Her heart sank as she recognized the low rumble of Alex's voice. Though he was speaking too low for her to make out his words, Glynis had no trouble hearing the woman.

"Where do ye want to meet, then?" Mary asked.

Nay, this could not be happening. Glynis squeezed her eyes shut and took openmouthed breaths, trying to gain control. Somehow, she had to go back inside without looking as if she'd had her guts sliced open and ripped from her body like a caught fish.

"I was made for trouble" was the last thing Glynis heard. The words rang in her ears as she stumbled blindly to the door.

Now she knew what Alex's "usual sort" of woman was like—she was the kind who was soft and easy and incited a man's lust.

A woman made for trouble.

CHAPTER 39

Alex returned to the hall to find his wife's seat empty.

"Where is Glynis?" he asked his mother.

"She said Sorcha looked tired and took her upstairs," his mother said. "I told her I'd be happy to take Sorcha home with me, but Glynis wouldn't hear of it."

Damn. Damn. Damn.

"Ye can't leave as well when we have all these guests," his mother whispered.

"Ye invited them, Mother, so ye can entertain them."

Alex left without a backward glance and took the stairs two at a time. He expected to find Glynis tucking Sorcha into bed or telling her a story, but the room was black.

"Glynis, I know ye can't be sleeping yet," Alex said.

Glynis's voice came out of the darkness. "Shhh. You'll wake Sorcha."

"Then come out and talk to me."

"I have nothing to say to ye," Glynis said. "Sorcha is

in the bed with me, so ye can make yourself comfortable on the floor."

"I apologize for last night," he said in a low voice. "I wanted to make it up to ye tonight."

"To me and who else?"

"I don't deserve that," he said. "I haven't even had time to do anything I shouldn't, even if I were inclined—which I'm not."

"I don't believe ye," Glynis said. "And I don't want to talk about it tonight."

He tried to make Glynis see sense, but it was like bailing the sea with a creel. Eventually, he tired of talking to himself in the darkness, so he lay down on the cold floor and wrapped his plaid around himself. He was tempted to tell her there were other beds in this house that he wouldn't be turned out of. But he thought of his parents' vicious fights and bit his tongue.

Clearly, he wouldn't be getting his deepest desires fulfilled tonight.

After tossing and turning on the hard floor all night, he awoke abruptly to a room filled with sunlight and sat up. The bed beside him was empty.

So, for the second morning of his marriage, Alex went looking for his wife. As he was crossing the hall, his mother poked her head out from behind the screen.

"Get your father," she said. "I must speak with the two of ye alone."

Being trapped alone with his mother and father was the last thing he needed right now. "Later, Mother. Have ye seen Glynis?"

"It's about her that we need to speak," she said. "This is important, Alex, so get your father. Now."

His father was in his bedchamber—alone, for once. A short time later, the three of them were sitting at the small table that was behind the screen in the hall. Alex would rather be boiled in oil than sit with the two of them in a small space, but here he was.

His father leaned back in his chair and crossed his arms on his chest. In the surly tone he reserved for Alex's mother, he said, "What is it, Mòrag?"

His mother opened her mouth to shout at him, but with an effort she stopped herself.

"Fergus, ye must remove every woman from this house who our son has bedded at one time or another." His mother made this astonishing statement in a calm and reasonable voice, as if she were saying they were out of salt or needed another barrel of wine.

Alex and his father exchanged glances, but they were both too startled to say a word.

"Are ye men such fools that ye can't see what is happening?" she asked.

"I've no idea what ye are talking about, Mother."

"It comes as no surprise that your father is wholly lacking in consideration for a new bride," his mother said. "But, Alex, can ye no see how it hurts Glynis to have these women about?"

"What is it ye think I've done?" Alex felt self-righteous, which was a rather new sensation for him. "I've not touched a woman since I was wed." Hell, he had not even touched his wife.

"I am relieved to hear that," his mother said, pressing her hand to her chest. "Then it isn't too late to mend things with Glynis and convince her to stay with ye."

Alex felt as if the ground were shifting under him. He

knew Glynis was upset, but was she planning to leave him already?

"What are ye saying, Mòrag?" his father asked.

"That the two of ye are mistaken if ye don't think these women have found ways to let Glynis know they've been in Alex's bed before—and expect to be again," she said, and Alex had the impression she was talking about herself as a young wife as much as she was about Glynis. "Ye don't help matters, Alex, by being an even worse flirt than your father."

"I joke with them," he said, lifting his hands. "It means nothing."

"And just how is Glynis supposed to know that?" his mother asked.

"I gave her my promise."

"Just as every philandering husband in the Highlands has done before ye," she said, "including her first husband and your father."

"I will no change my household to suit ye, M—"

"Ye will do it, da," Alex said, cutting his father off. Then he left them to find his wife.

*　*　*

Alex found Glynis walking alone on the beach. She was barefoot, his island lass. Seeing her like this, he felt a deep longing for her that had nothing to do with salvaging his pride or needing a mother for his daughter. Alex wanted this woman at his side, and to have her look up at him with a smile in her eyes.

When Glynis saw him, she stood still and waited for him, with the wind blowing her hair and skirts.

She looked so pretty, but her eyes were sad.

"Sit with me?" he asked.

She gave him a tight nod and let him take her hand. He led her up the beach to sit in the tall grass where it was dry. Still holding her hand, he told her about his conversation with his mother and father.

"I'm going to try to explain this to ye and be truthful," he said, rubbing his thumb over the back of her hand, "though ye won't like part of what I have to tell ye."

"I want the truth," she said.

"All right," he said. "From the time I was a young lad, my father told me that men like us needed women like we need the sea—and that one woman would never do for us. So there were always women about my father's house. Willing women, if ye catch my meaning."

He glanced at Glynis. She was staring out to sea, but she was listening.

"That was just how it was," he said. "I thought nothing I did before we wed should matter. But I didn't realize how it might seem to ye, being here."

Glynis was thoughtful for a long moment. Finally, she turned to him and said, "Would ye want to share a house with men I had bedded?"

"I had the impression there was only one man before me." And if Alex had his way, that man would be weighed down with chains at the bottom of the sea. Speaking very carefully, he asked, "Have there been many?"

This, of all things, brought a smile to her face. She touched his arm, and it amazed him how the slight gesture could soften him. She had him in the palm of her hand. God help him if she ever knew it.

"There was only the one," she said. "And he was worthless."

Alex had the sense not to tell Glynis how much this pleased him, but he lifted her hand and pressed it to his lips. "We'll leave for North Uist tomorrow, and we'll make ourselves a different kind of home there."

"For certain," Glynis said, and gave a short laugh.

"I told my father he must change his household if he wants us to ever come here again."

"He'll do that?" she asked.

"I suspect my mother will do it for him." Alex could almost hear her: *I'll stay just until Fergus's whores can be replaced with decent clanswomen—preferably toothless, elderly ones.* "She's been wanting to do it for years."

"I don't want the women to be turned out with nowhere to go," Glynis said.

Alex cupped her cheek with his hand. She was such a good woman—as Ilysa said, better than he deserved.

"I'll ask my mother to send them home to their families or find husbands for them." If Alex had to figure out how to deal with a wife, every man should.

"What about that woman, Mary?" Glynis asked in a quiet voice.

"I did bed her a few times, but I ended it before I went to the gathering at Shaggy Maclean's," he said. "I'm no proud of what I did, for she was married at the time, but I broke no vow."

"I heard ye with her outside," Glynis said, her voice still very low.

"I was asking her to leave." He took her hand and kissed it again. "Glynis, ye are the only one I want. Are ye determined to make me suffer longer, or will ye come to bed with me now?"

Glynis looked at him with her clear gray eyes. "I will."

Finally, he was taking his wife to bed—a place where he knew his ground.

CHAPTER 40

What are ye doing?" Glynis cried when Alex lifted her off her feet and started carrying her up to the house.

"I'm letting everyone know that I'm dying to ravish my wife," Alex said, grinning at her.

Glynis felt embarrassed and pleased at the same time by his intention to proclaim to the entire household that she was the one he'd chosen, the woman he wanted. The guests who had stayed overnight cheered as Alex carried her around the hall—overjoyed, no doubt, that they would have a fine story to tell. As Alex carried her toward the stairs amid the shouts, Glynis caught a glimpse of Sorcha sitting between his parents. All three were clapping, and Alex's parents both looked happy for once.

"Ye can put me down now," she said when they reached the bedchamber door.

"Hell no," he said. "I'm no risking the bad luck that lurks in doorways a third time."

She rolled her eyes, but she couldn't help laughing

when he kicked the door open and carried her through. As soon as he set her on her feet, he swung the door shut and pressed her against it. The laughter died in her throat when she saw the longing in his eyes.

"Ach, I've been wanting ye so much," he said, holding her face in his hands.

Her eyes closed as his mouth met hers. For a long, long time, he just kissed her, not as a step to something else, but as if he wanted to do it forever. His fingers slid into her hair and supported her head as their tongues moved against each other in deep kisses.

Glynis felt adrift and breathless as he kissed her cheeks, her eyelids, her hair.

"*Cronaím thú,*" he said. I missed you.

His hands slid down her shoulders and arms. As they fell into deep kisses again, he held her in a firm grasp with his hands splayed over her ribs and back. Her breasts ached for his touch. Desire swept through her. She reached between them and rubbed her hand over the length of his erect shaft, drawing a deep groan from him and a sigh of her own.

"*O shluagh,*" he said, calling on the fairies for mercy.

Alex's mouth grew hungry, feverish, devouring hers as he ground his hips against her, pinning her to the wall. His fingers dug into her hips, and still they could not get close enough. When he lifted her up, she wrapped her legs around his waist. He ran his hands under her gown along the bare skin of her thighs until he cupped her bottom.

Through their clothes she felt his erection against the sensitive spot between her legs. She clung to him, urging him closer, but there was too much fabric between them.

It had been days and days since he'd been inside her. She wanted to meld into his heat, to go to the dark depths of passion with him. She rocked against him, begging. *Please, please, please.*

Tension radiated between them as he tugged at her bottom lip with his teeth in barely controlled violence. But she wanted to feel the full force of his desire for her, unleashed, unshackled, freed of all restraint and caution.

He had one hand on her breast, massaging and kneading, as he held her buttocks with the other. His tongue and breath were hot in her ear. "You've too many clothes on. I must feel ye."

She heard the ping of buttons as he pulled her bodice down.

"Aye," she breathed when his rough palm cupped her bare breast. Her head fell back against the door. She was lost in a haze of desire as he squeezed her nipple and dragged his tongue and lips along the side of her throat.

"I need ye now," he said, panting against her ear. "Oh, please, Glynis, right now."

Aye. Now. She tugged at his shirt, but they were pressed too tightly together. His mouth covered hers again as he moved his hips away just long enough to jerk his shirt up.

"Oh!" She felt the tip of his shaft against her. When he paused, squeezing his eyes shut, she dug her fingers into his shoulders. "Now, Alex. *Now.*"

He made a strangled sound, and in one deep stroke, he was inside her. She wrapped her legs tighter around his hips. She bit his shoulder as Alex's control broke, and he rammed against her, again and again. Her back banged against the door, and she didn't care.

"Harder, harder," she cried, as their bodies slammed together. She heard herself scream as he surged against her, and a shattering rapture shook her.

Alex collapsed against her, his body hot, his breathing harsh against her ear. She shivered as he ran his hands along her thigh and over her hip.

"Hold on to me," he said, and then he carried her to the bed. With one hand, he pulled the bedclothes back and then fell sideways with her across the bed.

"By the saints, ye nearly killed me," he said. "But it was like touching Heaven."

He enfolded her in his arms and slung his leg over her as well. She fell sound asleep surrounded in his warmth.

Glynis didn't know how long she had been sleeping when she was awakened by a breeze tickling her face. She opened her eyes to find Alex blowing on her.

"Why are ye doing that?" she asked with a slow smile.

"I woke up and wanted your company," he said. "Do ye mind?"

"Nay."

"Ye see, I've been lying here thinking of ways to make up for being useless the night of our wedding." He had a devilish glint in his eyes that made the room suddenly seem warm. "I probably know a few things we haven't tried yet."

It would be easy to let him distract her, but Glynis had a serious question.

"Why did ye get so drunk that night?" she asked.

"I hadn't seen Connor, Duncan, and Ian in a long while and—"

"I think it was something else," she said.

Alex looked away and did not speak for a while. Finally, he said, "Ye know I had never wanted to marry—you've met my parents, so now ye know why."

Her stomach tightened, but she had asked the question so she should have been ready to hear the answer.

"When they arrived at Dunscaith, it brought all that back to me—the bickering and fighting, the endless misery between them." He turned his gaze back to her and touched her cheek with the back of his fingers. "It worried me for a bit, but it didn't last."

"I'm glad ye told me the truth," she said. "I want ye to promise ye will never lie to me."

"I won't lie to ye," Alex said. "And now I'll tell ye what I want."

"What's that?" she asked.

"I am happy to fight my clan's enemies—in truth, I enjoy it—but I don't want to fight with you."

"We might argue once in a while," she said.

He shrugged. "I want things peaceful between us."

Glynis suddenly felt uncomfortable with her gown bunched around her. She sat up on the edge of the bed and tried to untwist it. "I hope I can find a needle and thread so I can fix my gown myself. If I have to ask one of the servants to do it, they'll be talking about us for weeks."

"Let's take your gown off all the way," he said, trailing his finger over her bare shoulder. One light touch, and she was like soft butter. What this man did to her.

He sat up and unfastened the rest of the buttons down her back and then pressed soft, warm kisses down to the base of her spine. Then he pushed her gown down farther and nipped at her bottom, sending little thrills of sensation that echoed in a tightening of her womb.

"Stand up so we can get this off ye," he said.

When she rose up, he helped her step out of her gown. Then with sure hands on her hips, he pulled her back to sit between his legs. He moved her hair to one side and kissed her neck while one hand fondled her breast and the other inched up the inside of her thigh.

"When ye said ye wanted company," she said, "I thought ye meant ye wanted someone to talk to."

"I do," he said. "I want ye to tell me all the ways ye want me to touch ye."

"This is good," she managed to say, as he started stroking and circling between her legs. She let her head drop back against his shoulder.

"Ye are beautiful like this," he said in a hoarse whisper, as his fingers worked their magic. "I want to hear ye keen and moan when ye find your release."

She gripped his leg as the sensations grew stronger. His shaft was hard against her buttocks, but he seemed intent on her pleasure. When her breathing changed, he sucked on her shoulder and stuck his finger inside her. All the while, he was rolling her nipple between his thumb and finger. She arched her back as the tension grew inside her until she feared she might snap in two.

But this was Alex in control, the skilled lover who knew how to please a woman, any woman.

"Stop," she said, pulling his hand away.

"What's wrong?" he asked.

She turned and pushed him back on the bed.

"I want to feel ye inside me, with nothing between us," she said, as she leaned over him. "I want to touch ye in a way no other woman has. I want to touch your heart."

"Glynis, I can't—"

"I'm no saying ye have to love me right away," she

said. "But I can't do things halfway, Alex. I'm not that sort of person."

"Ah, Glynis, don't."

"I love ye, Alexander Bàn MacDonald," she said. "I won't say it again because I know it makes ye uncomfortable to hear it. But ye need to know that ye hold my heart in your hands."

She straddled him and slid slowly down onto his shaft.

"Jesus, Glynis," he said.

"It means ye can hurt me badly," she said. "And if ye do, I won't be able to forgive ye. Not ever."

"I won't hurt ye," he said as if it were a plea, as they began to move together slowly. "I won't."

CHAPTER 41

Alex stood on the wall of Dunfaileag Castle with Tormond, the crusty old warrior who had become his right-hand man in overseeing the rebuilding of the castle's defenses.

"We'll be done patching this last hole in the wall today," Tormond said, as they examined the work.

"'Tis a shame this old castle wasn't built on an off-shore island," Alex said, not for the first time. Unlike many castles in the Western Isles, including Dunscaith and the MacNeil stronghold, Dunfaileag sat on a rocky hill above the shore, where it was accessible by land. "We'd have trouble withstanding a large attack by another clan."

"Not much risk of that here, is there?" Tormond said. "Now that it's patched up, Dunfaileag will do fine against raiders."

The pirates relied on stealth and speed, usually attacking with a small group of men. When Alex first arrived, he had regular skirmishes with raiders. They ventured onto his side of the island less and less now. But he hadn't seen Hugh's ship at all, and he wondered why.

Alex smiled when he turned and saw his wife and daughter on the beach below the castle. It reminded him of the first time he'd seen Glynis without her disguise on the beach at Barra. He chuckled to himself, remembering the blotches of red clay sliding down her face. What a determined woman his wife was.

These days, Glynis focused that determination on turning Dunfaileag Castle into a home that ran smoothly and was a comfort to all who lived and worked within its walls. She thrived on being in charge of a large household.

The weeks had flown by. Alex didn't even know how it had come to pass that he could no longer imagine his life without her. She had come upon him slowly, insinuating herself like a warm summer mist permeating his skin, his senses, and his very soul until he needed her like air to breathe.

"Take over for me here," Alex said to Tormond. "I'm going to have a wee visit with my wife and daughter."

Tormond nodded. "Ye are a lucky man to have those two."

But luck was a fragile thing that could turn on you in a moment. Alex knew that a sinner like him did not deserve his good fortune, but he was praying that mending his ways counted for something.

He went down the steps and then followed the trail to the beach. When Sorcha saw him, she ran to him holding out an oyster shell.

"I see ye found a magical shell." Alex held it up, examining it carefully. "This one came all the way from Ireland on the back of a dolphin."

Sorcha laughed and snatched it back. Her laughter came more and more frequently now, and sometimes she seemed within a breath of speaking. Before long, he would hear his daughter's voice, he felt certain.

When Sorcha went off in search of more treasures, Glynis took his arm, and they walked along the shore. Ah, life was very good.

"Have ye noticed how Peiter, the young fisherman who brings fish up to the castle sometimes, stops what he's doing every time Seamus's sister walks by?"

Seamus was the ten-year-old lad who followed Alex around like a young pup. At Glynis's suggestion, Alex had finally given the lad the job of cleaning his weapons.

"Seamus's sister?" he asked.

"Aye, she's that pretty lass with the golden hair," Glynis said. "Her name is Ùna."

"Hmm." Though Glynis had come to trust him, Alex took care not to say or do anything that might change that. For the same reason, he didn't find it necessary to tell Glynis that all his men stopped working to watch that particular lass when she came to the castle.

"Peiter wants to wed her," she said, looking up at him with a soft look in her eyes.

"And how would ye know this?"

"I asked him, of course."

Alex chuckled, wondering how she had wrung this confession out of the young man. Unfortunately, his wife appeared to see Peiter's lovelorn state as a problem that needed fixing.

"Would ye consider speaking to her father on his behalf?"

Alex groaned. "You've only to ask, and I'll fight a hundred men for ye. But matchmaking ... ach."

"Ye act in your chieftain's place here on North Uist," Glynis said in her most reasonable tone. "And one of a chieftain's duties is to approve marriages—and even encourage them at times."

"Connor failed to mention this duty to me." Alex didn't bother pointing out that she had not appreciated it when her own father exercised that particular chieftain responsibility.

Glynis leaned against him and smiled up at him. "I want them to be happy like us."

"I'll talk to Pieter first. And if he says he wants me to, I'll speak to the father." Alex sighed and kissed her nose. "Now we both know there is nothing ye can't get me to do."

*　*　*

Alex kept his eye on Peiter the next time Seamus's sister came up to the castle. The poor fool stood with his mouth open and didn't hear Alex until he'd said his name twice.

"Ùna is a pretty lass," Alex said to him.

"Aye," Pieter said on a sigh, as he followed her across the castle yard with his eyes.

"Have ye tried speaking to her?" Alex asked.

"We were good friends as children," Pieter said. "But she won't even look at me now."

Alex watched how the young woman kept her gaze fixed on the ground and didn't greet any of the men, though she must have known most of them all her life. But as shy as she was, she came to the castle often. Seamus was old to have his sister fetch him, but the lad was always glad to see her. Despite their age difference, the two seemed unusually close.

"Is it marriage ye have in mind, then?" Alex asked Peiter.

"All I want in this life is to marry Ùna," Peiter said, his gaze fixed on the lass's back as she went out the castle gate with her brother. "I've asked her father, but he refuses to consider me, though I could provide for her better than he does."

Alex had met Ùna and Seamus's father and disliked him on sight. He was not surprised to hear that the man was not a good provider, for although he was a powerfully built man, he had a reputation for being both lazy and overly fond of his whiskey jug.

"Has her father made an arrangement with another man to wed her?" Alex asked.

"Nay, he's just a selfish bastard," Pieter said. "He told me he needs Ùna to keep house for him because his wife is dead."

Alex made himself drag the words out, "Would ye like me to speak to him?"

"I would be forever grateful," Pieter said, turning pleading eyes on him. "Ùna is the only lass who will ever do for me."

Ach, the young man was in a bad way.

* * *

"I saw Seamus and Ùna's father with some other fishermen on the shore today and went down to have that talk with him," Alex reported to Glynis a few nights later while they were lying in bed. "It did not go well."

"Ye have the chieftain's authority so ye could order the match," Glynis said. "But I suppose that wouldn't be wise, at least not yet."

Alex was glad Glynis understood that forcing a lass's marriage against her father's wishes would cause a good deal of grumbling among the men.

"I'll see to the marriage in time, provided Ùna wants it as well, but my first duty is to protect the MacDonalds on North Uist," Alex said. "To lead my clansmen here, I must gain their trust."

"I'd follow ye anywhere," Glynis said, and kissed his cheek. "Most of the men already know ye are a good man and a strong leader, and the rest will soon."

Alex's chest swelled at her compliment as if he were a young lad instead of a seasoned warrior. So long as Glynis had faith in him, he could do anything.

*   *   *

A week later, Alex was practicing in the bailey yard with the other men when he noticed Seamus had a black eye. The lad was keeping his head turned, as if he did not want anyone to see it.

"That's enough for today," Alex called out to the men. "Good work."

Alex strolled over to where Seamus was leaning against the castle wall.

"Ye get into a fight?" Alex asked.

Most lads are proud to have something to show for a fight, but Seamus's head sunk even lower into his shoulders.

"Come now, what happened to your eye?" When Seamus pressed his lips together and shook his head, Alex put his hand on the lad's shoulder. "I'll do what I can to help, whatever it is."

Seamus ventured a sideways glance at Alex. "In private," he whispered. "No one can know. Ye must promise me."

"Ye have my word," Alex said. "Here, take my shield, and we'll go into the armory."

Once they were alone in the armory, Alex sat beside the boy on a low wooden bench. He pretended to study the axes and other weapons hanging on the stone wall in front of him while he waited for Seamus to speak.

"'Tis about my sister," Seamus choked out.

Ach, family troubles, the worst kind. "What about Ùna?"

"My da...my da..." Seamus couldn't get the words out, and various thoughts whirled in Alex's head, none of them pleasant.

"Has your father hurt her?" he asked.

Seamus nodded without looking up.

Alex forced himself to keep his voice calm. "I suppose ye got that black eye trying to protect her?"

When the lad nodded again, Alex clenched his teeth against the blinding rage that roared through him. Seamus's father was a foot taller and twice the lad's weight. Alex wanted to murder the man.

"I know what it's like to be angry with your father," Alex said, though his own father only laid a hand on him when it was well deserved, and then it was always measured. "How has your father hurt your sister?"

Alex pretended not to see the tears that started spilling

down the lad's face and took a deep breath. This was even worse than he'd first thought.

"You're a brave lad, but ye don't have the size or the years to handle this problem yourself," Alex said. "When our chieftain made me keeper of Dunfaileag Castle, he made the safety of every member of our clan here on North Uist my responsibility—that includes you and your sister. Ye must tell me what the trouble is so I can do my duty."

"I don't know exactly," Seamus said, fidgeting. "But he gets drunk and sends me out of the cottage. He bars the door so I can't get back in, but I can hear my sister screaming."

Alex's stomach turned sour. Oh, God, there was evil in this world.

"When he lets me back in," Seamus said, his voice barely above a whisper, "Ùna is on the bed weeping. Da tells her to keep her mouth shut, or he'll do it again."

The man should go straight to hell, and Alex wanted to hurry him on his journey.

"Ye did well to tell me," Alex said, and the lad's shoulders relaxed as if a weight had been taken from them. "I'm going to pay a visit on your father."

"He's gone fishing in deep waters," Seamus said. "We don't expect him back for a few days."

May he drown and save me the trouble.

"The two of ye will stay at the castle until I can sort this out with your father," Alex said. "We'll go get Ùna and your things now."

"I don't know if she'll come," Seamus said. "Men frighten her. Best let me talk with her first."

"I'll bring my wife," Alex said. "She'll be able to persuade Ùna."

"But ye promised ye would tell no one!" Seamus's eyes were panicked. "Ye gave me your word."

"All right, I won't tell my wife just yet," Alex said, putting his hand up to calm the lad. "Go home and talk to Una, and I'll come get the two of ye after supper."

With their father out to sea, waiting a couple of hours should make no difference.

CHAPTER 42

I must see to a matter with one of the tenants," Alex said at the end of supper. He got up and kissed his wife's forehead. "It shouldn't take long, but don't wait up."

The wind swept over the tall grass, making it move like an amber sea, as Alex crossed through it in the growing darkness. Ahead of him, weak candlelight shone through the window of the small cottage at the edge of the sea. Sadness seemed to weigh down its sagging thatched roof.

Alex knocked on the cottage's weathered door. When his knock was met by silence, he knocked again. "Seamus, it's me, open up."

Silence again. Unease settled in Alex's gut. He gave them another moment, and then he opened the door.

Alex was a warrior, and he'd fought since he was almost as young as Seamus. And yet, he stood staring for a long moment at the chaos in the one-room cottage before he could take it in. Questions flooded his mind as his gaze traveled over the broken crockery strewn across the floor, the broken table and overturned benches, before coming to rest on the body.

Seamus's father lay on his back in a pool of blood with a knife stuck in the middle of his chest.

The smell of burning herring finally penetrated Alex's thoughts. As he crossed the small room to the hearth, he wrapped his shirt around his hand, then lifted the flaming pan from its hook over the fire and set it on the dirt floor. The pan hissed and smoked as he doused the flame with a jug of water that had miraculously survived the maelstrom.

Alex waved the smoke away from his face and looked about the cottage again. Mother, Mary of God, where were the children?

His heart missed a beat when he saw a still, bare foot under the edge of the bed. When he dropped to his knees amid the broken crockery, he saw a tangle of arms and legs under the bed. He prayed hard for a sign of life.

"'Tis safe to come out," he said, speaking in a low voice. "It's me, Alex."

When Seamus's head and shoulders popped out from under the bed, relief coursed through Alex's body. He pulled Seamus out and held him on his lap as if he were a bairn Sorcha's age.

Ùna rolled out from under the bed with a fire poker in her hand. The lass was covered in blood. When she saw Alex holding her brother, she blinked several times and then slowly dropped her arm with the poker to her side.

"I did it, not Seamus," she said. "I killed him."

"Ye had good cause, lass," Alex said. "No one who knows what your father did to ye will blame ye." Whether everyone would believe it was another question.

"I would die of shame if anyone knew," Ùna said. "I don't want anyone to know what he did. *Not ever.*"

Ùna had started shaking, and Alex did not have the heart to cause the lass any more suffering. He took a deep breath as it became clear what he would have to do.

"If you and your brother can pretend that none of this happened," he said, "then no one need know that ye killed your father or why."

Both of them nodded. Keeping secrets about what happened in this house was not new to them.

"I'll take his body out to sea in his boat," Alex said. "Fishermen are lost all the time. When he fails to return home in a week or two, folks will assume he drowned."

Seamus and Ùna looked at Alex as if he were the second coming.

"Can ye clean up here while I'm gone?"

"Aye," the girl said.

"Seamus, I'll need a rope and a shovel," Alex said, as he took off his boots. "Bring them down to the boat."

Alex hefted the body over his shoulder and carried it down to the boat, which he found on the beach just below the cottage. Their father had kept the boat in such poor repair that none of the fishermen would be surprised when it washed up on shore with a hole in it. A body with a knife wound, however, could be a problem. Alex grunted as he lifted a heavy rock onto the boat.

Seamus came out of the darkness and put the shovel and rope in the boat.

"I'll be back in a few hours." Alex squeezed the lad's shoulders. They felt frail and bony beneath his hands. "It will be all right."

After sailing down the coast a bit, Alex took the boat

straight out to sea for a mile or more. He tied the stone to the body and dumped them both over the side. Damned if he'd say a prayer for the man.

After ramming a hole in the boat with the shovel, Alex dove over the side. He was a strong swimmer, so the worst part of the long swim was the cold. Still, it seemed to take forever to reach shore. When he did, he was so cold he was shaking. He was barefoot and soaking wet, but he warmed up as he made the long walk back by starlight.

By the time he reached the cottage, the sky had the gray cast of predawn. Thankfully, the children—though Ùna was seventeen, Alex could not help thinking of her as a child—had a good fire going. Alex stood before it to dry his clothes as long as he dared.

"Ye did a good job cleaning up," he said, as he put his boots on.

"I burned what I was wearing," Ùna said.

"Good. Now get some rest." They were both too pale and had dark circles under their eyes. "I'll come back to check on ye tomorrow."

Alex was exhausted when he returned to the castle just as dawn was breaking. The guards at the gate were men who had come with him from Skye. He suspected they might think he had been in some woman's bed, as in former days, but he could not very well tell them he'd spent the night disposing of a body at sea—and he was too damned tired to think of a better explanation. He would set them straight in the morning.

Praise be to the saints that Glynis was a sound sleeper. All the same, before easing the bedchamber door open Alex took off his boots and then set them down carefully just inside the door. After hanging his damp clothes over a stool, Alex slipped under the bedclothes and wrapped himself around Glynis. After the hellish night, peacefulness settled over him, as it always did when he fell asleep with his wife in his arms.

* * *

Glynis lay on her side watching the pink dawn sky through the narrow window. Her husband's arm felt heavy slung across her ribs. With every breath she took, the weight seemed to grow heavier and heavier until she felt as if she were wheezing. But she knew it was not his arm, but the weight on her heart that made it so hard to breathe.

She told herself not to rush to judgment. There could be a dozen reasons why Alex crept into bed with the dawn. And yet, she could think of only one. It throbbed in her head. *Another woman, another woman.*

She squeezed her eyes shut and prayed. *Please, God, don't let it be true.*

If Alex had planned to meet a lover, that would explain why he was distracted all through supper last night. And then there was his vague explanation about needing to visit a tenant, something he never did in the evening. And his parting words: *Don't wait up.*

Alex was sleeping like the dead—or like a man who had spent the night sating himself.

Glynis could not lie here a moment longer waiting for Alex to wake up and tell her where he'd been all night. When she threw off the bedclothes and sat up, the first thing she saw was his boots. Alex had stood them neatly by the door instead of tossing them on the floor by the bed as he always did.

Her husband had taken pains not to wake her when he came in.

Glynis was so upset that the thought of breakfast made her ill. After grabbing an oatcake for her pocket from the kitchen, she headed out for a walk on the beach. She bid good day to the men on guard as she started through the gate, then she stopped.

"Were ye here when my husband came in early this morning?" she asked one of the men. Her stomach sank as the guard looked away and shifted his weight from side to side.

"Aye," the man said, then quickly added, "but he didn't say where he'd been."

Apparently, Alex did not need to say for the man to guess.

CHAPTER 43

Alex awoke with the sun shining on his face. He blinked to clear the images of the bloody cottage from his vision and looked about the empty bedchamber. *Good God, how late had he slept?*

He was not used to waking up without Glynis, and he didn't like it. And where in the hell were his boots? He was on his knees looking under the bed before he remembered leaving them neatly by the door. He smiled thinking how that must have pleased his orderly wife.

His stomach rumbled, and his muscles ached as he drew a clean shirt over his head. It was a long swim last night, and he was starving.

When he went down to the hall, Sorcha ran across the room to him. It must be noon already, for everyone was sitting at the tables, waiting for him to start the midday meal—everyone, that is, except his wife.

He picked Sorcha up and rubbed her head with his knuckles. "Where's your mother?"

Sorcha pointed in the direction of the beach.

"She must have lost track of time," Alex said. "She does love her walks."

The others were waiting to eat, and the men had work to do, so Alex sat down and signaled for the meal to begin. He missed having Glynis beside him at the table, but it was just as well. He was anxious to see how Seamus and Ùna were faring. As soon as he had seen them, he would find Glynis and explain the situation to her.

Poor Ùna. Alex hoped the lass was strong enough to recover from this horror. As he crossed the meadow to their cottage, he picked a few wildflowers for her. Most of the flowers were gone, but there were still some knapweed and devil's bit blooming. When he reached the cottage and knocked, Ùna opened the door. She looked at the flowers he held out to her as if they were some strange gift from a fairy hill.

"Thank ye," she finally said in a soft voice and took them.

Tears were streaming down her face. God help him, had the lass seen so little kindness in her young life that a handful of flowers could touch her so? Alex laid a hand on her shoulder and stepped inside.

"The cottage looks good," he said. "Shame about the table and chairs. I'll bring tools next time and fix them for ye."

"'Tis no the first time they've been broken," Seamus said.

"For now, the two of ye must act as if nothing unusual has happened," he reminded them. "Seamus should come up to the castle as usual. Then, after a few days, ye can ask the other fishermen if they've seen your father's boat. Do ye think ye can do that?"

"I can't ask anyone about him," Ùna said, shaking her head violently.

Seamus took his sister's hand. "I'll do the asking."

Alex was starting to worry that the lass would give them away.

"I need to tell my wife the truth about what happened," he said. "I can't have secrets between us."

"Don't! Please!" Ùna said and backed away from him.

"Hush now, it's all right," Alex said, trying to calm her.

"I hate that ye know about it." Her voice was shaking, and she was wringing her hands. "I can't bear to have anyone else know. I can't, I can't!"

Alex could not risk having the lass fall apart—she might end up telling everyone about murdering her father, and then he'd have an even worse mess to clean up. And Glynis couldn't lie to save her life. If he told her, the truth would be all over her face every time she looked at Seamus or his sister.

"All right, I won't tell my wife just yet," Alex said. "I'll give ye a day to think on it, and then we'll talk again."

* * *

As Glynis paced the beach, she reminded herself that Alex had given her no cause to doubt him until now. His friendly, easy manner had deceived her at first, but beneath the charm and humor was a reliable man who took his responsibilities seriously. That was the reason his chieftain, who knew Alex as well as anyone, entrusted

Dunfaileag Castle and the safety of their clansman on this island to him.

Of course, a man could be loyal to his chieftain and not to his wife.

Glynis pushed that thought aside. Alex had shown no signs he was tired of her yet—in bed or out of it. He would have a good explanation for where he was last night, and she'd be annoyed with herself for getting upset over nothing.

And getting upset was not good for her baby.

Having finally talked herself into seeing reason, Glynis left the beach. She started up the path to the castle. But when she stopped and turned to take in the view, she saw Alex. He was walking with his back to her, but with his fair hair, tall frame, and long, easy stride, he could not be mistaken for anyone else.

Glynis ran to catch up with him. As she came closer, she saw that Alex had gathered flowers for her. Ach, her warrior had a soft heart. Glynis called to him, but he did not hear her over the wind. She smiled to herself as she decided to suggest they be truly wicked and make love outdoors in the middle of the day. They had not done that once since their journey to Edinburgh.

Glynis put her hand up to shield her eyes as Alex approached a small cottage. All the fears that she had spent the morning pushing away now slammed into her like a crashing wave. She waited, every muscle tense, to see who would greet her husband at this lowly fisherman's cottage.

When the door opened, Glynis recognized Ùna's dark golden hair. Dread clawed at her belly like a sea monster. When Alex held the flowers out to Ùna, Glynis sank to her knees in the tall grass. She felt as if a jagged blade was piercing her chest as her husband rested his hand on Ùna's shoulder, ducked under the low doorway, and shut the cottage door behind him.

Glynis was so light-headed that she dropped her head to her knees to keep from fainting. All the pieces fell into place. Alex's reluctance to arrange the marriage for Peiter. Ùna's daily visits to the castle. The lass did not avoid looking at other men because she was shy, but because she belonged to the warrior who was the keeper of Dunfaileag Castle.

Glynis covered her face with hands. The lass was so young!

Although Glynis had been lulled into trusting Alex, down deep she knew that she would never be enough for him. Eventually, Alex's desire for her would fade, and he would take another. And then another. But Glynis thought he would go to a woman like Catherine Campbell or that Mary back on Skye.

Ùna was just a poor fisherman's daughter. Glynis never, ever thought Alex would take advantage of an inexperienced young lass who was in no position to refuse him.

How had she been so mistaken about what kind of man her husband was?

Glynis vomited into the grass until there was nothing left inside her. Then she sat on the ground with her head between her knees. When she had the strength to stand, she rose on shaky legs.

Nothing in her life would be as hard as what she had to do now.

She did not allow herself to look back at the cottage

where her husband was sinning with a sweet, golden-haired lass. Instead, Glynis balled her hands into fists, stiffened her back, and started back up the path to the castle to pack her things.

She would leave this very day.

CHAPTER 44

Alex sensed there was a bad wind blowing his way as soon as he entered the gate. The men avoided his gaze, and the women sent him accusatory glances from the corners of their eyes. Surely, the body could not have been found already. Alex went over in his mind how he'd tied the rock to it.

He looked for Glynis in the hall. When he did not find her there, he went up to their bedchamber, taking the steps two at a time, and flung the door open. Glynis was on her knees before an open chest, surrounded by gowns. When she looked up, he saw that she had been weeping.

"Glynis, what happened?"

"Perhaps ye should tell me," she said in a strained voice. She picked up a gown and folded it into a neat rectangle with swift, sharp movements.

"Why are ye angry?" he asked. "And what are ye doing with your clothes?"

"I am leaving."

Panic rose in Alex's throat. "I thought we were past this, Glynis. Why would ye leave me? How can ye?"

When she looked up, her eyes were wet but sharp as daggers. "I told ye I would leave if ye took another woman."

"But I haven't!" Alex said. "I gave ye a promise, and I swear I haven't broken it."

"Another wife might not be troubled by it," she said, as she folded another gown into a perfect square. "But I told ye I would leave if ye were unfaithful, and I am."

"Who said something to make ye believe this?" he demanded. "Ye accuse me without even asking me for the truth."

"So I'll ask ye," she said, glaring up at him. "Where were ye last night?"

Ach, the one thing he could not tell her. He had given his word. Besides, Alex was not entirely certain Glynis would think any better of him for covering up a murder and dropping the body at sea. He scratched his neck as he tried to think how best to answer her. It crossed his mind to make up a good story, but he'd promised never to lie to her.

"I can't say now, but I will tell ye as soon as I can."

"I thought ye would be quicker with a lie, being such a good storyteller," she said. "But ye must be tired."

"I don't take well to being called a liar." Alex was starting to get angry himself. "And stop folding your damned clothes."

"Ye are a liar," she said, her voice breaking. "I saw ye myself this afternoon."

"Then your eyes deceive ye."

"Ye brought flowers to her cottage."

Alex could not believe what she was accusing him of. "Ye think I've taken *Ùna* to bed?" he said, spreading out his arms. "Why, she's just a child!"

"Seventeen is no child." Glynis pressed her lips together and resumed her methodical folding.

It felt like a blow to the chest to learn that Glynis believed he would lure a young lass to his bed who was so fearful of men she could not look one in the eye. After knowing him this long—after living with him as his wife—how could Glynis think so little of him?

"I won't be here when Ùna brings your child to the castle," Glynis said, as she slammed a pair of shoes into the chest. "Did ye think I would be happy to care for all your bastards?"

The blood in Alex's veins went as cold as January ice. "Is that how ye feel about my daughter?"

"Not Sorcha," Glynis said quickly. "But that doesn't mean I want a houseful of children reminding me of your infidelities."

Alex banged the lid of the chest shut with his fist and picked Glynis up by her arms. "I have done nothing wrong, so *ye will not leave.*"

* * *

Alex sat in the hall drinking. From here, he could see the stairs and be sure his wife did not leave the castle without his knowledge. When Bessie started into the hall with Sorcha, she took one look at him and hurried Sorcha outside. The rest of the household showed the good sense to leave him alone as well.

Outrage pounded through Alex's head, blocking out all

else. He had complied with Glynis's rules, done nothing to merit her accusations and ill regard. If she came down the stairs looking for a servant to carry her trunk to the nearest boat, they were going to have one hell of a fight.

All Alex had wanted was a peaceful home for his daughter. Was that too much to ask? No shouting matches, just a steady woman who wouldn't throw crockery—and who wouldn't abandon them. Instead, he had gotten exactly what he did not want: thrown out of his wife's bed, fighting and shouting, and his wife packing to leave him. He had spent his entire life trying to avoid living as his parents had, only to end up the same.

Hours went by. Alex heard noise coming from down below and suspected the entire household was crowded in the kitchen between the spits and the worktables eating their supper. And still, Glynis did not show her face. At least she had not attempted to leave.

Alex poured the last of his jug of whiskey into his cup and drank it down. Perhaps Glynis regretted her harsh judgment of him—as well she should. She was a prideful woman. Likely, she was stewing up there, gathering herself to apologize to him.

He deserved an apology.

And he was tired of waiting for it. He would go up there now, and they would settle this trouble between them. He marched up the stairs to their bedchamber door and lifted the latch. But when he pushed, the door did not open. He shook the handle, not believing she would do it.

Glynis had barred the goddamned door.

"Glynis!" he shouted as he beat his fist against it. "Open this door to your husband. Now."

"Go away." Her voice came faintly through the door.

"Ye will regret this, I swear it."

Alex never got upset, but he was upset now. Anger pounded through every bone and muscle as he stormed down the stairs, grabbed an axe from the wall, and stomped back up with it.

"Stand back from the door!" he shouted.

Crack! He swung the axe so hard that it reverberated up his arms. Glynis did not scream, proving his wife had ice in her veins.

Crack! Crack! Crack! His violence against the door felt good. When the boards gave way with a satisfying *crunch*, he reached his arm through the hole and slid the bar back. Then he kicked the door with such force that it swung open and banged against the wall.

And there, sitting on her trunk with her arms crossed, was his wife. He was a wronged husband, an angry man with an axe in his hands, and Glynis glared at him as if she had nothing to fear. She didn't, of course—but she should have had the good sense to look frightened. Did she not respect him at all?

He crossed the room and stood over her. His chest was heaving, his ears rang. The only sign that an enraged Highland warrior concerned Glynis one whit was a slight twitch in her left eye.

"Ye will not lock our bedchamber door to me again," he said.

"I told ye," she said, calm as could be, "I wouldn't share a bed with ye if ye took another woman."

"I promised ye I wouldn't take another woman," he said, "and I haven't done so."

"Ye expect me to believe that?" She stood up, clenching her fists at her sides. "A man like you will say anything."

"A man like me?" Anger tightened his throat, stretching out his words. "Just what do ye mean by that, Glynis MacNeil?"

"I mean a man whose word means nothing," she said. "I should have married Lord D'Arcy. *He* was an honorable man. *He* would have kept his vows."

Alex felt as if his head were exploding. Until now, he had believed D'Arcy had told her of his true intentions.

"Perhaps I'll take D'Arcy up on his offer now," she said.

"What, and be his whore?" Alex said. "Because that is what D'Arcy was offering ye. He would not have said vows to ye, as I did."

Upset as Alex was with her, he would not have told Glynis of D'Arcy's insult even now, except that he couldn't trust her not to go traipsing off across the breadth of Scotland to find the Frenchman.

"Nay, D'Arcy's intentions were good," Glynis said.

"Ye are a fool, woman," Alex said. "D'Arcy has a wife in France."

Glynis's lips parted, and she blinked several times. In a whisper, she said, "That cannot be true."

Her obvious disappointment cut Alex to the core.

"Aye, your white knight has a wife—probably one who came with a title," he spat out. "And when she joins him in Scotland, that sense of honor that ye so esteem would require D'Arcy to send ye away. Ye see, he would think it cruel to upset his wife by keeping his whore in his home while she was there."

Glynis sat down on the trunk with a thump.

"The French don't treat their bastard children like Highland men do," Alex continued. "Though D'Arcy might feel honor-bound to provide for any bairns ye had by him, he would never claim your children or allow them to set foot in his home and contaminate his legitimate heirs."

Alex saw the shock in her eyes, but it was nothing to the well of pain in his chest.

"I have much to answer for in this life," he said, "but ye are the one who has been unfaithful in this marriage."

"Me?" she said, slapping her hand against her chest. "I am not the sinner here."

"Ye kept another man in your heart, Glynis." He could see that now.

"I didn't—"

Alex cut her off—he didn't want to hear her excuses. "My promise was that I would not take another woman so long as ye shared my bed," he said. "I have needs like any man, and if ye won't have me…"

He let that hang in the air before he spelled it out for her.

"I know how to please a lass under the blankets," he said, leaning down close to her. "I'll have no trouble finding replacements for ye."

Alex wanted Glynis to lie awake thinking of him with another woman, making her scream with pleasure. He wanted her to regret what she'd done and call him back.

He turned on his heel and left her.

The axe was still in his hand.

CHAPTER 45

After dark, Alex went to the cottage to see how Seamus and Ùna fared. So far as he could tell, they were holding up better than he was. He did not want to sleep in the hall with all his men pretending not to notice that his wife had kicked him out of their bedchamber. So, instead of returning to the castle, he went down to the beach to make his cold bed in the war galley.

As he lay looking up at the stars, Alex could not help thinking about all the nights he and Glynis had slept together outdoors on their journey to Edinburgh. Ach, how had it come to this? He thought his threat to take other women to bed would bring Glynis around. It hurt more than his pride that it hadn't.

When he awoke in the morning, he sat on the beach staring out at the sea. He had worked hard every day for the last two months, rebuilding the castle, training the men, chasing pirates away from these shores. But he didn't feel like doing a damned thing today.

He heard a giggle and turned to see his daughter running toward him with her hair flying out behind her. When she crashed into him and flung her arms around his neck, he closed his eyes. At least he still had her. God, he loved this child.

Bessie was breathless when she caught up to her charge. "Sorcha, go to the kitchen and bring your father back some breakfast."

Sorcha appeared pleased to be entrusted with the task. When she had scampered off, Bessie remained with her feet planted in front of him.

"Do ye want to accuse me of something as well?" Alex asked.

"Nay." Bessie bit her lip, looking uneasy. "Mistress Glynis would no be pleased to have me tell ye this, but I think ye have a right to know."

The back of Alex's neck prickled. "What is it that I have a right to know?"

The woman fidgeted with her hands for a time before she finally spoke again. "Your wife is with child."

Pain seared through him, blinding him with its force. Glynis was carrying his child, and she had not seen fit to tell him. How long had she kept this from him—and why? Had she been planning to leave him all along?

* * *

"Have ye seen your father?" Glynis asked Sorcha when she came barreling up the steps of the keep.

Sorcha pointed in the direction of the beach.

"Don't run inside," she said, and touched Sorcha's cheek.

Glynis found Alex sitting alone on the beach. When she stood beside him, he did not acknowledge her.

"I am going home," she said.

"This is your home."

"I'm returning to my father's," she said. "Ye can supply a boat, or I'll steal one."

Alex continued staring off at the horizon as he spoke. "Did ye plan to leave and never tell me about the child?"

Glynis sucked in her breath. How did he know about the babe? Although he still did not look at her, she could feel the anger and hurt vibrating off him. Ach, it had been a mistake not to tell him.

"I haven't known long," she said in a soft voice. "My fluxes have always been irregular, and I thought I was barren, so I didn't believe it at first. I wanted to be certain before I told ye."

"But ye did know, and ye kept it from me."

Glynis had wanted to save him from the disappointment if it turned out she was wrong. But she had been going to tell him soon.

"I'm sorry," she said, "But it doesn't change anything."

"It doesn't?" he said, his voice dangerously low. He turned to face her, and his eyes burned through her like a torch to parchment.

"I can't live with ye now." Her voice shook, despite herself. "I want to go to my father's."

"If you're that set upon it," Alex said, his eyes hard as ice, "then I will allow ye to leave after the child is born."

"After? But that's months away," she said. "Ye can't keep me here."

"As I said, ye may leave after the child is born, if that is what ye want," Alex said. "But the child stays here."

"Ye can't mean it," Glynis said, her voice coming out high-pitched. "Ye wouldn't try to force me to stay by threatening to keep my child."

"I'm no threatening, and ye can do as ye like," he said. "But the child *will* remain here."

"Ye wouldn't do that to me," Glynis said, looking into his face for a bit of softness and finding none. "Nay, ye can't hate me that much."

"Ye are the one leaving. I asked ye to stay." Alex got to his feet. "If ye are separated from our child, it's by your own choice. I won't take the blame for that."

"I won't let ye keep my child from me," Glynis said, clenching her fists.

"Under Highland law, it is a father's right."

"But most fathers don't enforce it—at least not when the child is young." Glynis grabbed his sleeve, but he shook her off. "Alex, ye wouldn't do this."

"Since ye believe I would seduce that poor, frightened lass, Ùna," Alex said, glaring down at her, "than ye know I'm capable of anything."

CHAPTER 46

The tension was so thick between her and Alex at the table that Glynis could not eat. It had been like this for a week now, and she was feeling the strain—as was the entire household. When she set down her eating knife, she felt Alex's eyes on her and could not help giving him a sideways glance. There were lines around his eyes, and his expression was grim.

Smiles rarely graced his countenance these days—except when he was playing with Sorcha. Unlike most fathers of daughters, he paid close attention to her. He treated her as the special and unexpected gift that she was to him. If Glynis took her new babe away with her, she would be denying the child a wonderful father. But it was worse to separate a babe from its mother, was it not?

Nothing she did would be right.

Glynis got up from the table without eating a bite and left the hall. She was going down the steps of the keep when Alex caught her arm and spun her around.

"God damn it, Glynis, ye have to eat," Alex said.

"Ye wouldn't care if I starved to death, except for the child I carry."

Alex took a step back, as if her words had dealt him a physical blow. "After all that was between us, how can ye say that to me?"

It was a harsh thing to say, and she would not have if she were not so tired. She found it hard to sleep in their bed alone.

"Ye win, Glynis." Alex sank onto the steps and held his head in his hands. "I've tried to do what I thought was best, but nothing has turned out as I wanted it to."

Win? She could not feel worse. Oh, God, she hated to see him like this.

"Are ye saying you'll let me go?" she asked.

"Aye. And take Sorcha with ye," he said, sounding as though the words were wrenched from him. "I can't provide her with the family she needs."

Glynis sat beside him on the step. "Nay, Alex. I cannot do that."

"You've become a mother to her," Alex said. "Sorcha needs ye more than she needs me."

"Ye know I love her with all my heart, but I could never ask ye to give her up."

He turned, and his gaze settled on her like a cold sea mist. "And yet, ye asked me to give up my other child with no hesitation."

"I didn't think—"

"Do ye believe I will care less for that child?" he demanded. "That the babe we made together would be any less precious to me than Sorcha?"

Glynis dropped her gaze to her lap and shook her head.

"If ye know that," Alex said, "then how can ye believe I would risk everything that matters to me for a tumble with some lass I barely know?"

"Ye were never particular before," Glynis said in a low voice.

"I had nothing to lose before." Alex stood up. "Go when ye wish. I'll not stop ye."

*   *   *

Sorcha flicked her eyes from her father to her mother and back again. Their sadness weighed down on her chest. She squeezed what was left of her doll. Bessie tried to hide Marie, but Sorcha always found her again.

She knew her parents had been waiting for her to speak. Sometimes when she was alone she could make the words that were always in her head come out of her mouth. But that was before she learned her mother was leaving. She'd heard whispers about it all over the castle.

Sorcha wanted to tell her mother not to leave them. She wanted to ask if it was her fault that she was. But her chest grew tighter and tighter, trapping the words inside.

CHAPTER 47

Glynis was leaving tomorrow.

As Alex had always suspected, he was incapable of keeping a woman happy for long, incapable of being the good husband and father he wanted to be. *Blood will out.*

But he missed Glynis so much his heart ached with every step. He had tried shouting at her, reasoning with her, and threatening her, and he had come very close to begging her. Now he would make one last attempt.

He wanted her to stay with him because she trusted and respected him. *Ah hell*, he wanted her to stay because she cared for him. But with her leaving in the morning, Alex was desperate enough that he didn't care if she stayed with him for the wrong reasons—so long as she stayed.

It was time to play to his strengths. He would get her into bed. And then he would drive Glynis so mad with passion that—against her better judgment and despite the lies she believed about him—she would take him back.

And even if she did not, Alex would have one last night with her.

*   *   *

Glynis sat by the window stitching because she had finished her packing and had nothing else to do. Although she'd rather be outside, it was better for both her and Alex if she avoided him until she boarded the boat tomorrow. It was one of those fine autumn days when they had a lull between storms and the sun shone as if it was summer. But in her heart, there was no break in the rains.

Alex's laughter floated through the window, and her needle stopped. Alex was by nature full of good humor— and yet, how long had it been since she'd heard his laugh? She'd missed the sound of it.

Had he sought out another woman because Glynis drained the joy out of him? She was all hard edges and strong opinions. If she were easy and sweet-natured like her sisters, perhaps Alex would not have strayed. Or perhaps she could live with his straying.

But she was the difficult, demanding person she was.

Glynis set aside her stitching and picked up the silver medallion of Saint Michael from the table beside her. She twirled the medallion by its heavy chain and watched it spin, thinking of the day it had caught her eye in one of the shops that her aunt and uncle had dragged her into. When she left Edinburgh in a rush, she had tucked it away in her bag and forgotten it until she came across it while packing today.

She stopped it spinning and rubbed her thumb over it. She had traded one of her rings for the medallion because the image of Saint Michael, the warrior angel, looked so much like Alex.

Alex's laughter came in through the window again. Drawn by the sound as if it were a string tied to her heart, Glynis set the medallion on the table and went to the window. The sight of Alex in the castle yard below stole her breath away. With graceful, swift movements, he was demonstrating the use of the claymore to a few of the older lads.

Alex with a sword in his hands was pure masculine beauty in motion. Glynis's throat went dry as he danced and spun and sliced his blade through the air with deadly force. Her fingers itched to touch the powerful muscles of his chest, arms, and back as he swung the heavy sword from side to side with sure, smooth strokes.

When the men stopped to rest, Alex slapped one of the lads on the back. His broad smile, showing even white teeth, reminded her again of how little she had seen it of late. Long after Alex disappeared from view and the voices of the men faded, Glynis remained at the window. She stared off at the sea, remembering how Alex used to look at her with a sparkle in his eyes.

"Glynis."

Her heart went to her throat at the sound of his voice behind her. When she turned, Alex stood in the doorway, his long, lean body propped against the door frame. He had not put on his shirt, and his skin glowed as if it still retained the warmth of the sun.

"I didn't hear ye," she said stupidly, as she dragged her gaze to his face—which was no safer than his body.

She loved everything about that face, from his stubbled jaw, to the strong planes of his cheekbones and forehead, to his wide, sensuous mouth. When she met his green eyes, they sizzled with the knowledge of every inch of her body.

Did Alex say more than her name? Glynis's heart was banging so hard against her chest she could have missed it.

She tensed, trying desperately to convince herself to stop him if he came nearer. But then, a knot of disappointment tightened in her stomach when he did not. Instead, he crossed the room to the chair, watching her from the corner of his eye. From the way his mouth quirked up at the corner, Alex knew precisely the effect he had on her. Ach, he was a devil.

Alex sat in the chair, put his hands behind his head, and stretched out his long, muscular legs. Her breathing grew shallow as he let his gaze burn over her as if she wore nothing.

"Come sit on my lap, Glynis," he said, crooking his finger. "Ye know ye want to."

"I don't," she said, though her body was tilting toward him like a flower to the sun. How she longed for his touch.

Alex laughed. "Ye have always been a poor liar."

"That is no a bad quality," she said, stiffening.

"Aye, 'tis one of your charms," he said, giving her a smile that sent a wave of desire through her. "I have a proposition for ye."

"A proposition?" Her life had changed the last time he had said that to her.

"Come sit with me, and I'll tell ye what it is."

He was not angry and yelling at her. Alex was his old, lighthearted self, so without stopping to ask herself why, she went to stand beside him. Instead of trying to pull her into his lap, he ran his finger slowly up her arm. She could hardly push him away for such a small gesture, and yet the slow, light touch set all her senses alight. Her entire being focused on the course of his finger sliding up her arm under her loose sleeve.

When his hands enclosed her waist and lifted her onto his lap, no word of objection would come out of her mouth. She longed to close her eyes and lean against his solid frame. Why, why, why could she not just accept his nature, take the good with the bad? Alex could not help that women were drawn to him like flies to honey. He was who he was.

And yet, Glynis wanted to be the only one. She had to be.

"This is no so bad, aye?" he asked, as he played with her hair.

She bit back a sigh when his fingers grazed her neck. Finally, she remembered to ask, "What is this proposition?"

"I know ye miss me in bed," Alex said. "And God knows, I miss you."

He missed her. It should not please her so much to hear him say it.

"That's not enough," she said—though at the moment, it nearly was.

When she said it, she thought she saw a flash of pain cross Alex's face, before he covered it with another easy smile.

"I'm a sentimental man," Alex said, as he brushed his knuckles across her cheek. "I think we should have one more night together to remember each other by."

"Nay" caught in her throat when she felt his breath on her ear.

"I know how to please ye," he whispered.

When Alex nuzzled her neck the way she liked, Glynis leaned her head back. Alex did know how to please her. She ached for him to touch every valley and crest of her body.

His nearness worked an enchantment upon her. She could form no clear thoughts while his hands slid over her and he lowered his mouth to hers. When his lips touched hers, she sank into him. Everything about him—his smell, his kiss, his heat—was familiar and filled the empty spaces he had left inside her.

Alex moved slowly, as if he were afraid of waking her from her dream. She was so lost in him that she barely noticed when he carried her to the bed. He touched her with a tenderness that made her heart bleed. No matter what he did with someone else, she knew he did care for her. It was in the way he held her.

They were naked without her knowing or caring how it happened. He said her name over and over as he ran sweet kisses down her arms and pressed her palm against his rough cheek. With his gentleness, he shattered every defense she had erected against him. She squeezed her eyes shut, feeling too much to bear looking into his face.

Even while he was in her arms, she was grieving for the loss of him. She hurt inside, and she knew she was hurting him badly, too, but she didn't see a way to stop wounding each other except by leaving.

Glynis held him tightly to her, her deep need for him filling her with a quiet desperation. If he told her now that he loved her, she would believe him.

"Ye won't forget me," he said before he thrust inside her.

"I could not," she whispered. "Not ever."

"Ye will think of me in the night." He held her face between his hands and forced her to look into his eyes. "And ye will wish I was there."

"Aye." She wrapped her arms and legs around him and clung to him as he moved against her. She dug her nails into his back as her need for him grew until she felt as if she would burst with it. Tears rolled down the sides of her face as emotions too big to contain swirled inside her. She felt as if she were drowning in her love for him.

Why didn't he love her? Why did he not care *enough*?

As her body shook with the force of her release, she felt as if she touched both Heaven and Hell.

"Oh, God, Glynis, how can ye leave me?" Alex said just before he exploded inside her—and she knew he had not meant to make this last, heart-wrenching plea.

Afterward, he held her with his face buried in her hair. She wanted to give in, to tell him what he wanted to hear, to stay in the warmth of his arms and never leave. If he had ever once said he loved her, she would not have held out. But he did not.

* * *

When Bessie came in the next morning, Glynis sat up quickly and dried her face on the bedclothes.

"Tormond is ready to take ye in the war galley," Bessie said. "'Tis no my place to say it, but what are ye doing leaving such a fine man? 'Tis no making ye happy."

"I don't know what I'm doing," Glynis admitted. "I

haven't even told Sorcha yet. I suppose I was waiting until I was certain I wouldn't change my mind."

But Sorcha was a child who knew things without being told.

"It will break her heart to leave her father," Bessie said.

With that indictment ringing in her ears, Glynis dressed and went downstairs. She was so full of doubts that she did not know if she still intended to get on the boat or not. She should have given herself more time to think this through instead of insisting on leaving right away. For once, she wished she knew how to do things by halves.

She found Alex sitting alone with Sorcha downstairs. The hall was rarely empty so it was evident everyone had left to give him time with his daughter.

"Your mother and I need to talk," he said to Sorcha. "Have one of the stable lads take ye to visit the horses, and I'll come find ye there as soon as we're done."

Sorcha shifted her gaze back and forth between them, her face far too solemn for such a young child. Then she kissed her father's cheek and left the hall with her feet dragging.

"Tell Sorcha whatever ye think best," Alex said, pain etched on his face as he watched Sorcha leave. "She seemed close to speaking not long ago. I'm hoping she will once ye have her settled."

Glynis opened her mouth to tell him that she was not sure she wanted to go, but Alex held his hand up.

"This is hard, so let me finish and be done with it," he said. "If our babe is a boy, I want ye to send him to me for his training when he is old enough. Our world is dangerous, and a boy must have fighting skills to survive and to do his part to protect his clan. I know your father is dear to ye, but he's growing old. I'll train your brother as well, if ye wish to send him to me."

Alex was not the shallow charmer she had once thought him, though the man could charm a saint out of her shift. He would do anything for his children—even give them up. Although Glynis had always prided herself on having the resolve to do what was right, she doubted she had the strength of character to make that sacrifice.

Was she wrong about Alex in other ways as well? He never denied his philandering past—but had he changed? Glynis was always decisive and certain in her opinions, but for once, she did not know what to believe or what she should do.

"I won't be the one to set aside the marriage," Alex said in a calm, steady voice. "And I'm asking ye to wait the full year before ye do it."

Another man would not put his pride aside and leave the door open to her like this, after she was the one to leave. Glynis felt as bleak as November rains as Alex stood and walked away. She wanted to trust him. She was almost sure she had misjudged him.

And despite her doubts, she realized she could not face life without him.

"Alex!" she called out.

But her voice was drowned out by the shouts coming through the open door of the keep. When Alex ran outside, she followed him out. She came to an abrupt halt at the top of the steps.

A war galley had entered their small bay and was sailing straight for the castle.

CHAPTER 48

It's our chieftain's ship," Alex called out to his men.

When he ran down to the shore to meet it, Glynis picked up her skirts and followed with all the others. She reached the beach in time to see Connor climb down from the galley, followed closely by Ian and Duncan.

"What's happened?" Alex asked after thumping his old friends on the back. "Ye wouldn't bring so many warriors from Skye for just a friendly visit."

"We can't wait any longer to deal with my vile uncles," Connor said.

"What have they done now?" Alex asked.

"Angus and Torquil were guests at Banranald's home while he was away," Connor said. "And Angus tried to rape Banranald's wife."

"Banranald's is not far from here," Alex said. "How did ye hear before I did?"

"The wife Angus tried to rape is a Clanranald, like our mothers," Ian said, taking over the story. "She fled to her

Clanranald kin, and their chieftain sent an official emissary to Connor at once demanding justice."

Glynis could not help interrupting the men to ask, "Magnus Clanranald has stirred himself over an offense against one of his clanswomen?"

"The Clanranalds removed Magnus from the chieftainship," Duncan told her. "They went so far as to ban his line from the chieftainship forever."

Glynis had never heard of such a thing—but if anyone merited such treatment, it was Magnus.

"So who is their new chieftain?" Alex asked.

"That is the one piece of good news," Connor said. "The chieftainship fell to our mothers' cousin and your namesake, Alexander. As ye know, he's a good man. He wants both Angus and Torquil delivered to him for punishment—and I want Hugh. They'll be together."

"While we search the outer isles," Ian said, "the Clanranalds are looking for them in the isles to the south and east."

"I haven't seen your uncles' ships," Alex said. "Have ye heard where we might find them?"

No one answered, but Duncan, Connor, and Ian all avoided looking at Glynis.

"Barra?" Glynis asked, her heart slamming against her chest. "They're going to Barra?"

"We don't know that for certain," Connor said. "But we have heard rumors that my uncles are planning a big raid on the MacNeils with both their ships."

"Your father will need our help," Alex said, touching Glynis's arm, before he turned to the others. "My men will be ready to sail in a quarter of an hour."

After shouting orders to his men, Alex took Glynis by

the arm and led her up the beach a short distance away from the others.

"It's too dangerous for ye to go to your father's just now," he said. "And I need ye here while I'm gone."

"Of course."

"I'll leave half my men here to protect you and the castle. With the pirates sailing toward Barra, that should be sufficient," Alex said, but he looked uneasy.

"We'll be fine," Glynis assured him. "But ye must save my brother and my sisters. The girls are delicate. They can't—"

"Shh, don't fret," Alex said, and touched her cheek. "I won't let anything happen to them."

"I'm so grateful to ye for going to them."

Even though she was leaving him, Alex was honoring the bond he had made to protect her family and her clan. Glynis hated to have him sailing off into danger with things so wrong between them. As he left her to rejoin the other men, she remembered that she was wearing the silver medallion. She had put it on when she dressed, to comfort herself.

"Wait!" she called after him. "I have something for ye."

She ran to where he stood at the water's edge and stretched up on her toes to put the chain around his neck.

"It's of Saint Michael, God's warrior angel," she said, holding the medallion up for him to see. "He's supposed to give special protection to both horsemen and sailors."

"Ah, Glynis, that's sweet of ye," Alex said and put it inside his shirt, next to his heart. "But there's nothing to worry about."

"Be safe," she said, as she rose up on her toes to kiss

his cheek. When Alex's arms came around her, she rested her head against his shoulder. She felt his chest rise and fall in a deep breath, then he kissed her hair.

She loved him so much.

Alex released her as Sorcha came running down to the beach, her hair flying out behind her. When she flung herself at Alex at full speed, he lifted her in his arms.

"I must go chase some pirates," Alex said to her, making it sound like an adventure—which he probably thought it was. "But your mother will be here to look after ye."

He kissed Sorcha and handed her to Glynis. Then he took his shield and his claymore from Seamus, who had carried them down to the shore. By now, the entire household had assembled on the beach, and Alex chose which men would go and which would stay.

As Alex's ship set sail behind the other war galley, he stood at the rudder, his hair whipping in the wind. He waved his sword at them, looking like a Viking king.

Glynis held Sorcha's hand and watched until Alex's boat disappeared over the horizon. When she finally turned away, the only one left on the beach besides her and Sorcha was Seamus.

"Seamus, will ye take Sorcha up to Bessie at the castle for me?" Glynis asked.

She should have been brave enough to do this before. As soon as the two children were gone, Glynis found the path that led to the cottage where she had seen Alex take the flowers that awful day. Sweat broke out on her palms as Glynis remembered sitting in the tall grass with her head between her knees trying to get her breath back. But she had to find the truth.

When she reached the ancient cottage with the sagging roof, Glynis knocked before she could lose her nerve. No one answered for so long that she thought no one was home. But then the door finally creaked open, and Ùna stood in the doorway.

Ach, she was a lovely lass.

"I saw the ship sail," Ùna said. "Is he gone?"

"My husband?" Glynis was surprised at the lass's willingness to speak about Alex to her. "Aye, he's gone."

Ùna bit her lip and dropped her gaze to the ground. In a voice barely above a whisper, she asked, "Did he ask ye to come?"

"Why would he do that?"

Ùna looked up, her eyes wide. "So he didn't tell ye about me?"

Glynis was about to ask why in the name of all that was holy did Ùna find it surprising that her lover had not told his wife about her...but nothing was fitting. The lass's demeanor was all wrong.

"He said he wouldn't tell," Ùna said, dropping her gaze again. "I should have trusted him."

"Perhaps we both should have." *O shluagh, what have I done?* "Let me come in, and we'll have a talk."

Glynis was persistent, and before long, she got the whole tragic story out of the lass. As Ùna wept on her shoulder, Glynis felt a murderous rage against the man who called himself a father and committed unpardonable sins against this poor lass.

"Why did Alex not tell me?" she said under her breath.

"He kept telling me how good ye would be with me," Ùna said. "But I made him promise not to tell ye because I was afraid."

"You and Seamus will move into the castle today," Glynis said, as she rubbed Ùna's back. "Your father has been gone long enough, and with so many of our warriors off, it's safer for ye there."

Alex should have told her all about this. Ùna seemed so fragile, however, that Glynis could understand that he may have been afraid to add to her distress. And he had given his word to Ùna. As she was learning, he was a man who kept his promises.

But Glynis knew those were not the only reasons Alex had not told her. Her husband had wanted her to believe in him, to trust him without needing proof.

And she had failed him.

*   *   *

Three days later, Glynis and Sorcha were again on the beach below the castle. The wind was sharp enough to sting her face, but Glynis felt closer to Alex with just the sea between them.

"Your father will be home before long," Glynis said, putting her hand on Sorcha's shoulder. "All will be well with our family then."

Sorcha's face lit up like the sun breaking through the clouds. Although Glynis had never told Sorcha about her plan to leave Alex, the child had sensed the tension between them.

A short time later, Sorcha squatted beside a tide pool and, bouncing with excitement, waved Glynis over. Glynis was leaning over and squinting at the spiny sea urchin that Sorcha was pointing at when the castle bell began to ring.

Gong. Gong. Gong.

Glynis's heart went to her throat. The bell was reserved as a warning for danger. When Glynis looked up at the castle, several of the men were shouting at her from the wall and pointing out to sea. She turned and saw a ship coming around the headland into the bay.

"Run!" She grabbed Sorcha's hand, and they flew across the beach to the path.

Gong. Gong. Gong. The bell's toll echoed off the hills and vibrated through Glynis's bones. She had seen that ship before. But where?

As they scrambled up the steps carved into the rock beneath the castle, Glynis glanced at the horizon. Fear jolted through her limbs. There were three sails now.

"Faster, Sorcha!"

A guard ran out the gate to carry Sorcha the last few yards. As soon as they passed through it, others slammed the gate behind them. Inside, men were rushing to fetch weapons from the armory. Bessie was waiting for them and took Sorcha from the guard.

"Take her inside the keep," Glynis said to Bessie. Then she saw Tormond, the man Alex had left in command, hurrying toward her. He was a man of fifty with bulging biceps and iron-gray hair.

"Do ye recognize the ships?" Glynis asked him.

"Two of them belong to the MacDonald pirates," Tormond said.

So it was Hugh MacDonald's ship she had recognized from the time he had attacked Barra while Alex and Duncan were there.

"I have my suspicions about the third," Tormond said. "I was hoping ye could take a closer look at it."

"Me?"

Glynis could not imagine there was a ship she would know better than he, but she climbed up onto the wall with him. The three ships were much closer now. She held her hand up to shade her eyes—and gasped.

"Aye, I know that ship." Glynis could not mistake the distinctive red dragon painted on the sail. "It is Magnus Clanranald's."

CHAPTER 49

Alex says ye have both courage and good sense so I'll give ye the plain truth," Tormond said. "They'll have fifty men on each of those ships. It will be a miracle if we can hold the castle."

"God help us," Glynis said and crossed herself.

"Since we are clansman of the MacDonald pirates, I expect they'll let us live, though they'll strip the castle bare." Tormond paused. "But they don't respect women-folk. They've raped their own clanswomen before."

"I'll send the women into the hills," Glynis said.

"We'll hold them off as long as we can." Tormond touched her arm, an unexpectedly gentle gesture from the crusty man. "Alex warned us that Magnus is a special danger to ye, so take the child and hide yourself well."

Glynis found most of the women gathered in the hall with Bessie and Sorcha. She counted them and came up two short.

"Everyone follow Bessie out the back!" Glynis

shouted. "Ye must all run to the hills and hide as quick as ye can. Now hurry!"

"What about you, mistress?" Bessie asked.

"I'll follow as soon as I've found the others," Glynis said, pushing at Bessie's back. "Go! Go!"

Glynis ran from room to room shouting. She finally found the two missing serving women hiding under a table in the kitchen and sent them to join the others.

Oh, God, she had forgotten about Ùna and Seamus. She could not let the pirates get their hands on poor Ùna. Glynis picked up her skirts and ran out of the keep, hoping to find them in the stables. Arrows fell around her as she ran across the bailey yard.

Seamus saw her coming and stood in the open doorway to the stable, waving her inside. Fortunately, Ùna was right behind him.

"Ye must come with me out the back," Glynis said, grabbing Seamus's hand. "Now hurry!"

The small door that led to the fields was hanging open. As they ran toward it, Glynis looked up and saw men fighting on top of the wall.

She shoved Ùna and Seamus out ahead of her and screamed at them, "Run as fast as ye can and hide!"

When Glynis ducked through the doorway behind them, she saw the women and children she'd sent out earlier scattered over the hills running for their lives. But one woman had turned around and was running back toward the castle.

By the saints, it was Bessie! Glynis ran out to meet her in the field. When she reached Bessie, they were both gasping for air.

"Sorcha isn't with ye?" Bessie asked.

"I sent her with you." Fear ran down Glynis's limbs. "What happened?"

"I'm so sorry, mistress," Bessie said, tears rolling down her cheeks. "I was taking the other women, like ye told me to, but Sorcha wanted to come with you. I thought ye were just upstairs, and she couldn't miss ye. But after I came out, I started to worry, so I watched for ye."

"I'll find her," Glynis said. When Bessie hesitated, Glynis pushed her. "I can't be worrying about you as well, so go!"

When Glynis reentered the castle, she was met by the sounds of battle—the clank of swords on the top of the walls and the steady pounding of a battering ram reverberating against the front gate. *Bang, bang, bang.*

"Sorcha, Sorcha!" she called, as she ran through the keep, pausing to look behind doors and under benches and tables.

Where was the child? *God, please, I must find her.*

Glynis ran up the stairs. If Sorcha was hiding somewhere else in the castle, Glynis was losing precious time. The shouts of men fighting came in through the windows as she ran by them. The sounds were far too close—some of the attackers must have made it over the wall and into the castle yard.

"Sorcha! It's me, Glynis," she called out, as she searched the bedchamber she shared with Alex. She snatched her dirk from the side table, then dropped to her knees to look under the bed. Sorcha was not there. Time was running out. As she got up, her gaze fell on the chest at the bottom of the bed.

She rushed to it and threw open the lid—and saw Sorcha's shining head of hair. Her daughter was tucked into a ball with her head down, and she was shaking violently.

"Sorcha, love, I'm here," Glynis said, resting her hand on her back.

The child looked up at her with Alex's green eyes. Then she sprang to her feet and threw her arms around Glynis's neck. Glynis held her tight. *Praise God*, she'd found her.

Glynis jumped at the sound of wood cracking. It was followed by a roar of voices. She rushed to the window, carrying Sorcha with her. Ach, no. Pirates had broken through the gate and were pouring into the castle yard below.

It was too late to escape.

The scene below was chaotic, with men shouting and swinging their claymores. Glynis could not tell who was winning—or even who was on which side.

And then she saw Magnus, and the breath went out of her.

He stood alone in the middle of the yard, ignoring the fighting that was going on all around him. His claymore was drawn and ready, but he stood still, scanning the castle grounds with his black eyes. A chill went through her.

Magnus was looking for her.

When his gaze turned toward them, Glynis jumped back into the shadows with Sorcha. As he started toward the keep with a determined stride, Glynis forced back the urge to run blindly. They were trapped with nowhere to go.

She had to think. She must find a way to protect Sorcha.

"Ye found the best place in the whole castle to hide," Glynis said, running her hand over the girl's hair. "I'm going to put ye back inside the chest and cover ye up."

Sorcha shook her head and dug her fingers into Glynis's arms.

"Your da needs ye, so ye will do as I say and be a brave lass," Glynis said in a firm voice. "No matter what ye hear, ye must not come out until these bad men are gone."

Loud male voices sounded in the hall below.

"Ye *must* do this for me," Glynis said, holding Sorcha's face.

Glynis heard boots coming up the stairs and dropped the child into the chest. Her heart pounded in her ears as she flung off her cloak and laid it over Sorcha.

"I love ye," she whispered, and closed the lid an instant before the door burst open.

When she turned, Magnus Clanranald filled the doorway.

"Glynis, my dear wife," Magnus said, "ye have much to answer for."

CHAPTER 50

Damn, where are they?" Alex said, as he scanned another empty bay. After finding the MacNeils safe and
sound behind their castle walls, they had sailed into every
inlet and loch on Barra.

"We've been led on a merry chase." Duncan slammed
his fist against the rail. "I'd wager Hugh put the word out
that he intended to raid Barra to divert us from his true
plan."

"And he succeeded," Connor said with his gaze fixed
on the horizon. Someone who did not know him well
would not guess from his calm exterior that the chieftain
was as angry as Duncan. "We have little chance of finding
Hugh until he strikes again. He and his men could be hiding in any of a thousand inlets in the Western Isles."

"They could have gone to North Uist." Alex's heart
started pounding as the thought struck him. "While we
sailed south, along the west side of the islands, Hugh and
his men could have sailed north on the east side."

"Alex, they could be anywhere," Connor said.

"Hugh has gone to attack my home." The certainty of it settled over Alex like a cold, heavy fog. "We must go back at once."

Connor did not look convinced, but he signaled to the men to turn the ships north.

"It does make sense that Hugh would attack Dunfaileag Castle," Ian said. "It would be his way of thumbing his nose at ye, Connor. Your uncle knows ye have too many loyal men at Dunscaith now for him to take it, so instead he lures ye to the outer isles. And then, while he has us looking the other way, he takes the one castle we hold here."

Hugh would enjoy making Connor look the fool by raiding Dunfaileag Castle while Connor—and his castle keeper—were close by with two war galleys full of men.

"I left my wife and daughter unprotected," Alex said as he stared north at the endless sea.

He had feared all the wrong things: that he would not know how to keep Glynis happy, that he would hurt her, that she would steal his heart. All those things had come to pass, but they were nothing to this. In his vanity, it had never occurred to him that he would fail to protect his wife and daughter. That was the one duty a man had above all others.

Duncan came to stand beside him at the rail and rested a hand on Alex's shoulder. "Even if Hugh has gone to Dunfaileag, he doesn't have enough men to take the castle."

* * *

From the corner of her eye, Glynis saw her dirk on the bed, where she must have set it when she went to open the chest. When Magnus took a step toward her, she lunged and grabbed it. Then she jumped back, holding it in front of her with both hands.

"Stay away from me, Magnus," Glynis said. "I've knifed ye once, so ye know I have the nerve to do it."

"I was dead drunk at the time—and fool enough not to expect my own wife to take a blade to me," Magnus said. "I'm neither now. Put the blade down before ye get hurt."

If it were not for Sorcha, she would have fought him anyway, as hopeless as that would be. But Glynis did not want her daughter to hear her being hurt.

"I'll put it down," she said, "as soon as ye tell me why ye are here and what ye plan to do with me."

"Ye belong to me," he said. "I'm taking ye away from your false husband."

"But why? Ye never liked me."

"What has that to do with it?" Magnus said, his face turning an ugly red. "Ye are my wife, and ye don't leave unless I say so."

She had been desperate at the time, but Glynis could see now that she should have found a quieter way to leave him. Cutting Magnus with a blade and stealing a boat was as foolish as poking a mad bull with a stick.

"Alex will find me and bring me back," she said, trying to keep up her courage.

"No one has found us yet," Magnus said with a sneer. "Our camp is hidden away behind an island on Loch Eyenort on South Uist."

"Leave me here." Though she knew pleading never

worked with Magnus, she could not help herself. "Ye don't want me for your wife. Ye never did."

"Aye, I don't want ye—you're too dirty for me now," he said. "But I will enjoy watching the other men share ye."

Magnus would do it, too. He hated her that much.

"Put down the dirk, or you'll die in this room," Magnus said. "Make your choice quickly, for I'm sorely tempted by the notion of Alex MacDonald finding ye dead in a pool of blood on his bedchamber floor."

Alex finding her would be bad enough, but it would be Sorcha who saw her body first. Glynis let her dagger clatter to the floor.

"Ye weren't quick enough." Magnus took two long strides toward her and put his boot on her dropped blade. "I saw how Alex MacDonald looked at ye—at *my* wife— and I want him to come home to find his bed soaked with your blood."

The venom in Magnus's black eyes made Glynis's heart freeze in her chest.

"He might not recognize ye at first," Magnus said, fingering the blade in his hand. "But eventually, he'll know ye by the ring on your finger or a lock of your hair. And then he'll spend the rest of his nights imagining how your screams filled his bedchamber."

CHAPTER 51

Alex stared at the outline of Dunfaileag Castle in the distance. A thin reed of smoke rose from behind its walls. He tried to tell himself that there could be a dozen causes of fire in a castle—a turned lamp in the stable, a grease fire in the kitchen—all of them easily controlled and put out. And there were no ships in sight. Surely that was a good sign.

But as they sailed closer, he saw the broken boards of the gate. The pirates had been here and gone.

Duncan pushed the man at the rudder aside and guided their galley in with his sure hand, while Ian and Connor stood on either side of Alex without saying a word. And still, it seemed to take half his lifetime to sail the remaining distance to shore.

"Look," Ian said, pointing. "There are women on the beach."

Alex's knees felt wobbly with relief. Tormond must have had time to send the women to hide in the hills. Slowly, Alex let his breath out.

Before the boat scraped the bottom, he was over the side and running to shore. The women surrounded him. None seemed hurt, but they were all talking at once. "Pirates! Pirates were here!"

Neither Glynis nor Sorcha were with the women, so they must be up at the castle. Several of his men were coming down the rock steps. Tormond, who was in the lead, was limping and had a long gash down the side of his face and a bloody sleeve.

"Ye did well to get the women out," Alex greeted him. "Did we lose many men?"

"We fought as long as we could, but it was clear we couldn't hold the castle," Tormond said. "Once I thought the women were well away, I surrendered in the hope of saving as many men as I could."

"Ye did right." Alex started up the steps. He was anxious to see with his own eyes that his wife and daughter were safe.

Tormond followed behind him. "The pirates locked us in one of the storage rooms along the wall while they looted the castle."

Alex reached the top and saw the smashed gate. Getting oak boards to replace it would take a long time, but there were worse things. He stepped through the gaping hole into the castle yard.

"How many attackers were there?" Alex asked, but he was wondering why Glynis and Sorcha were not running out to meet him.

"There were three ships, each full of men."

"Three?" Alex asked, turning back to Tormond. "Who were they?"

"Two belonged to Hugh Dubh and his brothers," Tormond said. "The third was Magnus Clanranald's."

Magnus's? Alex felt as if the ground were sinking under him.

"Where is Glynis?" When Tormond did not answer right away, Alex grabbed him by his torn shirt and shook him. "Where is my wife?"

"We've searched everywhere." Tormond could not meet Alex's eyes. "But we couldn't find her—or your daughter."

*   *   *

Glynis's spirits sank lower the farther they sailed into Loch Eyenort. God protect her, for it could be weeks before Alex found her. Loch Eyenort had so many bays and islands that even if Alex came here on his search, he could easily miss her.

Glynis rubbed the blood on her forehead with her sleeve. At least she was not on the same boat as Magnus.

"If ye leave that cut alone, it might stop bleeding."

Glynis looked up to find Hugh Dubh standing over her. Though Hugh's weathered face made him look older than his thirty-odd years, he had the powerful build of a man in his prime.

"If ye are worried I might die on ye," Glynis snapped, "then ye should give me something to bind this wound."

All she'd suffered was a nick—and a long moment of terror in which she believed she would die at Magnus's hands. Hugh had pulled Magnus off of her just in time. In the argument that ensued between the two men, Hugh had taken the position that a live hostage was of greater value than a dead one.

"Ye could show a wee bit of appreciation after I saved your life," Hugh said, giving her what he must have believed was a charming smile.

"Ye didn't do it for me," she said. "Ye did it for the gold my husband and father will give ye for my return."

"I'll be getting more than gold for ye, lass," Hugh said, as he leaned back against the rail and folded his arms across his broad chest.

Hugh was baiting her. Glynis knew it, and yet she had to ask. "What else?"

"I want vengeance, just as Magnus does," Hugh said. "But Magnus is a simple man, sorely lacking in patience. Unlike him, I'll enjoy the game, get my revenge on my nephew, and end up with the gold as well."

Hugh was vain. If she could prick his pride, he might tell her what this game was.

"Ye believe ye can get the better of Connor?" Glynis asked. "They say he is verra clever."

"He is that, but Connor also has a great weakness." Hugh nodded to himself as he looked off into the distance. "Connor would give his life without hesitation for any one of those three—Alex, Ian, or Duncan."

That was true of each of the four men. Glynis wondered how Hugh intended to use Connor's loyalty against him.

"Everyone in the isles knew of Alex's vow never to wed," Hugh said. "So when I heard he'd taken a bride, I knew it could only be because Alex had found a woman he simply had to have or die."

"It wasn't like that." Glynis said, giving him a sideways glance. "Alex needed a mother for his daughter, and I was close at hand."

Hugh barked out a laugh. "'Tis usually men who are the fools."

Glynis had been a fool, but she wasn't admitting it to Hugh. "The opinion of a thieving pirate means less than nothing to me."

"Alex must like a sharp tongue." Hugh was drumming his fingers on the rail, jarring her nerves. "I believe he'll do anything to get ye back. And my nephew Connor would do anything for Alex."

"Connor is a good man," Glynis said. "I don't see how the two of ye can share the same blood."

"I confess I find it surprising myself," Hugh said, scratching his beard. "Loyalty is a flaw in a Highland chief—and it will cost Connor his life."

Glynis turned to face Hugh. "His life?"

"Aye." Hugh had the golden eyes of a wolf. "And you, lass, are the bait in my trap. The four of them will come together for ye, and I'll be waiting."

Hugh had planned it all along. He had lured Connor and the others to the outer isles for the very purpose of trapping them.

"This is the perfect place." Hugh pointed to a small island in the loch as they sailed into the narrow channel between it and the shore. "I'll have half my men hidden on the island, there, across from my camp. We'll have two chains below the water between the island and the shore that we'll pull up to trap their boat in the middle so they can't escape."

"They're keen warriors—they'll sense trouble," she said, hoping it was true.

"They'll sail right into the trap when they see ye tied to a log on the beach, half naked," Hugh said, smiling to himself. "Ach, that's sure to drive Alex blind with rage."

"You've wasted your time. Alex won't come for me," she said, trying her best to keep her voice steady. "Ye know his reputation. He's tired of me already."

"If that's the case, I'll be so disappointed that I'll give ye to Magnus—after my brothers have a turn." Hugh laughed. "But then, I'd planned to do that in the end anyway."

* * *

The words were important. In the blackness, Sorcha practiced them over and over in her head so she would not forget them. Then she whispered them, testing the sounds with her mouth.

She had almost forgotten the dark, dirty room with the big mice where her father found her. But the memory came back to her in this small, dark place and threatened to push the words out of her head again. She breathed in the smell of her mother in the clothes that surrounded her.

She heard voices, but they were not her father's, so she covered her ears and mouthed the words until the voices went away. Still, the pounding of her heart made it hard to hear the words.

But she would be strong like the warrior queen, Scáthach.

She would be strong like her mother.

CHAPTER 52

Your wife was taking the women out the back gate," Tormond said. "I thought she was safe with the others."

"Glynis is probably still hiding in the fields," Ian said.

Tormond shook his head. "The woman Bessie said that Sorcha disappeared, and the mistress went back into the castle to find her."

Nay. It can't be that I've lost them both. As Alex's gaze traveled over the bailey yard, he saw dead and injured men—but no women or children. He tried to think. Where could they be?

"We searched everywhere," Tormond said.

"Then look again!" Alex ran to open storeroom doors along the wall. He found sacks of grain torn open, and the wine and ale barrels were all gone.

"Glynis! Sorcha!" he called again and again as he searched. He could not let himself consider that he might be looking for their bodies.

Mary, Mother of God, protect them. He made promises

to God as he searched for them. *Take me—just keep them safe.*

Alex's hands shook as he entered the keep. The weapons on the walls were gone. Tables were overturned. The hall was eerily quiet, except for the crockery crunching under his feet.

"Glynis! Sorcha!" The answering silence closed in on him.

His boots echoed on the stone steps as he climbed the stairs to the bedchambers above. Would he find them dead? His wife's body, broken and used by the foul men who had destroyed their home? Alex did not think he was strong enough for that, but he kept walking.

When he pushed their bedchamber door, it creaked open slowly, revealing the room inch by inch. In contrast to the rest of the keep, the bedchamber was neat and tidy. It looked as if Glynis had just stepped out.

Except for her dirk lying in the middle of the floor.

Alex sank to his knees and picked it up. There was no blood on it, praise God. But if Glynis and Sorcha were not here, that meant the pirates and Magnus had taken them—and their purpose could only be evil. Alex had to find his wife and daughter before they were harmed, but he did not know where to look.

Alex pounded the floor with his fists. "Where did they take ye?" he shouted. "Where? Where?"

A *creak* right next to him brought him upright. When he saw his wee daughter standing in the chest holding the top up, Alex swept her up into his arms. He ran his hands over her to assure himself the fairies were not playing tricks on his eyes, and then he held her tightly against him. *Sweet Jesus and all the angels, thank ye.*

Alex thought he heard a small voice in his ear, saying, "Aye."

He leaned back. "Was that you, Sorcha?"

She looked at him with her clear eyes and nodded. In the midst of a day of dread and despair, the miracle of hearing his daughter's sweet voice for the first time over-whelmed him.

"What was that ye said, *mo chroí*?" Alex asked, as he brushed her hair back with his fingers.

"Eye." He had thought she was saying *aye* before, but this time when she said the word she rested the point of her finger next to her eye.

"Did something happen to your eye?" he asked.

"That's where the bad man took Mother."

His daughter spoke in perfect Gaelic, but Alex had no idea what she meant.

"Eye snort," Sorcha said. "That's where the bad man said he was taking her."

Eye snort? What in the name of heaven was...

"Eyenort Loch?" he asked. "On South Uist?"

"South Uist," Sorcha repeated, and nodded.

Alex gave her a big kiss on her forehead. "What a blessing ye are."

"Mother called him Magnus," Sorcha said. "She doesn't like him."

"That's verra helpful, little one," Alex said, keeping his voice calm with an effort. "Do ye remember anything else?"

"Another bad man came, and they argued."

"Did ye hear the second man's name?"

Sorcha gave him a solemn nod. "Hugh."

"Ye did verra, verra well," Alex said as he started down

the stairs with her. "Now I must leave ye with Bessie while I go fetch your mother."

"Bring her home," Sorcha said, hugging his neck.

"I will."

Alex had just had one miracle. And now he needed another.

CHAPTER 53

I'll let your husband stew for a few days," Hugh said, as he tied her wrists to the mast. "I need my bait live 'til then, so I'm leaving a man here to guard ye from Magnus. Ye made an enemy with that one, lass, though I can't say I blame ye for sticking a blade in him. Magnus is an arse."

"*Aithníonn ciaróg ciaróg eile,*" Glynis said. A beetle recognizes another beetle.

Hugh hit her so hard across the face that Glynis saw stars and swayed on her feet.

"Mind that tongue of yours if ye want to keep it," he said.

She had been foolish to goad him—her stepmother always told her that she did not know when to be quiet. Because Hugh had protected her from Magnus, she'd relaxed her guard around him. She'd do well to remember that Hugh was a ruthless man who killed innocents and stole food from the mouths of children.

"If Magnus sets foot on my boat against my orders, kill him," Hugh said to the man with him. "I could use another boat."

While Hugh hoisted himself over the side of the galley, Glynis eyed her guard. He was a huge, muscular man with unkempt hair, a scarred face, and only one ear. When the guard turned, the look he gave her sent alarm racing through her veins. Glynis felt helpless to defend herself, tied like a dog to the mast. She tugged at the ropes, but they held fast.

* * *

A heavy fog rolled in over the loch as evening turned to night. Although Alex could not see the shore, the raucous laughter of the pirates' camp carried clearly across the still water. Hugh had grown lax.

Behind the laugher, Alex heard the clank of cups and the snap of the fires. Hugh's and Magnus's men would outnumber them, but they had surprise on their side. Judging from the sounds, Hugh's men were well into their cups, celebrating with Alex's whiskey and ale.

Alex, Duncan, Ian, and Connor stood at the front of his galley and would go first. While the others were fine warriors, the four of them had long years of fighting together. And they were the best.

Alex nodded to the others, and the four of them dropped over the side of the boat with a soft splash. He paused to listen, but the pirates carried on as before. As soon as he gave a low dove call, the other men began dropping into the water behind them. They moved silently through the chest-high water, holding their shields and claymores over their heads. As he neared shore, Alex could see the glow of campfires through the thick fog.

He and Connor hid in the brush near the shore, while Duncan and Ian led most of the men behind the encampment. Duncan and Ian's group would attack from behind so the pirates could not escape inland. Their plan was to trap the pirates between the devil and the deep blue sea.

Before giving the signal, Alex and Connor's task was to make certain Glynis and any other hostages would not be caught in the middle of the attack. They crawled forward on their bellies until they were close enough to see the faces of the men gathered around the fires. Alex saw Hugh and Connor's other uncles, Angus and Torquil.

But he did not see Magnus. Or Glynis.

Alex's blood went cold as he saw one man come out of a tent that had been set up and another go in. Either that was where the whiskey was—or they were taking turns with a woman. When Alex heard a woman cry out, he was off the ground before Connor grabbed his arm to stop him.

No, Connor mouthed and shook his head. He nodded in the direction Duncan had gone, to tell him that Duncan was closer and would deal with it. The blood pounded in Alex's head. In his mind's eye, Alex could see Duncan slipping into the back of the tent and then holding his hand over the man's mouth to keep him quiet while he slit his throat.

The man did not come out of the tent. Aye, the four of them knew each other very well.

It was not Glynis that he had heard cry out. Alex scanned the rest of the camp, but he did not see her or any other prisoners who would be in harm's way when they attacked. But where was Glynis? Had she also been in the tent, raped by a dozen men?

Or was she dead?

Alex forced himself to focus on the battle ahead. When Connor touched his arm, Alex made another low bird call to alert the men with Ian and Duncan that it was time. An instant later, he and Connor rose to their feet, shouting the MacDonald battle cry, "*Fraoch!*"

Their men across the fire echoed their ferocious cry. *Fraoch! Fraoch! Fraoch!*

Alex channeled his pent-up rage and his fear for his wife into his blade, slicing through one man after another. Battle fever burned in his veins like blue fire. He whirled and swung like a madman, until Duncan's voice penetrated through the battle sounds around him.

"Connor needs help!" Duncan shouted from across the fire.

Alex turned and saw that Hugh and several of his men were closing in on Connor. Alex leaped to his defense, and the two fought back to back, as they often did. Despite everything, Alex began to enjoy himself. He was made for this. No one could match the pair of them as fighters—except perhaps Duncan and Ian.

Hugh was a strong and cagy fighter, but he was always willing to risk the lives of his men before his own. When it was clear that Alex and Connor were winning the fight, Hugh slipped away into the darkness.

"I'll get Hugh," Connor shouted. "Angus is running for their boats—catch him before he escapes."

Through the fog, Alex could just make out the back of a man running hard for the loch. Alex charged after him and brought him down to the ground, crashing on top of him with a thud.

"Where is she?" Alex shouted, as he sat on Angus's chest with his dirk against the man's throat. When Angus did not answer quickly enough, Alex pressed the blade deeper, drawing a line of blood. Enunciating each word, he said, "Where is my wife?"

"On the boat," Angus gasped.

"Which boat?"

"Hugh's," Angus said. "He put her there to keep her away from Magnus."

"If I find ye laid a finger on her, Angus," Alex said between clenched teeth, "I'll come back and gut ye."

Alex had no time to tie Angus so he picked up the nearest rock and hit him on the head.

* * *

Glynis's wrists were raw from struggling to get the ropes off, but she kept at it. She glanced over her shoulder at her surly keeper, wondering if there was a way she could get his dirk off him. He had an oil lamp beside him, but the fog was so thick that she could see little more than his dim outline, sitting with his legs propped up on the side of the boat.

Somehow, she must get free and warn Alex and the others before they fell into Hugh's trap. She had not seen a village or even a cottage when they were sailing to the camp. Once she escaped, she would have a long way to travel before she found someone to help her, but she would walk to hell and back if she had to.

Suddenly, there were shouts and the sounds of fighting

on the beach. Glynis could not see what was happening through the fog and darkness, but she had not heard a boat arrive. It didn't surprise her that the pirates had started fighting among themselves. Hugh and Magnus were uneasy allies. Neither trusted the other, and with good reason.

"Arrgh..."

The horrible gagging sound was close. Was that her guard? Glynis leaned forward as far as the rope would let her and squinted into the darkness at the far end of the boat.

The figure of a man slowly emerged from the night fog, carrying his long claymore blade before him. Even before she could see his face, she knew who it was.

She was alone on the boat with Magnus.

* * *

The others were still caught up in the battle, and Alex could not wait for them. He ran through the dense fog, sucking the heavy air deep into his lungs. When he reached the edge of the loch, he saw a wavering light over the water.

God, no! One of the boats was aflame.

Alex splashed into the water. The three pirate boats loomed out of the fog like ghost ships, dimly lit by the glow of fire on the middle ship. Alex could just make out the carved serpent head affixed to its bow. It was Hugh's ship that was burning.

He clamped his dirk between his teeth and swam the rest of the way to the boat. He found a rope hanging over the side near the burning bow. As he hauled himself up, he strained to listen, but he could hear nothing over the crackle of flames and the sounds from the ongoing battle on shore. When he rolled over the side into the boat, he fell onto something soft.

A body. His mind whirled at the possibilities, and a cold fear settled in his belly. Magnus must have killed the guard. Through the flames, he caught glimpses of the back of a man. Then he heard a deep, angry voice. Magnus's voice.

"Ye made a fool of me before all my clan," Magnus said. "That is why they took the chieftainship from me. They lost respect for me because of you."

"They took the chieftainship from ye because ye were cruel to your own people."

Ach, that was his wife—arguing with a vicious man with a blade in his hand.

God help him, Magnus was far too close to her. Alex moved forward cautiously, knowing he would have but one chance. If Magnus heard him coming, he could kill Glynis before Alex could reach her.

"All my troubles started with you," Magnus said, waving his blade in the air like a madman. Flames were licking at his feet, but he was so enraged he didn't seem to notice. "I should have dragged ye back by your hair and fooked ye til I got ye with child."

Alex crept forward, his own rage barely under control.

"Everyone was already laughing at me because of what ye did," Magnus said. "So when I heard ye didn't leave Shaggy's with your father, I went looking for ye. I couldn't let my wife run off with another man."

"I'm no your wife!" Glynis said.

Alex sensed Magnus was about to attack her. The fire

was so hot now that sweat rolled down his face as he crept closer. He must take his chance soon.

"It was while I chasing after ye that they took the chieftainship from me," Magnus shouted. "They never would have had the ballocks to do it if I'd been there. Because of you, they took everything from me!"

When Magnus swung his arm back, Alex was already running through the flames.

* * *

"Glynis!"

Everything seemed to happen at once: Glynis heard Alex's voice shouting her name; a dirk flew through the air and landed with a *thunk* above her head; and Magnus flung his arms out and arched back, howling in pain.

Through the flames, she saw Alex charging across the boat toward them with his hair flying out behind him. *All the saints be praised!* He looked like one of the legendary heroes of his tales.

Magnus, a famed warrior himself, recovered in time to block Alex's sword, though his arms shook and his knees bent with the effort. When he turned, she saw the dirk sticking out of his shoulder. Remembering the one above her head, Glynis reached up and worked it out of the wood. Turning the blade toward her, she sawed awkwardly against the ropes holding her wrists. It seemed to take forever, but at last she cut through them.

Glynis backed out of the way as the men fought in the cramped space, knocking over barrels of ale and sending captured pigs squealing. Their swords clanked and scraped the wood of the boat as flames rose higher around

them. As the heat seared her face, Glynis feared they
would all be consumed in the blaze.

Her hands shook, but she held the dirk in front of her,
looking for a chance to stick it into Magnus. But the
two men were moving too quickly for her to be sure she
wouldn't strike Alex by mistake. And then Magnus was
charging straight at her through the flames, his face con-
torted with black rage. Just before he reached her, Alex
jerked him backward by the back of his shirt.

Pain seared Glynis's leg. When she looked down, her
skirts were on fire. She leaned over and beat at the flames
with her hands. But her hair swung down over her shoulders. When it caught on fire, she shrieked.

Alex appeared out of the flames at a full run.

The next Glynis knew they were flying through the air.
They hit the water hard, knocking the breath out of her.
The last sound she heard as they plunged beneath the sur-
face was the sizzle of flames meeting the water.

She swallowed water and came up coughing. Water
streamed down her face, and the charred smell of burned
hair filled her nose as Alex carried her to shore. She
rested her cheek against his chest and listened to the reassuring sound of his thundering heart.

"*Mo chroí*, did he hurt ye?" he asked. "Are ye all
right?"

"I am now."

Alex came to a halt. "I love ye so much. I couldn't bear
it if I lost ye."

She let the words wash over her. Alex loved her.

"You'll never lose me," she said. "Never."

CHAPTER 54

No more whiskey!" Glynis pushed away the cup Alex held to her mouth.

Duncan, Ian, and Connor were all hovering over her as well, like a bunch of mother hens.

"A burn is the worst kind of wound," Alex said. "No need to be brave now."

She'd let the men ply her with whiskey—the man's cure for everything—last night, but she wanted to arrive home sober, for heaven's sake.

"My leg barely pains me at all now," Glynis said, though it hurt like the devil. "I won't have our daughter see me stumbling off the boat."

"Ye won't stumble because ye won't be walking," Alex said, in a tone that told her there would be no arguing the point.

"Ye have quite a gathering of folks to welcome ye home," Ian said.

Glynis ignored her husband's protests and stood. It

looked as if everyone from the castle and the nearby cottages had come down to the beach to greet them. She smiled up at Alex and squeezed his hand.

When Alex carried her off the boat, the people waiting on the shore cheered—which very nearly made her weep. Alex set her on her feet as Sorcha ran up. Glynis dropped to one knee on the sand and held out her arms to her daughter.

"Mother," Sorcha said, as she threw her arms around Glynis's neck. "I knew da would bring ye home."

As she held Sorcha tightly against her, Glynis did shed a tear now. She would always remember this moment when she heard her daughter's voice for the first time, calling her Mother.

"Your mother has a battle wound that proves how brave she is," Alex said, as he helped Glynis to her feet again. He rested his hand on Sorcha's head. "Wait til ye see it—it's a beauty."

Glynis laughed because she knew he meant it.

"We'll bid ye farewell now and join our men on the other ship," Connor said.

"Ye can't stay?" Glynis asked, looking from Connor to Ian and Duncan.

"We must deliver Angus and Torquil to the new Clanranald chieftain for their punishment," Connor said. "The Clanranalds, at least, will have justice."

"I know ye feel badly about Hugh escaping again." Alex clasped Connor's shoulder. "But I appreciate what ye did."

When Alex had carried her to the shore from the burning ship, they had met Connor running hell-bent toward the loch. They learned later that Connor had been fighting one-on-one with Hugh, when Hugh told him that Glynis was on the flaming ship.

"Ach, ye didn't need my help," Connor said.

"But ye thought I did," Alex said. "Ye left Hugh to help me save my wife."

"You'd do the same for me." Connor paused and then gave him a crooked smile. "If I had a wife."

"It's time ye did," Alex said. "Shall I make ye a list?"

The other men laughed so hard that Glynis suspected she was missing part of the joke.

"No need for that yet," Ian said, and elbowed Duncan hard in the ribs. "We have it all planned out, and Duncan's next."

"Don't believe it," Duncan said in Glynis's ear when he leaned down to kiss her cheek good-bye.

"All the same," she whispered back, "I'd advise ye not to wager that galley ye stole from Shaggy."

* * *

Alex was relieved to have his wife home. He hoped she would stay.

Although Glynis had told him she would never leave him, she'd been a breath away from being burned alive the moment before. As a warrior, he'd often heard men make pledges when they looked death in the eye that were soon forgotten once the danger was passed.

He wanted to hear Glynis say it again.

On the ship, they'd had no opportunity to speak alone. As soon as Connor and the others set sail, Alex turned, intending to lift Glynis in his arms and carry her to the castle. But he froze in place when he saw Úna running straight toward him down the beach. Ach, Glynis was sure to think the worst. But when Ùna reached them, she took Glynis's hands.

Alex's heart started to beat once more. Apparently, the two had met and talked in his absence.

"I'm so glad you're safe," Ùna said to Glynis.

"Do ye see Peiter there?" Glynis said, nodding in the direction of the young fisherman, who, as usual, was looking at Ùna with calf eyes.

"Aye," Ùna said, her cheeks going pink.

"I know you're not ready. But when ye are, Peiter is a good man ye can trust." Glynis put her arm through Alex's and leaned into him. "Like my husband."

Alex's chest swelled, even as he was amused that his wife was setting the household to rights before they had even left the beach.

"She needs her rest," Alex said, waving off the other well-wishers.

"I'm well," Glynis said, as carried her to the castle.

"I want ye alone," Alex said, giving her a wink. "I have something to give ye."

"Is this the sort of gift that usually involves taking our clothes off?" she asked, waggling her eyebrows at him.

He laughed. "I do believe ye are feeling better, wife."

Once he had her upstairs in their chamber, he set her on the bed and tucked pillows behind her back and another under her injured leg.

"I spoke with your father when we stopped on Barra looking for Hugh and the others," Alex said, as he sat on the edge of the bed to have a look at her leg. The burn was healing well, praise God. "I believe I've convinced him to make his peace with Colin Campbell and submit to the Crown."

"Oh, that is a good present," Glynis said, leaning forward to touch her fingers to his cheek.

"That's not your present," he said, as he reached into his leather pouch. "We wed so quickly that I didn't have time to find a ring, so I asked Ilysa to help me. She found someone to make what I wanted, and Duncan brought it with him."

Alex took her hand and slipped the silver ring on her finger.

"Oh, Alex, it's lovely!" she said. "Are those two herons carved on it?"

"Aye," he said. "Herons mate for life, and that's what I want."

She looked up at him with wet eyes. "I'm sorry I didn't trust ye. I'll never make that mistake again."

"Don't ever leave me," he said, gathering her in his arms, "because I love ye *go síoraí*." Forever. It was still hard for him to say it, though it had been true for a long time.

When he released her, she held out her hand and smiled as she examined the ring again.

"I suspect Ilysa and Teàrlag put all sorts of magical charms on it," he said.

"Ye don't need magic charms to keep me." Glynis took his hands and looked straight at him with her dead-serious gray eyes. "Ye know how stubborn I am. Ye couldn't be rid of me now if ye tried."

Alex felt himself relax. Glynis was the most determined woman he'd ever known, and she'd decided to keep him.

Her expression softened, and she said, "We'll make a home for our children that's filled with love, *mo shíorghrá*." My eternal love.

Alex took his wife's face in his hands and kissed her long and slow.

EPILOGUE

I missed ye," Alex said, kissing his wife's cheek again as she walked up with him from the beach. He had just returned from a meeting with Connor and the others at Dunscaith.

"Ye shouldn't have sailed across the Minch to Skye this time of year," she scolded.

"I have Saint Michael to protect me," he said, placing his hand on his chest where the medallion rested. "Besides, it's been a mild winter."

He wrapped his plaid more tightly around Glynis's shoulders. Judging from the sharp wind coming off the water, they were in for a change in weather.

"There's a wee bit of commotion in the hall," Glynis warned him. "So tell me the news now, before we go in."

"Angus and Torquil are dead," Alex said. "The Clanranald chieftain had Angus tied in a sack and dropped at sea, straight off, since he was the one who offended their clanswoman."

"What about Torquil?"

"He was kept prisoner for a time, but then he bragged about how fast he could run. When they let him run on the beach to prove it, he tried to flee. He was shot in the leg with an arrow."

"He died from that?"

"Well...," Alex said, "they decided the wound was incurable and put him to death."

"Hmmph. And how is Connor?"

"Hugh has vowed to take bloody vengeance for his brothers' deaths," Alex said. "And if that is no enough, there's a rumor floating about that the MacLeods and the Macleans have secretly advised the Crown that they are willing to switch sides in the rebellion—for a price."

"For a price?"

"Aye, and the price is usually someone else's lands," Alex said. "And then, Connor's heard that his sister Moira is being treated poorly by her husband."

"Ach, that's terrible," Glynis said. "What will he do?"

"He's sent Duncan to Ireland to find out if it's true," Alex said, giving her a sideways glance.

"That's a lot to ask of Duncan," Glynis said.

"I haven't told ye the most startling news," Alex said, still not believing it himself. "My parents are living together—and they're acting like a pair of lovebirds."

Glynis laughed and squeezed his arm as they climbed the steps to the keep.

"They still think of no one but themselves, but they're more pleasant to be around."

"I'm glad ye made it home in time to celebrate Saint Brigid's Day," Glynis said, as he opened the door for her.

Alex had no idea it was Saint Brigid's Day.

When they entered the hall, he saw Sorcha with the group of women and children at the long table. They had made the traditional figurine of the saint from sheaves of grain and were in the midst of decorating it with ribbons and shells.

"Da!" Sorcha ran to greet him and tugged at his hand. "Come see Saint Bridget."

Alex dutifully admired the doll in all her finery.

"Come, children," his wife said, "and I'll tell ye about Saint Bridget's Day."

As the children gathered around her by the glowing hearth, Glynis rested her hand on her swollen belly and smiled at him. They were both so happy about this baby.

"Saint Bridget's Day comes at a time when the sheep get their milk in preparation for the birthing of new lambs," she told the children. "Although winter is not over, we see the first glimmer of spring. We celebrate new life, the reawakening of the land, and our hope for good fishing after the stormy season. No spinning or other work involving a wheel is permitted because the wheel of time is turning between the seasons."

Alex chuckled to himself. Like most Highland feast days, this was a pagan celebration wrapped in the guise of a Christian saint.

"The fishermen gathered seaweed for fertilizing, while we women spent the day cleaning," Glynis continued. "And then we placed live limpets outside the four corners of our clean houses to foster good fishing."

Glynis met his eyes over the children's heads and gave him another warm smile. "Saint Bridget's Day is the day we celebrate home, hearth, and family."

This was the kind of home that Alex had dreamed of

when he was a child. He sighed with contentment as he glanced at the faces of the folk who had gathered in the old keep that Glynis had made into a home. He nodded at Tormond, who—if he wasn't mistaken—had his hand on Bessie's leg beneath the table.

Glynis sent Sorcha to the door to call out, "Brigid, come in."

"Welcome, Brigid," the other women chanted. "Your bed is ready."

Glynis took the doll from the table, and everyone gathered around as she laid it in a bed of rushes by the hearth.

"This is called Brigid's wand," she explained, as she tucked a smooth, straight birch stick in with the doll. "The saint uses the wand to bring earth back to life."

"I think I know what the stick is supposed to represent," Alex whispered in her ear.

She gave him a mock-severe look and then handed Ùna a bowl of water and a bowl of salt. "Set them outside for the saint to bless. We'll use them all year in medicines, for Saint Brigid's Day is also a time of healing."

Alex knew she chose Ùna for the task because the lass had a special need for healing.

"These will bring healing and protection to each of us in the months ahead," Glynis said, as she cut a strip of cloth for every member of the household to leave outside the door for Saint Brigid to bless.

Alex took his to please her, though Glynis had already healed his wounds.

The last ritual of the night, after the feast, was for the head of the household to smother the fire and rake the ashes smooth. In the morning, they would look for signs of the saint's visit in the ashes. Alex made quick work of the task, for it was the last thing between him and taking his wife upstairs to bed.

Later that night as he lay with her in his arms, Alex thought of his blessings and the many changes wrought in his life over the past months. As Teàrlag predicted, Glynis had fulfilled his deepest desires.

"Ye gave me everything I longed for but didn't believe I deserved," he told her. "And ye made me a far better man than I thought I could be."

"I look forward to every day with ye," she said, as she rested her palm over his heart. "Ye make me so happy."

He did make her happy. But then, Glynis had surprised him from the start.

HISTORICAL NOTE

One of the joys of doing research for a historical novel is discovering real-life characters and events that no one would believe if you made them up. Happily, sixteenth-century Scotland is a treasure trove of such finds, and I included a number of them in this book. After five hundred years, many details are unavailable or disputed, and the line between historical fact and legend blurs. This, of course, gives a fiction writer room for imagination.

Shaggy Maclean and Catherine Campbell did marry. The incident with the tidal rock, including Shaggy's subsequent visit to the Campbells, is a well-known tale, though these events occurred a few years later than I make them. In 1523, Shaggy was murdered in Edinburgh, probably dirked in bed. It was generally believed that John Campbell, Thane of Cawdor, was responsible.

John Campbell's wife, Muriel, is also a real historical figure. According to the stories, Muriel was stolen by the Campbells from outside Cawdor Castle when she was

very young, was raised in the Campbell chieftain's household, was married to John at twelve, and had a happy
marriage. I was lucky enough to visit Cawdor Castle and
see a carved mantel commemorating their marriage.

James IV's death in the Battle of Flodden led to a long
minority rule by his son, which fostered factional fights
for power. Under the dead king's will, Margaret Tudor,
who was his widow and also Henry VIII's sister, ini-
tially served as regent. The Douglas chieftain, who makes
an appearance in *The Guardian* and is mentioned in this
book, became her lover in a bid to control the Crown.
Douglas overplayed his hand, however, when he married
her. As a result, Margaret Tudor lost the regency. While
Margaret took refuge in England, Douglas helped himself to her funds and took up with another woman. His
marriage never recovered, but for three years, he held his
teenage stepson, James V, as a virtual prisoner and ruled
on his behalf.

Antoine D'Arcy, a French nobleman known as the
White Knight, was a real person who came to Scotland
to assist the next regent, the Duke of Albany. Apparently,
D'Arcy had visited Scotland earlier to participate in
jousting tournaments. As with the other historical figures,
I filled in his personality to suit my story.

My character Connor's half uncles are loosely based
on the real sons of Hugh, the first MacDonald of Sleat
chieftain. Because Hugh named two of his sons Donald
and two Angus, I changed most of their names to reduce
confusion. My version of how two of these men were captured is wholly fictional, but the manner of their deaths is
consistent with stories told about them.

I based Magnus Clanranald on a Clanranald chieftain

named Dougal. The real Clanranald chieftain was actually assassinated by members of his own clan, and his
sons were excluded from the succession to the chieftainship.

I adjusted travel times as well as the dates of some
events to suit my story. Except for Dunfaileag, all of the
castles mentioned in this book existed, though some are
in ruins now. There is a Loch Eynort on South Uist, but I
have no idea if it has secret bays and inlets. I hope I can
visit it one day and find out.

Look for the third book in
this sizzling series featuring
fearless Highlanders!

Please turn this page
for a preview of

THE WARRIOR

Available in November 2012

CHAPTER 1

Duncan MacDonald could defeat any warrior in the castle—and yet, he was powerless against his chieftain's seventeen-year-old daughter.

"As soon as my father leaves the hall," Moira whispered, leaning close enough to make him light-headed, "I'll meet ye outside by the ash tree."

Duncan should refuse her, but he may as well try to stop his heart from beating.

"I've told ye not to speak to me here," he said, glancing about the long room filled with their clansmen and the chieftain's guests from Ireland. "Someone might notice."

When Moira turned to look straight at him with her midnight-blue eyes, Duncan felt as if a fist slammed into his chest. That had happened the first time she looked at him—*really* looked at him—and every time since.

"Why would anyone take notice if I speak with my brother Connor's best friend?" she asked.

Perhaps because she had ignored him the first seventeen years of her life? It was still a mystery to him how that had changed.

"Go now—Ragnall is watching us," he said when he felt her older brother's eyes on him. Unlike Moira and Connor, Ragnall took after his father—he was short-tempered, fair-haired, and built like a bull. He was also the only warrior in the clan Duncan was not certain he could defeat at arms.

"I won't go until ye say you'll meet me later." Moira folded her arms, but amusement quirked up the corners of her full lips, reminding Duncan that this was a game to her.

But if her father learned that Duncan was sneaking off with his only daughter, he'd murder him on the spot. Duncan turned and left the hall without bothering to answer—Moira knew he'd be there.

As he waited for her in the dark, he listened to the soft lap of the sea on the shore. There was no mist on the Misty Isle of Skye tonight, and Dunscaith Castle was beautiful, ablaze with torchlight against the clear night sky. He had grown up in the castle and seen this sight a thousand times—but Duncan took nothing for granted.

His mother had served as nursemaid to the chieftain's children, and he and Connor had been best friends since the cradle. From the time they could lift wooden swords, the two of them and Connor's cousins, Alex and Ian, were trained in the art of war. When they weren't practicing with their weapons, they were off looking for adventure—or trouble—and they usually found it.

Moira had always been apart, a coddled princess dressed in finery. Duncan had little to do with the lovely, wee creature whose laughter often filled the castle.

Duncan heard the rustle of silk skirts and saw Moira running toward him. Even in the dark and covered head to toe in a cloak, he could pick her out of a thousand women. Though she couldn't possibly see what was in her path, Moira ran headlong, expecting no impediment. No stone tripped her, for even the fairies favored this lass.

When Moira threw her arms around his neck, Duncan closed his eyes and lost himself in her womanly softness. He breathed in the scent of her hair, and it was like lying in a field of wildflowers.

"It's been two whole days," she said. "I missed ye so much."

Duncan was amazed at how unguarded Moira was. The lass said whatever came into her head, with no caution, no fear of rejection. But then, who would refuse her?

The chieftain had sent Duncan to attend university in the Lowlands with Connor and Connor's cousins, and he'd learned about Helen of Troy there. Moira had a face like that—the kind that could start a clan war. And worse for his jealous heart, she had lush curves and an innate sensuality that made every man want her.

But for Duncan, Moira was the bright spark in his world.

Moira pulled him down into a deep kiss that sent him reeling. Before he knew it, his hands were roaming over the feminine dips and swells of her body, and she was moaning into his mouth. They were in danger of dropping to the grass at their feet, where anyone could happen upon them, so he broke the kiss. One of them had to keep their head—and it wouldn't be Moira.

"Not here," he said, though he knew damned well what they would do if they went to the cave. Anticipation caused every fiber of his being to throb with need.

For the first weeks, they had found ways to please each

other without committing the last, irrevocable sin—the one that could cost Duncan his life if his chieftain knew of it. He felt guilty for taking what rightfully belonged to Moira's future husband. But it was a miracle that he'd held out against her as long as he had.

At least he was confident that Moira wouldn't suffer for it. She was a clever lass—she wouldn't be the first to spill a vial of sheep's blood on her wedding sheet. And Moira was not one to be troubled by guilt.

Once they were inside the cave, they spread the blanket they kept there and sat close together.

"The Irish chieftain's son is rather amusing," Moira said, poking his side with her finger.

Moira's father had not taken another wife after Connor and Moira's mother died. So when they had guests, Moira sat on one side of her father, charming them, while her older brother Ragnall sat on his other side, frightening them.

"The man was looking down the front of your gown all through supper." And Duncan thought Moira let him. "I wanted to crush his head between my hands."

All his life, he'd minded his temper, both because he was bigger than other lads and because his position was precarious. He hated the way Moira made him lose control.

"That's sweet." She laughed and kissed his cheek. "I was trying to make ye jealous."

"Why would ye do that?"

"To make certain ye would meet me because we need to talk." Her voice was serious now. "Duncan, I want us to marry."

Duncan closed his eyes and, for one brief moment,

let himself pretend it was possible. He imagined what it would be like to be the man so blessed as to sleep with this lass in his arms each night and to wake up each morning to her sunny smile.

"It will never happen," he said.

"Of course it will," she said.

Moira was accustomed to having her way. Her father, who had no other weakness, had spoiled her, but he would make his own choice on such an important matter.

"Your father will never permit his only daughter to wed the nursemaid's bastard son," he said. "He'll use your marriage to make an alliance for the clan."

Duncan pulled out his flask of whiskey and took a long drink. With Moira talking such nonsense, he needed it.

"My father always lets me have what I want in the end. And what I want," she said, her breath warm in his ear as she ran her hand up his thigh, "is you, Duncan Ruadh MacDonald."

With all his blood rushing to his cock, he couldn't think. He pulled her into his arms, and they fell across the blankets, their legs tangled.

"I'm desperate for ye," she said between frantic kisses.

He still found it hard to believe Moira wanted him—but when she put her hand on his cock, he did believe. For however long she wanted him, he was hers.

*   *   *

Duncan ran his fingers through Moira's hair as she lay with her head on his chest. He fixed every moment of their time together in his memory to retrieve later.

"I love ye so much," she said.

An unfamiliar sensation of pure joy bubbled up inside Duncan.

"Tell me ye love me," she said.

"Ye know I do," he said, though it made no difference as to what would happen. "I'll never stop."

His feelings didn't come and go like Moira's. One week, she loved her brown horse, the next week the spotted one, and the week after that she didn't like to ride at all. She had always been like that. They were opposites in so many ways.

Duncan forced himself to sit up so he could see the sky outside the cave.

"Ach, it's near dawn," he said and cursed himself. "I must get ye back in a hurry."

"I will convince my father," she said as they dressed. "He's no fool. He can see that you're a warrior who will one day be known throughout the Western Isles."

"If ye tell your father about us," he said, cupping her face in his hands, "that will be the end of this."

Moira could not be as naïve about it as she pretended.

"He would let us wed if I carried your child," she said in a small voice.

Duncan's heart stopped in his chest. "Tell me ye are taking the potion to avoid conceiving?"

"Aye," she said, sounding annoyed. "And I've had my courses."

He brushed his thumb over her cheek. It was strange, but he would love to have a child with her—a wee lass with Moira's laughing eyes. He had no business having thoughts like that. It would be years before he could support a wife and child, and he'd never be able to provide for a woman accustomed to fine clothes and servants.

The scare she gave him made him resolve, once again, to end it. Moira could hide the loss of her virginity, but a child was another matter.

"If my father won't agree, we can run away," she said.

"He'd send half a dozen war galleys after us," Duncan said, as he fastened her cloak for her. "Even if we escaped—which we wouldn't—ye would never be happy estranged from our clan and living in a humble cottage. I love ye too much to do that to ye."

"Don't doubt me," Moira said, gripping the front of his shirt. "I'd live anywhere with ye."

She believed it only because she'd never lived with hardship. And Duncan knew that even if he could give her a castle, he could never keep her. Moira was like a colorful butterfly, landing on his hand for a breathless moment.

The sky was growing light when they reached the kitchen entrance behind the keep.

"I love ye," Moira said. "And I promise ye, one way or another, I will marry ye."

Duncan was a lucky man to have her love, even for a little while. He pulled her into one last mindless kiss and wondered how he would last until the next time.

He lived on the precipice of disaster, never knowing which would befall him first—getting caught or having her end it. And yet, he had never felt happier in his life. He had to stop himself from whistling as he crossed the castle yard to his mother's cottage.

Damn, there was candlelight in the window. Duncan was a grown man of nearly twenty and didn't have to answer to his mother. Still, he wished she were not awake to see him come in with the rising sun. She would ask questions, and he didn't like to lie to her.

Duncan opened the door—and his stomach dropped like a stone to his feet.

His chieftain and Ragnall sat on either side of his mother's table with their long, claymore swords resting, unsheathed, across their thighs. Rage rolled off them. With their golden hair and fierce golden eyes, they looked like a pair of lions.

Duncan hoped they would not kill him in front of his mother and sister. Though he didn't take his eyes off the two warriors dwarfing the tiny cottage, he was aware of his mother hunched on the floor in the corner, weeping. His eleven-year-old sister stood with her hand on their mother's shoulder.

"The old seer foretold that ye would save my son Connor's life one day." The chieftain's voice held enough menace to fell birds from the sky. "That is the only reason I did not kill ye the moment ye walked through that door."

Duncan suspected he would be flogged within an inch of his life instead. But a beating, however bad, meant nothing. He was strong; he would survive it. What weighed down his shoulders was the realization that he would never again hold Moira in his arms.

His chieftain was speaking again, but Duncan found it hard to listen with the well of grief rising in his chest.

"I suspect Connor and my nephews knew ye were *violating my daughter*!"

When the chieftain started to rise from his chair, Ragnall put his hand on his father's arm.

"We are taking Knock Castle from the MacKinnons today, so fetch your sword and shield," Ragnall said. "As soon as the battle is over, you, Alex, and Ian will sail with

Connor for France. Ye can hone your skills there, fighting the English."

"By the time ye return," the chieftain said, his eyes narrow slits of hate, "Moira will be far from Skye, living with her husband and children."

Duncan had known from the start that he would lose Moira. And yet, he felt the loss as keenly as if he'd been the expectant bridegroom whose bride is torn from his arms on his wedding night.

The bright spark was gone from his life forever.

THE DISH

Where authors give you the inside scoop!

♥ ♥

From the desk of Jill Shalvis

Dear Reader,

It's been a fun, exciting year for my Lucky Harbor series. Thanks to you, the readers, I hit the *New York Times* bestseller list with *The Sweetest Thing*. Wow. Talk about making my day! You are all awesome, and I'm still grinning from ear to ear and making everyone call me "N-Y-T." But I digress...

In light of how much you, the readers, have enjoyed this series, my publisher is putting *Simply Irresistible* and *The Sweetest Thing* together as a 2-in-1 volume at a special low price. CHRISTMAS IN LUCKY HARBOR will be in stores in November—just in time to bring new readers up to speed for book three, *Head Over Heels,* in December.

When I first started this series, I wanted it to be about three sisters who run a beach resort together. I figured I'd use my three daughters as inspiration. Only problem, my little darlings are teenagers, and they bicker like fiends. Some inspiration. But then it occurred to me: Their relationships are real, and that's what I like to write. Real people. So I changed things up, and the series became about three ESTRANGED sisters, stuck together running a dilapidated inn falling down on its axis. Now *that* I could pull off for sure. Add in three sexy alpha heroes to go with, and voilà...I was on my way.

So make sure to look for CHRISTMAS IN LUCKY HARBOR, the reprint of books one and two, available both in print and as an ebook wherever books are sold. And right on its heels, book three, *Head Over Heels*. (Heels? Get it?)

Happy reading and holiday hugs!

Jill Shalvis

www.jillshalvis.com

♥ ♥

From the desk of Margaret Mallory

Dear Reader,

Bad boys! What woman doesn't love a rogue—at least in fiction?

I suspect that's the reason I've had readers asking me about Alex MacDonald since he made his appearance as a secondary character in *The Guardian*, Book 1 of the Return of the Highlanders series.

Alex is such an unruly charmer that I was forced to ban him from several chapters of *The Guardian* for misbehavior. Naturally, the scoundrel attempted to steal every scene I put him in. I will admit that I asked Alex to flirt with the heroine to make his cousin jealous, but did he have to enjoy himself quite so thoroughly? Of course, if there had been any real chance of stealing his cousin's true love, Alex would not have done it. A good heart is hidden beneath that brawny chest. All the same, I told the scene-stealer he must wait his turn. When he laughed and refused to cooperate, I threw him out.

Now, at last, this too-handsome, green-eyed warrior has his own book, THE SINNER. I hope readers will agree that a man who has had far too many women fall at his feet must suffer on the road to love.

The first thing I decided to do was give Alex a heroine who was as loath to marry as he was. In fact, Alex would have to travel the length and breadth of Scotland to find a lass as opposed to marriage in general, or to him in particular, as Glynis MacNeil. Glynis's experience with one handsome, philandering Highland warrior was enough to last her a lifetime, and she's prepared to go to any lengths to thwart her chieftain father's attempts to wed her to another.

Alex has sworn—repeatedly and to anyone who would listen—that he will *never* take a wife. So the second thing I decided to do was surprise Alex partway through the book with an utterly compelling reason to wed. (No, I'm not telling here.) I hope readers appreciate the irony of this bad boy's long, uphill battle to persuade Glynis to marry him.

Helping these two untrusting souls find love proved an even bigger challenge than getting them wed. Fortunately, the attraction between Alex and Glynis was so hot my fingers burned on the keys. The last thing I needed to do, then, was force them to trust each other through a series of dangerous adventures that threatened all they held dear. That part was easy, dear readers—such dangers *abound* in the Highlands in the year 1515.

I hope you enjoy the love story of Alex and Glynis in THE SINNER.

Margaret Mallory

www.margaretmallory.com

♥ ♥ ♥ ♥ ♥ ♥ ♥ ♥ ♥ ♥ ♥ ♥ ♥ ♥ ♥ ♥ ♥ ♥ ♥ ♥

From the desk of Cara Elliott

Dear Reader,

Starting a new series is a little like going out on a first date. I mean, doesn't every girl get a little nervous about meeting a guy who is a complete stranger? Well, I have a confession to make: Authors get the heebies-jeebies too. Hey, it's not easy to waltz up to a hunky hero and simply bat your eyelashes and introduce yourself!

Okay, okay, I know what you're thinking. *How hard can it be?* After all, unlike in real life, all I have to do is snap my fingers (or tap them along my keyboard) and presto, as if by magic, he'll turn into a knight in shining armor, or a dashingly debonair prince, or...whatever my fantasies desire!

Strange as it may sound, it doesn't always flow quite so smoothly. Some men have minds of their own. You know...the strong, silent, self-reliant type who would rather eat nails than admit to any vulnerability. Take Connor Linsley, the sinfully sexy rogue who plays the leading role in TOO WICKED TO WED, the first book in my new Lords of Midnight trilogy. Talk about an infuriating man! He snaps, he snarls, he broods. If he didn't have such an intriguing spark in his quicksilver eyes, I might have been tempted to give up on him.

But no, patient person that I am, I persevered, knowing that beneath his show of steel was a softer, more sensitive core. I just had to draw it out. We had to have a number of heart-to-heart talks, but finally he let down his silky dark hair—er, in a manner of speaking—and allowed me to share some of his secrets. (And trust me, Connor has some *very* intriguing secrets!)

I'll have you know that I am also generous, as well as patient, for instead of keeping my new best friend all to myself, I've decided to share this Paragon of Perfection. I hope you enjoy getting to know him! (Pssst, he has two very devil-may-care friends. But that's another story. Or maybe two!)

Please visit my website at www.caraelliott.com to read sample chapters and learn more about this Lord of Midnight.

Cara Elliott

❤ ❤ ❤ ❤ ❤ ❤ ❤ ❤ ❤ ❤ ❤ ❤ ❤ ❤ ❤ ❤ ❤ ❤ ❤ ❤

From the desk of Jami Alden

Dear Reader,

I first met Krista Slater in my first romantic suspense for Grand Central, *Beg for Mercy*. All I knew about her then was that she was tough, no nonsense, dedicated to her work and committed to right, even if it meant admitting she'd made an enormous mistake in sending Sean Flynn to death row. But it was only after I'd spent about a month (and a hundred pages) with her in my latest book, HIDE FROM EVIL, that I learned she's also an automobile expert who can hotwire a car in less than sixty seconds.

And I knew Sean Flynn was loyal and honorable, with a protective streak a mile wide. I also knew that when he was forced into close quarters with Krista, he'd fall and fall hard, despite the fact she'd nearly ruined his life when she prosecuted him for murder. However, I didn't know he listened to Alice in Chains until he popped in his earbuds and clicked on his iPod.

After I finish every book, I'm amazed at the fact that I've written three hundred plus pages about people who exist only in my head. For about six months, I spend nearly every waking hour with them. Even when I'm not actually writing, they're always around, circling the edges of my consciousness while I think up a sexy, scary story for them to inhabit.

When I first started writing, I read books that said I shouldn't start writing until I knew absolutely everything about my hero and heroine. And I mean EVERYTHING—stuff like the name of their best friends from kindergarten and their least favorite food. So I would try to fill out these elaborate questionnaires, wracking my brain to come up a list of my heroine's quirks.

I finally came to accept the fact that it takes me a while to get to know my characters. We need to spend some time together before I get a sense of what makes them tick. It's like getting to know a new friend: You start with the small talk. Then you hang out, have conversations that go beyond the surface. You start to notice the little details that make them unique, and they reveal things from their pasts that have molded them into the people you're coming to know.

That's when things get interesting.

It was definitely interesting getting to know Sean and Krista in HIDE FROM EVIL. Especially finding out why, despite their rocky past, they were absolutely meant for each other. I hope you have as much fun with them as I did.

Enjoy!

Jami Alden

www.jamialden.com